Horror Fiction

Also available in this series:

Native American Literatures: An Introduction, by Suzanne Lundquist
American Gothic Fiction: An Introduction, by Allan Lloyd-Smith
Irish Fiction: An Introduction, by Kersti Tarien Powell
Fantasy Fiction: An Introduction, by Lucie Armitt

Forthcoming in this series:
Crime Fiction: An Introduction, by Alistair Wisker
Science Fiction: An Introduction, by Pat Wheeler

CONTINUUM STUDIES IN LITERARY GENRE

Horror Fiction:
An Introduction

GINA WISKER

continuum
NEW YORK • LONDON

2005

The Continuum International Publishing Group Inc
15 East 26 Street, New York, NY 10010

The Continuum International Publishing Group Ltd
The Tower Building, 11 York Road, London SE1 7NX

www.continuumbooks.com

Printed in the United States of America

Library of Congress Cataloging-in-Publication Data

Powell, Kersti Tarien.
Wisker, Gina, 1951–
   Horror fiction : an introduction / Gina Wisker.
      p. cm. — (Continuum studies in literary genre)
   Includes bibliographical references and index.
   ISBN 0-8264-1560-1 (hardcover : alk. paper) — ISBN 0-8264-1561-X
(pbk. : alk. paper)
   1. Horror tales, English—History and criticism.   2. Horror tales,
American—History and criticism.   I. Title.   II. Series.
   PR830.T3.W55 2005
   823'.0873809--dc22

                                                              2005014781

Contents

Chapter One: What Is Horror Fiction?   1

Chapter Two: Timeline   15

Chapter Three: Reading Horror Writing   25

Chapter Four: The Best and the Best Known   39

Chapter Five: Major Themes, Movements, and Issues   145

Chapter Six: Key Terms   217

Chapter Seven: Horror Criticism and Ways In   225

Chapter Eight: Key Questions   251

Chapter Nine: Bibliography and Further Reading   257

Index   287

Chapter One

What Is Horror Fiction?

'I'm giving serious thought to eating your wife.' (Harris, *Hannibal* 226)

So Dr Hannibal Lecter, connoisseur, cannibal, torments Commendatore Pazzi (a 'patsy') with two threats, both of possession, sexual and bodily, just prior to disembowelling and stringing him up from one of Florence's historical seats of religion and art. In one of Michael Arnzen's short stories, the protagonist's young daughter, playing among the plastic balls in the fast food café, suddenly emerges with the first of many human skulls ('Diving In', 2004), tossed as casually as the 'stars' tennis balls' (Webster, *The Duchess of Malfi* [Act V, Scene 4]). Impossible? Unlikely? Look at the newspapers and the TV headlines. Horror is both an everyday occurrence—terrorism, the cannibal next door, torture—and a way of dramatising our hidden fears and desires through fantasy that takes the everyday that few steps further.

> It's in black-jacketed books and lurid movie posters. It's in police reports from murder sites and tearful recollections from battlefields. It's in our nightmares. It's in our secret ambitions. (Barker, *A–Z of Horror* 16)

This chapter establishes the characteristics of the genre of horror fiction, its social, cultural, and fantasy elements. It looks at the appeal of the genre—the entertainment of shock and repulsion, facing up to what we fear, the enjoyment of being terrified, the humour of horror, the need to stake the vampire, shut the coffin, close down the horror and restore order, manage the nightmare, the death, reassure ourselves, however temporarily, that we can indeed keep out the night, tame and understand the alien and Other, and defy death. It makes a case for its appeal to different readers/audiences, over time. So:

> Horror constitutes the limit of reason, sense, consciousness and speech, the very emotion in which the human reaches its limit. Horror is thus ambivalently human. (Botting, *The Gothic* 131)

> But is there any common thread of subject matter that connects all these manifestations? Maybe. Perhaps the body and its vulnerability. Perhaps the mind and its brittleness. Perhaps love and its absence. (Barker, *A–Z of Horror* 16)

Clive Barker highlights horror's rich potion of the violent eruptions of the ordinary and those of the nightmare. Horror is located in both the real and the nightmarish imaginary, and an important ingredient in its success is the ability to entertain, terrify, problematize, and provoke politicized, philosophical engaged thought. Important also is its embodying that of which we cannot speak, our deep-seated longings and terrors, and then, once they have been embodied, acted out, they are managed. Order is restored (if only temporarily).

H. P. Lovecraft, an earlier master of horror and expert on the psychology of fear, takes us further into the 'weird' (his term) in his definitions of the ways in which horror of the weird tale homes in on our ancestors' primitive fear of the dark, the unknown, the inexplicable, the uncanny and supernatural. He speaks of:

> the genuineness and dignity of the weirdly horrible tale as a literary form. Against it are discharged all the shafts of a materialistic sophistication which clings to frequently felt emotions and external events, and of a naively inspired idealism which deprecates the aesthetic motive and calls for a didactic literature to "uplift" the reader toward a suitable degree of smirking optimism. (Lovecraft, *Supernatural Horror in Literature* 12)

Horror, nurtured in the fears we have of pain and death, and in our dark fears of the unknown, is a taste acquired by those with sufficient imagination to see beyond, beneath, and through what we take for granted as normal and familiar, to the sources of their other 'real', our imaginations and the 'imaginary' of culture, and our psychological, emotional, and intuitive elements of experience.

> The appeal of the spectrally macabre is generally narrow because it demands from the reader a certain degree of imagination and a capacity for detachment from everyday life. (Lovecraft, *Supernatural Horror in Literature* 12)

Since 'pain and the menace of death' are more vividly remembered than pleasure, and formalized religion has captured the pleasant, beneficial elements of the unknown, so the 'darker and more maleficent side of cosmic mystery' figures in the tales of folklore and the supernatural, weird tales, and horror, depicting 'peril and evil possibilities' (Lovecraft 14).

Horror Elements—Appeal in Different Genres

When I was five I saw *20,000 Leagues Under the Sea*. I saw it again about nine times. Kirk Douglas, dashing American sailor, jauntily sings a sea shanty celebrating life at sea while behind him and fully within our gaze emerges a terrifying sea monster. Captain Nemo's submarine, an art deco mechanical sea beast, then a figment of Verne's futuristic imagination, is no monster but an elegant place of escape for Nemo/no one/nameless, who steers a course beneath the sea, meting out justice against his enemies, including illegitimate, materialistic, cruel governments holding people in slavery. Undersea, the submarine is grand, embellished, and Gothic in its location and splendour, and the role of Nemo and his sub is dark but moral, exposing the steamy underside of politics and power. This is the politicized side of Gothic horror. The other monster of the deep, the gigantic octopus that battles with the sub, its motives without human intellect or justice, its aim pure destruction (to eat?), is the unknown; emerging from one of the two truly unknown Gothic places—down there (the sea floor) as opposed to up and out there (space)—it revives our terror of the Other. Both the sub and the octopus are the predecessors of the monster shark in Peter Benchley/Steven Spielberg's *Jaws*; Mother, the pod-laying, body-invading bug-based alien in the *Alien* films; and the medusa/hydra, toothed, snaky terror that devours unwitting passengers, looters, ship breakers, and hapless crew in *Deep Rising* (1998). And this Jules Verne classic, not usually defined as horror, launches us into most of horror's categories, aims, intentions, effects, successes, formulae, and forms.

Horror is pretty much everywhere. Horror is entertaining and educational. Horror is contradictory, paradoxical; it combines opposites, destabilises, and challenges, but often does so in order to restore order, however order is culturally constituted at that particular time and place. It is social, cultural, political, psychological, emotional, spiritual, supernatural, natural, and part of the human condition:

> Horror constitutes the limit of reason, sense, consciousness and speech, the very emotion in which the human reaches its limit. Horror is thus ambivalently human. (Botting, *The Gothic*, 131)

Clive Barker finds it in the daily monstrousness of politics, terror, violence, Fascism, murder, rape, and most particularly in the seemingly safest places:

> As soon as we begin to delve into the nature of horror, or attempt to list its manifestations in our culture, the sheer scale of the beast becomes apparent. Horror is everywhere. It's in fairy tales and the evening headlines, it's in street corner gossip and the incontrovertible facts of history. It's in playground ditties (*Ring-a ring o' roses* is a sweet little plague song), it's on the altar, bleeding for our sins ('Forgive them, Father, for they know not what they do'). (Barker, *A–Z of Horror* 15)

Horror, sourced in primitive fears, possesses our imaginations and reappears throughout our histories.

> No amount of rationalism, reform, or Freudian analysis can quite annul the thrill of the chimney-corner whisper or the lonely wood. (Barker 12)

Lovecraft identified a history to weird tales and horror in the United States:

Supernatural Horror in Literature is in a sense the collective of a movement in the history of popular literature in the United States. The field of weird fiction, as exemplified in the magazine *Weird Tales* (and its less successful rivals, *Ghost Stories, Tales of Magic and Mystery*), paralleled and even slightly preceded the development of its mechanistic sister, science-fiction. The readers of *Weird Tales* had a feeling of fraternity and community, a feeling of participating in a development. (Bleiler, ed., *Supernatural Horror in Literature* vii)

Representation

Horror is in everyday reality, but it is also a genre, a construction, and a representation of what terrifies and disgusts, what we fear and secretly desire. Herein lies the difference, subtle and necessary to define, especially when discussing reception and the links between imaginative projects, embodiments, and literal actions, between the real and our projection from it, construction of it, and representation and interpretation of it in genre fictions. An event can be horrific and our response one of horror, recognizing in acts of terrorism and torture, characteristics of the monstrous, vile, violent, dehumanizing elements that the genre itself uses, manages, dramatises, and represents in order both to entertain and to comment. But horror fiction is a genre and a construction, projection, and representation. Its elements have meanings, their roots in popular consciousness and the popular unconscious, their representation in popular fictional forms from fairy tale and parable (Grimm, Perrault) to full-blown Hollywood blockbuster (*Silence of the Lambs, Jaws*). Horror fiction draws attention to itself by being fiction, whether in written, visual, or film text. Horror fiction tends to gain its effects from its imaginative strategies—pace, characterization, narrative, settings, perspectives, and so on, and both its tone and appeal lie along an axis from the very realistic to the supernatural, fantastic, and weird. As Linda Holland-Toll puts it:

Horror fiction will be handily defined as any text which has extreme or supernatural elements, induces (as its primary intention and/or effect) strong feelings of terror, horror or revulsion in the reader, and generates a significant degree of unresolved disease within society. (Holland-Toll, *As American as Mom, Baseball and Apple Pie* 6)

It generates just enough 'disease' (dis-ease) that it cannot merely be glossed over and returned to 'business as usual'. Horror tells us fundamental truths about what we fear, what we desire, and the dangers of complacency.

Reading Horror

But can horror fiction be taken seriously? We are reminded here of the African-American journalist and writer of vampire mythic fictions, Tananarive Due, who feared that she would not be respected if she wrote horror—presumably the supernatural horror, the vampire rather than the average massacre. As readers, we are likely to locate ourselves along a continuum of response to horror, some more troubled, provoked, and finally, perhaps, reassured by the documentary realism, others by the supernatural, fantastic, the weird. For many, fictions that uneasily straddle the documentary real and the fantastic are the most troublesome, lacking resolution:

> fiction which cannot be marginalized, pre-defined as fantastic and thus easily resolved and categorized, is much more threatening than a fiction which actually occupies the margins, which is clearly demarcated by the fantastic. (Holland-Toll 6)

One of the most crucial questions we need to ask when considering horror is how we read it—and here enter the issues of censorship; the role of popular culture in our society; readership and reading practices that are informed, critical, or uncritical; taking the actions on the screen (perhaps literally) as a blueprint for violent action; or judging and interpreting what is recognised as an imaginative lesson.

In learning and teaching terms, the main issue of horror's functions and the kinds of reading or viewing practice related to it is a crucial 'threshold' concept. If the reading and viewing public take it all at face value alone, horror can be entertaining, maybe scary, dangerous, and destabilising, perhaps a recipe for monstrous actions. But it cannot really be thought provoking in terms of questioning those essential philosophical and political concerns, such as what is defined as real, whether there is a shared real, what the self is/selves are and how they are constructed, freedom and power, relationships between imposed and internalised order, censorship, free speech, independence, anarchy, dictatorship and tyranny. In the recognition of the representational nature of horror, the significance, the symbolism, the conceptual, meaningful element underlying and informing it, lies the crucial element of both intentionality and reading practice (see chapter 3, 'Reading Horror Writing').

When I was young, *20,000 Leagues Under the Sea* troubled and fascinated me. So, too, did the other horror film I saw as a child, *The Fly*, where it seems science could accidentally turn an intelligent human being into a disgusting insect. Body horror and mad scientists combine in one film focusing on identity and questioning issues about what is good, what is evil. The abject, the disgusting, and our right to destroy the evil in us, whether extruding or invading, are all explored in this groundbreaking film (originally 1958, remade in 1986 with Jeff Goldblum as Seth Brundle).

Gothic Roots of Horror

One clue to the disease and disturbance, the closeness of horror to the real but its appearance as fantastic, can be found in its origins in the Gothic as well as in the expression of everyday monstrosities. Horror has its roots in the Gothic, historically both an entertaining form—Gothic romances—and a culturally and psychologically disturbing form—socially engaged; a location for exposing undersides, alternatives, and contradictions; and an outlet for paradoxical forces and disturbances of the safety of the routine, the normal. Gothic destabilises, offers and dramatises alternatives that can be terrifying but which tend also to shine a powerful light into the cracks and fissures of what we smugly take for granted or that which is imposed upon us as natural, to be obeyed. It provides personal, emotional, psychic, and energetic release.

A branch of Gothic writing, horror uses many of its formulae but is more likely to use violence, terror, and bodily harm than the Gothic. Both are disturbing, pointing out paradoxes and contradictions, hypocrisies and deceits, sometimes to thrill, sometimes to teach us not to be complacent and too comfortable—to entertain and act as a social critique. Both Gothic and horror use settings of dungeons, attics, corridors, and terrifying and unpleasant threatening spaces. Horror disturbs our sense of what is comforting and normal.

Horror embodies what is paradoxically both desired and feared, dramatising that which is normally unthinkable, unnamable, indefinable, and repressed. The Gothic also looks at such dualisms and dichotomous responses, but horror is more likely to dwell 'on the connections between violence and sexuality' (Punter, *The Literature of Terror* 361) and on punishing the fatally attractive; it is 'closely interlocked with the rather belated spread of Freudian theory' (Punter 348):

> Horror is evoked by encounters with objects and actions that are not so much threatening as taboo: what is least avowable in oneself, what is symbolically least palatable or recognizable, may be the most horrible. Horror appears when fear comes a little too close to home. (Botting, *The Gothic* 124)

Freud's 'The Uncanny' (1919) is a key piece exploring such issues. Freud influenced psychoanalytic readings of fantastic and horror literature, showing ways in which they engage with and enact the uncanny or '*unheimlich*', the intrusion of the unfamiliar when the familiar is expected (see chapter 6, 'Key Terms'). In using 'the uncanny', horror exposes and enacts dread and apprehension. It concentrates on making the homely frightening and revealing what is concealed and unexpected: alternative versions of self, relationships, and family, energies that might burst out or intrude on and threaten everyday life. What results is a projection of something repressed, embodied in a demon spirit, ghost, monster, or disruptive energies, hence those films of houses that start to explode (*Poltergeist*) because they are built over desecrated graves, and children possessed by demons (*The Exorcist*, *The Omen*).

Horror names and dramatises that which is otherwise unthinkable, unnamable, indefinable, and repressed. Split selves, false identities, erupting bodies, unsafe spaces, and hospital or scientific operations and experiments that go horribly wrong (*Frankenstein, The Island of Dr Moreau, The Fly, Kingdom Hospital*) are all terrors explored and dramatised in horror. Frequently, domestic settings and the nurturing relationships within the family are locations for horror in women's writing in particular. Mark Jancovich defines the role of conventional horror and its pleasures:

> It is claimed that the pleasure offered by the genre is based on the process of narrative closure in which the horrifying or monstrous is destroyed or contained. The structures of horror narratives are said to set out from a situation of order, move through a period of disorder caused by the eruption of horrifying or monstrous forces, and finally reach a point of closure and completion in which disruptive, monstrous elements are contained or destroyed and the original order is re-established. (Jancovich, *Horror* 9)

Horror Is Political

Horror explores the fissures that open in our everyday lives and destabilizes our complacency about norms and rules. Much conventional horror has always been conservative, of course, and merely entertaining. However, the radical edge of horror began appearing as early as the horror comic campaigns of the 1950s. Then, the destabilization of norms on which horror (particularly *Tales from the Crypt*) focused was claimed by both the writers of this radical (left-wing) horror and the oppressive political censors, who recognised its dangerous edge and so clamped down on it, designating it as merely disgusting rather than politically and ideologically challenging and anarchic.

The comfortable dismissal of horror as merely entertainment or silly, scary monsters avoids its well-established, politicized role as exposer of social and cultural deceits and discomforts, deriving from the Gothic. Conventionally, Gothic finally shuts down these disturbances and restores order. Horror, drawing from the impulse and forms of the Gothic, but its more violent and psychologically, physically disturbing and invasive, destructive relation, acts as a vehicle for us to face up to and face down what we avoid, repress, ignore, or can see no escape from. However, just like Nemo and his submarine, the objects and subjects of horror are not always what they appear to be and are very often socially, politically, and culturally transgressive and challenging. Restoring order, which is itself dubious and questionable, destructive, and illegitimate (oppressive gender roles, slavery, imperialism, capitalism, etc.), is not always the aim of the radical horror writer. Here emerges one of the problems of horror, which links it to the political and the horror comics scare of the 1950s (see Martin Barker's *A Haunt of Fears*, 1984). Challenges to the cultural, gendered, social, political, emotional, etc. status quo destabilise, but sometimes this instability is a vehicle for imaginative change, equality, rewriting forms and relations of power, and reimagining otherwise. Would it be necessary to close down a horror scenario if it exposed the comfortable collusion with the daily investment in oppression and lies? Many radical horror writers have refused such closure, not merely so that there can be a sequel to sell the novels and fill the cinemas but to make a point about our continued need to take less for granted, and to question and challenge some of the seamier sides of everyday life.

In the late 1950s, American-originated (U.K.-imported) horror comics, notably *Tales from the Crypt* among others, were banned in Great Britain following a moral panic originating in the fears of teachers and parents that stories of demonic knife sharpeners and shop owners, monstrous neighbourhood and family behaviours, were not merely terrifying the nation's children but warping their imaginations. These comics were seen as morally dangerous by those in power, operating a kind of political domestic and Christian censorship. The comics were burned, their readers seen as perverse. Martin Barker, identifying the source of the threat of the comics in the tempting and liberating of the imagination in its darkest spaces, aligns the anti-horror comic campaign with the McCarthy witch hunts. There is to some extent a political radicalism in horror comics, which were seen as a moral terror to be suppressed.

William Friedkin's movie *The Exorcist* (1973) provides another case in point. Not merely did it send thousands from the cinema terrified and sickened, but religious leaders found it blasphemous. The film was released in 1973, condemned by Rev. Billy Graham, banned in the wake of the 1980s 'video nasties' scandal (toddler James Bulger's murderers were found to have been watching *Child's Play 3*, and connections were made straightforwardly between video nasties and brutality and abuse), and finally released on video in the 1990s. Many found the scene of masturbation with a crucifix disgusting, terrifying, and soulless. However, it has since been recognised that the actualisation of powers of religious good and evil and the representation of demonic possession sent thousands to the Catholic church ('The Fear of God: 25 years of the Exorcist', BBC TV, 1998, in Jones 2002, 7). This tapping into the imaginative needs for both spiritual and demonic, perhaps a simplified imaginative good and evil, benefited the Church.

Feminist Horror

There are other readings. Feminist readings identify in *The Exorcist* an expression and acting out of patriarchal forces controlling the emergent (seen as monstrous) sexuality of the adolescent girl Regan. Regan's disturbing shaking, vomiting, and shrieking 'Fuck me, fuck me' disgusted and disturbed censors, doctors, and religious leaders—but it can be seen as an acting out through the metaphor of horror (exacerbated by being dramatised onscreen realistically, in front of us) of the unknown, the threat of emerging female sexuality (Regan is on the point of puberty).

Horror is often defined by Gothic experts to be more a male than a female form, since terror is the form favoured by women (it is claimed). Terror is localised and easily overcome, horror more far-reaching, deep-seated, and troubling.

> Horror suggests that rationalist, consumerist socio-modernity produces alienation from the body and denial of desires and terrors. Usually, the remedies proposed are conservative depending not on new attitudes towards the repressed or abject, but on violent confrontation, ritual cleansing, re-discovery of lost heroism and authenticity, and re-imposition of order. (Kerridge 1998, 282)

Women have always written horror. Mary Shelley's *Frankenstein* (1818) was an early example, but so, too, was the romantic Gothic of Ann Radcliffe. Women's contributions to the genre have frequently troubled underlying bourgeois and patriarchal assumptions. They have very often been at odds with a conventional society that would silence and marginalise them as a matter of course. One key element in this marginalising is to rename and then dismiss and devalue women's versions of horror. Lisa Tuttle describes being amazed at a World Fantasy convention where a panel of men discussed 'why women don't write horror' based on their assumption that it is a largely male preserve:

> Women writers tend to be seen either as rare exceptions, or redefined as something else—not horror but Gothic; not horror but suspense; not horror but romance, or fantasy, or something unclassifiable but different. (Tuttle, ed., *Skin of the Soul* 2–3)

Horror tales frequently expose elements of the familiar and the self that we might prefer to keep secret. What results is a projection of the monstrous side of the trusted familiar. J. Laplanche and J. B. Pontalis note this gesture of outward projection and abjection as:

> qualities, feelings, wishes and objects which the subject refuses to recognise or rejects in himself . . . expelled from the self and located in another person or thing. (Laplanche and Pontalis, *The Language of Psycho-Analysis* 25)

Julia Kristeva (*Powers of Horror* 1982) theorises both the conventional representation of women in horror and therefore the challenge of much feminist horror. She identifies abjection as a stage in the infant's development when it rejects that which is not self in order to begin to recognise and define the limits of self. What is rejected (faeces, and then that Other, the body of the mother) is considered disgusting. Growing up, the child extends this projection to women in general, Kristeva argues. Disgust and fear at women's bodies, sexuality, and power follow rapidly from attraction, displacing it. Disempowerment and engulfment are conventional (male) fears that derive from abjection. This, clearly, is not an attractive prospect for the woman writer or reader, who finds herself the object, location, and source of horror and disgust, of the abject.

Horror fiction and film draw from perspectives of gender and power, utilising the language of text and film to explore and problematise what is considered normal and what troubles us.

Conclusion

Horror is an interpretation of local and global cruelties and tragedies. It embodies what is paradoxically both desired and feared, dramatising that which is normally unthinkable, unnameable, indefinable, and repressed. Horror, a branch of the Gothic, also dramatises dualisms and dichotomies but is more likely to dwell 'on the connections between violence and sexuality' (Punter, *The Literature of Terror* 361) and on punishing the fatally attractive; it is 'closely interlocked with the rather belated spread of Freudian theory' (348):

> evoked by encounters with objects and actions that are not so much threatening as taboo: what is least avowable in oneself, what is symbolically least palatable or recognisable, may be the most horrible. Horror appears when fear comes a little too close to home. (Botting, *The Gothic* 124)

Horror fictions range from those that come dangerously close to resembling reality and the documentary real of our home-based evening TV viewing: torture, rape, murder, poisonings, suicide bombs, deadly diseases from eating burgers, approaching comets, madmen in power, to the more metaphorical, allegorical, and fantastic. The latter intrude themselves into our unconscious, homing in on our inherited fears of the unexplained, the night, Otherness, the unexpected, the unfamiliar, that which we can neither comprehend nor control, the stuff of folktale and nightmare. The supernatural and fantastic enter here, also, historically identified as the 'weird', and if horror is a continuum from the real or realistic to the weird and supernatural, then readers might well find themselves more comfortable at different points on that continuum.

The current revival of horror is in direct relation to the increase in interest in the Gothic and the recognition of instability and multiplicity, of which elements of postmodernism have forced us to become aware. Beliefs of identity, self, social, and cultural norms, even overall worldviews have, themselves, been questioned in the postmodern period, revealed as constructions and constrictions, necessary to sanity, but fictive and artificial in themselves. Horror grows from this destabilisation. Whether it then returns its readership or audience to renewed stability with comfortable closure, packing away the disturbances it unleashed, or whether it refuses such closure and demonisation of these disturbances depends on the political and ideological intentions of the writers themselves. What we do with what we read depends on ourselves as readers.

Chapter Two

Timeline

700	*Beowulf*
1564	William Shakespeare born
1580	John Webster born
1600	William Shakespeare, *Hamlet*
1605	William Shakespeare, *King Lear*
1606	William Shakespeare, *Macbeth*
1612	John Webster, *The White Devil*
1614	John Webster, *The Duchess of Malfi*
1616	William Shakespeare dies
1625	John Webster dies
1765	Horace Walpole, *Castle of Otranto*
1792	Mary Wollstonecraft, *A Vindication of the Rights of Woman* (nonfiction)
1794	Ann Radcliffe, *Mysteries of Udolpho*
1796	Matthew Lewis, *The Monk*
1797	Mary Shelley born
1798	Charles Brockden Brown, *Wieland*
1840	Edgar Allan Poe, *Tales of the Grotesque and Arabesque*

1845	J. M. Rymer, *Varney the Vampire*
1847	Bram Stoker born
1848	Disturbances at the Fox Household, Hydesville, New York State: origins of spiritualism
1849	Edgar Allan Poe dies
1850	Edgar Allan Poe, *Collected Works*, ed. R. W. Griswold (3 vols)
1851	Nathaniel Hawthorne, *The House of the Seven Gables;* Mary Shelley dies
1854	Oscar Wilde born
1861	Start of American Civil War
1865	S. Baring-Gould, *The Book of Were Wolves;* End of Civil War
1866	H. G. Wells born
1869	Sheridan le Fanu, 'Green Tea'
1872	Sheridan le Fanu, *In a Glass Darkly* (3 vols)
1875	Founding of the Theosophical Society
1876	Madame Blavatsky, *Isis Unveiled* (nonfiction)
1879	Mary Baker Eddy founds Church of Christ, Scientist
1882	Society for Psychical Research founded (Great Britain); Charlotte Perkins Gilman, *The Yellow Wallpaper*
1886	Vernon Lee, *A Phantom Lover;* Robert Louis Stevenson, *The Strange Case of Dr Jekyll and Mr Hyde*
1888	Robert Louis Stevenson, *The Phantom Rickshaw and Other Eerie Tales;* Madame Blavatsky, *The Secret Doctrine* (nonfiction)
1889	F. W. Murnau born

1890	Vernon Lee, *Hauntings*
1891	J. K. Huysmans, *La Bas*; Ambrose Bierce, *Tales of Soldiers and Civilians*; Oscar Wilde, *The Picture of Dorian Gray*
1893	Edith Nesbit, *Grim Tales*; Ambrose Bierce, *Can Such Things Be?*
1894	Arthur Machen, *The Great God Pan*
1895	R. W. Chambers, *The King in Yellow*; Arthur Machen, *The Three Imposters*; John Meade Falkner, *The Lost Stradivarius*
1896	Mary Molesworth, *Uncanny Tales*; H. G. Wells, *The Island of Dr Moreau*
1897	Bram Stoker, *Dracula*; Arthur Machen, *The Hill of Dreams*; Richard Marsh, *The Beetle*
1898	Henry James, *The Turn of the Screw*
1899	Bernard Capes, *At a Winter's Fire*; Alfred Hitchcock born
1900	Oscar Wilde dies
1902	W. W. Jacobs, 'The Monkey's Paw'
1903	A. C. Benson, *The Hill of Trouble*; Bram Stoker, *The Jewel of Seven Stars*
1904	M. R. James, *Ghost Stories of an Antiquary*
1906	Algernon Blackwood, *The Empty House and Other Ghost Stories*; Arthur Machen, *The House of Souls*
1907	R. H. Benson, *A Mirror of Shalott*
1908	Morley Roberts, 'The Fog'; William Hope Hodgson, *The House on the Borderland*; Algernon Blackwood, *John Silence: Physician Extraordinary*; G. K. Chesterton, *The Man Who Was Thursday*
1911	Bram Stoker, *The Lair of the White Worm*; M. R. James, *More Ghost Stories*; (George) Oliver Onions,

	Widdershins; Gaston Leroux, *The Phantom of the Opera*; F. Marion Crawford, *Wandering Ghosts*
1911	Opening of Hollywood
1912	E. G. Swain, *The Stoneground Ghost Tales*; William Hope Hodgson, *The Night Land*; Bram Stoker dies
1914	Bram Stoker, 'Dracula's Guest' (posthumous); Start of World War I; Ambrose Bierce 'disappears' in Mexico
1915	Gustov Meyrink, *The Golem*
1918	End of World War I
1919	Sigmund Freud, 'The Uncanny' (nonfiction); Robert Weine, *The Cabinet of Dr Caligari*
1920	Paul Wagener, *The Golem*
1921	Marjory Bowen, *The Haunted Village*
1922	Jessie Douglas Kerruish, *The Undying Monster*; F. W. Murnau, dir. *Nosferatu: Eine Symphonie des Gravens* (unofficial adaptation of Bram Stoker's *Dracula*)
1923	H. P. Lovecraft, 'The Rats in the Walls'; first issue of H. P. Lovecraft, *Weird Tales*; E. F. Benson, *Visible and Invisible*
1925	H. P. Lovecraft, 'The Horror at Red Hook'; M. R. James, 'A Warning to the Curious'
1926	H. P. Lovecraft, 'The Call of Cthulhu'; Cynthia Asquith, *The Ghost Book*
1927	H. P. Lovecraft, *The Case of Charles Dexter Ward*; Edward Lucas White, 'Lukundoo'
1928	H. P. Lovecraft, 'The Dunwich Horror'; H. Russell Wakefield, *They Walk at Night*; A. J. Alan, *Good Evening Everyone*; W. F. Harvey, 'The Beast with Five Fingers'

1931	F. Tennyson Jesse, 'The Railway Carriage'; Charles Williams, *The Place of the Lion*; M. R. James, *Collected Ghost Stories*; F. W. Murnau dies
1933	W. F. Harvey, 'The Ankardyne Pew' (Moods and Tenses); Guy Endore, *Werewolf of Paris*; Marjory Bowen, *The Last Bouquet*; Aleister Crowley, *The Book of the Law* (nonfiction)
1934	Elizabeth Bowen, 'The Cat Jumps'; E. F. Benson, *More Spook Stories*
1935	Charles G. Finney, *The Curse of Dr Lao*; Oliver Onions, *Collected Ghost Stories*; Dennis Wheatley, *The Devil Rides Out*
1936	Arthur Machen, *The Children of the Pool and Other Stories*; R. E. Howard dies; M. R. James dies; White Eagle Lodge founded (Great Britain)
1937	H. P. Lovecraft dies
1939	H. P. Lovecraft, *The Outsider and Others*, ed. August Derleth (first publication of Arkham House Press); Start of World War II; Wes Craven born
1940	Harry Price, *The Most Haunted House in England* (nonfiction)
1943	Fritz Lieber, *Conjure Wife*; William Beaudine, dir. *The Ape Man*
1945	Evangeline Walton, *Witch House*; Charles Williams, *All Hallows' Eve*; End of World War II; Start of Cold War
1946	H. G. Wells dies
1947	French legislation regarding children's 'horror' comics; Aleister Crowley dies; Arthur Machen dies; Stephen King born
1948	Charles Barton, dir. *Abbott and Costello Meet Frankenstein*
1949	Horror comics banned in Canada

1950	William M. Gaines (pub.), *Tales from the Crypt*, etc.
1954	Richard Matheson, *I Am Legend; Weird Tales* magazine closes
1955	Children and Young Persons (Harmful Publications) Act (Great Britain); Jack Finney, *The Body Snatchers*; Gerald Kersh, *Men Without Bones*
1957	Roger Corman, dir. *Attack of the Crab Monsters*
1958	Terence Fisher, dir. *Dracula*
1959	Robert Bloch, *Psycho*; Shirley Jackson, *The Haunting of Hill House*; Herbert Van Thal, *Pan Book of Horror Stories*
1960	Obscene Publications Act (Great Britain);
1962	Robert Bloch, 'Yours Truly, Jack the Ripper'
1964	Start of Vietnam War
1967	Ira Levin, *Rosemary's Baby*
1968	George A. Romero, dir. *Night of the Living Dead*
1969	Kingsley Amis, *The Green Man*; Angela Carter, *Heroes and Villains*
1971	William Peter Blatty, *The Exorcist*; Michael Crichton, dir. *The Andromeda Strain*
1972	Angela Carter, *The Infernal Desire Machine of Doctor Hoffman*; Wes Craven, dir. *Last House on the Left*
1973	End of Vietnam War
1974	Stephen King, *Carrie*; James Herbert, *The Rats*; Tobe Hooper, dir. *Texas Chainsaw Massacre*
1975	Stephen King, *Salem's Lot*; Harlan Ellison, *Deathbird Stories*
1976	Anne Rice, *Interview with the Vampire*
1977	Joyce Carol Oates, *Night-Slide*; Hugh B. Cave, *Murgunstrumm and Others*; Bernard Taylor, *Sweetheart, Sweetheart*; Stephen King, *The Shining*;

Julia Briggs, *Night Visitors* (nonfiction); Wes Craven, dir. *The Hills Have Eyes*

1978   Stephen King, *The Stand*; Whitley Streiber, *The Wolfen*; George Hay (ed.), *The Necronomicon*; Philip Kaufman, dir. *Invasion of the Body Snatchers*; George A. Romero, dir. *Dawn of the Dead*; Meir Zarchi, dir. *I Spit on Your Grave*

1979   Angela Carter, *The Bloody Chamber*; Virginia Andrews, *Flowers in the Attic*; David Morrell, *The Totem*; Ramsey Campbell, *The Face that Must Die*; Peter Straub, *Ghost Story*; Werner Herzog, dir. *Nosferatu: Phantom der Nacht*

1980   Stephen King, *The Shining*; Julia Kristeva, *Pouvoirs de L'Horreur* (nonfiction); Suzy Mckee Charnas, *The Vampire Tapestry*; David Punter, *The Literature of Terror* (nonfiction); Lewis Teague, dir. *Alligator*; Alfred Hitchcock dies

1981   Rosemary Jackson, *Fantasy* (nonfiction); Stephen King, *Danse Macabre* (nonfiction); Angela Carter, *The Bloody Chamber*; Sam Raimi, dir. *The Evil Dead*; John Landis, dir. *An American Werewolf in London*; Greenham Common Women Protesters

1982   Shaun Hutson, *Slugs*; Frank Henenlotter, dir. *Basket Case*

1983   Susan Hill, *The Woman in Black*; Arthur Machen, *Tales of Horror and the Supernatural*

1984   Clive Barker, *The Books of Blood*, vols 1-3; Robert Holdstock, *Mythago Wood*; Julia Kristeva, *Powers of Horror* (nonfiction); Wes Craven, dir. *Nightmare on Elm Street*

1985   Clive Leatherdale, *Dracula* (nonfiction); Anne Rice, *The Vampire Lestat*; George A. Romero, dir. *Day of the Dead*

1986   Lisa Tuttle, *A Nest of Nightmares*; David Cronenberg, dir. *The Fly*

1987	Whitley Strieber, *Communion* (nonfiction); Clive Barker, *Weaveworld*; Stephen King, *The Tommyknockers, Misery*; Ramsey Campbell, *Dark Feasts*; J. Gerald Kennedy, *Poe, Death and the Life of Writing* (nonfiction) James Herbert, *The Magic Cottage*; Virginia C. Andrews, *Flowers in the Attic*; Alan Parker, dir. *Angel Heart*; Peter Jackson, dir. *Bad Taste*
1988	Robin Cook, *Mortal Fear*; Dean Koontz, *Watchers*
1989	Robin Cook, *Mutation*
1990	Lisa Tuttle (ed.), *New Horror Stories by Women*; Richard Dalby (ed.), *The Virago Book of Ghost Stories*; Manuel Aguirre, *The Closed Space* (nonfiction); Brian Stableford, *The Werewolves of London*
1991	Peter James, *Sweet Heart*; Brian Docherty (ed.) *American Horror Fiction* (nonfiction); Jewelle Gomez, *The Gilda Stories*; End of Cold War
1992	David Morris, *The Masks of Lucifer* (nonfiction); Carol Clover, *Men, Women, and Chainsaws: Gender in the Modern Horror Film* (nonfiction); Poppy Z. Brite, *Lost Souls*; Joss Whedon, dir. *Buffy the Vampire Slayer*
1993	Clive Bloom (ed.), *Creepers* (nonfiction); Barbara Creed, *The Monstrous Feminine: Film, Feminism, Psychoanalysis*; Poppy Z. Brite, *Drawing Blood*; *The X-Files* (TV)
1994	Kenneth Grant, *Outer Gateways* (nonfiction); Ken Gelder, *Reading the Vampire* (nonfiction); Michael Arnzen, *Grave Markings*; Poppy Z. Brite, *Wormwood (Swamp Foetus)*, *The Crow*; Stephen King, *The Stand* (TV movie)
1996	Clive Bloom, *Cult Fiction* (nonfiction); Poppy Z. Brite, *Exquisite Corpse*
1997	Robin Cook, *Invasion*; *Outbreak*

1998   Poppy Z. Brite, *The Lazarus Heart*; Poppy Z. Brite, *Are You Loathsome Tonight?*; Pam Keesey, *Daughters of Darkness: Lesbian Vampire Stories*

1999   David Punter, *A Companion to the Gothic* (nonfiction); Michael Arnzen, *Paratabloids, Fluid Mosaic and Other Outre Objects D'art*; Ken Gelder, *The Horror Reader*; Adam Simon, dir. *American Nightmare*; Mary Harron, dir. *American Psycho*; Adam Simon, dir. *American Nightmare*

2001   Caitlin R. Kiernan, *Threshold*; Arthur Machen, *The Three Imposters and Other Stories: The Best Weird Tales of Arthur Machen*, vol 1 (*Call of Cthulhu Fiction Series*); The War in Afghanistan

2002   Arthur Machen, *The Hill of Dreams*; Danny Boyle, dir. *28 Days Later*; Marc Evans, dir. *My Little Eye*; Stephen Spielberg, *Taken* (TV)

2003   Michael Arnzen, *Once Upon a Slime*; Poppy Z. Brite, *The Devil You Know*; Eli Roth, dir. *Cabin Fever*; Ronny Yu, dir. *Freddie vs Jason*

2004   Michael Arnzen, *100 Jolts: Shockingly Short Stories*; Arthur Machen, *The White People and Other Stories: The Best Weird Tales of Arthur Machen* (*Call of Cthulhu Fiction Series*, 6035); Arthur Machen, *The Terror and Other Tales: The Best Weird Tales of Arthur Machen* (*Call of Cthulhu Fiction Series*); Tess Gerritsen, *Under the Knife*; Stephen King, *Kingdom Hospital* (TV)

Chapter Three

Reading Horror Writing

Reading Horror Writing—Text and Film

We love to read or view horror because we enjoy the chill with which it disturbs our sense of comfort and equally enjoy the way it then finally, monsters banished, returns us to that comfort, secure. We actually *like* to be frightened. But we also like to be reassured that what frightens us—monsters, dark corners, vampires, axe-wielding murderous neighbours—can be controlled. Where does this love of being frightened come from? It appears in our nightmares and dreams, and it seems to creep out as a disturbing thought about all those people and things we need to feel comfortable and safe with—the most familiar—family, partners, and our home. It appears in myths and fairy tales—ogres eating children, terrifying tales such as that of Perrault's Bluebeard, who marries a series of young women and murders them when they open his locked door (behind which they find dead former wives), or Grimms' story of Hansel and Gretel, the 'babes in the wood' abandoned by their parents to starve, almost cooked in an oven by a wicked witch in a delicious-seeming gingerbread house. Much horror even today retells those tales. The 1999 film *The Blair Witch Project* is partly based on the 'babes in the wood' plot, for example. Horror in fiction and film is endlessly popular, reviving these myths, fairy tales, and legends, these hidden fears. It is immensely entertaining. Often it makes us laugh as well as shudder.

Horror also, by exposing and exploring what we fear, by disturbing our complacency and what we take for granted, starts to enable us to face up to contradictions and disturbances in our everyday lives. It acts as a vehicle for exploration of the mind and for exposure of the conflicts and contradictions in society.

Horror has a history in myth, fairy tale, and nightmare, and it also has literary grandparents. The literary Gothic underpins horror and conventional horror, like the Gothic has been used as a vehicle to explore potentially disruptive, hidden fears and desires underlying our sense of security, our social conformity (see chapter 4).

The literary Gothic works by using metaphors and imagery usually of extremes and opposites, gaps, losses, and things hidden, exposing contradictions in our lives and in society. Much literary Gothic focuses on romance, its dangers and final rewards. It uses spaces that are dangerous, at the edge, such as cellars, dungeons, attics, and haunted castles, illustrating and enacting how we push worrying elements of our lives into safe, distant places. The Gothic disinters and exposes these worrying elements, enabling readers to explore contradictions before being returned to security. Horror texts, particularly from the Hammer studio of the sixties and after, use Gothic settings and stories. Horror is a more violent version of the Gothic; it faces us with our desires and our fears—mostly our fears. Explored, dramatised, worked through in a horror fiction, these desires and fears can be sorted out, resolved, and safely returned to the subconscious. For us, as readers and audiences, life goes on. Those who enjoy horror fictions and films, it is argued, do so partly for this formula—the excitement of the disturbance and the comfort of finally reaching 'a point of closure and completion in which disruptive, monstrous elements are contained or destroyed and the original order is re-established' (Jancovich, *Horror* 9). And what is terrifying is often that which is most familiar: We fear potential disruption to our security of self, of place, and of relationships. In more radical horror, however, there is no comfortable return to a (questionable) 'normality', with problems exposed and sorted out.

Guilty Pleasures

Horror is a very popular genre. It increasingly seeps or explodes from our TV and film screens, provides seemingly casual reading for a surprisingly diverse range of readers, crossing social and cultural divides with extraordinary ease. The office temp and the professor, the teenager and our parents (probably more likely our fathers) all read horror. But for me, as an academic in a university and a person living and working in a local community (Cambridge, U.K.), enjoying and discussing it with myself and others has always been something of a guilty pleasure. Horror fiction and film are popular fictions that still attract a great deal of suspicion from the literary critics and provide a great deal of (guilty?) enjoyment for their varied readerships. They seem to offer pure violent and often absurd pleasures, pleasures that some of us would not like to own up to and that some of us find quite nauseating. Other popular fictions (science fiction, romance, crime) are being 'rescued' for literary study, recognised as offering readers certain dialogues with culture and pleasures of multiple readings that provide not only entertainment but a critical dimension. Horror fictions, however, still retain their rather marginal status. This is particularly true when they are read, taught, and written about by the feminist reader, who might be expected to be shocked and irate at the level of abjection in which women are so frequently placed in horror fiction. Women are typically helpless, shrieking victims (damsels in distress, hapless baby-sitters, women walking alone at night) or the cause of the horror-hags, witches, Medusas, monsters, and femmes fatales. Deciding to read a horror fiction or watch a horror film seems a rather sick choice at best, at worst, something quite perverse.

A woman reading a popular romance on the beach, round the pool, or on the commuter train causes few confused responses. You are presumed to be a dupe for the promises romances offer—a bored housewife and escapist office worker. If you are a feminist, you can at least get away with arguing that you are reading romances in order to critique them. This has become a commonplace response, even if we readers are secretly enjoying some of the formulae we read. Reading crime novels has much the same response: no lifted eyebrows or double takes from those around you. But reading a horror novel is very different. What, those who notice you wonder, is going on in your head to make you want to read something deliberately nasty, absurdly fantastic, gruesome, and disgusting (possibly even pornographic)? It is not something easy to own up to among friends and acquaintances, and it is even more difficult to admit among academics. Or it was. I have spent some time wondering myself why I enjoyed and sought out 'horror comics' and the *Tales from the Crypt* alongside *Superman* and *Batman*. There was a particularly surprising disclosure of the oddity of my tastes when, visiting my mother's parents in Hull, North of England, on an extremely rare visit from our life abroad, I tried to buy a horror comic at the Hull station. The woman at the kiosk visibly blanched and stared at my mother as if she were some kind of monster. Such comics had been banned in the U.K. I settled for a *Superman* comic and wondered what had produced this criminalisation of my favourite pursuit (I was nine years old). Later, Martin Barker (*A Haunt of Fears*, 1984), in tracking the alignment between the radical critique of horror comics and the repressive politics that shut them down in the fifties and sixties, began to make connections between horror's pleasures and its potential as an ideologically engaged, critical vehicle.

Popular fictions of all kinds have attracted critical scrutiny about our motivations for reading, our cultural reading practices, and the pleasures we derive from this. As Janice Radway's work *Reading the Romance: Women, Patriarchy and Popular Literature* suggests, '[T]he act of reading can carry quite separate meanings from the texts themselves' (Radway 1991, 139).

Radway's readers describe reading romances as restorative, relaxing. Horror also provides a forum in which to explore life's problems and potential. Romance offers the projection of a variety of idealised scenarios. Horror is more cathartic; its explorations lead to dead ends (which can restore a sense of peace after a crisis), to fantasy escapes, and, like science fiction, to alternative readings of our worlds. Horror is essentially a subversive form that destabilises the complacent and the popular alike, allowing creative freedoms to see things differently, to encourage imaginative projections of both what we desire and what we fear, which are frequently the same.

For our own age, aware of the constructedness of our beliefs and behaviours, of the performances we play and of the cracks and contradictions opening up in all of these, horror is a perfect fit, a fantasy space for our needs, for exploration of such contradictions and for projection of new possibilities. Horror is the ultimate creative, imaginative, and subversive mode. This should not be surprising, for its roots are in the Gothic, which, also, conventionally destabilised norms and offered alternatives in the very rigid society of the eighteenth century in Britain and Europe, where it first made its literary appearances. In the 1960s and 1970s in the United States, the Gothic was revived in the midst of the Vietnam War, enabling scepticism to be embodied, and for Middle America and then middle England to question their own complacencies. It is this marvelous potential for subversion, irony, and imaginative space that enables horror to appeal to the whole of society, people with imagination as well as the average taxpayer. This enables a critique of what is comfortably taken for granted at our peril, a very healthy critique.

Horror's potential for both enjoyment and critique resides in its subversion and its ironizing tendencies, its exposure of alternatives, its destabilising of the stable, and its defamiliarisation of the completely familiar. Horror provides such a marvelous opportunity for a rich reading response. I would argue that our enjoyment of horror takes those two linked responses, pleasure and subversion, and pleasure at subversion. We can enjoy what frightens and destabilises us, and that can enable us to see things as other than they appear to be, and to choose to live our lives in our own ways rather than be forced to do so, as moral dupes easily thrown by the slightest crack in the seeming coherence of our society.

Clive Barker comments:

> Of course, there's the 'guilty pleasure' aspect of all this: that while I love well-turned phrases and great cinema, I also have a sentimental fondness for the literary or cinematic equivalent of *Titus Andronicus*. Indeed, there are times when the sheer artlessness of a Z-grade zombie flick can tellingly reveal the root of the genre's fascination in a fashion that a more sophisticated piece of work may conceal. (Barker, 19)

In the context of the 'casual cruelty of our world', taking comfort in the fantastic representations of such cruelty might, Barker argues, reduce distress and provide a sense of control. He also raises the problem of horror's potential (it is claimed) to encourage, even wallow, in violence and the deliberately nasty:

Bathing for a time in the red rivers of violence and retribution that feed the heart of this fiction may indeed wash away some part of our insanity; discharging our anger by indulging our private monsters. But if it doesn't—if we're simply making ourselves all the crazier by inflaming these appetites—then I humbly suggest that it's the way of the world and perhaps our culture, in its fall from faith and certainty, *needs* to go through a dark night of the soul, in which the atrocities of street and battlefront, and those conjured by storytellers, becoming one seamless nightmare . . .

Only this seems certain: the subject is part of our psyche from childhood, enshrined in innumerable tales as a force that helps us understand the primal battle of our natures. The abomination, whether it comes in the form of a fairy tale dragon, a serial killer, a piece of special effects or a crazed terrorist, is a necessary part of the human story. It defines what the best in us despises; and reminds us how close to it we come in our most forbidden thoughts. (Barker, 19–20)

The dangerous pleasures offered by horror attract us from both sides of the night. It is wild and alternative; its energies—slow, relentless, creeping, exploding—match and encourage the release of our own. It is a catalyst, a catharsis. In horror, events, people, and actions move from the unthinkable into a bodied-forth version of the unbearable, one you can see, experience, suffer, and ultimately handle. Its rhythms match ours. It is a slow buildup to an explosion of something terrifying; the relentlessness of the unstoppable; continuing to and beyond the unbearable; the sudden intrusion or extrusion of the unexpected and the violent; the stupefying feeling of having what you took for granted exposed as quite different, quite the opposite. And in horror we face up to this and either explain it and close it down, return it to order, or, in more radical contemporary horror, recognise it as a projection of a part of ourselves, not Other to us. Then closing it down would be absurd and futile. In such variations on and developments of horror, we see this very Otherising as an ultimately blinkered, destructive defence mechanism, and the characters, events, actions, settings of horror become reinvested with insight and social critique. Horror figures—

vampire, werewolf, femme fatale, a host of monsters—are recuperated, celebrated, or at least tolerated and recognised.

The release of energies horror involves exposes pomposity; hypocrisy; power games; the artifice of respectability, hiding deception and violence; and the falseness of romantic relationships of family life and of social, political, and work hierarchies. This radical, deviant, wild energy assaults and exposes the lies upon which we either base our sense of security or by which others, defended by a status quo that claims to be 'right', ordered, logical, good, healthy, and in control, controls us.

Poppy Z. Brite's alienated, punk, post-Vietnam youth (*Lost Souls, Swamp Foetus*) erupted from the dark, repressed side of a society that sent its young men to die fruitlessly for a dubious political cause. The escape onto highways, into small towns, and alternative religions and cultures of Caitlin Kiernan's America (*Silk*) cannot keep the trapdoor shut on the cellar of social and individual horrors, darkness, abuse, and the abyss of pointlessness and absurdity. If you are terrified of scuttling things just out of eyesight, hovering on the edge of consciousness, keeping spiders helps you feel you control it; so might mantras, friends, or lifestyles. Hot dinners on the family table and pretty clothes do this for others, such as Virginia Andrews's families (*Flowers in the Attic*), but horror fictions expose your tenuous attempts to keep the terrors at bay: 'we keep the wolf outside by living well' (Angela Carter, 'The Company of Wolves').

Angela Carter, contemporary feminist Gothic and magic realist, reread and rewrote fairy tales, exploring, exposing, and overturning their sexual and gendered messages. For me, as for so many others, Carter brought horror into perspective as a vehicle for psychoanalysis and social critique as part of 'legitimized' academic study. She bridged the gap between 'high art' and 'popular culture', a gap which was very firmly demarcated even in later years of the twentieth century, but which has, thankfully, been eroded now, giving us leave to reread even the classic fictions, or hidden fictions by classic writers, in a different way. So, we discover/rediscover George Eliot's *The Lifted Veil*, Edith Wharton's ghost stories, Virginia Woolf's haunting *A Haunted House*, and we enjoy and critically speculate about the arguments explored within and by a diverse range of popular fictional forms, from comic strip to film, to prizewinning 'great literary' novels (Margaret Atwood's *The Robber Bride*, with the vampiric Zenia, for example).

Feminist critiques of horror and contemporary feminist horror writing are critically engaged and provocative. They can both expose cultural constructions that feed into conventional horror's disempowering, constricted roles for women and can also (with Carter, Jewelle Gomez, and others in the lead) provide a carnivalesque opportunity to overturn and criticise relationships of power and accepted certainties. The energy of overturning is a release of fun. The critique is enabling: We can imagine creative possibilities.

Reading Frankenstein—*a Classic Horror Tale*

We have probably seen films and read comics that portray Frankenstein as a monster, bolts sticking out of his neck, bandages waving, as he slaughters people and walks with a lumbering mechanical walk. He is huge, terrifying. In fact, of course, in the original tale, Frankenstein is the name of the scientist who creates the monster rather than the monster itself.

Mary Shelley started to write *Frankenstein* when she and her friends—including her husband, the poet Percy Bysshe Shelley; Byron; and the British writer and doctor John Polidori—were holidaying by the side of Lake Geneva in Europe. Each member of the party decided to write a Gothic tale, there were thunderstorms and lightning, and Mary produced *Frankenstein*. We all know the story. The mad scientist Dr Frankenstein decides he will dedicate himself to creating life. He raids graves for body parts, slaves long hours in his laboratory, and brings to life the monster he makes using lightning/electricity. The monster is so hideous that Frankenstein rejects it. Gradually, it learns that everyone fears it because it seems so ugly, huge, and strange, and then, initially by accident, unaware of its own strength (and later in planned revenge), it kills people. Hunted down, the monster escapes on an ice floe.

So why do people like to watch *Frankenstein* films and read the novel? And what would we read for in considering the text as horror (as opposed to autobiography, journal, or science fiction)? It is a very well written novel using letters and journals written by the scientist, Dr Victor Frankenstein, his friend Walton, and the monster himself (surprisingly well-expressed entries by the monster . . .). Our responses of horror to the monster are based in deep-seated fears about things that are not human, which seem Other, different from ourselves, and which we assume wish to harm us. The horror in this tale also derives from disgust and fears at daring God and nature and creating life artificially. This is partly why we are also currently worried about genetically modified crops and cloning of animals and, worse still, of people. *Frankenstein* uses natural descriptions derived from the language of the literary Gothic—blasted landscapes, extreme weather, lightning, ice, and storm. The novel also invites a variety of readings, each related to troubling elements of our lives, thoughts, and society. It questions what it means to be human, or monstrous, what identity is (is the monster a criminal? A person? A dubious side to the scientist Victor Frankenstein?); the devastating effects of social, personal, and nature-related mistakes (lack of 'parental' love turns this noble savage dangerously wild); guilt, revenge (felt by the monster towards Frankenstein); and physical violence (Justine and Elizabeth as well as several vulnerable others die). Shelley's tale is entertaining as well as frightening and able to raise such philosophical personal and social issues.

Reading 'The Company of Wolves'

Horror is not only a branch of the literary Gothic; much of it lies on the borderline between terrible truths using historical realism, cold-blooded tales, and real elements for its shocks and conjuring up latent terrors from the darkness and fireside of our ancestral histories, the supernatural and the weird. The ability to read horror lies in recognizing the ways in which it (1) is engaged with our imaginations, our psychology, our inner selves, and (2) manages and dramatises images and versions of what it means to be human, the social/cultural dimensions and concerns. Representation—the metaphorical and analogous, the symbolic—is a threshold concept in the study of literature and the arts per se. So, too, is the concern with what can be constructed and performed as 'normal', 'everyday', or radical, questioning and problematising that 'normality'. We need to identify metaphorical, representational characteristics, the ways in which by looking into the imaginary, our subconscious, and imaginations, horror engages fundamentally with our hidden desires, fears, sense of reality or otherwise, and our humanity or lack of it. 'The Company of Wolves' tells a story and suggests, represents, signifies. As imaginative literature, it disturbs complacency with the ordinary, problematising what is taken for granted and releasing creativity. The form of writing in which this story challenges the taken for granted and encourages creative, imaginative probing and thinking is also important.

David Lodge has pointed out (*The Modes of Modern Writing*, 1977) that writers tend to position themselves along a continuum. At one end lies the symbolic, the utterly fantastic, quite removed from reality, and at the other, the factual documentary, of which Hansard, that word-by-word record of parliamentary speech, is the prime example—as close as we can get through the shifting medium of language to actually capturing what is real (though what is real even here is mediated by language—spoken then written). Angela Carter's 'The Company of Wolves' is one of those texts that engages readers on both sides of the boundary between the realistic/historical and the metaphorical/imaginary/supernatural. This it does through its utilisation at first of the language of journalism and realism, gathering documented case histories, and then its use, parallel to this, of the language of the imagination, the Gothic or deepseated unease that disturbs the prosaic recording of how many and who were dismembered by what wolves. Here enters the notion that these wolves of which we read, the wolves of storytelling and fairy tale of 'Little Red Riding Hood', are wolves of our imagination, representatives of our fears of what cannot be controlled or kept at bay, understood, prevented, or denied. They might be wolves who are our other selves, werewolves in fact.

'The Company of Wolves' (1981) rewrites the traditional fairy tale of 'Little Red Riding Hood', exploring its potential for horror and exposing its base in patriarchal power relations. The boundaries between myth and historical record are troubled in the opening pages, as incidents of confrontations with werewolves are detailed with the historical accuracy of nineteenth-century local historians such as Rev. Sabine Baring-Gould, who records incidents of werewolves and vampires (Baring-Gould, *The Book of Werewolves*). It is realistic: 'There was a hunter once, near here that trapped a wolf in a pit' (Carter 111), but in death the wolf metamorphosed into a man.

The process, once begun through the familiar 'Little Red Riding Hood' tale, is so self-aware of its own constructedness that the terrors and resolutions of the original are put in perspective. Young women arriving at puberty should fear roving, predatory men. It is a horror tale to terrify young women, constructed of the father's fear of his daughter's violation and loss of chastity, of worth, and the threat to lineage and property ownership. The girl's growing sexuality is signified in the red cloak, the predatory undependable male in the wolf, and the resolution and restoration of patriarchal order in the woodcutter who eventually prevents the wolf's rape/devouring of the girl.

Rosaleen is marked as a potential sacrificial victim, her red (blood) hood contrasted against white (virginity). The dual nature of the dashing young stranger she meets is indicated in the ambiguity of his description:

> When she heard the freezing howl of a distant wolf, her practiced hand sprang to the handle of her knife, but she saw no sign of a wolf at all, nor of a naked man, neither, but then she heard a clattering among the bushwood and there sprang into her path a fully clothed one, a very handsome young one. (Carter 114)

The conflation of wolf and young man is obvious, and werewolves, the tale suggests, are really only versions of ourselves: 'The worst wolves are hairy on the inside' (Carter 114). Rosaleen falls for the 'commonplace of a rustic seduction' from the young man whose eyebrows tellingly meet in the middle (one sign of a werewolf) (117).

Despite her grandmother's precautions—'we keep the wolves outside by living well' (117)—the invasion of hearth, home, and body is a consistent threat. The red, nocturnal, predatory eyes are unperturbed by latched doors, banked fires, Bibles, and other domestic insurance: 'night and the forest have come into the kitchen with darkness tangled in its hair' (116).

Rosaleen spots traces of her missing, devoured granny like a trained sleuth, and although she fears the blood 'she must spill' (117) (his or hers?), she answers the wolf/man back, forgets her fear, and throws both their clothes in the fire, having undressed him. His practiced moves and lines are absurd; he thinks he is in control:

> 'All the better to eat you with.'
>   The girl burst out laughing; she knew she was nobody's meat. She laughed at him full in the face, she ripped off his shirt for him and flung it full in the fire, in the fiery wake of her own discarded clothing. (Carter 117)
>   Every wolf in the world now howled a prothalamium outside the window as she freely gave him the kiss she owed him. (Carter 118)

Sleeping between the paws of the tender wolf, Rosaleen has her sexual partner tamed her own way. The horror/fairy tale has a resolution that returns sexual power to women.

Angela Carter's young Rosaleen reveals herself as an equal partner in the sexual games the werewolf initiates. If werewolfishness connotes unleashed sexuality, Rosaleen's answering of his standard questions and her burning all their clothes, trapping them in their werewolf condition, connotes her desire to embrace and take control of her own sexual fate. In a closure in which women's sexuality is allowed energetic free rein despite male attempts at control (rape and devouring, or rescue), the result is a new celebratory howling. The trajectory of the cautionary horror tale is evident until the end of the story. A restoration of normality and order at the story's end *doesn't* return Rosaleen as the daughter of patriarchy but instead rewards her sexual energies. There is harmony without restoration of the status quo.

Radical and feminist (although she would have baulked at the description), Carter exposes much of horror's collusion in conformity, complacency, and conservatism—instead she empowers her Rosaleen/Little Red Riding Hood to recognise the beast in herself and the lover in the beast.

Carter's tale serves as a paradigm for much radical women's horror and for reading horror more generally. It utilises the tropes and trajectory of a conventional horror tale: threats amid the familiar, the deceptiveness of what seems attractive and safe, the instability of ordered lives and norms (Granny's precautions, warnings to Rosaleen) to protect from real danger, but it then disturbs them, with

Rosaleen's embracing of werewolfishness and so of her own sexuality. Pam Keesey's collection *Women Who Run with the Werewolves* (1996) unleashes further eroticised werewolf encounters.

In teaching Carter's 'The Company of Wolves', it is at the point where the handsome young man is revealed as a werewolf, and the tale identifiable as being about ways in which patriarchal authority, colluded in by women, controls young girls' sexuality, that readers pass between and can handle simultaneously both kinds of writing, the factually realistic and the imaginatively representative. In so doing, they/we engage imagination, enjoyment, and our social and textual critical functions. Through the medium of a horror scenario, the language and imagery of Gothic horror, we appreciate a social dialogue between the conformist 'normal' (young girls need sexual obedience and restraint; wolves are wolves and there are no such things as man/wolves or werewolves) and the creative and imaginative revelations or problems, questions, and issues to be considered. Especially in terms of sexuality, men and women can be like animals—is that so bad? Those you think you 'know' (e.g., young men, others) could hide alternative selves; we are not so safe as we feel we are just by maintaining a civilised exterior and domestic order (Granny is devoured first).

'The Company of Wolves' specifically uses the characteristics of horror to ask questions about sexuality, liberty, and convention. It considers an arena of vulnerability and danger for conventional families, where ownership of the woman could pass indiscreetly to another man, one not licensed by the family, or worse still, be governed by the decision-making process of the girl herself. Carter's Rosaleen/Little Red Riding Hood is warned about wolves and about young men whose eyebrows meet in the middle. Clearly, the wolf is a man, but even when Granny has been devoured and conventional, regulated behaviours and beliefs about civilisation have failed her one after another, we recognise that like the catechism or spaniel ornaments (rather than real dogs), they are merely constructions we agree to believe in.

Carter's text enables her readers to engage at the level of storyline *and* metaphor; in so doing, it exemplifies how horror uses a variety of strategies to enable us to see what we desire and fear— sometimes to exorcise having it dramatised, and sometimes to recognise that the threat born of our own instabilities will linger beyond any story precisely because it is our own product. Here, horror is being read to terrify and entertain, to challenge the constructed borderline between reality and fantasy, and to identify ways in which we can imagine handling what we worry about socially, culturally, and personally: body invasion and challenges to our conventional behaviours and beliefs in identity, family, humanity, and self.

If we return to the question of how we read horror, there are several answers. We read horror for entertainment, shock, the enjoyment of being scared and thrilled, and the satisfaction of closure once the monster has been destroyed, buried, or staked through the heart or the haunted house has been burned to the ground, the chainsaw unplugged. But the lingering pleasure of horror is its constant destabilising influence rather than its tendency for resolution. We read it as an index of the cultural, imaginary values, threats, and potential threats, and as a cultural critique disturbing complacencies and fixities, thus returning to us our potential to be on edge and so deal with risks, problems, and differences in these descriptions. Horror can be a very conditional and conservative genre or one that is more deeply radical. It also provides for readers ways into appreciating philosophically and politically the constructedness of all representations and the power of metaphor and the imaginary. In the end, horror uses image and metaphor to embody what we fear. It is up to us to be able to track back and recognise the sources of these embodied fears; the way we might handle them is not exactly to overcome them. Missing the metaphorical in reading horror, reading it as merely a mirror to reality, is a huge imaginative and critical loss; reading it as a blueprint for action is potentially highly dangerous. However, there are those who dismiss horror just as entertaining and despicable, pointless splatter (and some of it is, of course!).

Chapter Four

The Best and the Best Known

This chapter explores key horror fictions through time, explaining their lasting power, the kinds of characteristics they have established in the genre, and the reasons why they have lasted. It considers major horror writers, providing brief profiles of their work and the major works of horror directors, producers, and studios.

History

Horror of different forms has always been with us as a dark accompaniment to the comforts and certainties of developing civilisations. It appears in sagas, tales by the fire, by the bedside, in the terrors of *Beowulf*, the ogres and monsters of myth and fairy stories, and the figure of Satan himself, the devil, from the Bible, and in different guises but playing a similar role—incarnate evil—in other cultures. The genre of horror has been labeled as such most likely only since the emergence of the tales of the great horror master, Edgar Allan Poe. From Poe we can then read backwards and identify its characteristics in earlier work. Historically, until relatively recently, for many writers, it was unlikely that their work would be recognised as horror because the genre itself had other names—the Gothic, fantasy, weird—or because it was not considered a genre sufficiently polite or highbrow with which to recognise the work of great writers. It is a revelation, then, to discover that so many of the canonical poets and novelists wrote what we could broadly define as horror, from the ghost stories of Dickens and Wharton, the vampire and succubus tales of the romantic poets Keats and Coleridge, to the supernatural moments in arch-realist George Eliot, specifically in *The Lifted Veil* (1859). Redefinitions return to us a variety of rich horror texts hidden until now as the secondary, unknown, or improperly defined work of their authors.

H. P. Lovecraft, acknowledged master of the genre, identifies a variety of horror antecedents in what was probably the first critical text to attempt to define the genre, concentrating as it did on the supernatural or weird arenas of horror. In *Supernatural Horror in Literature* he notes that:

> Most of the ancient instances, curiously enough, are in prose; as the werewolf incident in Petronius, the gruesome passages in Apuleius, the brief but celebrated letter of Pliny the Younger to Sura, and the odd compilation *On Wonderful Events* by the Emperor Hadrian's Greek freed-man, Phlegon. It is in Phlegon that we first find that hideous tale of the corpse-bride, *Philinnion and Machates*, later related by Proclus and in modern times forming the inspiration of Goethe's *Bride of Corinth* and Washington Irving's *German Student*. (Lovecraft 20)

Tracing the genre further back into sagas and ancient tales of cosmic and real violence and anger, Lovecraft recognises:

> The Scandinavian Eddas and Sagas thunder with cosmic horror, and shake with the stark fear of Ymir and his shape-less spawn; whilst our own Anglo-Saxon Beowulf and the later Continental Nibelung tales are full of eldritch weird-ness. (Lovecraft 20)

Jacobean revenge dramas, including many of Shakespeare's own tragedies, contain a rich variety of horror, so Webster's *The Duchess of Malfi* (1623) and *The White Devil* (1612) demonstrate many of the characteristics we have later come to recognise as true to hor-ror. In *The Duchess of Malfi*, a beautiful, sexually active woman becomes a threat to her domineering, possessive, and sexually jeal-ous, powerful brothers, ostensibly because of the threat she repre-sents to good behaviour and their position (one is a cardinal). The tenor of the play, however, suggests that maintenance of the fam-ily's good name is not the main motive of revenge when their sister takes a young courtier, Antonio, first as a lover, then as her husband. Ferdinand, in particular, uses the language of lust and incest to evi-dence his mixed desire for his sister and his disgust at her sexuality, which, as it is conventionally represented, is both socially unacceptable (women were meant to be obedient and not display their sexual activity) and the cause of such troubling desire in him. Pre-Freud, Lacan, and Kristeva, this represents a convincing case of the transferred guilt and disgust that leads to labelling women femmes fatales, whose transgressive actions invite punishment and destruction. Apart from grave digging and carrying corpses over his shoulder by the legs, in his madness (lycanthropia: Ferdinand's actions are said to spring from his latent tendency to express the characteristics of a wolf—in modern terms we would designate him a werewolf) Ferdinand is also a potential incestuous lover scorned and the guardian of the family honour. In one of the very first examples of what soon became a conventional twist of horror, most popular in film noir, Ferdinand and the Cardinal must first torment and destroy all that is dear to her—her husband and children—and then kill their sister. In psychoanalytic terms, much later to be defined by Julia Kristeva (1982), they have literally abjected the duchess, created and constructed her, laden with desire and disgust, and rejected her from their lives through murder. Through these acts, theoretically explored/explained within the psychoanalytic frame, the brothers have absolved themselves of any guilt, sexual perversity, or lust, and they figure themselves as some kind of valiant upholders of moral virtue and conformity.

This horror turn of abjection and destruction typically does not only single out the representation and treatment of women (see chapters 5–7). Fundamentally, it focuses on the sense of feeling threatened by everything that is not self and which could destabilise the wholeness of the self. It comes into being in horror as that which we must create first from our *own* terrible desires and imaginings and then, having objectified and extradited it to a space well outside our own actions and culpability, destroy it and put it to rest. In identifying that we create this abjected Other from ourselves (Kristeva 1988), we should be able to recognise the objects and events of horror emerging from our fears and desires and so avoid the complacency that they can be ignored, forgotten, and killed off permanently.

H. P. Lovecraft does not analyse Jacobean revenge dramas from a feminist or a psychoanalytical standpoint but instead recognises a dramatisation of the demonic in the figure of Webster's terrible brothers. Elsewhere, in Shakespeare's work, for example, we see horror in the devilish malice of Iago, who plays upon the racially constructed insecurities of Othello, and in *Macbeth*, where greed and desire for promotion are embodied in the deceptive, frightful allure of the witches on the blasted heath. Their imaginings conjure up a future where Macbeth will be Thane of Cawdor, then King, and secondly, where his line will fall to that of Banquo, thus setting Macbeth off on a murder spree abetted by his wife, whose more overt ambition is, like his, embodied as an outside force in the three graceless ones, the witches or hags.

Lovecraft identifies the contemporary links with witchcraft and magic, close beneath the surface of everyday lives in the Elizabethan and Jacobean periods:

> In Elizabethan drama, with its *Dr. Faustus*, the witches in *Macbeth*, the ghost in *Hamlet*, and the horrible gruesomeness of Webster, we may easily discern the strong hold of the demonic on the public mind; a hold intensified by the very real fear of living witchcraft, whose terrors, wildest at first on the Continent, begin to echo loudly in English ears as the witch-hunting crusades of James the First gain headway. To the lurking mystical prose of the ages is added a long line of treatises on witchcraft and demonology which aid in exciting the imagination of the reading world. (Lovecraft, *Supernatural Horror in Literature* 20–21)

Demonology inspires Oberon in *A Midsummer Night's Dream* also, but his powers are mitigated by the comic moment and lightness of some of the play's elements. Lovecraft's history of the stronghold of supernatural horror on the common mind and on creative writers' expression moves through ballads and legends in the following centuries up to the horror tales of the great nineteenth-century authors, including Defoe and Dickens.

> Through the seventeenth and eighteenth century we behold a growing mass of fugitive legendary and balladry of darksome cast; still, however, held down beneath the surface of polite and accepted literature. Chapbooks of horror and weirdness multiplied, and we glimpse the eager interest of the people through fragments like Defoe's *Apparition*

of Mrs. Veal, a homely tale of a dead woman's spectral visit
to a distant friend, written to advertise a badly selling the-
ological disquisition on death. (21)

The Romantic poets are a prime example of the literary Gothic and
its characteristics of horror, featuring vampire women and figures of
terror such as Christabel and the terrible haunting memories of the
Ancient Mariner. Lovecraft notes:

> The shadow-haunted landscapes of *Ossian,* the chaotic
> visions of William Blake, the grotesque witch dances in
> Burns' *Tam O'Shanter,* the sinister daemonism of
> Coleridge's *Christabel* and *Ancient Mariner,* the ghostly
> charm of James Hogg's *Kilmeny,* and the more restrained
> approaches to cosmic horror in *Lamia* and many of Keats'
> other poems, are typical British illustrations of the advent
> of the weird to formal literature. Our Teutonic cousins of
> the continent were equally receptive to the rising flood, and
> Burger's *Wild Huntsman* and the even more famous dae-
> mon-bridegroom ballad of *Lenore*—both imitated in
> English by Scott. (23)

The main antecedent of the horror genre lies in the literary Gothic,
developed as a response to the cold reason of the Enlightenment,
which denied the value of anything not quantifiable, measurable, or
provable in cold daylight reason. In this respect, the Gothic and horror, its more violent and disturbing relatives, provide a healthy anti-
dote to the somewhat complacent attitudes of the Enlightenment,
attitudes that we must remember also denigrated non-white
Europeans and Others of all kinds.

The Literary Gothic

Beginning in the eighteenth century, with novels such as Horace
Walpole's *The Castle of Otranto* (1765) and Ann Radcliffe's
Mysteries of Udolpho (1794), the literary Gothic explores contradictions and unease in social conventions. It enables readers to question what is taken for granted, such as families, identity, love, and
inheritance. It works by using metaphors and imagery usually of
extremes and opposites, gaps, losses, and things hidden, and so

exposes contradictions in our lives and in society. Much literary Gothic focuses on romance, its dangers and final rewards, and so many romantic fictions have used Gothic settings, stories, and stereotypes. Much Gothic uses spaces that are dangerous, at the edge, such as cellars, dungeons, attics, and haunted castles—illustrating how we, in our minds, push those elements of our lives about which we are concerned into ostensibly (temporary, of course) safe, removed places. The Gothic brings them out again, exposes them, and enables readers to explore contradictions before being returned to security. In modern times, many horror films in particular use Gothic settings and stories, such as the British Hammer studio films of the sixties and after.

Horror is a branch of the Gothic and so we would expect to see many Gothic elements in much contemporary horror, although the more documentary-type realistic horror—*The Texas Chainsaw Massacre, 28 Days Later*—contains fewer Gothic traces than do the full-blown inheritors, such as *Dracula* and its various spawn—legions of vampire films and stories. Gothic settings can be recognised in the fetid cabin of horrors containing dismembered travelers and body parts in *Wrong Turn* (2003), where inbred cannibalistic backwoodsmen ensnare then devour pleasure- or action-seeking travellers wandering off course.

Women's Horror

Mary Shelley is one of the most important originators of what has become modern horror, but oddly women are often not thought to actually write horror at all, their work being described as something else, such as ghost stories or the fantastic. However, women figure in conventional horror in a variety of roles, including hags and witches, victims, bimbos, and femmes fatales. These different versions of women in horror spring from certain social and individualised fears. Hags and witches are the construction of the Bad Mother rather than the Good Mother, one who seems nurturing but in fact tricks, devours, overwhelms. The seemingly kindly witch in the gingerbread house in 'Babes in the Wood' becomes the evil witch in *The Blair Witch Project*; mothers in the mould of Medea prevent their children from growing up, stifle, murder, and devour them (Virginia Andrews, *Flowers in the Attic*). Femmes fatales and alluring, dangerous women derive from the myth of Eve but also from the legendary sirens who sang to Ulysses and his men, aiming to lure them onto the rocks and to their deaths.

We might expect that women horror writers would themselves sometimes replicate these stereotypical representations of women, and sometimes abhor and baulk at their limitations, deciding instead to write differently, reverse the stereotypes, deny them, delving into what horrifies or disturbs women in particular. Often, indeed, women horror writers can be seen to explore and then exorcise very different configurations of horror, investing different spaces, places, and relations with the powers of horror. Looking at such differences, Lisa Tuttle in the important collection of contemporary women's horror *Skin of the Soul* (1990) notes:

> Territory which to a man is emotionally neutral, may for a woman be mined with fear, and vice versa. For example: the short walk home from the bus-stop of an evening. And how to understand the awesome depths of loathing some men feel for the ordinary (female) human body? We all understand the language of fear, but men and women are raised speaking different dialects of that language. (Tuttle 41)

Contemporary women Gothic horror writers work to critique assumptions underlying male sexualised terrors (see Chris Baldick, *The Oxford Book of Gothic Tales* xiv). They reverse roles, imbricate different scenarios with the texture and atmosphere of horror, and celebrate that which is so often the wellspring of male sexualised horror, women's sexual energies. Sexual oppression and claustrophobic spaces are tackled by contemporary women's horror, although different results often follow from those found in more conventional horror.

Women horror theorists and critics such as French feminists Julia Kristeva and Luce Irigaray theorise both the gendered sources of horror and ways in which these can be challenged and undercut (see chapter 7). Kristeva recognises that we construct and project out of our own fears and need for identity those things and elements of self that terrify and disgust, so that we might attack and destroy them. She exposes them as a way of overcoming our fears and owning up to them, admitting to their location and source in our own lives, as parts of ourselves. In this respect, much of women's horror challenges not only the furniture, events, and characterisation common to conventional horror but also the psychoanalytical and social impulses behind it. By recognising the source of horror as a projection of elements of self, fears that a calm order that might actually constrict women's lives might be disturbed, these writers challenge the forms and shapes of horror. Much women's horror refuses the closure and punishment, the restoration of order, insisting on this recognition of ourselves in the construction of that which has conventionally been seen as Other, as disgusting and rejected, as abject.

Considering horror and abjection, Kristeva (1982) defines the abject as those substances that the body needs to reject, make Other, in order for the subject to be able to recognise itself. She argues that the first abjected Other is the mother, so mothers and, by contagion, women, are constructed as Others, borderline creatures fascinating because of their difference from the self, but engulfing and destructive, overwhelming the self. In *The Powers of Horror: An Essay on Abjection* (1982), Kristeva identifies a particularly male-derived imaginative response that fears women's generative powers and their potential for engulfment, responding for self-preservation, with destructive acts, attempting to destroy the Other. In this economy, women and sexually active women, in particular, can be constructed as dangerous, desirable but destructive— the femme fatale, Medusa, a myriad of demonised female figures, dramatised. Such Otherising is followed by destroying the perpetrator, the woman. As Kristeva and others indicate, however, it is the male who creates this kind of female figure from his threatened psychical position.

This recognition of the Other, the impulse to abject, can be turned to positive effect in contemporary women's horror. Recognising that the Other is our other half, that we offload fears of death onto this monstrous female construction, can liberate. Celebrating our Other is empowering. It can undercut binary oppositions by showing they are twin sides of the same: yoked. For some writers, this yoking of opposites is actually enacted through the language, as in Angela Carter and Poppy Z. Brite. Theirs is often confrontational, oppositional, and carnivalesque contemporary women's horror. In their work, horror provides an entertaining and provocative vehicle for interrogating gender representations and assumptions, as well as other configurations of power.

The Best and Best-Known Writers

Mary Shelley (1797–1851)

Mary Shelley was the daughter of William Godwin (*Caleb Williams*), great Enlightenment thinker, and Mary Wollstonecraft, great proto-feminist. Wollstonecraft's *Vindication of the Rights of Woman* (1792) took to task and demolished the reasoning behind Rousseau's work *Emile*, which matched the differing education of men and women to their (in his view) clearly hierarchically different, 'natural' capabilities. With two great thinkers as her parents (though Mary Wollstonecraft died in childbirth), her father's library at her command, and a Romantic poet, Percy Bysshe Shelley, for her husband, Mary Shelley married her understanding of the arguments of the Enlightenment—reason, order, and logic—to her critique of its shortcomings and her love of the Gothic, the imaginative, metaphorical, creative, problematising, and problem-solving creativity and speculation of the Romantic period and its creative writers.

Frankenstein (1818)   *Frankenstein* is one of the classic original horror tales—replayed, reinterpreted, and misrepresented in popular fictions ever since it was written. *Frankenstein* has also been recognised as the birth (or a rebirth) not only of the horror tale but also of science fiction. Interestingly, *Frankenstein* appeared on the popular stage many times during the nineteenth century. Jancovich acknowledges:

> The Gothic novel which has enjoyed the most enduring popular success is without doubt Mary Shelley's *Frankenstein* (1818). . . . Part of the reason for the novel's success is that it extends its critique of the separation of spheres beyond the sexual politics of the middle-class family, and relates it to the horrors of modernity and scientific rationality. It does not simply identify the horrific or monstrous with the creature, who is presented as a sympathetic

character, but also identifies it with Frankenstein's own scientific activities. (Jancovich, *Horror* 25)

Mary Shelley's astonishing narrative of the dangers of scientific hubris in a post-Enlightenment age is also a birth trauma tale, one where the 'mother', here Victor Frankenstein, is disgusted and repulsed by what he has given birth to and rejects it with disastrous consequences. Shelley wrote *Frankenstein* while sequestered with Byron, Shelley, and Polidori on the shores of Lake Geneva, each writing a Gothic tale in a terrifying storm at the height of the Gothic era (an event portrayed in Ken Russell's elaborate and excessive film *Gothic*, 1986). One of the lingering fascinations of *Frankenstein* is the way in which it touches on our terrors of man as monster or automaton, dehumanised, dangerous, and let loose (a theme explored in later android or robot films questioning the nature of what it means to be human, including *Blade Runner* [1982] and *I, Robot* [2004]). The monster turns destructive when rejected by its creator, thus encouraging a social constructivist reading of the text. This interpretation sits alongside the reading of the story as a challenge to the Enlightenment belief that science and reason explain everything, that you can construct and challenge anything, and that there are no mysteries, even mysteries of life, so life can be created as a challenge to the power of God.

Frankenstein also critiques the notion that education is good for its own sake, since Victor Frankenstein's education has led to his inability to care for others and to his practising of science without morality. As a Gothic text, the novel also moves beyond the merely popular, such as William Dicey's broadsides and the popular 'blue books' or 'shilling shockers'—cheap productions of Gothic tales of the supernatural or of violent crime. Even with added moral comments, these were sensational and considered a threat to the innocent, unguided minds of middle-class schoolboys, young women, and newly literate working classes. *Frankenstein* also deviated from the romantic and sentimental Gothics influenced by Anne Radcliffe's work.

Early readers of *Frankenstein* seem concerned with culture, the formation of character, and the role of reading. 'It inculcates no lesson of conduct, manners, or morality; it cannot mend, and will not

even amuse its readers, unless their tastes have been deplorably viti-
ated' (*The Quarterly Review* 385). Another reader notes it is philosophical: 'All these monstrous concepts are the consequences of the
wild and irregular theories of the age' (*Edinburgh Magazine* 253).
Sir Walter Scott (unsigned review in *Blackwood's Magazine*) saw the
work as intellectual, a 'more philosophical and refined use of the
supernatural', mixing pleasure with a concern for human conduct
('Remarks on Frankenstein' 613). *Frankenstein* provides a major
comment on human nature, morality, education, and ways of man-
aging experience to control social development. Mary Shelley deals
with the working class as a possible mob if uncontrolled (they burn
Frankenstein's house); she also looks at the role of women, insofar
as she highlights the dangerous usurpation of the maternal role by
Victor Frankenstein, the fate of Justine, rescued and educated by
Victor's mother, and finally, conventional Elizabeth, Victor's wife
and the monster's victim. Structurally, the novel uses three different autobiographies of Victor, his friend Walton, and the monster.
Both men are ambitious, Walton more reflective than Victor initially, and the monster more eloquent than one would imagine given
his circumstances.

Each narrator explains himself in terms of his childhood education and his reading. The monster is a model for Rousseau's noble
savage, rejected and abandoned by the 'father' Victor, self-educated
in a rural hovel, then cast out on an ice floe threatening eternal
revenge on his maker.

Most readers are more likely to be familiar with the countless
films of *Frankenstein* than with the novel. The 1931 Universal
Studios film, directed by James Whale, is the most famous.
Responding to current thoughts about human character, development, and control, Whale made the monster brute power (lacking
the linguistic abilities of the monster in the novel) and Frankenstein
the model for the mad scientist. Henry Frankenstein and Fritz, his
hunchbacked assistant, use dead, hanged bodies to construct the
monster's body; the opening sequence features their cutting down
a hanged man to see if his brain can be used in the monster. This
unnatural brain (as it is called) leads to the monster's criminal
intent, hence contributing to debates about nature and nurture—

the monster is naturally and inherently bad because of the criminal brain. Frankenstein only rejects his monstrous creation after it has murdered Fritz and menaced Henry himself.

Changing versions of the story reflect cultural shifts, fears of the lower classes, of eugenics, of the lack of ethics of a science that invested in bomb making and nuclear war instead of working for the benefit of human health. Film remakes engage with issues of patriarchy, colonialism, and imperialism when suggesting that more educated peoples renege at their peril on their duty to appropriately educate and care for 'lesser' others (the working class, children, and women).

Lee E. Heller comments on the novel's concerns for:

> what these new readers, especially from the lower classes, might bring with them in the way of criminality threatening to run amok; and, for twentieth-century ideologies of human personality, on fears of the uncontrollable insanity and criminality imprinted in our animal being. In our post atomic culture genetic engineering suggests both a new way to control human destiny and an even greater sense of the physical determinism behind the illusion of choice. (Heller online)

Highly popularised versions of *Frankenstein* confuse the man and the monster rather tellingly and lead to 'family member' versions of the monster in *The Munsters*, the long-running comic TV serial that gave us a family of vampire, monster, and witch/femme fatale, among others. Margaret Atwood's *Oryx and Crake* (2003) takes the mad scientist a step further. Brilliant rationalist Crake sees human emotions and the art as useless, engineering a Rousseauistically simple race (the Crakers) and releasing a deadly biological weapon to wipe out messy humans.

Selected Bibliography

Mary Shelley's Frankenstein, dir. Kenneth Branagh, 1994.

Frankenstein, dir. James Whale, 1931.

Frankenstein, Mary Shelley, 1818.

Edgar Allan Poe (1809–1849)

Edgar Allan Poe is acknowledged as the originator of the horror genre, likewise crime fiction, and his dark tales introduce us to demonic pledges ('Never Bet the Devil Your Head'); walled-in corpses ('The Cask of Amontillado'); living death, curses, body horror, and contagion ('The Masque of the Red Death'); and natural terrors turned weird ('A Descent into the Maelstrom'), probably fueled by his own fears of being buried alive ('The Premature Burial'). Edgar Poe was born in Boston on January 19, 1809, to Elizabeth ('Betty') Arnold Hopkins, an English actress, and David Poe, an Irish actor, who then deserted his family of four when Edgar was still an infant. His mother died when Edgar was three, the first of the tragedies plaguing his life. The children were adopted by John Allan, a wealthy tobacco exporter in Richmond, Virginia, and raised by his wife, Frances, and her elderly servant, Nancy.

Poe was educated at a boarding school in London, at a private school and an academy in Richmond, and at the University of Virginia, where, although he was outstanding at French and Latin, he was sent down after just a year for drinking and gambling. Returning to Richmond, Poe wrote his first serious poem, 'Tamerlane' (his first published work), a heartbroken response to the marriage of a woman he loved. He enlisted in the army under an assumed name and in 1832 published his first short story, the occult 'Metzengerstein', in *The Philadelphia Saturday Courier*, followed by four other pieces. In 1833, six short stories, collected as *Tales of the Folio Club*, were submitted to a contest sponsored by the *Baltimore Saturday Visitor*. 'MS. Found in a Bottle', one of the first ever science fiction stories, won a $50 first prize and acclaim for its twenty-four-year-old author. Poe began experimenting with opium, published regularly, and in 1835 became editor of the *Southern Literary Messenger* in Richmond. In 1836, he married Virginia, his thirteen-year-old cousin.

Poe's drinking and womanising led to his dismissal from the *Messenger*, though it continued to publish his work, including the serialised *Narrative of A. Gordon Pym of Nantucket* (a tale of Antarctic adventure inspiring sequels from Jules Verne and H. P. Lovecraft). In 1840, *Tales of the Grotesque and Arabesque* was published, collecting in two volumes twenty-five of his best stories. The 'grotesque' tales are humorous pieces, Gothic satires, while the 'arabesques' are the better-known horror stories.

In 1841, Poe began *The Penn Magazine*, which failed. He went to work for *Graham's Magazine* and in April published 'The Murders in the Rue Morgue', called 'the world's first detective story'. 'A Descent into the Maelstrom' was published in 1841, influencing Jules Verne's Captain Nemo in *20,000 Leagues Under the Sea*.

Virginia's health was failing, and in 1842 her tuberculosis led to hemorrhaging while singing. Poe produced the classic 'The Masque of the Red Death' and 'The Pit and the Pendulum'. In 1843, he wrote 'The Tell-Tale Heart', 'The Black Cat', and the mysteries 'The Gold Bug' and 'The Mystery of Marie Roget'. In 1844, the Poes returned to New York, where Poe perpetuated his famous 'Balloon-Hoax' in the pages of the *Sun*. (Poe's story first appeared in the *New York Sun* in the guise of an actual article reporting on a balloon crossing of the Atlantic.) Freelance work was followed by Poe taking a job on the staff of the *Mirror* newspaper, which published 'The Raven' in January 1845. Poe's success was then so spectacular that by October he acquired ownership of the *Journal* and in November Wiley & Putnam published *The Raven and Other Poems*. In January 1847, Virginia died of tuberculosis, and Poe never really recovered from this loss. Alan Gullette comments:

> Poe's creative writing transformed and extended Romanticism and Gothicism, while his critical theory pre-saged Symbolism. Translated by Baudelaire, he was much admired by the French, strongly influencing the aesthetic schools of the Decadents and Symbolists, and was also revered by the Surrealists. (Gullette online)

Poe is best remembered for his horror tales, including the poem 'The Raven'. H. P. Lovecraft devotes a whole chapter to Poe in *Supernatural Horror in Literature* (1927, 1933), acknowledging his mastery by calling him the 'deity and fountain-head of all modern diabolic fiction' (p. 58).

During the period within which Poe was writing, there was considerable social transformation and turmoil in America. The emergence of the Northern industrial bourgeoisie was threatening the power of the planter class of the pre-capitalist South, where racial conflict was also erupting. Much of this, it is claimed, fed into the unease in Poe's tales.

Master of the horror tale that has become the contemporary model for horror, Edgar Allan Poe is also credited with developing the first fictional detective. He also established several of the main formulae of horror and the standard tales of terror. Poe's tales are well crafted and often start with storytelling or an everyday opening, building up layers of suspense, defamiliarising the ordinary, and using a mix of psychological horror, body horror, the supernatural, and the realistic. In 'Never Bet the Devil Your Head', an arrogant wager leads to decapitation—in the world of the devil, his word should not be taken in vain. In 'The Cask of Amontillado', a wine cellar owner manages to wreak a terrible, lingering revenge on an enemy who has criticised him publicly. Relying upon the man's greed for fine wine and sherry, he lures him into the vault and walls him up. The tale's origins lie in Poe's own fear of being buried alive. The event replays itself in a variety of tales and movies and even appears as a tale where a man is bricked up behind a cellar wall for revenge in an episode of the TV series *Homicide*, set in Baltimore, where Poe lived and died.

His own personal tenuous hold on what is living or dead, augmented by a fear of social chaos, underpins Poe's horror fiction. He represents time and history as processes of disintegration and loss, and many of his stories are founded upon a desire to repeat the past and move back to a state of stasis and order. In his fiction, time is denied or questioned by either reanimating the dead or embracing death. In 'The Masque of the Red Death' (made lavishly as a Hammer horror movie starring Vincent Price in 1964), contagion is a metaphor for retribution following a feudal lack of care for the rural populace. In a castle where the fancy-dressed rich overindulge themselves in dancing, eating, and sexual entertainment, while the poor die outside of the plague, Death, dressed in red, is the unwelcome guest who passes the plague between them all.

Some of the stories are social in object, many more personal, built on grudges, wagers, and terrors about the proximity of death to life. 'Ligeia', a ghost story, is a model for tales of returned former wives and lovers. A husband witnesses his first wife return to life in the reanimated body of his second wife. This is an early example of undying and potentially deadly love, a common horror theme (see chapter 5, 'Major Themes, Movements, and Issues'). Poe's ghostly femme fatale is fascinating and lovely. However, she has a deadly hold not only on her living husband but on the hapless second wife. Daphne du Maurier's *Rebecca* both replays and to some extent over-turns the narrative when the young nameless second wife turns into a shadowy version of the dead Rebecca but colludes with Max, the murdering husband, to maintain a life of relative comfort through hiding Rebecca's death.

Another wife wastes away and dies as her husband immortalises her life and beauty in paint in 'The Oval Portrait'. Poe's characters are frequently removed from, or reject, the public social spheres, pre-ferring to seal themselves off in castles or in dark, enclosed rooms whose windows either block out the world beyond or alter it through artifice. In such rooms, often libraries, characters become engaged in studying the past and interpreting potentially dangerous antique texts (characteristics found in work by Algernon Blackwood, Dennis Wheatley, and in the TV series 'Buffy the Vampire Slayer').

In 'The Fall of the House of Usher', a domestic horror tale (see Chapter 5) focusing on inheritance and lineage, Poe depicts the fear of time as a process of fragmentation and loss. Roderick Usher's break-ing down is figured in the cracks in the house itself, a mix of spatial and family horror, a model for domestic horror and the deceptive-ness of security offered in family, home, lineage, and inheritance. The tale works at the level of the realistic and metaphorical by embodying the house as family and, visually, as a head. Illegitimacy and hidden family secrets emerge as cracks and fissures, presaging the eventual destruction of the house. Poe's house builds upon its literary Gothic antecedents, dungeons and great halls in *The Castle of Otranto*, for example. We find a spoof of the genre and location in Jane Austen's *Northanger Abbey*, where to Catherine Morland's (romance-fed, overheated) mind, every creak and seemingly locked chest seems to offer the potential to reveal dark family secrets. In contemporary forms, it reappears in *Poltergeist*, *The Amityville*

Horror, The Shining, and numerous tales where the location of the house or home enacts and embodies the dubious destructive secrets of past actions, and present covert or overt tyrannies are its legacy.

Selected Bibliography

'The Fall of the House of Usher' (1839)
'The Masque of the Red Death' (1842)
'The Pit and the Pendulum' (1842)
'The Cask of Amontillado' (1846)

Poetry
'The Haunted Palace' (1839)
'The Raven' (1845)
'Annabel Lee' (1849)

Bram Stoker (1847–1912)

Bram (Abraham) Stoker was born November 8, 1847, in Dublin. His father was a civil servant and his mother a charity worker and writer. A sickly child, Stoker spent much time in bed, where his mother told him horror stories. He studied Maths at Trinity College, Dublin, graduating in 1867, becoming a civil servant and working as a freelance journalist, drama critic, and editor of the *Evening Mail.* In 1876, Stoker met the famous actor Sir Henry Irving, accepted a job as his personal secretary, published his first book *The Duties of Clerks of Petty Sessions in Ireland* (1878), and travelled to England. Here he met and in 1878 married aspiring actress Florence Balcombe. Their son, Noel, was born in 1879. While in England he began writing a series of novels and short stories starting with *The Snake's Pass.* Stoker wrote eighteen books before he died aged 64 in 1912.

Dracula (1897)   *Dracula* is one of the two best-known horror tales in the Western world, the other being Mary Shelley's *Frankenstein* (1818). Like *Frankenstein, Dracula* has been replayed and misrepresented countless times in tales and films, testimony to its imaginative grip on public consciousness. Stoker would have been aware of the myths of vampires prevalent in Ireland and across Europe, some of which were collected by the Rev. Sabine Baring-Gould around the time of Stoker's writing *Dracula*. He decided, however, to base his tale on an initially less local terror, the historical figure of Vlad the Impaler (or Vlad Dracul), the Romanian count who brutally murdered thousands and impaled the heads of his victims on spikes around his castles. Myth has it that Vlad drank the blood of his victims. *Dracula*, probably the most popular literary Gothic horror tale of all, is the main source of the formulae for legions of contemporary vampire fictions and films. It unites the age-old myth of vampires, to be found in most cultures in different guises, with a host of both nineteenth-century and lasting terrors. Stoker's Count is a foreigner who invades the blood of pure English women and wishes to buy up property in London, importing and creating vampire hordes in the heart of the British Empire. In this respect, he represents fear of the culturally different Other, of invasion, and a threat to heredity, the ownership of land, as well as ownership of the purity and sexuality of the women of the family. Racial and sexual insecurities, insecurities about inheritance, heredity, and continuity are all brought to life by this tale. *Dracula* deeply disturbs our appreciation of the religious and natural laws of mortality. The vampire is an undead creature whose very existence denies that boundary between life and death. While Christ's resurrection of Lazarus and himself can be celebrated as miracles, the nightly resurrection of a fanged predator who kills for food and can spawn future monstrous predators at will is clearly a demonic construct, undermining the appreciation of the need and importance of the life/death boundaries.

Vampires disgust and attract simultaneously. Stoker's Count is a host whose qualities are fascinating and compelling. He causes prosaic ordinary men (Harker) to behave in prurient and morally dubious ways, frolicking with a trio of vampire women, and inspires the women on whom he preys to loose their hitherto reined-in Victorian sensuality and sexuality to dangerous effects.

Harker, the estate agent, arriving at the Count's castle, is invited in by his seemingly conventional, if a little strange-looking, generous client and host. Crossing this boundary or threshold represents all those other crossings between life and death, moral and exces-

sively sexual, dangerous behaviour. Beset by voluptuous temptresses
—female vampires—Harker is prey to his Transylvanian host.
Ironically, the most exotic, foreign, and dangerous vampire woman
reminds Jonathan of Mina, his love back home. The unfamiliar
recalling the familiar tests any easy investment in the safety of home
and loved ones.

> I was not alone . . . I saw them, for although the moonlight
> was behind them, they threw no shadow on the floor. They
> came close to me, and looked at me for some time, and then
> whispered together. Two were dark, and had high aquiline
> noses, like the Count, and great dark, piercing eyes that
> seemed to be almost red when contrasted with the pale yel-
> low moon. The other was fair, as fair as can be, with great
> wavy masses of golden hair and eyes like pale sapphires. I
> seemed somehow to know her face, and to know it in con-
> nection with some dreamy fear, but could not recollect at
> the moment how or where. All three had brilliant white
> teeth that shone like pearls against the ruby of their volup-
> tuous lips. There was something about them that made me
> uneasy, some longing and at the same time some deadly
> fear. I felt in my heart a wicked, burning desire that they
> would kiss me with those red lips. It is not good to note this
> down, lest some day it should meet Mina's eyes and cause
> her pain; but it is the truth. (Stoker 11)

Dracula has become the archetypal sexual horror tale, replete with
sexual disgust and attraction, that very English mix of love and
death. Stoker's Jonathan Harker epitomises the dichotomous
Victorian response to sexuality and power, particularly as it focuses
on structures of marriage, inheritance, and property. In the horror
sequence above, Harker's reactions and Stoker's descriptions figure
voluptuous, sensual women as deadly and predatory. Sin and sex are
linked; a dark longing links with fear and guilt. These sexual, disquieting responses must be covered up so as to maintain the purity
of betrothal and the betrothed. Mina, however, is herself figured in
one of the vampire women and ultimately tainted by the Count.
Harker's deferral of his longing and fear finds embodiment in the
vampire women. The taboo is tempting, a heated product of male

imagination terrifyingly rendered real in the foreign castle. As the Mina-like, fair girl advances, Harker is both paralysed and entranced:

> There was a deliberate voluptuousness which was both thrilling and repulsive, and as she arched her neck, she actually licked her lips like an animal, till I could see in the moonlight the moisture shining on the scarlet lips and the red tongue as it lapped the white sharp teeth. (Stoker 13)

As in a dream sequence, he is enthralled into a passivity both longed for and feared. The seductive vampire beauty with her red lips and sharp teeth on his highly sensitised skin is both desired and an abject creature, bestial, terrifying in her destructive Otherness masquerading as allure, a creature sprung from man's wildest fantasies. Her teeth are sharp; her tongue is 'lapping', then licking, churning. These words specifically relate to animals about to feed, confusing recognised categories of language, images of seduction and devouring. The Count, of course, exerts his male power of ownership and furiously wrenches away his transgressive partner, not to save Harker but to claim Harker as his own. His homoerotic 'This man belongs to me!' is matched in terms of the disgust and fear it can produce in a conventional reader with the women's soulless laughter and 'ribald coquetry'. All social and sexual behavioural norms upset, the women are tossed a child in a bag to devour in compensation.

Stoker's *Dracula*, a text for popular readership, now features in countless degree courses. The sexually lively sixties and early seventies gave us *Cosmopolitan*-type Countess Draculas and partners for the Count. In the nineties, Francis Ford Coppola re-recognised the myth of eternal undying love. But as a testimony to the Victorian response to sex, power, Otherness, and women, *Dracula* is the place to initially locate any discussion of the Victorian supernatural, vampires, the sexuality of foreigners, and women. All the longings and the hang-ups, all the Gothic license, exploration, wallowing, and middle-class moral tidying up of lurking desires and fears fuel this tale. *Dracula*, like so many other Victorian and modern examples of supernatural horror, backs up its claims of authenticity in the trustworthiness of its narrator—and in the testimony of diary and letter records. And what could be more terrifying than corruption and depletion of the very lifeblood—of Harker, of Victorian and British norms and values as represented in both warping the purity of the betrothed Lucy, poisoned and hypnotised into excess sexuality and most unchristian behaviour, and in the terror of foreigners polluting the neighbourhood by moving in next door or invading the sanctity of the home by coming in through the window (preferably but not necessarily open).

The fevered brain produces these vampire women from the terrifying figure of the late nineteenth-century New Woman. In Stoker's *Dracula*, we have a direct piece of ideological attack on this figure that threatens patriarchy even beyond the grave. David Punter notes that:

> Stoker appears from the text to be almost traumatised by a specific sexual fear, a fear of the so-called 'New Woman' and the reversal of sexual roles which her emergence implies. (Punter, *The Literature of Terror* 261)

Mina, the author's other mouthpiece, is afraid of developments in women's freedoms, too, and voices Harker's/men's horrors in a diatribe against these devouring, sexually voracious monsters. Although her skills with the typewriter and communication media help capture the Count, Mina remains conformist, her vulnerability dangerous. She is afraid that New Woman writers will upset the traditional relations within patriarchy.

> Some of the 'New Woman' writers will some day start an idea that men and women should be allowed to see each other asleep before proposing or accepting. But I suppose the New Woman won't condescend in future to accept; she will do the proposing herself. And a nice job she will make of it, too! There's some consolation in that. (Stoker 100)

It is Mina (somewhat tainted by her encounter with the Count) who eventually survives, while her sexually adventurous friend, Lucy, perishes.

Dracula may be an invading seductive foreigner acting out all sorts of xenophobic British traits, but he also represents an endless, soulless, naked desire, something Victorian writers could not openly acknowledge, especially if it involved their womenfolk.

The tale offers the opportunity to different ages and contexts to explore different desires and fears. F. W. Murnau's film *Nosferatu* (1922) replaces Dracula with Orlok and removes all sexual attraction, while from the Hammer horror studios Peter Cushing made the role both melodramatic and occasionally sophisticated (debonair in looks, at least). Dracula was a hissing, shaking melodramatic villain, lurking in a Gothic castle, then emerging a powerful mad invader. Frank Langella's (1979) frock-coated, wall-climbing version revives Dracula's sexual power and fascination in a kind of demonic James Bond entering a Victorian woman's boudoir. Coppola (1997) gave us a Count who was both victim of undying love, his dead countess revived in the figure of Mina (so emphasising Mina's own half-conscious collusion with the dangerous Other, sexual foreign invader) and hideous, shape-shifting creature, a mix of satyr and demon.

Wes Craven Presents: Dracula 2000 (dir. Patrick Lussier, UK title *Dracula 2001*) shows a newly disinterred Count enjoying the delights of consumerism in shopping malls, aligning him, perhaps, with the bloodsucking of materialistic society dominated by multinationals. Jancovich notes of *Frankenstein*, *Dracula*, and *The Picture of Dorian Gray* that:

> Writers such as King, Twitchell and others have read these three novels as embodying the three fundamental subgenres of horror and their monsters: the dual personality or werewolf; the vampire; and the thing with no name. (Jancovich, *Horror* 44)

Like Poe's work, these novels 'deal with transformation and doubling, but they are not produced by the anxieties of a failed or failing aristocracy, but an anxious bourgeoisie' (Jancovitch 44). Critical appreciations of horror frequently make political and cultural points (see chapter 7). Vampire tales are revived in the work of Anne Rice, Poppy Z. Brite, Suzy McKee Charnas, Angela Carter, and a host of others in the late twentieth and early twenty-first centuries, where the figure is sometimes used as a way of troubling gender and other boundaries, offering an opportunity to combine entertainment with social comment.

Selected Bibliography

Novels
Dracula (1897)
The Lady of the Shroud (1909)
The Lair of the White Worm (1911)

Stories
'Dracula's Guest' (1897)
'The Way of the Vampire by Professor Abraham Van Helsing' (1897)
'The Burial of the Rats' (1914)

Filmography (Dracula)
Nosferatu (F. W. Murnau, 1922)
Dracula (Terence Fisher, 1958)
Dracula (John Badham, 1979)
Bram Stoker's Dracula (Francis Ford Coppola, 1997)
Dracula 2000 (Wes Craven, 2000)

H. G. Wells (1866–1946)

H. G. Wells is better known as one of the great early science fiction writers, but much of his work crosses the boundary between science fiction and horror. *The Time Machine* (1896) is Wells's terrifying cautionary tale about man's descendants, the Morlocks and the Eloi. It derives from Darwin's theory of evolution, and the second law of thermodynamics, the notion that the universe is cooling down and will run out of energy, or heating up and about to explode. Entropy is simplified and brilliantly deployed in the scene in which Wells's Time Traveller journeys thirty million years into the future to an earth dominated by giant crablike creatures under a dying sun feeding upon hapless, tentacled, bobbing scraps of life, humanity's mutated descendants.

Wells revels in nightmare. His dramatisation of the underworld, mutated, industrial masses, the Morlocks, falling upon the delicate Eloi and eating them, has been seen as taking revenge upon the upper classes for their oppression of the working class, including that suffered by his mother at the hands of her employers, who relegated her metaphorically and literally to a Morlock-like under-world. The Morlocks' subterranean tunnels and the ventilation shafts by which the Time Traveller descends to the realm are based on features of Uppark, in Sussex, where Wells's mother was employed as a servant. *The War of the Worlds* (1898) takes a theme later developed in the TV serial (1958) and film *Quatermass and the Pit* (1967) and features an alien invasion by monstrous Others, in this case huge machinelike creatures. Broadcast as a radio play in 1938, *The War of the Worlds* was taken literally as a government early warning, causing thousands to flee from their homes, testimony as to how easily we can believe horror enters our daily existence (and reminding us of some of those government early-warning films about nuclear war). *The Island of Dr Moreau* (1896) is another horror tale about evolution that questions the boundaries between the human and the animal, as mutation and surgical transposition produce human/animal mixtures.

Selected Bibliography

The Island of Dr Moreau (1896)
The Time Machine (1896)
The War of the Worlds (1898)

Women's Horror: Late Nineteenth and Early Twentieth Centuries

Towards the end of the Victorian and Edwardian periods in both the United States and the United Kingdom, many women wrote tales that employed some elements of horror or horror figures. There was a rise in the ghost story and tales that speculated upon psychological states of being. Virginia Woolf's 'A Haunted House' (1921), a gentle *not* horrific ghost tale, portrays caring, loving ghosts haunting a house in which the narrator drowses and the reader speculates as to their background anxieties as they murmur and move around in the heart of the house, seeking what they have left behind—their love. Charlotte Mew's 'A White Night' (1903) focuses on a gender- and imperialistic-related tale of oppression and manipulation in which two young men and a young woman observe the sacrifice of another woman dressed in white, the victim of a strange ceremony in a mountain vault. The men validate oppression of the woman.

Vernon Lee (Violet Paget) (1856–1935)   Vernon Lee (Violet Paget) focuses on classically based ghost and supernatural tales resembling horror in which domineering characters oppress the weak and unpleasant historical events imprint themselves upon places.

Vernon Lee was influenced by Italian Gothic settings. She provides details of the origins of two of these stories, 'The Virgin of the Seven Daggers' and 'A Wicked Voice', in her introduction to the 'five unlikely tales' included in *For Maurice*, dedicated to Maurice Baring, an author of supernatural tales.

'The Virgin of the Seven Daggers' was sketched during a short visit to Granada in 1889, where Lee was bored and in low spirits. Madonnas, suffering, and antique and Renaissance art lie behind the tales deriving from:

> a temperamental intuition that there is cruelty in such mournfulness and that cruelty is obscene. All of which aversion came to a head . . . and just in proportion to that natural devotion of mine to the Beloved Lady and Mother, Italian or High Dutch, who opens her scanty drapery to suckle a baby divinity, did that aversion concentrate on those doll-madonnas in Spanish churches, all pomp and whalebone and sorrow and tears. (Lee 11)

There is a great deal of cult myth and ancient arts in Lee's tales, terrible voices from the bowels of the earth and magical incarnations.

> 'Osiris! Apollo! Balshazar!' he cried, and flung the cock with superb aim into the boiling cauldron. The cock disappeared; then rose again, shaking his wings, and clawing the air, and giving a fearful piercing crow.
>   'O Sultan Yahya, Sultan Yahya' answered a terrible voice from the bowels of the earth.
>   A colossal shadow appeared on the high palace wall, and the great hand, shaped like a glover's sign, engraven on the

outer arch of the tower gateway, extended its candle-shaped fingers, projected a wrist, an arm to the elbow, and turned slowly in a secret lock the flat-shaped key engraven on the inside vault of the portal.

The two necromancers fell on their faces, utterly stunned. (Lee 201)

Lee's tales are filled with occult power and Renaissance images.

Selected Bibliography

'A Phantom Lover' (1886)

'The Virgin of the Seven Daggers' (1889)

Mary Elizabeth Braddon (1835–1915)   Mary Elizabeth Braddon's vampire tale *The Good Lady Ducayne* (1896) features an aged, weak woman who drains a series of impoverished female companions for cosmetic purposes using a scientific contraption and the services of an immoral scientist.

Sylvia Townsend Warner (1893–1978)   Sylvia Townsend Warner's *Lolly Willowes* (1926) is a recognition of the positive celebratory impulses of being what has been marginalised and condemned, a witch. A loved maiden aunt, Laura, decides to reject a merely caring role as financial supporter of her brother's expenses and to escape London, moving to the countryside. She relocates to a Home Counties village, Great Mop, where all the villagers are part of a coven and every cat is a familiar. Here, Laura finds her sense of identity and meets the gardener/huntsman/devil who offers, in exchange for obeying his mastery, a genuine alternative to the constraints of domesticity, dependency, and a secondary female role. This is a horror tale that figures both witch and devil as positive, natural, and caring.

Edith Nesbit (1858–1924)   In the early twentieth century, some of Edith Nesbit's work utilised horror and ghost story strategies, including that of haunting—a familiar expression of latent fears and powers and most often a dramatic phenomenon. Nesbit wrote children's tales such as *Five Children and It* and produced undead and ghost stories for adults. In 'Hurst of Hurstcote', Hurst gives a flamboyant paper at Oxford on black magic, marries, and lives in a ghoulish, Gothic house in which he is visited by the narrator, and where the Liberty prints in the rooms don't overcome the clematis that grabs at your hair.

When his lovely wife was alive, Hurst was mesmerised by her and he cannot imagine her gone. His bond with her lasts beyond death. She dies, or seems to die (catalepsy), and is seen nightly wringing her hands and begging that he let go. Hurst joins her in death, but the narrator, his friend, finds them both equally fresh— she was either a ghostly returner or one who did not actually die. Eternal love is terrifying.

May Sinclair (1862–1946)   May Sinclair's horror and ghost tales have a deftness of touch. She critiques conventional relationships and idealised nonsenses between men and women. In 'The Token', Cicely, a languishing woman, suffers a husband who snaps at her and fails to tell of his love. The excuse she hears is:

> 'He's Scotch, my dear. It would kill him to tell you.'
> 'Then how'm I to know! If I died tomorrow I should die not knowing.'
> And that night, not knowing, she died. (Sinclair, 'The Token' 41)

Cicely returns to sit endlessly in her husband's forbidden study until he acknowledges that he loved her. Undying love rules again in 'The Nature of the Evidence', a tale retold by many different authors about fixation upon a powerful, attractive, dead first wife. When Marston's first frail, passionate wife, Rosamund, dies, he agrees he will never replace her. The highly sensual second wife, Pauline, finds she cannot gain Marston's physical love because Rosamund's phantasm interposes itself between them even in bed. Marston loses Pauline, but the phantasm is enough for him. Their love, like that of Cathy and Heathcliff (*Wuthering Heights*), is eternally consummated. 'You have to get rid of your bodies first', he insists (122).

This is a case of possessiveness and possession, literally. 'The Villa Desiree' is another tale featuring a couple and ghosts.

Twentieth-Century Male Masters of the Craft of Horror

H. P. Lovecraft (1890–1937)

H. P. Lovecraft was born and lived in Providence, Rhode Island. Although not widely famous for his work during his lifetime, he has left a lasting influential legacy. Lovecraft's 'Cthulhu Mythos' and many of his tales underpin and inform a very wide range of writers after him, as well as leading to films and TV versions. Darryl Jones says Lovecraft made a 'bizarre but nevertheless significant contribution to High Modernism' (Jones, *Horror: A Thematic History in Fiction and Film* 128), comparing him with Yeats, because of a similar *fin de siecle* fascination with the occult and a distaste for modernity. Like Yeats, Lovecraft developed his own symbol system and mythic world. This cosmology, the 'Cthulhu Mythos', features a universe governed by a monstrous race of 'elder gods' who, although banished to another dimension, are sensed, called upon, and constantly threaten to return through various fissures in our own world, bringing with them eternal chaos. In his famous 'The Dunwich Horror' (1928) Lovecraft notes of them, 'Those great Ones . . . were not composed altogether of flesh and blood. They had shape . . . but that shape was not made of matter. When the stars were right, they could plunge from world to world through the sky' (80), but they are held in place by spells in stone houses in the city of Rlyeh, throughout aeons, until that moment should come. In 'The Call of Cthulhu' (1926), the monstrous 'Great Cthulhu' (gigantic octopus creature) emerges through such a fissure onto a multidimensional island in the South Seas, his appearance sensed by many in dreams, visions, and terrible imaginings, leading often to suicide and violence. The tale is constructed from a number of scholarly sources, manuscripts, and testimonies collected by the narrator's great-uncle, who dies mysteriously. The main source is a forbidden book, the 'Necronomicon of the Mad Arab Alhazred', consulted at one's peril.

Although the book and the 'old ones' are fictions, many writers and fans have perpetuated them beyond Lovecraft's own work. Apart from numerous Web sites and writings, there are some clear examples of impact on a variety of writers. Borges wrote, 'There Are More Things' to Lovecraft, creating a posthumous Lovecraft story. This kind of a constructed myth, details of which can be found in great, dangerous, terrifying, and informative tomes, features in the world of a range of horror writers in text and film; for example, such features can be found in the tales of Dennis Wheatley, where the goat of Mendez and other horrors are conjured by Satanists (*The Devil Rides Out* [1934], *To the Devil a Daughter* [1953]), and in the consultation of occult texts and the release of demonic powers from 'the Hellmouth' in *Buffy the Vampire Slayer*. Lovecraft's tales always suggest a lurking, creeping horror, appearing momentarily at windows, taking away companions in the night. His language is heavily laden, static, rich, threatening, ancient, including words such as 'bequested', 'pithecanthropoid', and 'annals', or filled with words he himself coined such as 'eldritch'. Lovecraft's language is rich, his scene-setting and suggestiveness powerful, his landscapes blighted:

> It was not a wholesome landscape after dark, and I believe I would have noticed its morbidity even had I been ignorant of the terror that stalked there. Of wild creatures there were none—they are wise when death leers close. The ancient lightning-scarred trees seemed unnaturally large and twisted, and the other vegetation unnaturally thick and feverish, while curious mounds and hummocks in the weedy, fulgurite-pitted earth reminded me of snakes and dead men's skulls swelled to gigantic proportions. (Lovecraft, *At the Mountains of Madness and Other Tales of Terror* 1–2)

'The Dunwich Horror' (1928), considered by many his best story, is a 'wrong turn' tale of incest, illegitimacy, parallel worlds, and cannibalism. Dunwich is located in a kind of marginal, lonely, familiar, then defamiliarised, forbidding area near Ayesbury, Massachusetts. There are no signs or maps; the traveller is off course in a region where the inhabitants are degenerate, inbred, and dangerous. 'Repellently decadent, having gone far along the path of retrogression common in many New England backwaters' (101), they have formed their own race, furtive, vicious, and monstrous, whose 'annals reek of overt viciousness and of half-hidden murders, incest and deeds of almost unnameable violence and perversity' (101). Living among them are monstrous, other-dimensional brothers, Wilbur Whateley (nine feet tall, with twenty penises) and his brother, who is the size of a house. This tale of wrong turns into dangerous backwaters is set in America but hints at the Gothic, Celtic locations Lovecraft also deploys elsewhere. Here, we find his dubious theories of eugenics, developed into fully fledged racism in other tales. Cannibalism appears in the Poe-influenced 'The Rats in the Walls' (1923), in which American, Delapore, (a variant upon Poe's name), upon returning to his ancestral home in Exham priory in Wales, discovers piles of historical bones beneath the priory and, haunted by the loss of his son in the First World War, degenerates and turns to cannibalism, eating his neighbour.

Lovecraft's horrors do not always emerge full-blown in the tales. It is enough to see what they leave behind them or hear from terrified survivors that the description is too disgusting and terrifying to detail. In this way, what he leaves to our imaginations plumbs the depths of nightmare:

> The disordered earth was covered with blood and human debris bespeaking too vividly the ravages of demon teeth and talons; yet no visible trail led away from the carnage. (Lovecraft, 'The Lurking Fear' 3)

Slime also has a place. Lovecraft's horrors reappear in a huge range of contemporary films as bugs, the *Alien* acid slime, winged creatures, and demons, all preying upon the unwary human who chances to step off the path, stay too long in the ruin, and uncover the entombed. That the horror is indescribable, unnameable, hooks into our subconscious in a distinctly unpleasant way:

> No—*it wasn't that way at all*. It was everywhere—a gelatine—a slime—yet it had shapes, a thousand shapes of horror beyond all memory. There were eyes—and a blemish. It was the pit—the maelstrom—the ultimate abomination. Carter, *it was the unnameable!* [*sic*] (Lovecraft, 'The Lurking Fear' 106)

Lovecraft also authored the surprisingly largely unknown *Supernatural Horror in Literature* (1928), which established and defined a critical context and structure for horror, identifying supernatural horror as the most elevated form, while that dependent upon the real was less imaginative and important. Lovecraft's own term 'weird tales' influenced the production of much writing in 1950s America in the horror comics that were subsequently banned (see Martin Barker's *Haunt of Fears*, 1984).

Lovecraft's *Supernatural Horror in Literature* was produced in and tracks his development of a critical approach to horror writing. He focused on the field of weird fiction, as exemplified in the magazine *Weird Tales* (and other less successful rivals, *Ghost Stories* and *Tales of Magic and Mystery*), whose readers felt they were taking part in a development of critical and creative work on the supernatural, predating science fiction in most cases.

The only other critical work preceding Lovecraft's was Edith Birkhead's *Tales of Terror* (1921), which covered the Gothics fairly well but in a rather limited and scholarly fashion. Lovecraft identifies how powerful and permanent the attraction of horror is because it recognises humankind's fear:

> The oldest and strongest emotion of mankind is fear, and the oldest and strongest kind of fear is fear of the unknown. These facts few psychologists will dispute, and their admitted truth must establish for all time the genuineness and dignity of the weirdly horrible tales as a literary form. Against it are discharged all the shafts of a materialistic sophistication which clings to frequently felt emotions and external events, and of a naively inspired idealism which deprecates the aesthetic motive and calls for a didactic literature to 'uplift' the reader toward a suitable degree of smirking optimism. But in spite of all this opposition the weird tale has survived, developed, and attained remarkable height of perfection; founded as it is on a profound and elementary principle whose appeal, if not always universal, must necessarily be poignant and permanent to minds of the requisite sensitiveness. The appeal of the spectrally macabre is generally narrow because it demands from the reader a certain degree of imagination and a capacity for detachment from everyday life. (Lovecraft, *Supernatural Horror in Literature* 12)

At his best Lovecraft creates a terrifying scene utilising the full range of nightmare horrors. Many of these images and strategies have been dramatised in films such as *Van Helsing* (2003) (in the harpies), *Underworld* (2002), and, for tentacled octopus monsters, even the comic-originated *Hellboy* (2004) and *Spiderman 2* (2004).

Lovecraft's language is terrifying, visceral, and demonic.

> Madness rides the star-wind . . . claws and teeth sharpened on centuries of corpses . . . dripping death astride a bachanale of bats from night-black ruins of buried temples of Belial . . . Now, as the baying of that dead fleshless monstrosity grows louder and louder, and the stealthy whirring and flapping of those accursed web-wings circles closer and closer, I shall seek with my revolver the oblivion which is my only refuge from the unnamed and unnameable. (Lovecraft, 'The Lurking Fear' 98)

Selected Bibliography

'The Rats in the Walls' (1923)
'The Shunned House' (1924)
'The Call of Cthulhu' (1926)
'At the Mountains of Madness' (1948)
'The Dunwich Horror' (1963)
'The Lurking Fear' (1971)

Algernon Blackwood (1869–1951)

Algernon Blackwood was a prolific fantasy and horror writer of more than 200 short stories, twelve novels, a couple of plays, poems, an autobiography, and children's books. Born in Kent, U.K., he travelled a great deal: New York, Switzerland, Canada, Italy, Egypt, and all over Europe. Blackwood worked in Switzerland as a secret agent after World War I, visiting a spiritualist camp, exploring haunted houses, and discussing spiritual and philosophical ideas with Gurdjieff and Ouspensky. (George Ivanovitch Gurdjieff [1872–1949] was born in Russian Armenia. He spent years searching in Central Asia, North Africa, and other places for a hidden tradition whose traces he had encountered in youth. During this search he came into contact with certain esoteric schools. In the early 1900s he brought to Europe a teaching that he had developed from the results of this contact. The Gurdjieff pupil who is best known in the West is P. D. Ouspensky, who expounded 'the System' in England and America from the early 1920s until his death in the late 40s. Ouspensky's book, *In Search of the Miraculous*, which narrates the years from 1915 to 1924, was published posthumously with Gurdjieff's authorization.) Blackwood received the CBE (Commander of the British Empire) in 1949. His books are mostly out of print, but he is far from forgotten. Emotionally intense, Blackwood's writing locks the reader into the narratives. Supernatural elements are carefully woven into plots that often turn the ordinary and familiar into something mysterious and threatening. Many of his tales take place outdoors in natural beauty, the wilderness of Canada, the swamplands of the Danube, or the Black Forest in Germany. He deals in mysterious, immortal, strange worship, nature spirits, haunted houses, the spirits of the dead, and other ancient sorceries.

Lovecraft said of him, 'He is the one absolute and unquestionable master of weird atmosphere' (*Supernatural Horror in Literature* 95). 'The Willows' effectively describes another dimension impinging upon our own, reckoned by Lovecraft to be both 'foremost of all' Blackwood's tales and the best 'weird tale' of all time.

Blackwood wrote a series of stories and short novels featuring John Silence, a 'physician extraordinary' or psychic detective. In 'Secret Worship', a man takes the opportunity of a business trip to revisit the German mission school where he once studied. Travelling deep into the forest, he affectionately recalls the extremely stern Brothers of the order. The place is difficult to find, the Brothers remarkably familiar, unaged, and he is welcomed. Gradually, he realises that these are genuinely the same people he used to know. They begin to involve him in a strange ritual in which, it seems, he has offered to be a willing victim. The mood is vague, overwhelming, ghostly, blurred; his energies are removed, but his mind fills with terror.

> And then the room filled and trembled with sounds that
> Harris understood full well were the failing voices of others

who had preceded him in a long series down the years. There came first a plain, sharp cry, as of a man in the last anguish, choking for his breath, and yet, with the very final expiration of it, breathing the name of the Worship—of the dark Being who rejoiced to hear it. The cries of the strangled; the short, running gasp of the suffocated; and the smothered gurgling of the tightened throat, all these, and more, echoed back and forth between the walls, the very walls in which he now stood a prisoner, a sacrificial victim. The cries, too, not alone of the broken bodies, but—far worse—of beaten, broken souls. And as the ghastly chorus rose and fell, there came also the faces of the lost and unhappy creatures to whom they belonged, and, against that curtain of pale grey light, he saw float past him in the air, an array of white and piteous human countenances that seemed to beckon and gibber at him as though he were already one of themselves. (Blackwood 91)

Luckily, he escapes, aided by a fellow traveller, only to discover that the Brothers and their terrible secrets of strange worship, pain, and sacrifice have been long gone. Was this a nightmare, or was it real?

Blackwood is described as conjuring horror tales set indoors, and there is a series of tales set in constricting circumstances, redolent with the atmosphere of threat.

Certain houses, like certain persons, manage to somehow proclaim at once their character for evil. In the case of the latter, no particular feature need betray them; they may boast an open countenance and an ingenious smile; and yet a little of their company leaves the unalterable conviction that there is something radically amiss with their being: that they are evil. (Blackwood 315)

In 'The Listener', the narrator is almost entirely taken over by the dead previous tenant, who turns out to have been a leper, and whose terrible haunting presence removes all his energy and will, threatening his sanity and health until rescued by a friend who reveals all. The house seems claustrophobic and destructive:

In spite of the chillness of the night there was something in the air of this room that cried for an open window. But there was more than this. Shorthouse could only describe it by saying that he felt less master of himself here than in any other part of the house. There was something that acted directly on the nerves, tiring the resolution, enfeebling the will. He was conscious of the result before he had been in the room five minutes, and it was in the short time they stayed there that he suffered the wholesale depletion of his vital forces, which was, for himself, the chief horror of the whole experience. (Blackwood 328)

Not fully defining what terrifies and exerts its energies over the protagonist is a tactic of horror and ghost stories, involving the reader directly as a victim himself.

In 'The Empty House' the narrator visits a haunted house in which a murder has been committed. He and his aged aunt unwisely spend the night there as if to test the existence of ghosts —something we might all be tempted to do, since even avid readers of horror might actually be sceptics. This is nearly fatal for them, confirming the existence of the terrible memories of the house in which a young maid was assaulted and murdered.

In the hall they saw nothing, but the whole way down the stairs they were conscious that someone followed them; step by step; when they went faster IT was left behind, and when they went more slowly IT caught them up. But never once did they look behind to see; and at each turning of the staircase they lowered their eyes for fear of the following horror they might see upon the stairs above. (Blackwood 334)

Like Lovecraft, Blackwood is a master of the atmospheric and suggestive horror tale.

Selected Bibliography

'The Empty House' (1906)
'The Insanity of Jones' (1907)
'The Listener' (1907)
'The Willows' (1907)
'Secret Worship' (1908)
'The Wendigo' (1910)
'The Man Who Found Out' (1921)
'Ancient Sorceries' (1927)

Arthur Machen (1863–1947)

Born Arthur Llewellyn Jones in Caerleon-on-Usk, Wales, and called 'The Apostle of Wonder', Machen was the author of *The Great God Pan* (1894), *The Three Imposters* (1890), *The Novel of the White Powder* (1895), *The Novel of the Black Seal* (1895), *The Hill of Dreams* (1907), *The Terror* (1917), and other supernatural horror. He was an essayist, a journalist, a Shakespearean actor, a translator, and an occultist. With Blackwood, Yeats, and Aleister Crowley, Machen was a member of the Hermetic Order of the Golden Dawn —a complex body of teaching and ritual magical practice bringing together Kabbalistic cosmology, the Rosicrucian initiation system, ritual magic, Egyptology, astrology, tarot, and various other such magical and occult streams. Under its twin founders S. L. 'MacGregor' Mathers (1854–1918) and William Wynn Westcott (1848–1925), these were woven into a single all-embracing metaphysical and practical system (www.kheper.net/topics/Hermeticism /GoldenDawn.htm).

Of Lovecraft's four 'modern masters' of supernatural horror (Machen, Algernon Blackwood, Lord Dunsany, and M. R. James), Machen was considered the greatest creator of cosmic fear raised to an 'artistic pitch'. His prose style is lyrical and expressive. Lovecraft considered *The White People* the best weird stories, though Carl van Vechten preferred the highly autobiographical *Hill of Dreams*, which Machen called 'a *Robinson Crusoe* of the mind' and 'an interior tale of the soul and its emotions'. Genre historian E. F. Bleiler regarded Machen as 'probably the outstanding British writer of *fin de siecle* supernatural fiction, highly important historically'.

On November 1997, the fiftieth anniversary of Machen's death, a plaque was unveiled on the house where he was born. The Arthur Machen Society functions still.

Selected Bibliography

The Three Imposters (1890)
The Great God Pan (1894)
The Novel of the Black Seal (1895)
The Novel of the White Powder (1895)
The Hill of Dreams (1907)
The Terror (1917)

William Hope Hodgson (1877–1918)

William Hope Hodgson was born one of twelve children on November 15, 1877, in Blackmore End, Essex, England. His father was an Anglican clergyman who was often transferred with his family to remote locations such as Galway, Ireland.

Hodgson loved the sea and at age thirteen ran away to be a sailor, was retrieved, and became a cabin boy in the merchant marine in 1891. Treated badly by a cruel second sate, he learned judo and began bodybuilding to protect himself. In 1895, Hodgson attended a technical school in Liverpool, acquiring a third mate's certificate, then returned to the sea around 1897. He distinguished himself by rescuing a shipmate drowning in shark-infested waters and was given the Royal Humane Society award for heroism. He set up a darkroom and photographed the sea and storms, sailed around the world three times, then decided that he hated the sea, which appears as a horror in nearly all his writings.

In 1904, Hodgson devoted himself to creative writing, supplementing his income with photography. His first published story was 'A Tropical Horror' in *The Grand Magazine* (June 1905). Possibly his finest tale, 'The Voice in the Night' appeared in *The Blue Book Magazine* (November 1907). His episodic novel *The Boats of the "Glen Carrig"* (1907) featured weird events at sea. *The Ghost Pirates* (1909) is the best-crafted of Hodgson's novels, using realism as a backdrop for supernatural events, but his second novel, *The House on the Borderland* (1908), is his masterpiece, called by Lovecraft 'a classic of the first water'. A version of 'cosmic horror', imaginative, filled with the atmosphere of sustained fear, it concerns a house on the coast of Galway, perched above both a physical and a psychic or metaphysical abyss from which emerge strange, swinelike creatures, assaulting the narrator, who travels to the future, witnessing the destruction of the solar system.

Like M. P. Shiel and Algernon Blackwood before him, Hodgson created a sort of supernatural detective. 'Carnacki' was the subject of at least nine 'ghost-busting' adventures in which he usually refutes claims of hauntings or other supernatural elements.

Hodgson is often accused of sentimentality, and his protagonists, as in *Glen Carrig* and *The Ghost Pirates*, for instance, frequently survive supernatural horrors. At the outbreak of World War I in 1914, Hodgson returned to England, training as a lieutenant with the

Royal Field Artillery. He received a serious head injury, recovered, and was sent to the front lines near Ypres, Belgium, volunteering for highly dangerous (in his case, fatal) duty as a forward observer. After his death, Hodgson fell out of popularity, until interest in his writing was revived by H. C. Koenig, who reprinted *The Ghost Pirates* in *Famous Fantastic Mysteries*. 'The Hog' appeared in *Weird Tales*. Derleth, at Arkham House, brought out an omnibus collection of all four Hodgson novels in 1946.

In 1958, Alfred Hitchcock's television mystery and suspense series *Suspicion* adapted Hodgson's 'The Voice in the Night'.

Selected Bibliography

The Boats of the "Glen Carrig" (1907)
The House on the Borderland (1908)
The Ghost Pirates (1909)

Ambrose Bierce (1842–1914)

Ambrose Gwinnett Bierce was born June 24, 1842, in Meigs County, Ohio. A prolific reader, he became a printer's devil at fifteen, enrolling in the Kentucky Military Institute at seventeen, where his map-reading skills led to Civil War service in 1861, providing him with firsthand experience of death. After the war, Bierce moved to San Francisco to write. His poems, prose, and humorous satirical articles and essays appeared in the *Californian*, the *Atla California*, the *Golden Era*, and the weekly *News-Letter and California Advertiser*. Inspired by contemporaries Brette Harte and Mark Twain, then the satire of Swift, Voltaire, Pope, and Juvenal, Bierce's style enabled him to work as a writer and editor, beginning with the December 5, 1868, *News-Letter*'s 'Town Crier' page. Bierce became a newspaper editor at twenty-six, married in 1871, and honeymooned in England, where he joined the 'Fleet Street Gang' of prominent authors, critics, editors, and 'pubcrawlers'. In July 1872, J. C. Hotten published Bierce's first book, *The Fiend's Delight*, a collection of his California writings. He gained notoriety for his acid wit, becoming known as 'Bitter Bierce'.

In 1880, Bierce spent the year gold mining and shotgun-riding in the Black Hills of South Dakota for Wells Fargo & Co., then moving to San Francisco and writing for the *Wasp* in 1881. In 1891, Bierce's first collection of stories appeared—twenty-six horror stories entitled *Tales of Soldiers and Civilians*. Chatto and Windus reprinted the collection in England as *In the Mist of Life*.

In 1892, Adolphe Danzinger (Adolph de Castro), W. C. Morrow (author of *The Ape, The Idiot and Other People*), Joaquin Miller, and Bierce formed the Western Authors Publishing Co., which only produced one volume, *Black Beetles in Amber*, Bierce's venom in rhyme. In 1893, *Can Such Things Be?*, Bierce's second, most famous, fiction collection was published.

Bierce wrote ninety-three short stories, fifty-three of which are supernatural, concerning telepathic power, survival on Earth after death, among other strange events, which he called 'escapes'. Much of his work features twists near the end of the story, a format popularised by Saki and O. Henry. Ghostly revenge is a favourite, appearing in 'An Arrest', 'Two Military Executives', and 'The Middle Toe of the Right Foot'. Another favourite ghost story formula features apparitions who attempt to warn someone of danger, as in 'A Diagnosis of Death', 'The Stranger', and 'A Wireless Message'. Bierce also focused on existence beyond life in 'The Thing of Life', 'A Jug of Sirup', and 'The Isle of Pines'.

'The Other Lodgers', The Secret of Macarger's Gulch', 'A Cold Greeting', 'Beyond the Wall', 'A Fruitless Assignment', and other tales consider the reenactment of a crime or other disturbing event. Blackwood's 'The Empty House' and 'A Haunted Island' are influential in Bierce's work, an important example of which is 'An Occurrence at Owl Creek Bridge', filmed in 1962. Here a lynched man reviews events in the buildup to his death. 'The Boarded Window' and 'A Horseman in the Sky', 'The Applicant', 'The Man and the Snake', and 'The Affair at Coulter's Notch' are also shocking, while 'The Coup de Grace', 'George Thurston', 'One Kind of Officer', and 'Killed at Resaca' satirise common human failings.

Other supernatural stories use a variety of themes, including lycanthropy, hypnosis, telepathic influence, 'mysterious disappearances', and 'psychic' themes ('The Death of Halpin Frayser', 'A

Psychological Shipwreck', 'One of Twins', 'John Bartine's Watch', et al.). A few are influenced by Lovecraft, such as 'The Damned Thing' and 'The Vine on a House'. 'At Old Man Eckert's' and 'The Spook House' deal with the dislocation of time and space, while 'Moxton's Master' features a lively, insubordinate automaton.

Ambrose Bierce's stories are very short (often less than 300 words) and characterised by subtlety, abruptness, and meticulous detail. Bierce was influenced by Poe but was less literary and more observant of human behaviour, focusing on the human mind and behaviour as sources of horror, while utilising elements of the Gothic and Victorian ghost stories. He influenced Blackwood, Arthur Machen, M. R. James, W. C. Morrow, Robert W. Chambers, Lord Dunsany, and Lovecraft.

The 1960s saw a revival of interest in Bierce. In 1964, Dover issued a collection of ghost stories; in 1966, the *Collected Works* were reprinted in facsimile by the Gordian Press of New York; and in 1967, a new Richard O'Connor biography appeared and Carey McWilliams's 1929 biography was reprinted, along with the Pope edition of *Letters*. Three Doubleday publications came out: *The Enlarged Devil's Dictionary* (1967), *The Ambrose Bierce Satanic Reader* (1968), and *The Complete Short Stories* (1870; reissued in 1971 as a two-volume paperback by Ballantine Books).

Selected Bibliography

'A Psychological Shipwreck' (1870)

The Complete Short Stories (1870)

'Killed at Resaca' (1964)

'The Affair at Coulter's Notch' (1966)

'The Applicant' (1966)

Collected Works (1966)

'The Damned Thing' (1966)

The Enlarged Devil's Dictionary (1967)

The Ambrose Bierce Satanic Reader (1968)

'The Death of Halpin Frayser' (1985)

'One Kind of Officer' (1985)

M. R. James (1862–1936)

Cambridge Don M. R. James is renowned for his ghost stories told to his students and colleagues in front of his study fire and that frequently begin with the traditional opener of a reliable witness recalling incredible events while emphasising their credibility. M. R. James was headmaster of Eton, Provost of Kings College, Cambridge, Vice Chancellor of the university, and Director of the Fitzwilliam Museum. His tales are scholarly, formalised, ambiguous about their trustworthiness and resolution, and usually take place within his own cloistered locations of colleges, country house, library, and rectory. William Hughes ('James, Montague Rhodes (1862–1936)', in *The Handbook to Gothic Literature*, M. Mulvey-Roberts, ed. 143) sees him as constructing 'an almost idyllic, late Victorian and Edwardian world', and Julia Briggs says he fails to focus on mental states: '[P]sychology is totally and defiantly excluded' (Briggs, *Night Visitors the Rise and Fall of the English Ghost Story* 135). Punter finds that the stories are structurally identical— which actually could be seen as a strength—readers enjoying the formulaic will find it here. The most famous, 'Oh Whistle and I'll Come to You My Lad' (1904) takes its title from a Burns poem and begins with a dispute at high table between Professor Parkins and Mr Rogers about the existence of ghosts. Parkins doubts their existence, but upon meeting a very creepy, ghostly body, perhaps revises his opinions. The tone is formal, asserting truth in a very reliable fashion; however, in utilising the rather traditional white-sheeted ghost this story mixes the highly unlikely with the asserted real:

> Parkins, who very much dislikes being questioned about it, did once describe something of it in my hearing, and I gathered that what he chiefly remembers about it is a horrible, an intensely horrible, face of *crumpled linen*. What expression he read upon it he could not or would not tell, but that the fear of it went nigh to maddening him is certain.
>
> But he was not at leisure to watch it for long. With formidable quickness it moved into the middle of the room, and, as it groped and waved, one corner of its draperies swept across Parkins's face. He could not, though he knew how

perilous a sound was—he could not keep back a cry of disgust, and this gave the searcher an instant clue. (James 105)

Another famous tale is 'Casting the Runes', filmed as *Night of the Demon* and *Curse of the Demon* by Jacques Tourneur. Like several others of his tales that begin with or build on the discovery of demonic ancient texts, this story features a damned runic parchment, which results in the death of whoever holds it at the specific hour of the demon's visitation. Kasrewel, an alchemist and author of *The Host of Witchcraft*, chooses as his newest victim a hated reviewer of his work, Dunning. Andy Smith (*Diagesis* 2004) recognises that James revives an earlier eighteenth-century Gothic tradition suggesting the presence of barbarism in the comfortable cloisters of Oxbridge. In 'The Mezzotint' (1904), Cambridge University museum archivist Dennistoun recalls a strange tale told him by his colleague William, while being shown a mezzotint in the mausoleum/museum. It seems lifeless, but as he and others discern a Gothic narrative dramatised in it, it gains new life. They research the details and discover it tells of a drama from 1802 in which the engraver, Arthur Francis, had his son abducted by the ghost of the murderous Gawdy. In 'The Haunted Dolls' House', historical research reveals the deaths of children in a dolls' house and the tale repeats itself daily at one o'clock. Smith argues against Julia Briggs's sense that James distances himself from any psychological involvement when he notes that Dillet, a Gothic reader and collector of antiques who bought the dolls' house, is traumatised by the experience. The demonic and the Gothic are revived in James's ever-popular work, dramatised for U.K. TV's Christmas season in the early twenty-first century.

Selected Bibliography

'The Haunted Dolls' House' (1904)

'The Mezzotint' (1904)

'Oh Whistle and I'll Come to You My Lad' (1904)

'Casting the Runes' (1911)

Daphne du Maurier (1907–1989)

Daphne du Maurier is a key figure in the various developments of women's horror in the mid-twentieth century.

Du Maurier's father, Gerald, was a famous actor, and so she grew up among the trappings of the stage and public performance. Her marriage to 'Boy' Browning led to travelling abroad for much of her adult life, living in forces postings (army bases), the social life of which she found rather artificial and stifling. Having seen Menabilly in Cornwall a few years earlier, she bought it and settled there, continuing to write.

Often labeled a romance writer and best known for the disturbing, haunting *Rebecca* (1938), Daphne du Maurier is also a writer of horror, particularly the short fictions 'Don't Look Now' and 'The Birds', which have been made into compelling and disturbing films. In her own correspondence, she identifies a need to recognise, dramatise, and exorcise the horror within us.

> The evil in us comes to the surface. Unless we recognise it in time, accept it, understand it, we are all destroyed, just as the people in 'The Birds' were destroyed. (Daphne du Maurier, letter to Maureen Baker-Minton, July 4, 1957)

In du Maurier's writing we see a dialectic between the popular and the conservative, the predictable and the transgressive, which haunts her work and contributed to her lapse in popularity in more minded times. But the dialectic that structures the narratives turns our attention to the fractured spaces and fissures, the refusal to reward and punish in a satisfying way along conventional lines, to replace the spectre of unease in its comfortable coffin at the narrative's end. As Alison Light points out, it is:

> exactly the unruly and the ungovernable, those objects of official distrust and fear, which she captures with most energy and which dominate her novels, almost against her better judgement, as it were. (Light, *Forever England: Femininity, Literature and Conservatism between the Wars* 157)

Du Maurier wishes both to confirm conventional beliefs and behaviours and to deconstruct them, testing their limits, questioning received interpretations and securities, whether of behaviour in the natural world or of the stability of body, time, and space. These are precisely the same kinds of impulses lying behind much horror.

The strength of what lingers beyond any restoration of order is deeply disturbing and attests to the tenuousness of all boundaries and natural laws. Clairvoyance, spirit transfer, animals and nature unleashing uncontrollable powers, transgressive sexuality influencing beyond the grave—these troubling existences refuse the comforting closure of conventional popular fictional narrative forms. The confirmation of fissures in what we consider trustworthy, stable, and ordinary links du Maurier's horror very clearly with the interventions and undermining of the status quo found in contemporary women's horror writing.

Her version of the imagination is of 'an unconscious force locked within the individual' (Light 189). She is interested in ESP and time travel, altered states, regression, and ways in which forces of evil and latent power can reach out and influence people's minds.

In Daphne du Maurier's horror, we don't get buckets of blood and an invasion of demons. Hers is a version of horror that builds on the Gothic as critique and subversion of the conventional and the taken for granted. Her writing develops a dialectic between the familiar and the transgressive. Its investigation into the powers of the imagination, the crossing of boundaries between the normal and the destabilised, violent, troubled, and subversive aligns du Maurier's work at times with that of more contemporary feminists such as Angela Carter and Jeanette Winterson. Much of du Maurier's work was written between the wars and just after World War II in a conservative era. Her exploration of values and resolutions seems to wish to confirm our need for conventional safety and classic horror closure. Yet her work is troubling: It leaves us unable to bury the spectre of discomfort that arises from psychic powers; 'unnatural' wild acts by animals, birds, and people; surprise murders; and unruly sexuality, which the works enact and explore.

Through the gaps in conventional readings of romantic fictions, historical romances, and vignettes of everyday relationships, events and behaviours gradually appear that question women's roles under patriarchy and, related to this, questionings of the stabilities of identity, meaning, time and space, and the continuity and solidity of the body. As in ghost stories and sensation fictions of the late nineteenth and early twentieth century, new readings open up across the old and familiar, between the lines. Inherent contradictions are exposed in romantic love. Taking anything for granted is dangerous.

'The Birds' (1952)   'The Birds' is a chilling example of body horror, fear of creatures (in this instance of birds), and disgust at the intrusion of the abject. Bodily space is invaded by marauding birds whose behaviours are defamiliarised, no longer safe and ordinary. The story's horror is based on the natural world's potential for unpredictability and violence. The familiar turns into the monstrous and humankind is powerless.

Much of the story's power lies in its relentless buildup. There is little calm or release as the abnormal attack develops from disturbing peckings of small numbers of birds to a determined invasion. The doomed, puny, human attempts to ward off the birds leave readers feeling helpless.

In horror, power roles are frequently reversed, the animate becoming inanimate and vice versa. Here the possibility that intelligent birds might act as an invading force is menacing and inadequately explained by both the male protagonist, Nat, and the media as merely the swift descent of a 'black winter'. Warlike, massed ranks of gulls 'in formation' ride waves off the coast, awaiting some signal. This is wartime, but fatally inadequate precautions are taken. Curfew and boarded-up windows are no match for clouds of massed birds as nature's power is unleashed. Our sense of security, as readers, is disturbed, and what we take for granted in the world of our own, others', and animal behaviour destabilised. 'The Birds' has been seen as a metaphor for the gradual invasion of communism or any other force. This is a planned attack; 'They've been given the towns', thought Nat, 'they know what they have to do. We don't matter so much here. The gulls serve for us. The others go to the towns'. However, while there is an allegorical layer to du Maurier's story, it is also a fine example of our disgust and terror at the invasion of the body by creatures or others.

As in a nightmare, other people seem unable either to comprehend or act, rejecting advice, overlooking the obvious. The farmer and family who refuse the precautions of boarding up windows and punily believe they can shoot any irritating birds fatally underestimate the horrifying extent of the problem. Finally demolished, the ominously empty farmyard is evidence of the birds' power and violence. Threat and suspense build up relentlessly for the reader, while our comfortable beliefs in humanity's superior intelligence and determination are shattered: Nothing civilised and rational can stop the birds' repeated attacks.

'The Birds' also builds on the abject. Anything that breaks the boundaries of the self or threatens to overwhelm and disempower it terrifies. Wings, feathers, and beaks are disgusting qualities of the beast that overwhelm and engulf, undermining the space of the self, the individual's sense of identity and safe normality. The film (Hitchcock, 1963) capitalises on terror inspired by defamiliarisation. Flocks of birds around the small American town increasingly close in and destroy, their intense invasive fluttering in enclosed spaces threatening engulfment. It is a powerful, terrifying tale/film that lingers in our nightmares. The tale is influenced by E. T. A. Hoffmann's 'The Sandman', dramatising a fear of castration since 'anxiety about one's eyes . . . is often enough a substitute for the dread of being castrated' (Freud, 'The Uncanny' 352). The birds go for people's eyes; they enter through any crack and cover any space, blinding in different ways. The male protagonist Nat's disempowerment exemplifies masculinity's limitations and the grander, complete undermining of what we take for granted as normal, rational, and secure: 'life as we know it'.

The terror lives on beyond the story. Radio news breakdown is a sign of the birds' successful takeover and the end of the world. Daphne du Maurier refuses to restore order and normality.

'Don't Look Now' (1971)   'Don't Look Now' is a tale of domestic horror and defamiliarisation, employing powerful horror tactics of compulsion and suspense. It was filmed (Nicholas Roeg, 1973) starring Julie Christie and Donald Sutherland. The couple loses a daughter and travels to Venice for his work as a restorative architect. Here, they are haunted by the possible presence of their dead daughter, a supernatural comfort dangerously misinterpreted and invested in by the husband, who is led to his death by looking at the wrong signs at the wrong moment. The title suggests danger, uncertainty lurking beneath the ordinary.

Throughout, a clever use of the shifting signifier constantly keeps us, and John, the husband, off balance. 'Don't look now' starts the story, perhaps only a phrase between the couple or actually hinting at something important, unmissable, a pantomime 'Look out behind you!' or an indication of something terrible. The story is structured by deferrals, questionings, denials, misinterpretations, keeping it tightly knit and us as readers constantly uneasy, misdirected, and unsure. Like John, we are off balance, tricked into thinking something is dangerous and evil (such as two old ladies in a guesthouse) when it is not and safe when it is fatal. For the practised horror reader, there are hints and misinterpretations enough to weave for us a network of terrifying and unpleasant possibilities hidden in each person and each event at least as complex and contradictory as the mazelike streets of Venice, spatialised versions of the twistings of mind and plot. Viewers are as confused as John by the time he misinterprets the sight of a fleeting small figure in a red pixie hood as his daughter returned from the dead.

In the film, this first sighting is visually linked but separated from a threatening cry. John's own suppressed torment at his daughter's loss transfers into a desire to see this child safe. We make the same connections as he does, 'It was a child, a little girl', but unease at the juxtaposition of the strangling cry and the sure-footed child lingers on. The coffinlike boats, the houses, and threatening alleyways ('with the shutters closed each one of them seemed dead') are rendered safe by John's assurances: 'I know exactly where we are'. But his interpretations emerge as undependable, as a rift grows between his familiarising and the defamiliarising of the narrative voice. As with Ian McEwan's later, ill-fated visitors to Venice in *The Company of Strangers* (McEwan, 1981), unfamiliar holiday territory causes misreadings of atmospheres and events. The horror turn suggests that reassuring ourselves our reactions of fear are in excess of the situation, products of its novelty, can actually lure us into real danger. Defamiliarisation, fragmentation, and chaos rule.

The alleyway of interpretation John goes down is literally a dead end. As the story gathers momentum, we are locked into his misinterpretations with no alternative readings. All our certainties and his are refused and misdirected. John plays out a patriarchal, paternalistic fantasy of control, rescue, and restoration of order (in the film the fairy tale of 'Little Red Riding Hood' is invoked by the red hood), intent on rescuing the vulnerable little girl in the pixie hood, ostensibly fleeing a male attacker. But the thickset woman dwarf who turns, monstrous and grinning, to face him in the final shuttered room down the final alleyway is the third weird sister, a figure of his fate. The death throw of her knife is one continuous movement in the sentence, his reaction following it, enacting the scene.

> The creature fumbled in her sleeve, drawing a knife, and as she threw it at him with hideous strength, piercing his throat, he stumbled and fell, the sticky mess covering his protective hands. (du Maurier 55)

A final false security and misreading: The hands are not protective; John is fatally wounded. As it all coheres, premonition and death, he thinks, 'O god . . . what a bloody silly way to die' (55).

A psychological horror tale, 'Don't Look Now' undermines conventional logic, consistently disturbs and transgresses, replaying masculine terrors.

***Rebecca* (1938)**   *Rebecca* is also filled with horror elements, focusing as it does on the haunting of the second wife by the radical behaviour of the first, Rebecca herself.

The fatal attractiveness of the ostensibly innocent and lovely but treacherously dangerous, castrating woman is explored fully in Rebecca. The story plays out male terrors of vulnerability while also replaying the haunting or ghosting of contemporary women by those of the past, particularly one's husband/lover's past partners, and whose traces linger on in house and behaviours. Rebecca is the dead first wife of Maxim de Winter, owner of a palatial home with a sweeping drive who has swept his mousey second wife off her feet, 'taking her away from all this' into what seems an ideal romantic scenario, to be mistress of the grand house. However, the first wife cannot be exorcised to enable the second wife to develop any sense of identity or power for a number of reasons, all of which trouble the romantic fiction formulae, leaving readers similarly troubled.

The second wife is vampiric, feeding off Rebecca's image, snaky-haired, in a dream sequence:

I got up and went to the looking glass. A face stared back at me that was not my own . . . and then I saw that she was sitting on a chair before the dressing table in her bedroom, and Maxim was brushing her hair. He held her hair in his hands, and as he brushed it he wound it slowly into a thick rope. It twisted like a snake, and he took hold of it with both hands and smiled at Rebecca and put it round his neck. (du Maurier 396)

Rebecca herself is also vampiric, lingering, undead: 'But Rebecca would never grow old. Rebecca would always be the same. And her I could not fight. She was too strong for me' (244). The paradox for reader and author as much as for the second wife is the fascination Rebecca holds for us, however 'incapable of love, of tenderness, of decency' (283) she might be. Her transgressive potential lives beyond her, well after Manderley has burned and the novel has been closed. Rebecca's selfishness and beauty enthral. She 'did what she liked' and 'lived as she liked', 'cared for nothing and no one', in Max's judgement. 'She was not even normal' (283), but her attraction, beyond this repulsive image, persists as 'Rebecca seizing life with her two hands; Rebecca triumphant, leaning down from the minstrel's gallery with a smile on her lips' (284).

Rebecca, a rewrite of *Jane Eyre*, ostensibly romantic fiction, is also a Gothic text questioning the status quo, the stability of relationships, and the curtailing of women's power and sexuality. Patriarchal punishment of women's powerful disruptive sexuality would provide a traditional closure to the novel, with the second wife and Maxim enjoying a comfortable and loving partnership freed from the monstrosity of the scarlet woman. But the disturbances Rebecca and her power bring into their world and into the narrative trouble any neat ending.

In *Rebecca*, we see women's horror of the invasion by another. Horror also leaks out in the deception underlying the lie of a romantic escape and fulfillment, offered and maintained by a murderer, Max. There is horror in the concealed murder, in the power that has concealed it and lives on in the couple's collusion, in the haunting and invasion of the self-image and future sense of identity of the second wife by the first, and both in the death of Rebecca and the silence that produces and maintains her ghostly presence. But the story is not merely *Jane Eyre* with the sexual transgression's compulsive attraction more fully explored; it is also 'Bluebeard' rewritten, with the second wife triumphing.

Daphne du Maurier established a woman's form of psychological horror that has fully flourished since the 1970s. Her work represents continued fascination with transgressions defined as demonic by patriarchy. She frequently utilises the familiar horror formulae of entrapment, engulfment, invasion, and altered states to investigate and question our comfortable complacency about relationships, identity, and everyday life. Boundaries are crossed; divisions, questions, and fixities of time, space, and being are troubled. If there is any return to normality at the fiction's end, and this is rare, nothing is the same again. Like contemporary women writers of horror, many of whom she has influenced, du Maurier's horror fictions might contain conservatism and nostalgia, might critique and punish transgressions, but in the embodiment and exploration of these transgressions there is vitality, questioning, and a compulsive attraction that goes deeper and beyond any narrative closure. Our fascination with Rebecca lasts, as it does for the second wife, way beyond the grave, and it tells us more about ourselves perhaps than we would like to recognise.

Selected Bibliography

The Birds and Other Stories (1952)
Don't Look Now and Other Stories (1971)
Rebecca ([1938] 1992)

Dennis Wheatley (1897–1977)

They could see the cabbalistic characters between the circles that ringed the pentacle, and the revolving bookcase, like a dark shadow beyond it, through the luminous mist. An awful stench of decay . . . filled their nostrils as they gazed, sick and almost retching with repulsion, at a grey face that was taking shape about seven feet from the floor. The eyes were fixed upon them, malicious and intent. The eyeballs whitened but the face went dark. Under it the mist was gathering into shoulders, torso, hips.

. . . He knew that his prayer was answered. His fingers closed on the jewel. His arms shot out. It glittered for a second in the violet light, then came to rest in the centre of the circle.

A piercing scream, desperate with anger, fear and pain, like that of a beast seared with a white hot iron, blasted by the silence. (Wheatley, *The Devil Rides Out* 99)

Dennis Wheatley affected my own enjoyment of horror from an early age. His scenarios have influenced countless writers. They tend to be populated by monstrous figures and heroic British males. Most often, a hideous, devilish monster lurches into view, serving its Infernal Master, and determined to devour or destroy everyone. A sign of the cross and it shrivels and disappears, like the wicked witch in *The Wizard of Oz*, who dissolves in ordinary everyday water (see Wisker's 'Horrors and Menaces to Everything Decent in Life: The Horror Fiction of Dennis Wheatley').

Not surprisingly, considering they were written mainly in the 1930s, 1940s, and 1950s, Wheatley's books contain attitudes, witting and unwitting, about racism, sexism, the class system, and all sorts of social stereotypes, as well as glaring and quite irritating (or satisfyingly predictable) examples of British middle-class ideology at a particular point in time. Wheatley is very much a middle-class Englishman's man, able to identify foreigners as dangerous and women as in need of sexual control. British heroes confront villains and devilish figures whose characteristics resemble those of the familiar 'enemy'. In Wheatley, clichéd phrases reinforce the security, the certainty that good will triumph, despite the might of the forces of evil. 'Right' is profoundly middle class and British, involving religion, good sportsmanship, and a middle-class code of ethics mixed with superstition. Right wins, and the formula is comfortingly straightforward: 'As we go past, throw your crucifix straight at the thing on the throne. Then try and grab Simon' (*The Devil Rides Out*, 100). Established religion is here used as a token. Good carries a protective aura, authorised by religion, weapons, and chalices. Evil is always megalomaniac, dark, and ugly. Those like Simon, who have been tricked into the camp of evil by false promises, subterfuge, and deceit, can be physically rescued by smart, fast-driving automotive power, enabling escape through the conversion of belief into technical action.

> The car slid forward, silently gathering momentum as it rushed down the steep slope. Next second they were almost upon the nearest Satanist. The Duke let in the clutch and Rex switched on the powerful lights of the Hispano.
>
> With the suddenness of a thunderclap, a shattering roar burst upon the silence of the valley—as though some monster plane were driving full upon the loathsome company from the cloudy sky. At the same instant, the whole scene was lit in all its ghastliness by a blinding glare which swept towards them at terrifying speed. (Wheatley, *The Devil Rides* 100)

In *The Ka of Gifford Hillary*, Hillary, suspected of the murder of his wife's lover, writes convincingly in diary and statement to explain that he could not have been so involved, as he was disembodied while it took place. Protagonists like the Duke rescue and clarify, while there is always another central character, a potential victim, drawn from Gothic fiction. In both *The Ka of Gifford Hillary* and *The Haunting of Toby Jugg*, this potential victim encourages reader belief through personal testimony certified true by diary or statement form.

Wheatley's Duke de Richlieu is an aesthete whose choice wine drinking and cigar smoking are the embodiment of masculine values and medieval chivalry, mixed with a Sherlock Holmes investigative nature. His companion and sidekick is his friend Rex, ugly and built like a bull, yet a jolly good chap.

> Rex, giant-shouldered, virile and powerful, his ugly, attractive, humorous young face clouded with anxiety, the Duke, a slim, delicate-looking man, somewhat about middle height, with slender, fragile hands, and greying hair, but with no trace of weakness in his fine distinguished face. (Wheatley, *The Devil Rides Out* 100)

Together they rescue Tanith, power-hungry, sold to the devil (a scenario similar to that of *To the Devil a Daughter*, 1953), from giving herself to the dark rites. The powerful, honest giant Rex solves all her problems with promises of a long life spent with him, thus reinforcing romantic fiction: 'If you want them, my days are yours.' Similarly, in *The Satanist*, Mary, presumed dead after escaping various rites, is rescued by Barney, whom she believed hated her but who of course loves her. Near dead, she smiles, and, 'Then their icy breath mingled as their lips met in a long kiss' (Wheatley 107).

Selected Bibliography

The Devil Rides Out (1934)
The Haunting of Toby Jugg (1948)
To the Devil a Daughter (1953)
The Ka of Gifford Hillary (1956)
The Satanist (1960)

John Wyndham (1903–1969)

John Wyndham was born in Knowle, Warwickshire, in 1903, married Grace Wilson in 1963, and died in 1969. With his apocalyptic outlook, Wyndham rose to prominence as a science fiction writer after World War II.

The Day of the Triffids (1951), like H. G. Wells's *War of the Worlds* (1953), uses alien invasion as a horror strategy. Innocent-seeming plants try to conquer the world. This is a disaster tale that critiques the refusal of ordinary folk to accept potential dangers and to act in time. The image of the monster triffids picking up their roots and stalking and devouring hapless plant lovers and travellers is still terrifying for contemporary audiences who spend their spare time in garden centres.

The novels *The Kraken Wakes* (1953), *The Chrysalids* (1955), *The Midwich Cuckoos* (1957), *Trouble with Lichen* (1960), the short story collections *Jizzle* (1954), *Tales of Gooseflesh and Laughter* (1956), and *The Seeds of Time* (1956) look at social ills, while some of his short stories, such as 'Consider Her Ways', discuss the social values of Wyndham's day. Ostensibly, *Chocky* (1968) seems to have a happy ending but actually could be Wyndham's most pessimistic novel.

When we read of Wyndham's blinded masses or his rather beautiful blond alien children, we are reminded of the bomb, of the Cold War (see, for instance, the 'communist' pods in *Invasion of the Body Snatchers*), and of the mindless consumerism of the 1950s. Wyndham didn't need an external agent to create his speculative fiction; he had reality and contemporary terrors.

Selected Bibliography

The Day of the Triffids (1951) aka *Revolt of the Triffids*
The Kraken Wakes (1953)
The Chrysalids (1955) aka *Re-Birth*
The Midwich Cuckoos (1957)
Trouble with Lichen (1960)
Chocky (1968)

Filmography

Village of the Damned (Wolf Rilla, 1960), based on *The Midwich Cuckoos*
The Day of the Triffids (Steve Sekely, 1962)
Children of the Damned (Anton Leader, 1963), sequel to *Village of the Damned*
In 1995, John Carpenter remade *Village of the Damned* to mixed reviews.

Robert Bloch (1917–1994)

Robert Bloch was born in Chicago, Illinois, and educated at public schools in Maywood and in Milwaukee. At the age of nine, Bloch saw his first horror movie, *The Phantom of the Opera*, starring Lon Chaney, and for a long time afterwards slept with the light on. *Weird Tales* became his favourite reading. Bloch started writing stories in high school, and during the Depression could not find other work so he became a full-time writer between 1934 and 1942. He also did stand-up nightclub work, selling gags to radio comedians. Many of his early stories show the influence of Edgar Allan Poe or H. P. Lovecraft, with whom Bloch had corresponded since 1932. Much of his fiction between 1935 and 1938 has connections with Lovecraft's 'Cthulhu Mythos'. A member of the 'Lovecraft Circle', his correspondence with Lovecraft (edited by S. T. Joshi and David E. Schultz, with an introduction by Bloch) was published by

Necronomicon Press (1993). Following his first publication in *Weird Tales* in 1935, Bloch's work appeared in such classic pulps as *Amazing Stories, Famous Fantastic Mysteries, Strange Stories,* and *Unusual Stories.* Altogether Bloch wrote over 220 stories collected in over two dozen collections, two dozen novels, screenplays for a dozen movies and three *Star Trek* episodes, a volume of essays, and the award-winning *Once around the Bloch: An Unauthorized Autobiography* (1993). His tales focus on voodoo ('Mother of Serpents'), revenge ('The Mandarin's Canaries'), demonic possession ('Fiddler's Fee'), and black magic ('Return to the Sabbat'). 'Comedy and horror are opposite sides of the same coin,' he once said, and his work often uses slapstick humour.

In the 1940s, Bloch's fiction started to reflect a growing interest in the minds of psychopathic killers. In such films as Hitchcock's *Spellbound,* among others, psychiatric theories were used to explain the behaviour of characters. 'Yours Truly, Jack the Ripper' (1943) is a famous piece about this early serial killer. The radio adaptation (published in *Weird Tales*) resulted in Bloch's own radio series, 'Stay Tuned for Terror' in 1945. His first novel, *The Scarf* (1947), was narrated by a young man turned into a serial strangler by a childhood trauma. The story begins with the eerie lines: 'Fetish? You name it. All I know is that I've always had to have it with me . . . '

In 1954, Bloch published three novels. He wrote for *Lock-Up, Thriller, Star Trek, Night Gallery,* and from 1955 to 1961 for *Alfred Hitchcock Presents.* A horror, suspense, and science fiction writer and screenwriter, Bloche is best known for the novel *Psycho* (1959, filmed by Hitchcock in 1960). He says of his fascination with horror:

> I discovered, much to my surprise—and particularly if I was writing in the first person—that I could become a psychopath quite easily. I could think like one and I could devise a manner of unfortunate occurrences. So I probably gave up a flourishing, lucrative career as a mass murderer. (Bloch in Douglas E. Winter, *Faces of Fear*)

Bloch enlarged *Psycho* into a trilogy with *Psycho II* (1982), in which Norman Bates escapes from the mental asylum posing as a nun, and *Psycho House* (1990), in which the world outside the asylum becomes psychotic: 'Violence has become not only a cop-out in terms of being presented as self-explanatory—"this is human nature, that's the way it is, folks"—but it is also a drug. When you dose yourself with it, you find that you need increasingly bigger fixes' (Bloch, *Faces of Fear*).

Selected Bibliography

Psycho (1959)
Firebug (1961)
'Yours Truly, Jack the Ripper' (1943)
American Gothic (1974)
Psycho II (1982)
Twilight Zone: The Movie (1983) (novelization of screenplay)
The Jekyll Legacy (1990) (with Andre Norton)
Monsters in Our Midst (1993) (ed., with Martin Greenberg)

Joyce Carol Oates (1938–)

The Roger S. Berlind Distinguished Professor of the Humanities at Princeton University, Joyce Carol Oates is one of the United States' most prolific and versatile contemporary writers, the author of more than seventy books, including novels, short-story collections, poetry volumes, plays, literary criticism, and essays. Her writing has earned her much praise and many awards, including the National Book Award for her novel *Them* (1969), the Rosenthal Award from the American Academy Institute of Arts and Letters, a Guggenheim Fellowship, the O'Henry Prize for Continued Achievement in the Short Story, the Elmer Holmes Bobst Lifetime Achievement Award in Fiction, the Rea Award for the Short Story, and in 1978, membership in the American Academy Institute. She also has been nominated twice for the Nobel Prize in Literature.

Oates's early short-story collections established her achievement in horror. Since then, she has experimented with a number of genres and styles, earning praise for versatility and variety, and criticism for the violence in her work. Her fictional world is violent and tragic; her characters disturbed and unhappy, victims of emotional weakness and social starvation. Oates dramatises nightmare events

—waking up next to a dead husband, knowing you are the next victim for a seemingly romantic, literal collector of hearts.

In 'The Doll' (1994), while driving through Lancaster, Pennsylvania, Florence, an eminent lecturer whose life seems one of counterfeit, artifice, and manipulation, spots the house upon which her beloved dolls' house was modelled and longs to discuss the coincidence with the house owners. When she does, she meets polite confusion and hospitality mixed with growing threat. The man resembles her boy doll, red-haired, with a childishly old body. She is drugged and reverts to childhood memories: '[H]e began to smile at Florence, a sly accusing smile' (Oates 45), 'blaming her for making a mess then crying, in her face "Liar! Bad girl! Dirty girl!"' (Oates 46). But the next day, delivering her speech, she is unsure if this has been a dream or reality. This experience emphasises the mechanical nature of Florence's own behaviour, her insistence on a secure investment in the 'real', coupled with the infiltration of terrors of the past and the necessity of keeping up appearances. People become dolls. 'Why, Florence wondered, did she ever worry about her speech—her public self? Like an exquisitely precise clockwork mechanism, a living mannequin, she would always do well: you'll applaud too, when you hear her' (Oates 48).

Selected Bibliography

Because It Is Bitter, and Because It Is My Heart (1990)

Heat and Other Stories (1991)

Foxfire: Confessions of a Girl Gang (1993)

Haunted: Tales of the Grotesque (1994)

Zombie (1995)

We Were the Mulvaneys (1996)

Take Me, Take Me With You (2003)

As Rosamond Smith:

Lives of the Twins (1987)

Soul/Mate (1989)

Nemesis (1990)

Snake Eyes (1992)

Starr Bright Will Be with You Soon (1995)

Angela Carter (1940–1992)

Angela Carter uses horror to explore and expose relationships, particularly those of the family, or those based upon love, romance, and sex, destabilising and dislocating our certainties, showing them to be fabrications. Carter opens up the terrifying locked doors of relationships, focusing on the cruelties and deceptions behind romantic lies, on the perverse and sickening flip side of 'domestic bliss', exposing oppression and deception in ostensibly 'normal' families, dramatising latent sadism, illustrating how taboos are constructed from our fears of disorder. She recognises the Other in the self, retelling fairy tales, deconstructing and reconstructing myths, turning the tables and recuperating figures of horror—the werewolf, automaton, vampire—those products of our insecurities and identity confusions.

One favourite motif is of people reduced to the dehumanised status of puppets, dolls, and automata. Aunt Margaret (*The Magic Toyshop*, 1967) is silenced by her oppressive relationship with the post-Victorian, tyrannical puppeteer and patriarch Uncle Philip. Signs of disempowerment and rebellion appear as severed hands in kitchen drawers and incestuous relationships between silenced, oppressed Irish family members. Philip figures himself as godlike, enforcing phallocentric power as did Jove/Zeus when he raped a variety of lucky maidens in mythology, enabling each to bear a part-god, part-beast, part-human child. Melanie, the orphaned teenage protagonist, survives moments of fantasy donning her mother's wedding dress in the moonlit garden, but she is manipulated by the salacious uncle who wishes to control as well as abuse her youthful sexuality. Philip sets Finn on to observe and rape her (he refuses), playing to Melanie's childish memories of 'Swan Lake' and her dependent obedience to force her to take part in his show as human puppet. Melanie's identity is snuffed out in a farcical, horrible scene replaying the Leda and the swan tale (valorised by Yeats's poem and numerous Renaissance paintings). She is literally turned into the doll of Philip's imaginings and raped by the mocked-up, ludicrous swan. As in some of the more bizarre scenes of Jacobean revenge dramas, the scenario never underplays Melanie's vulnerability while debunking Philip's ridiculous, self-aggrandising power play. Farce and horror are played out in equal measure:

Well I must lie down, she thought, and kicking aside shells, went down on her knees. Like fate or the clock, on came the swan, its feet going splat, splat, splat . . . all her laughter was snuffed out. She was hallucinated. She felt herself not herself, wrenched from her own personality . . . and in this staged fantasy anything was possible. Even that the swan, the mocked up swan, might assume reality itself and rape this girl in a blizzard of white feathers. (Carter 142)

The description of the swan's mechanical movements emphasises both Philip's power and the potential reification of Melanie, losing control of self and reality. 'She felt herself not herself', disempowered, until Finn and Francie refuse further collusion. Carter makes the swan terrifying but empowers the reader by showing Philip is pompous, his power illegitimate, the swan ridiculous, 'its feet going splat, splat, splat', thus undercutting patriarchal power's hold on the imagination.

In 'The Bloody Chamber', Carter critiques romantic fiction, her Bluebeard figure relying upon both the genteel poverty of his newest, youngest bride and her latent sexuality, which he will pervert, then sacrifice. This version of the traditional story features an art connoisseur who selects his new wife as commodity, ornament, and feast for the eyes.

Rapt, he intoned: 'Of her apparel she retains/Only her sonorous jewellery.'
A dozen husbands impaled a dozen brides while the mewing gulls swung on invisible trapezes in the empty air outside. (Carter 121)

Threats of violence attract as they repel the new bride, who recognises her husband's 'connoisseur's look', inspecting her like meat on a slab. Carter aligns power and sex, showing how latent cannibalism informs relationships ruled by economics disguised as sexual equality: 'The strong meatify the weak' (Carter, *The Sadeian Woman* 138).

I saw him watching me in the gilded mirrors with the assessing eye of a connoisseur inspecting horseflesh, or even of a housewife in the market, inspecting cuts on the slab. (Carter 115)

Carter's women are sexually aware, rarely meek and obedient. She rewrites 'Bluebeard', identifying the gallant rescuer as the girl's Amazon warrior mother. In 'The Company of Wolves', rewriting 'Little Red Riding Hood', Carter uses the figure of the werewolf to express and dramatise hidden, socially unacknowledged passions, empowering the young girl, Rosaleen, to celebrate her sexuality, the 'beast' in herself. This story features a powerful reversal of the conventional werewolf myth in which women are often the victim, while the abject, the animal, is killed off. No woodsman can save Rosaleen since woodsman and wolf are the same. At the end of this rewriting of 'Little Red Riding Hood', Rosaleen and wolf unite. Discarding and burning her clothes, she gets into bed with the wolf, refusing to be a victim, celebrating her sexuality (see chapter 3, 'Reading Horror Writing').

'The Fall River Axe Murders' (1981), a true story/American urban myth of domestic entrapment, exemplifies the repression of Puritan American neighbourhoods and Lizzie Borden's claustrophobic family. The only response to repression and incarceration is eruption. Carter holds us in a terrifying stasis, awaiting Lizzie's violent explosion into the ostensibly calm domestic interior, murdering her family (see chapter 5). As a woman of her time and place, Lizzie is a social victim, a product of her puritanical upbringing, her undertaker father's capitalist insensitivities and dominance, her shuttered existence and dead-end future. Carter both dramatises this archetypal urban horror tale of the disruptive and destructive female and enables us to read its causes from the woman's point of view.

Rewriting figures of sexualised conventional horror, Carter demolishes established philosophical and cultural binary oppositions, that is, male/female, good/bad, day/night, normal/Other. Her horror fiction casts a critical eye on society and its myths, which consistently configure women as the desired or feared Other. Carter defamiliarises the (precariously) comfortable everyday world premised upon controlling women's sexuality, forms of social deviance, and other threats to social order. Social order is defined as the familiar manifestations of patriarchy: the domestic world, home ownership, white-male-controlled economic and sexual power, and so on. In undercutting the oppressive norms of patriarchy, Carter challenges what is considered the basis for horror, that is, whatever transgresses norms, subverts beliefs, and threatens security.

Celebratory excess moves beyond even carnival: 'the noise of negotiation and dialogue' (Donald, 'What's at Stake in Vampire Films?' 17). There's no need to put the circus away at the end of the show—everything changes. Carter's use of the carnivalesque, that subversive, energetic exploration of opposites, emphasises the comic, liberating alternative to established values and meanings. As such, it enables dialogue between beliefs and behaviours rather than insisting on one right way.

The oxymoron is Carter's favourite figure. It enacts at the level of language, character, event, and values the paradox and twinning of opposites, the attraction and terror of what could seem comfortably relegated to nightmare and myth but is immediate in its assault on our senses. In yoking opposites, self/Other, good/evil, and so on, she declines to privilege one version of the self and its values over another, showing this privileging to be a dangerous artifice. At the same time, Carter's fictional techniques—her balancing of documentary, historical realism, with the imaginative, the magical, and metaphorical—replays this yoking of opposites at the level of narrative, character, and theme. Carter's work is socially, politically, and sexually subversive, as well as entertaining and disquieting: magical realism with a healthy dose of sexual politics. She offers us the werewolf in the kitchen, the living doll in the bedroom, home sweet home.

Selected Bibliography

The Magic Toyshop (1967)
The Bloody Chamber (1979)
The Sadeian Woman (1979)
'The Fall River Axe Murders' (1981)

Melanie Tem

In American Melanie Tem's work, family relationships are a prime location for horror, an exposé of hypocrisy and simple repressive binary oppositions, taboos, and rituals, which prioritise some behaviours and exclude, demonise, and punish others. As a social worker,

Tem must have met many experiences of the closed cultures of families, each a law unto themselves, dangerous spaces for others to enter. Werewolves are used to represent the exclusivity of the family circle into which new partners are introduced at their peril. The 'sweetness and danger' of the embrace between Pam and Lydia in 'Wilding' (1992) represents the difficulty of presenting a lesbian lover to the family as literally throwing the loved one to the wolves. Lydia keeps her family carefully apart from her working life, gradually moving into a nurturing affair with Pam, a colleague. As the sole caretaker of her matriarchal family, Lydia keeps her own werewolf nature at home, crossing the boundaries between the working world and the charnel house of her domestic setting with relative ease. But she cannot introduce the two to each other. The story comments on what we hide, how we relate, and on the ultimate, conventionally submerged, hidden viciousness of the domestic. Lydia seeks salvation though her relationship with Pam, but the shortsighted, small-mindedness of the average suburban family fascinated with a lesbian couple is nothing compared to what these lovers face. Lydia's family return, like the three bears in 'Goldilocks'. As she slips in and out of her wolf/human nature she cannot choose and act decisively to save Pam, sacrificing her in her indecision:

> Neither wolf nor woman, Lydia ran away. She did not choose. In the house she left behind, the heart of her lover was devoured by someone else. (Tem 162)

Tem, like Carter, uses vampires to explore domestic horror. Vampire mothers are both figures of horror and a vehicle through which radical contemporary writers can undercut the stereotyping of conventional horror's gender roles. In Melanie and her husband Steve Tem's only collaboration, 'Mama' (1995), the title character is a non-nurturing vampire mother. A familiar figure, this never very effective but typically nagging mother's power is constant, her depression involving everyone:

> Everybody got exhausted trying to figure out what Mama wanted until they finally didn't have any life left for themselves. (Tem and Tem 78)

Elizabeth, the teenage daughter/narrator's sense of irritation and frustration at rules and regulations, curfews and demands, are as well rehearsed and familiar as her comparison of herself with her mother in whom she recognises repression and depression. Her father ominously points out that Elizabeth is more like her mother than her mother herself. This is the kind of ordinary thing people say in families, but in this instance it identifies the insidious power and stubbornness of mother and daughter. The mother literally desires both to be free from her daughter and to own her eternally. Upon the mother's death, we follow the girl's realisation that the returned vampiric figure, irritating and oppressive, is more demanding than she ever was in real life.

> 'You're grounded!' Mama yelled.
> 'You're dead!' Elizabeth yelled back. (Tem and Tem 80)

Her father is drained, spineless, and her mother something they need to hide, a shameful, dirty little family secret. 'Mama' is excessively friendly, referring to Elizabeth as 'sweetheart', her brother Matt as 'baby', and frighteningly desirous of a 'hug' with 'soft mothering arms', 'her mouth stained with something dark' (90) (blood!). Matt falls easy victim to this deadly embrace.

The interlacing of typical tension and interactions between teenagers and their parents with the arrival and combination of the vampire condition provides an interesting mix of normality and the abnormal, the *unheimlich*, creeping into the everyday. What can you tell others about your own dysfunctional family? Trying to explain that your dead mother has returned and now eats flies in the kitchen is impossible. Her father, caring and resistant, refuses complicity, remains a victim, and never rises into vampire existence. He is discovered in the bedroom, partially chewed, his bones jutting out.

In 'Lightning Rod' (1990), another secret revolves around the pain sustained by mother, passed to daughter, representing the strain of supporting the family. The terrible stress of nurturing and internalising the family's pains and needs are dramatised as the mother experiences becoming a lightning rod, wracked with electric spasms. Scars appear on her back, and the pain almost kills her, but she cannot help but respond to their sufferings. The daughter realises she, too, has these powers (or responsibilities) and removes some of her mother's pain, thus inheriting her excessive but typically female behaviour and moving herself into the self-destructive nurturing role. Tem uses the supernatural to explore and dramatise family interactions that enable survival at the expense of damage. Hers are dangerous, credible family circles.

Selected Bibliography

'Lightning Rod' (1990)
'Wilding' (1992)
'Mama' (1995)

Fay Weldon (1931–)

Fay Weldon uses comedy, parody, the grotesque, the carnivalesque, and a little horror to expose the social and cultural myths that conventional horror peddles about women. She deconstructs the roles women play, the gendered subtext that silences, victimises, and demonises women. Pacts with the devil are common—in *Growing Rich* (1992) and *The Life and Loves of a She-Devil* (1983). Sometimes this is a folly—if it offers only another male master, a blinkered buying into the consumerist lies that can constrain women socially. In *The Cloning of Joanna May* (1990), Weldon uses the topical horror of technologically engineered (cloned) body doubles, as a betrayed husband seeks to control his freed wife by cloning her, only to find several free-spirited, identical-looking women instead of the one. In *The Life and Loves of a She-Devil* (1983), Weldon empowers her incarcerated domestic housewife Ruth to cast off the stifling role of long-suffering wife. In taking revenge on her silly, unfaithful husband, Bobbo, she totally transforms her own life and body, deconstructing the lies of romantic fictions in the process. Ruth effectively sells her soul to the devil, refusing the domestic 'bliss' promised in her home in Eden Grove, seeking to shape herself in new ways, albeit physically in the fashion of Mary Fisher, the romantic novelist who stole the faithless Bobbo. The result has worried feminist readers because it seems to collude with romantic ideas of the perfect woman that Weldon set out to critique. However, Ruth is self-fashioned and controls Bobbo through her new power.

In *Growing Rich* (1992), the boredom of women's constrained lives in an average nowhere—the Fens in U.K., East Anglia—is temporarily countered. Three girls face future joblessness until Mephistopheles, the devil's agent, cruises past in a black BMW and offers Carmen beauty and a future in reward for loving multinational property developer Sir Bernard.

Carmen sees her body shape morph from ordinary to excessive pornography ideal and rebels. Eventually, she marries Sir Bernard and outwits the devil in a spectacular moment on the edge of the Fens when other histories emerge in the shape of long dead, buried corpses. The possibilities of demonic intervention surround the ordinary:

> But then nothing exciting ever happens in Fenedge these days. A tradition has grown up that you must never insult the town aloud, or hope too vehemently to escape it, in case the devil happens to be flying by, and overhears, and all hell breaks loose. (Weldon 250)

All Weldon's women, however critical and in league with the devil, seem stuck with the fictions of romantic love—as a message, perhaps, that, sadly, society and its myths are unchangeable.

Selected Bibliography

The Life and Loves of a She-Devil (1983)
The Cloning of Joanna May (1990)
Growing Rich (1992)

Susan Hill (1942–)

Mists and fogs, Victorian devices of confusion and location, appear in ghost and horror writer Susan Hill's London and the North. Hill's ghost stories replay conventional formulae, feature male protagonists, and concentrate on domestic tragedy (*The Woman in Black*, 1983) and the lingering deadly control of those who influence the young and blight their lives (*The Mist in the Mirror*, 1992). Hill's work has all the accoutrements of horror—mysterious doppelgangers, strange

characters hiding or leading to secrets, documents revealing tantalis-
ing and ultimately dangerous, threatening information, and revengeful ghosts. In *The Woman in Black* and *The Mist in the Mirror*, the
return of the repressed not only haunts but fatally disrupts the lives
of those unlucky enough to interact with the revengeful dead.

Rosemary Jackson (*Fantasy* 102) equates Hill's imagery of dark
enclosed spaces with the isolation and removal from daily life
demanded by artistic consciousness. Hill explores family claustrophobia, imprisoning parents and children, lives of denials and losses,
contained futures, a kind of living death. She creates threatened,
delicate social microcosms.

The Woman in Black (1983) utilises a traditional ghost story formula (familiar from M. R. James), the first-person narration of
Arthur Kipps, to authenticate strange tales told around the family
Christmas fire. Kipps begins, 'I heard a true story, a story of haunting and evil, fear and confusion, horror and tragedy. But it was not
a story to be told for casual entertainment, around the fireside upon
Christmas Eve' (Hill 21). Years earlier at the funeral of a client, Mrs
Drablow, he met suspicious silences and saw the figure of a young,
mysterious woman in black, spectral, gaunt in her thinness. She is
both vision and threat:

> [T]he thinnest layer of flesh was tautly stretched and
> strained across her bones so that it gleamed with a curious,
> blue-white sheen, and her eyes seemed sunken back in her
> head. . . . Nor did she look old. (Hill 49)

The apparition's stare is malevolent, passionately directing her
desire to punish any family in recompense for the tragic double loss
of her own son, once to her sister to be brought up, since she was
not considered a fit mother (unmarried, disturbed), and again when,
one terrible day, the carriage containing the beloved boy disap-
peared into the mist and sea, missing the narrow spit of land linking the mainland with the isolated Drablow house. A Gothic,
threatening atmosphere leads to haunting. Across the marshes
Kipps hears the sound of a ghostly pony trap:

> Baffled, I stood and waited, straining to listen through the
> mist. What I heard next chilled and horrified me, even

though I could neither understand nor account for it. The noise of the pony trap grew fainter and then stopped abruptly and away on the marsh was a curious draining, sucking, churning sound, which went on, together with the shrill neighing and whinnying of a horse in panic, and then I heard another cry, a shout, a terrified sobbing—it was hard to decipher—but with horror I realised that it came from a child, a young child. I stood absolutely helpless in the mist that clouded me and everything from my sight. (Hill 74)

Jenet Humphrey is the 'woman in black' and the boy, Nathaniel's, mother, and she watched and heard his death. Subsequently, she went mad, returning, a silent gaunt threat, presaging and ensuring the deaths of children. It's a terrible tale. The climactic point comes when the narrator's own wife and son go for a spin in a pony trap and notice, all too late, the woman in black, standing malevolently at one side, just before the trap crashes, killing the son and fatally wounding the wife. The novel gives a new slant on family ghost stories and is replete with tension, suspense, Gothic description, and sensitive handling of emotion and narrative. This spectral femme fatale curses with domestic tragedy.

Labyrinthine London streets, distant, haunted northern villages, and a school are locations for *The Mist in the Mirror* (1992), which adopts traditional ghost tale formulae and an archaic nineteenth-century tone, including Dickensian words such as 'dreech' and 'mizzle'. The tale told to the narrator by gaunt, beak-nosed Sir Jamie Monmouth after an evening in the club centres round brutality to Monmouth's own relative by an evil traveller, Conrad Vane.

Selected Bibliography

The Woman in Black (1983)
The Mist in the Mirror (1992)

Poppy Z. Brite (1967–)

Poppy Z. Brite was born in New Orleans on May 25, 1967. Her parents were from Kentucky, and her father was a professor of economics at the University of New Orleans. Upon their split in 1973, she moved to North Carolina, frequently returning to New Orleans to visit her father. Acclaimed as a splatterpunk writer, Brite has won prizes for homoerotic horror. (Splatterpunk uses decadent and shocking sexuality as a backdrop for horror. It is a type of extreme horror exploring the darker sides of sexuality and the full range of human and superhuman experience.) She wrote from childhood, editing her high school underground newspaper, *The Glass Goblin*, and selling her first story, 'Optional Music for Voice and Piano', at eighteen to *The Horror Show*. Upon being contacted by Stephen King's biographer, Douglas E. Winter, and asked if she had a novel in the pipeline, Brite dropped out of her first year at the University of North Carolina and wrote what became *Lost Souls* (1992), supporting herself in a surrealistic range of jobs, including artist's model, short-order cook, and stripper, but mainly cleaning up after mice in a research lab.

Brite moved to Athens, Georgia, and met her husband, chef Christopher DeBarr, at the 40 Watt Club in 1989. *Lost Souls* was published in 1992 to acclaim, followed by *Drawing Blood* (originally *Birdland*). She moved to New Orleans and compiled her short-story collection *Swamp Foetus* (1993), reprinted later by Dell as *Wormwood*. *Exquisite Corpse* followed two years later but was rejected by Dell due to its 'extreme' content. Penguin in the United Kingdom also declined to publish it because of the mix of journalism and a celebration of vampire-like characters. Caitlin Kiernan, Brite's horror fiction-writing collaborator, commented that it was a surprise no publisher had recognised vampires as serial killers. Courtney Love contacted Brite to write her biography, saying she would not officially authorise it. *Courtney Love: The Real Story* appeared 1996, followed by a volume of *The Crow*, *The Lazarus Heart* (1998), then *Self-Made Man* (formally published as *Are You Loathsome Tonight?*). Brite travelled the world. The untitled story from which *Lost Souls* grew, 'The Seed of Lost Souls', was published in 1999, as well as *Plastic Jesus* in 2000. Brite now focuses on gay male chefs rather than vampires in her writing.

Poppy Z. Brite's prose is luxurious, visceral, and florid. Her characters are drawn from adolescent and postadolescent underworlds of post-Vietnam, disaffected youth. Her vampire tales, in particular, home in on the rootlessness and pointlessness of the conformist

middle-class, aspirant existence of a society that sacrificed a generation of young men to dam the tide of communism in a faraway
unimaginable place (and lost). For Americans, Vietnam was a disaster that took over ten years to begin to acknowledge imaginatively
on screen and in fiction. For Brite's generation, the American dream
was a construction to rival other television constructions. Accom-
panying this, gender roles were seen as performance, easily undermined, while conformity and complacency were misled, mistaken,
if not dangerous. Her early writing days are the era of the gradual
emergence of films problematising war and the view that God is
always on the side of middle-class, capitalist white men.
Questioning national identities leads to testing the limits of what it
means to be alive, problematising and breaking lines between life
and death. Brite is indebted technically, in terms of turn of phrase,
some plotline, and values to H. P. Lovecraft, who predates her by
three-quarters of a century. With the popular reemergence of the
vampire myth—the film *The Hunger* (1983) making it radical, then
Anne Rice querying gender roles—Brite's entrance into the horror
scene was perfectly placed.

> The vampire is the only supernatural creature who has
> become a role model. (Brite, *Love in Vein 1*, ix)

Lost Souls is a Southern Gothic horror text located in alienated
youth subculture, whose lost youth wander through the emptied-
out suburbs and urban ribbon developments of Middle America.
Molochai, Zillah, and Twig pass as everyday Goths on the fringes of
taxpaying society but central to communities of young people hang-
ing around bars, gigs, and, more dangerously, street corners and dark-
ened suburban gardens. The generation a materialistic society
throws away joins the vampire community, a void at the heart of
white middle-class America. Lost children, strays, the neglected are
their victims. Missing Mile is a liminal space, a place you would hate
to get stuck in if driving through America.

Here, a vanload of vampires prey on twins, and a young man
named Nothing can be persuaded that the only way to belong to
some kind of family is to bleed his own best friend and others in
motels and houses devoid of parents, families, history, or continuity.

Children are abandoned by fathers, returning to where deaths took place; young couples prey upon each other; babies are sacrificed.

On the streets of New Orleans, legendary vampire home where cultures cross and dark swampy nights are filled with blended Creole and jazz music, vampire androgyny aligns itself with transgression. Molochai, Twig, and Zillah sport devilish and androgynous nicknames. Their behaviour is wild, performative. Contemporary, they survive on chocolate and relate to drug culture not vampire tradition. Those on the fringe of this rootless community, buying into the hype of fashion, performance, and radical chic of the vampire, are also most likely to end up victims. Brite utilises body horror and defamiliarisation of the real/unreal, safe/unsafe. Her performative young vampires *pretend* to be vampires in a hard rock group, mimicking and mocking the very thing, a living myth invested in as a construction by their audience. Only sacrifice can be real. Brite's is a Gothic subculture of drugs, rock and roll, bisexual encounters, magic, and death. Her language is brilliant, visceral, sensuous, erotic, and built on combinations of opposites—the oxymoron.

Vampires are creatures of cultural metamorphosis, indices of ways in which historical, political, and social change registers itself on the creative imagination of different people at different times. Brite's are aware of their own posing:

> The vampires got into town sometime before midnight. They parked their black van in an illegal space, then got hold of a bottle of Chartreuse and reeled down Bourbon Street swigging it by turns, their arms around one another's shoulders, their hair in one another's faces. All three had outlined their features in dark blots of makeup . . . they wished they had fangs but had to make do with teeth filed sharp, and they could walk in sunlight as their great-grandfathers could not. (Brite 59)

But the traditional polarisation between victim and predator is troubled in this new, gendered take on the vampire.

In *His Mouth Will Taste of Wormwood and Other Stories*, on the outskirts of the outskirts lurk Brite's horror characters, young gay men who, like Lovecraft's characters, seek ever more destructive, nihilistic thrills, eventually the thrill of death. Other lost souls, crazy women, and orphan children haunt the Gothic undercrofts of Grand Central Station, epitomising travelling rootlessness and aimlessness, emerging threateningly from the cavernous underground, themselves overtaken by the lives of insects existing in their hair, their brittle bodies hissing.

Set in New Orleans, 'His Mouth Will Taste of Wormwood' (1994) follows Howard and Louis, who drink the outlawed absinthe seeking 'the treasures and the pleasures of the grave'. These characters have moved beyond all manner of drink, drugs, straight and gay sex, fuelled by a need to satisfy nameless desires exceeding everyday youthful experiment. Death worship involves a collection of articles: Louis's mother's fetid suicidal head, the violet eyes of a dead girl. Hearing of a voodoo veve or talisman that could add to their mausoleum, they raid a grave, then, in the darkest of infernal nightclubs where the appropriately named band 'Ritual Sacrifice' are playing, they meet a terrifying youth with androgynous beauty:

> [H]is beauty was almost feral, but overlaid with a cool elegance like a veneer of sanity hiding madness. His ivory skin stretched over cheekbones like razors; his eyes were hectic pools of darkness. (Brite 55)

The boy overwhelms them both with passion and lust, leaving a taste of wormwood in Howard's mouth and Louis a desiccated corpse. But instead of horror and detestation, Howard responds with a desperate need to seek the boy, determining to desecrate the grave and see the blood-filled corpse. Howard is a victim of lust and desire generated in its victims by the vampiric embrace. The stranger holds out:

> his arms to me, inviting me to lie down with him in his rich wormy bed.
> With the first kiss his mouth will taste of wormwood. After that it will taste only of me—of my blood, my life, siphoning out of my body and into his. I will feel the sensations Louis felt: the shrivelling of my tissues, the drying-up of all my vital juices. I care not, the treasures and the pleasures of the grave? They are his hands, his lips, his tongue. (Brite 58)

The desire the vampire generates is a desire for the Other, who is also a version of self.

Selected Bibliography

Lost Souls (1992)

Drawing Blood (1993)

Swamp Foetus (1993)

His Mouth Will Taste of Wormwood (1995)

Exquisite Corpse (1996)

Courtney Love: The Real Story (1997)

Are You Loathsome Tonight? (1998)

The Lazarus Heart (1998)

Self-Made Man (formally published as *Are You Loathsome Tonight?*) (1998)

Anne Rice (1941–)

Born in New Orleans, Anne Rice was influenced by local ghost stories and vampire tales. When her mother died from alcoholism, the family moved to Dallas. Anne Rice married poet and painter Stan Rice in 1961, living in San Francisco. In 1966, their daughter, Michelle, was born. Diagnosed with leukaemia, she died before she was six, and Anne's despair at her loss led to an early version of *Interview with the Vampire*.

Rice's twenty novels have sold more than 100 million copies worldwide. It is to *Interview with the Vampire* (1976) that we turn to answer questions about the resurgence of the vampire myth in popular culture towards the end of the twentieth century. Although immediately successful with many, the novel's international success began some years after publication, as the reading public returned to fantasy and the vampire, in particular, as an icon of the paradoxes and potential of what it means to be human, especially in the self-questioning period immediately preceding the century's end. Rice's novel, then film (directed by Neil Jordan in 1994, starring Tom Cruise and Brad Pitt) spawned a huge cult following that has maintained momentum as she continues to produce new vampire and horror novels featuring witches, body snatchers, and other horror familiars. Rice maintains a public face aligned with her cult status and the imaginative constructions of her followers, wearing black Gothic outfits, appearing in TV shows in a New Orleans cemetery and on a Web site discussing death, giving explanatory interviews (Michael O'Reilly) and responding to fan requests.

Rice's family sagas and historical, supernatural horror deal with paradox and contradictions, both entertaining and encouraging moral and philosophical speculation. Like Poppy Z. Brite, Rice is a gay icon because of her treatment of homoeroticism, particularly in *Interview with the Vampire* and *The Vampire Lestat* (1985). Her work troubles boundaries and the often simplistic characteristics of gender, offering androgyny, bisexuality, and incest. She questions radical feminist rejection of all male power as evil (*Queen of the Damned*, 1988), while acting out/exposing the patriarchal tyrannies of the male-dominated 'Théâtre de Vampires' characters (in *Interview*). Rice's Catholicism might inspire some of the lushness of the language, the icons of blood and crucifixes in her books, but her engagement with contemporary critical issues of performativity place her directly with radical writers and filmmakers who highlight gender as performance, and with postmodernists who query notions of a shared reality. It is her ability to be read as contributing to and informed by complex literary and cultural theory and as entertainment—action, violence, lushness, sex, black humour, loss of blood—which ensures that she maintains such diverse readership. Influenced by Hawthorne, Dickens, Goethe, and Shakespeare, Rice usually produces horror or dark fantasy but has also written two historical novels and five erotic tales. She recycles and refocuses on the characters in her fictional universes so favourites return and play minor or major roles.

Daniel, a young interviewer, listens to the story of Louis, an initially reluctant vampire. A bored, decadent, mourning plantation owner, he was rescued from this despair by Lestat, who turned him into a vampire. Experiences of partying, devouring hapless partygoers, and finally burning the house to the ground take them from New Orleans to London and Paris, where they adopt Claudia, an orphaned, eternal child vampire who Louis saves from the plague. Claudia preys on other children and the caring hearts of adults, herself adopting a mother/sister/lover figure in Madeline. Her anger leads her to burn Lestat, a terrible vampire crime, but her escape with Madeline is short lived as they are left to die in the sun by the vengeful members of the Paris Théâtre des Vampires.

Much of the novel's fascination can be identified in its challenge to boundaries—life and death, sexuality, behavioural norms—and its focus on the performative and thinking vampire, a far cry from the husks of blood-draining Transylvanians met when seeking contacts with the extended vampire family in Eastern Europe.

Anne Rice's vampires are not easily categorisable as good/bad/ demonic/angelic. Their insecurities align them with the complexities of the postmodern world. They are aware they act roles and that all gendered roles are constructs. Their performative nature is most often employed as 'dressing to kill' as a vampire, fulfilling mortals' fantasies in their frock-coated disguises. As members of a parallel world parasitic upon our own, yet longer lasting, they enable us to scrutinise ourselves, to look closely at our equation of desire and disgust, love and death, and to recognise the vampire in ourselves.

Lestat, Armand, those of the blood religions in Anne Rice's *Vampire Chronicles*, play with the borders of death, defying it in their search for alternative reasons for existence. Rice's vampire fictions develop complex alternative mythologies, histories, family sagas, moralities, and relationships, refusing to punish the vampiric act or restore restrictive order, thus opening up liberating space for the rereading of relationships of power and interpretations of ourselves and our world. They also reinvest desire and the erotic with powerfully disruptive and creative forces. Lestat (*The Vampire Lestat, Queen of the Damned*) craves the limelight as a rock artist singing of his people's past, emphasising this factual past as invention to cover up his real activities.

In *Queen of the Damned*, Daniel and his vampire lover, the ever-youthful Armand, leader of the Théâtre de Vampires, live a life parallel to the mortals who flock to Armand's 'night island', a luxury shopping paradise filled with consumer items and mortal excess. The night consumers are scrutinised by Armand, who wanders among them, preying offshore on smugglers and drug runners from his 'sleek unlighted speedboat' (Rice 114).

> [Y]ou could buy anything on the Night Island—diamonds, a Coca-cola, books, pianos, parrots, designer fashions, porce-

lain dolls. All the fine cuisines of the world awaited you. . . .
Or you could live adjacent to it, in secret luxury, slipping in
and out of the whirl at will. (Rice 115)

Living close to mortals and mimicking their dress, lives, and the
mythic versions of vampires mortals fantasise about, vampires survive through the essential *artifice*, which, coupled with secular
investment in the reality of myth (the mythic made real) is their
safety. The novel suggests a creative congruence between the
metaphor and the 'real' spiritual and material.

Ken Gelder (*Reading the Vampire*) argues that claims of Rice's
postfeminism contradict her homoeroticism and politics of queer
theory. One of Rice's strengths could, however, be seen to be a
refusal of those very kinds of polarities. She explores the return to
the mother *and* the radical opportunities offered by queer theory in
fictional practice. She troubles other conventional divisions such as
male/female, straight/gay, life/death, self/Other, good/bad, etc. The
transgressive vampire is particularly well placed to explore and
enact such questioning and such queering, such disruptions.

Rice's exploration of relationships and the role of the mother
peaks with the story of Akasha, the archaic mother, and Enkil, her
husband (*The Vampire Lestat*). 'Those who must be kept', they are
the burden of memory and lore that sit enthroned, motionless
throughout the centuries, guarded by Marius, their keeper. The great
archaic mother's sexual powers are legendary, exercised (although
rarely, as Lestat is a favourite) beyond the tomb. As the life-giving and
devouring first mother of all, Akasha is a mythic and terrifying force.

Ancient blood rituals are enacted and the mother/destroyer is
exposed. Akasha's simplistic response to patriarchy's obvious evils
is to kill all men. But Lestat points out:

> History is a litany of injustice, no one denies it. But when
> has a simple solution ever been anything but evil? Only in
> complexity do we find answers. Through complexity men
> struggle towards a fairness; it is slow and clumsy, but it's the
> only way. Simplicity demands too great a sacrifice. It always
> has. (Rice, *Queen of the Damned* 522)

Don't you see? it is not man who is the enemy of the
human species. It is the irrational; it is the spiritual when it

is divorced from the material; from the lesson in one beating heart or one bleeding vein. (Rice 525)

The Mummy, intended to be a B horror movie TV romp, was latterly developed as a lively tale about an Egyptian king coming to life in Edwardian Egypt. *The Witching Hour* (1990) tracks the lives of the Mayfair Witches, a dynasty beset by poetry, incest, wealth, and corruption, that originates in Scotland and moves to New Orleans. *Servant of the Bones* (1996) is a classic ghost story involving a golem-like being in a terrorist plot with a lethal virus. *The Feast of All Saints* (1979) is a lavish masterpiece of historical fiction based in nineteenth-century New Orleans, focusing on the beautiful but doomed free people of 'color'. *The Tale of the Body Thief* (1992) is an out-of-body/swapping experience featuring Lestat. *Lasher* (1993) has witches and a seductively brutal demon. *Taltos* (1994) is another Mayfair Witches novel, and *Memnoch the Devil* (1995) is the last installment of the 'Vampire Chronicles' (as far as we know), where Lestat meets God and the devil in his quest for redemption. In *Blood and Gold* (2001), the great vampire Marius returns. *The Vampire Armand* (1998) and *Pandora* (1998) are the first in a new series of novels linked together by the vampire David Talbot, chronicler of the Undead. *Vittorio the Vampire* (1999) is the second of Rice's 'New Tales of the Vampires' and *Merrick* (2000) continues the saga of the Mayfair Witches, in which Rice interweaves the witches' world and the vampires' world, where magical powers and otherworldly fascinations are 'locked together in a dance of seduction, death and rebirth'. Rice's family and community sagas stretch through a myriad of horror figures, times, and places.

Selected Bibliography

Interview with the Vampire (1976)
The Vampire Lestat (1985)
Queen of the Damned (1988)

Jewelle Gomez (1948–)

Author of a variety of African-American lesbian tales, Jewelle Gomez used the vampire myth to cultural and political intent in

The Gilda Stories (1991). This novel refuses the Otherising of both women and black or Asian peoples, focusing instead upon a sisterhood of women vampires, the central figure of whom is Gilda, a role played serially by different women over time. The novel questions constructions of monstrosity and reframes notions of the horrific, of binary divisions. As Paulina Palmer notes:

> [I]t is in the construction of Gilda, her vampire protagonist, that Gomez takes the deconstruction of the normative and the related multiplication of representational as well as interpretive possibilities furthest. Gilda obviously 'stands out': as black, as a woman, as lesbian, as 'freedom fighter', and so forth. Yet she is also a being in a variety of disguises, a passing and trespassing figure, a queer (as) vampire who depends upon, and at times even delights in, 'mingling unobtrusively'. (Palmer, *Lesbian Gothic* 123)

Gomez valorises the lesbian or queer as protagonist and heroine, challenging binary oppositions that would denegrate her. Gilda has escaped from the horrors of history, her role as slave on a plantation in the Civil War, and joins a brothel of liberated and energised women. As in other tales by radical women vampire writers, the vampire sisterhood metes out justice only to the evildoers and polarises Others, celebrating black vampire women and lesbians.

Selected Bibliography

The Gilda Stories (1991)

Tananarive Due (1966–)

African-American journalist on the *Miami Herald* and daughter of civil rights activists, Tananarive Due writes horror that is also action-packed adventure questioning racial and gendered Otherising. In *My Soul to Keep* (1997) and *The Living Blood* (2001) she follows the tale of David/Dawit, a Life Brother, part of an African family of the blood religion (like vampires) living in a subterranean city, founded by one who rescued from thieves the bloodied clothing of Christ. They share the living blood that grants them eternal life and so have wonderful healing powers. At one level, the notion of a family of powerful Africans is celebratory but at another it is problematic, because these Brothers treat mortals and women in particular in a predatory, hierarchical manner, modelled on the brutal hierarchies of white on black, male on female, of racism and sexism in the time-bound world aboveground. David's mortal wife, Jessica, seeks out him and his family in the second novel, bringing their mixed-blood daughter, Fana, to be taught how to manage her powers for good, but she meets hostility and cultural discrimination as a mortal woman. Finally, they with a doctor, Lucas, intent on saving his son from a blood disease, and like-minded others escape oppressive violence. Together, they establish a new settlement in the United States that aims to counter divisions and destruction and bring people from religious and cultural groups to develop care, using the blood for good. Due's is an engaged saga, which, like Gomez's, challenges colour-coded hierarchies and gender race distinctions.

Selected Bibliography

My Soul to Keep (1997)
The Living Blood (2001)

Nalo Hopkinson (1960–)

Jamaican-born Canadian/Trinidadian Nalo Hopkinson has won a range of prizes for her novels and short stories. Her collection *Skin Folk* (2001) focuses on shape shifting, questioning the bodily shapes and roles that empower or disempower. In one tale, 'Greedy Choke Puppy' (2001), Jackie seeks the attention of men by remaining youthful, something she can only manage if she slips her own skin at night and flies, a soucouyant or hurtling ball of flame, to steal the blood and life of others, preferably babies. We gradually recognise that this murderer protagonist, sold on cosmeticised beauty, mercilessly draining others, must be stopped. Her grandmother, a wise woman who controls her own natural soucouyant tendency, peppers Jackie's discarded skin, so upon return Jackie cannot turn back into a woman, a punishment for her cruelty. *Brown Girl in the Ring* (1998) uses a child's singing tale as basis for fiction set in a future Toronto ruled by unscrupulous politicians and black posses. At the novel's centre is posse gang leader Rudy, set to obtain a new heart for the dying woman president. He buys support from other people to help him achieve this. This horror tale focuses on body and domestic horror involving strong women—a grandmother, a young mother with a vulnerable baby, and a mother, Rudy's wife, whom he turned into a duppy (ghost or spirit), enslaved, fed blood, forced to turn into a soucouyant and carry out cruel acts. After the death of her powerful grandmother, whose heart is stolen, Ti Jeanne, the young mother, learns her own powers and gains support from a gang of street kids to take revenge on Rudy. Nalo Hopkinson's tales explore shape shifting, power, gender, and race in culturally rich horror tales influenced by Caribbean myths.

Selected Bibliography

Brown Girl in the Ring (1998)
Skin Folk (2001)

Clive Barker (1952–)

A contemporary king of horror, Clive Barker writes novels, short stories, screenplays, TV shows, and survey-type criticism. His *A–Z of Horror* is both a book and a TV series exploring key players and themes in horror.

The Damnation Game, *The Hellbound Heart*, and 'The Last Illusion' are all reworkings of the Faust legend. 'Hell, I point out in *The Damnation Game*, is *reimagined by each generation*. So are the pacts and the pactmakers' (Barker 1988, quoted online).

Barker's writing is laden with sense impressions, emphasising the body and its vulnerability to decay. In *The Hellbound Heart*, smell overwhelms:

> the smell of burning was only the beginning. No sooner had he registered it than half a dozen other scents filled his head. Perfumes he had scarcely noticed until now were suddenly overpoweringly strong. The lingering scent of filched blossoms; the smell of paint on the ceiling and the sap in the wood beneath his feet: all filled his head.

He could even smell the darkness outside the door; and
in it, the ordure of a hundred thousand birds. (Barker, *The
Hellbound Heart* 13)

Body horror mixes with eroticism and terror with desire for death
in 'Scapegoats'. Images of draining and threat overwhelm:

I let it happen. I opened my mouth and felt it fill with cold
water. Salt burned my sinuses, the cold stabbed behind my
eyes. . . . Below me, two corpses, their hair swaying loosely
in the current, hugged my legs. Their heads lolled and
danced on rotted ropes of neck muscle, and though I pawed
at their hands, and the flesh came off the bone in grey, lace-
edged pieces, their loving grip didn't falter. They wanted
me, oh how dearly they wanted me. (Barker, 'Scapegoats',
in *The Books of Blood* 463)

However, Barker denies 'body disgust', celebrating decay as 'the
rearrangement of the flesh', noting bodily response to stimuli and
illness:

[H]ere we are sitting together, growing old, our flesh
minutely changing outside our control; our bodies responding to the alcohol we're taking in; our organs, for all we
know, growing tumorous. The flesh can decide to get sick,
to get upset, to make us desire. (Barker, 'Scapegoats' 463)

Barker's work often features metamorphosis, mutilation, aging, sexuality—the human condition laid bare. He uses metaphors to depict
the horrors of the human condition, laying bare the suffering and
doubt of the flesh. Barker also provides most useful inroads into
horror with his critical documentary work.

Selected Bibliography

The Books of Blood (1981)

Stephen King (1947–)

Stephen Edwin King was born in Maine in 1947. He attended the
University of Maine at Orono, where he wrote a weekly newspaper

column, was active in student politics supporting the antiwar movement, and graduated in 1970 with a B.A. in English. His first success was his short story 'The Glass Floor', sold to *Startling Mystery Stories* in 1967. King married Tabitha Spruce in 1971, and they lived on his earnings as a laundry worker and her student loan. One of his first major successes was the novel *Carrie*, accepted by Doubleday in 1973. To date he has written thirty-one novels and numerous short stories.

King's world highlights the paradox of the safety of the home, the threat lurking behind Middle America's values and lifestyles, so audiences can relate to his situations, characters, and events. He explores areas of the human psyche that are usually pushed to the back of the mind:

> I ask myself what is forbidden? What can't I write about? And then I write about it. (King, *Time*, 27 April 1992 62)

The reception of this immensely popular writer is one that cuts to the heart of the discussion about the acceptability of horror. King replays the insecurities of Middle America relentlessly in fiction and film and in so doing has produced some of the most remarkable horror.

His work exemplifies the power of horror from the psychological to the social. *Carrie* (1974) is an example of body horror in which the disturbing power of an adolescent girl is figured as telekinetic energy. Fear and disgust of female bodily functions and particularly the alignment of menstruation and divergence emerge in Carrie's powerful ability to control physical situations. She is odd, an outcast, but her brilliant evening as prom queen might restore her to a social position were it not for the malice of her peers who, in dousing her on stage with pigs' blood, dramatise abject disgust at women's blood, witchcraft, and domestic power. In her furious response, doors slam shut, fires start. The other teens who abjected Carrie are fatally punished. King demonises women throughout his work. In *Misery* (1987), every writer's nightmare, the sadistic 'best fan' is in control of the crash victim writer's body and his creative mind. King comments on the writer-reader relationship here but also on our shared terror of helplessness in the face of physical power, of entrapment, of being disempowered and made to disappear.

King is both an inheritor of the tradition of realism and a master of contemporary fantasy (see Regina Cross's unpublished Ph.D. thesis 'Stephen King and the Dark Tower', 2002). Cross identifies three kinds of women in King: the Sacrifice, a strong woman trying to find a place against all odds; the Destroyer, who often manipulates the destruction of the Sacrifice; and the Gunslinger, who is tragic but shapes the world to her own designs.

Annie, the psychotic fan in *Misery*, enslaves Paul, the novelist, who views her as unstable and evil: '[T]here's a borderline between the kinds of manageable and unmanageable psychosis. You're getting closer to that line every day . . . and part of you knows it' (King 144). Approaching subjects of interest to women, King gives us a victim of domestic abuse, husband murderer Dolores Claiborne, who protects her children until she snaps.

Gerald's Game (1992) and *Dolores Claiborne* (1992) are praised by critics for weaving characters and a narrative that captivate the reader without the traditional King trappings of horror, gore, and the supernatural.

Gerald's Game is about the twenty-eight hours of horror a woman endures after being handcuffed to a bedpost, and *Dolores Claiborne* is about an unloved wife or housekeeper accused of the death of her senile employer. King says of these two, 'When I write, I want to scare people, but there is a certain comfort level for the reader because you are aware all the time that it's make-believe. Vampires, the supernatural and all that. In that way, it's safe. But these last two books take people out of the safety zone and that, in a way, is even scarier. Maybe it *could* happen' (King in an interview with Esther Fein, *New York Times*, 18 November 1992).

Highly popular to TV viewers is *The Dead Zone* (1979), featuring a fictional setting reminiscent of Lovecraft's *Dulwich*. It aligns terms of place with psychological disturbance:

> set in an imaginary section of Maine and New Hampshire that feels exactly like the real thing, with its cozy little towns, its light-bulb-strung country fairs and its snow-stilled winters. And the detailing is consistently impressive: what

makes John Smith realize how long he has been in the coma is the fact that the first doctor to interview him after he wakes up is using a felt-tipped pen, an instrument that John has never seen before. The Dead Zone calls up images of carnage, of zombies, of hellish Dorésque underworlds; whereas in fact it refers to that tiny part of Smith's brain that no longer works after his accident, which of course affects in significant ways what he can see of people's future. (Lehmann-Haupt, *New York Times*, 17 August 1979)

Stephen King deploys the full range of horror types. The inanimate become demonically animate in one such favourite, *Christine* (1983), about an 'unholy' vindictive Plymouth car. King's is the voice of terrified Middle America seeing the demon in the mirror, the instability in family security. He exploits modern anxieties.

As Cross notes, 'King's fiction is rooted in his family' (Cross 62). In harnessing everyday domestic terrors and body horror, he deeply disturbs our necessary complacencies.

Like Barker and Lovecraft, King works critically to identify some of the strengths of horror. The genre functions as delight and:

'psychic relief' to the audience . . . but more important, such films provide a way of 're-establishing our feelings of essential normality.' . . . [*Danse Macabre*] has the effect of restoring the social order. (McCrillis 268)

King can be seen, on the one hand, as quite conventional—for example, his works reinforce fears of 'hysterical' women (*Carrie*)—or fundamentally culturally subversive, unleashing terrors—evil night visitors (*The Tommyknockers*), mad writers and readers, demonic chattering teeth and cars, revengeful dogs, and hospitals (*Kingdom Hospital*), where hidden histories leak upwards from Gothic underworlds and threaten sanity and safety only to restore order. King measures and critiques Middle America, enacting its fears using either psychological horror and/or the supernatural, restoring order but leaving lingering fears of reenactments and returns.

Selected Bibliography

Carrie (1974)
The Shining (1977)
The Dead Zone (1979)
Danse Macabre (1980) (nonfiction)
Cujo (1981)
Christine (1983)
Pet Sematary (1983)
Misery (1987)
The Dark Tower II: The Drawing of the Three (1987)
Dolores Claiborne (1992)
The Green Mile (2000)
Dreamcatcher (2001)
From a Buick 8 (2002)

Michael Arnzen (1967–)

Michael Arnzen is the master of minimalist horror fictions and poems. His short, sharp horror tales are filled with vile splatter and excess exploding from or invading everyday activities and relationships. Identifying horror's differences from crime fictions, he notes:

> Horror's mysteries are usually universally repressed truths, whereas suspense is a piano chord that can only be played so long. Horror bangs on the same piano as suspense, but it produces more chaotic chords. Cacophony, sometimes. Horror pounds the keys of the literary piano in staccato rhythm. Horror resides in the chirp of the *Psycho* soundtrack. The arc of Mother's knife. And the pulse-racing dribble and twist of the camera down the drain afterwards. (Arnzen, 'Minimalist Horror' 10)

Arnzen's minimalist horror provides a 'snapshot of terror' for immediate effect. In a café the protagonist's daughter plays among plastic balls only to retrieve the first of several human skulls. The bizarre pops up in the everyday:

Her favorite continent in Playland is the giant pen full of plastic balls which she loves to dive into and hide within, only to leap back out and scare other children whenever they enter the bin. You eat a burger and it's business as usual, until you hear her scream. Authentically. You turn, and for only a moment you think she's found some strange sort of puppet. But you quickly realize: your daughter holds a real human skull in her hands. (Arnzen, 'Diving In' 12)

In an unpleasant replayed version of 'Isabella; or The Pot of Basil' (Keats), Arnzen's wife figure turns revengeful gardener, clipping her husband's spinal cord, pruning, and finally saying, 'I turned him upside down and grew tomatoes in his potted head' (Arnzen, 'Gardener' 13).

Other plants eat children. Arnzen's is an unpleasant, violent everyday world.

Selected Bibliography

'Diving In', 'Gardener', 'How to Grow a Man-Eating Plant', and 'Introduction: Minimalist Horror' in *100 Jolts: Shockingly Short Stories* (2004)

Films and Film Studies

While horror fictions were popular throughout the nineteenth and early twentieth century, it was through film that most people came to recognise those two most popularised figures, Frankenstein and Dracula.

Key cinematic moments for horror are the use of fantasy by Méliès, T. S. Edison's version of *Frankenstein* in 1910, and the flowering of silent Gothic horror films in Germany.

Gothic Horror Cinema

Robert Wiene's *Das Kabinett des Doktor Caligari* in 1919 was one of the first Gothic horror films. Surreal sets transformed the usual Gothic locations and the film focused on life/death, blood, concealment, madness, dream, evil, and love in a compelling fashion.

This was followed in 1922 by the legendary, visually haunting *Nosferatu* by F. W. Murnau.

Murnau changed Count Dracula's name to Orlok, and although this undead, bald figure with his protruding fangs and elongated clawlike nails lacks the sex appeal of portrayals of Dracula from the 1960s onwards, the terrible image of his silhouette approaching the vulnerable sleeping girl is the stuff of nightmares. Murnau used German Expressionist techniques in his powerful film, set in Bremen. However, legal problems followed, as the film was too close to Stoker's own *Dracula*.

> The Count was portrayed by Max Schreck (whose last name is actually German for 'terror') as an undead bestial bloodsucker. In the story, the vampire can only be brought to rest by a virtuous woman who shall willingly give her blood to the beast until the sun rises, and the vampire turns to dust in a legendary scene. Many scholars describe *Nosferatu* as the best film ever made in the vampire genre. (Antti online)

Post-1960s vampires rarely seek rest from the vampire curse, instead celebrating the power it endows. Universal Pictures established the horror film genre in Hollywood. In 1931, Tod Browning developed Dracula as an elegant gentleman, Bela Lugosi dressed in a black and red satin cloak, and introduced the notion of sexuality and aristocracy to the role. Around the same time, 1931, James Whale popularised Mary Shelley's *Frankenstein* with Boris Karloff's square-headed monster, a warped noble savage with the potential for emotion.

In the 1960s, the wonderful Hammer horror movies began with Terrence Fisher's *Horror of Dracula*. With their creaking sets in British castles/mansions and the masterful work of Vincent Price and Christopher Lee they set a pattern for Gothic horror films. Lee's Count was based on Bela Lugosi's bloodsucker—aesthetic and powerful.

European auteurs included the Italian Mario Bava, who used brilliant Gothic imagery. Bava's films included *La Maschera del Demonio*, considered central to the genre. Many of the films starred Barbara Steele, who became known as 'The Queen of European Horror', a precursor to Ingrid Pitt, the Hammer horror beauty. In the 1960s, European directors followed Roger Vadim's *Et mourir de plaisir*, fairy tale Gothic with emphasis on soft-core pornography. French horrors, *Le Frisson des Vampires* and *Requiem for a Vampire*, were visually beautiful films with little storyline. Hammer contributed to the trend with *The Kiss of the Vampire* and a series of films based on *Carmilla*—*The Vampire Lovers, Lust for a Vampire*, and *Twins of Evil*, a successful trilogy that played a great part in popularising the subgenre of soft-core porn horror. Meanwhile, Roger Corman was writing, producing, directing, and shooting cheap exploitation films. Horror cinema's slide into soft-core pornography is aligned with the dual responses of desire and disgust that horror figures conjure up for their audiences, where voluptuous semiclad women (particularly identical lesbians as in *Twins of Evil*) offer delights clearly defined as dangerous, monstrous, and deadly, titillating the audience and finally reassuring them of their moral solidarity when all 'deviants' are punished at the film's end.

In 1960, Roger Corman began a series of Edgar Allan Poe film adaptations with *The Fall of the House of Usher, The Pit and the Pendulum, The Masque of the Red Death*, and *The Tomb of Ligeia*. Most starred Vincent Price and featured those fears that dogged Poe: family curses, being buried alive, and the return of the dead. These films took place in old, spooky castles and dungeons with rusty torturing equipment.

Alfred Hitchcock (1899–1980)

Alfred Hitchcock, son of East End greengrocer William Hitchcock, was known as the 'Master of Suspense'. He made mostly thrillers such as *The Lodger, The 39 Steps, Rebecca, Vertigo*, and *North by Northwest*, but Hitchcock also tested the boundaries between thrillers and horror with violent and unpleasant threatening scenes, peaking with *Psycho* (1960) and *The Birds* (1963). There are horror elements in *Marnie* (1964), the 'Alfred Hitchcock Hour' (1962) TV series, and *Rope* (1948). As such, he brought horror into prime-time viewing and filmed some of the most powerful stories of the twentieth century.

Robert Bloch's 1959 novel *Psycho*, the source of Hitchcock's most famous horror film, was based on the true story of serial killer and cannibal Ed Geins, whose mother fixation led him to disinter corpses and rebuild a version of his dead mother, brutally murdering another woman. This small-town Texas original shocked millions. Geins is actually the model for more than Norman Bates; his cannibalism and brutal dismemberment of people and corpses also fed into *The Texas Chainsaw Massacre* and *The Silence of the Lambs*.

> The horror was the horror of the Bates Motel. The horror was the horror of the insane brutality of it all. You didn't talk about dismembering people and cutting their guts out and doing things that they do today as a matter of course. You didn't want to hear that. Films were entertainment in those days. (Peggy Robertson [assistant to Alfred Hitchcock] in Clive Barker 29)

Psycho   Psycho is one of the most famous horror films ever made and is best remembered for its Hitchcockian set pieces, particularly the murder of Marion Crane (Janet Leigh) in the shower and the killing of Milton Arbogast (Martin Balsam) at the top of the stairs. Anthony Perkins gave a marvellously subdued performance as the lurkingly normal but weird, insane Norman Bates. The shocking discovery of Norman's mummified mother leads to the terrifying final scene of Norman talking in both his own and his mother's voices. During its original release, patrons were not allowed into the movie theatre after the screening had begun. Unforgettable is the brutal shower sequence—the woman's vulnerability, the knife attacking her, seemingly of its own volition, and the hiding of the murderer, his bizarre cross-dressing, and his fetish for his dead mother.

It is a problematic film that annoyed gay viewers in its alignment of homosexual cross-dressing and violent murder. Meanwhile, feminist critics are concerned that the woman's murder is tolerated because of her lax sexual practices and the mother fixation is blamed for Bates's psychosis and brutal actions. Bloch identifies *Psycho* as a classic tale of defamiliarisation of the everyday:

> But at the time I decided to write a novel based on the notion that the man next door may be a monster, unsuspected even in the gossip-ridden microcosm of small-town life. In order to become a successful serial murderer in a close-knit rural society, a man must adopt a reclusive exis-

tence: operating a motel on the outskirts of town seemed a solution. So I invented Norman Bates. I built him a motel and I installed a shower in it for him. (Bloch in Clive Barker 29)

The film impresses audiences with a healthy fear of seemingly safe places (motels and hotels) and the trustworthiness of ordinary folk.

Selected Filmography

Rebecca (1940)
Vertigo (1958)
North by Northwest (1959)
Psycho (1960)
The Birds (1963)
Marnie (1964)
Frenzy (1972)

Sequels to Psycho

Psycho II (Richard Franklin, 1983)
Psycho III (Anthony Perkins, 1986)
Bates Motel (Richard Rothstein, TV 1987)
Psycho IV: The Beginning (Mick Garris, TV 1990)

Invasion of the Body Snatchers *(1956)*

Look! You fools! You're in danger! Can't you see? They're after you! They're after all of us! Our wives . . . our children . . . They're here already! You're next!

So the threat ignored, a conventional horror moment, and humankind is doomed.

The Invasion of the Body Snatchers (novel, Jack Finney, 1954, film 1956, and remake 1978) captures our fears of the unfamiliar entering and disturbing the family and emphasises our need to invest in home, children, and friends. Here, these familiars seem to change, and instead of being reassured that this is just a temporary aberration, born of our *own* fears, instead we find they *have* changed.

Identical to the people we know, they are actually invaders, alien pods, replicates, soulless and emotionless replacements. After World War II, the Cold War and the threat of the Bomb dominated people's minds. These were enemies and fears that you could not recognise as Other, which could creep in at any moment, disguised as someone or something seemingly familiar and safe. Don Siegel's 1956 classic film *Invasion of the Body Snatchers* perfectly captured the ideology and politics of this period. The McCarthy witchhunt promised to identify and root out these hidden traitors to the American way.

> In *Body Snatchers*, the pod people, who, like McCarthy and the other red-baiters, look like typical, fine upstanding Americans, search out rebels like Miles who refuse to conform to what has been newly defined as the 'American way' —just as McCarthy and HUAC destroyed the lives of those who refused to knuckle under to their directives. The mob hysteria, the sense of paranoia, the fascist police, the witchhunt atmosphere of the picture certainly mirrors the ills of McCarthy's America. (Whitehead online)

The small California town of Santa Mira is infiltrated by pods from outer space that replicate and replace humans. Dr Miles Bennell (Kevin McCarthy) resists the invaders and their attempts to remove humanity from the face of the earth. Considered the greatest of all the horror and science fiction classics of the 1950s, the film brought science fiction into the public eye, ensuring it was seen as culturally and politically engaged. The book and film continue to fascinate modern filmmakers and have served as a model for many other films and television shows. Carmen Dragon's film score has also had a great influence on filmmakers and television directors alike, heard in *The X-Files* and *Buffy the Vampire Slayer*. Siegel's film focuses on the contemporary dehumanisation of the individual at a particular moment in history—the moment of brainwashing and the potential for humans being overtaken by Others (foreign, mechanical, with different value systems). It is both a film that defends the American way of life and one that questions it, since the majority become pods.

Body Snatchers merges the horrors of mad science with alien invasion and body horror. Fear of invasion following investigations and expeditions into outer space inform the film, as do fears of technology, excessive bureaucratisation, psychiatry, and other sciences. Jack Finney was interested:

> in the ability of technology, modernization and fragmentation to disenfranchise people and make them lose their ability to act human. (Whitehead online)

The 1978 version starring Donald Sutherland is set in San Francisco, so the invasion is centre stage in one of America's most radical cities. One of this ciy's major fears is bureaucratic control. Spores from outer space fall and hatch flowers, which are taken home by people by local government request. Everyone has one; you are extremely strange if you do not conform. City health department chemist Elizabeth Driscoll (Brooke Adams) confides in her colleague Matthew Bennell (Sutherland), a public health inspector, that her boyfriend seems strangely changed. Bennell comes across a restaurant owner whose wife seems not herself, and two friends find a blank, unformed body in their bathhouse, which takes on features as they sleep.

> The spookiest scene in the entire film though is the one where Sutherland dozes in his garden and the four pods, duplicates of he and the others, start to form, the pods oozing out naked bodies with a crunching, popping sound, forming into embryonic creatures. (Scheib online 1994)

Gradually, everyone is changed. The differences are that the pod people are emotionless and have a tendency to howl and point out traitors (non-pods). The film ends terrifyingly when Driscoll rediscovers Bennell, only to be howled and pointed at. No one escapes. This 1970s film is a cautionary tale about urban dehumanisation. Using *Star Trek*'s Leonard Nimoy as the psychiatrist reminds viewers of aliens appearing in our homes. He insists nothing is wrong.

This is an alien invasion/defamiliarisation/body horror tale. There can be no happy ending.

The Silence of the Lambs *(1991)*

Based on the best-selling novel by Thomas Harris and sequel to the underrated *Manhunter* (Michael Mann, 1986), *The Silence of the Lambs* is a psychological, body horror, classy cannibal film. Rookie FBI agent Clarice Starling (Jodie Foster) must gain the trust and use the knowledge of imprisoned psychotic psychiatrist Dr Hannibal Lecter (Anthony Hopkins won an Oscar as 'Hannibal the Cannibal') to track down the Ed Gein-like serial killer 'Buffalo Bill'. The film was a huge box-office hit and also won Academy Awards for Best Picture, Actress (Foster), Director (Jonathan Demme), and Adapted Screenplay (Ted Tally).

This most unsettling of films feeds on nightmares and terrible memories. Hannibal Lecter, cannibal doctor, interviewed by Starling, recognises her as part 'white trash' and homes in on her various insecurities. Lecter's aesthetic sense represents a contradiction that is also explored in *A Clockwork Orange* by Anthony Burgess (1962) and Stanley Kubrick (1971). In both texts/films, the lead male role is one that problematises any simplistic correlation between nastiness, evil deeds, horror, and aesthetic good taste. Both Alex in *A Clockwork Orange* and Lecter (suggesting T. S. Eliot's 'lecteur', someone of elevated taste and habits) love good music and beauty. Hannibal Lecter's penchant is for good food: 'A census taker once tried to test me. I ate his liver with some fava beans and a fine Chianti' is one of his famously disgusting delightful lines. But Hannibal only dines, in the main, on those who get in his way or, more aesthetically oriented, those bureaucrats, crooked cops, and management lackeys whose banality and limited roles irritate him. He might test Starling on her closeness to poverty, the gutter, and her nightmare memories of her uncle's farm and the cries of slaughtered lambs, but he would never harm her because of their parallel intelligence and obsessional qualities.

To capture Buffalo Bill, Starling negotiates with Lecter initially in all naiveté of the deceptiveness of the FBI, the system, and her immediate boss, who would like to exert psychological and some sexual control over his protégé (a characteristic he shares with Dr Lecter). The depiction of Buffalo Bill as a transgressive gay cross-dresser has received criticism from many quarters as reinforcing images of homosexual deviancy. Sold on gender as performance,

though a long way from Judith Butler, Buffalo Bill wishes to emu-
late the body image of a Hollywood starlet construction of woman
by sewing together different skin parts to make another skin,
another version of self. Starling must collude with the dubious relationship of verbal seduction and power wielded over her by the
imprisoned Hannibal Lecter in order to patch together clues as to
Bill's whereabouts and existence. Hannibal's vile acts of slaughter
and cannibalism repel—he tears off the face of a prison guard and
literally adopts him as a disguise—but his strange sense of preservation of and collusion with Starling uneasily turn this into a tale of
maker, master, and pupil, causing us to question power relations,
identity, and the safety of the familiar.

Hannibal, also by Thomas Harris, was filmed in 2002, reprising
the role of Dr Lecter as an art historian who takes revenge on those
who try to imprison him. Unpleasant moments with pigs devouring
people and dining on the brains of the living use both body horror
and nightmare images for their effects.

The Exorcist *(1973)*

> 'I made the film because it was a good story. I never
> thought of what psychological effect it would have on any-
> one.' (Friedkin in Clive Barker 41)

William Friedkin's classic adaptation of William Peter Blatty's best-
selling novel caused a storm of controversy when originally released.
The body of an apparently normal twelve-year-old girl, Regan
(Linda Blair) is dominated by an ancient demon. Neither mother
nor doctor can cure her fits, but alternative figures of male power,
an aged exorcist (Max Von Sydow) and a priest who questions his
own faith (Jason Miller), have the power to do so eventually. The
atmospheric opening desert scenes inform audiences of the source
of the demon, building on a horror standard of locating evil as
emerging from disinterred history somewhere exotic or alien, but
the climactic possession and exorcism cause the main shock. This is
one of the most frightening horror movies ever made. The shooting
was reportedly plagued with problems (actor Jack MacGowran
died) and the British censor subsequently cut the scene of Regan
masturbating with a crucifix, but it uses impressive makeup effects

created by Dick Smith and won Oscars for Best Screenplay and Best Sound.

> When *The Exorcist* first came out, people were saying it will ruin your life if you see this movie. How all these people saw it and killed themselves right afterwards, or were put in asylums. The *National Enquirer* was just filled with stories like, 'I saw *The Exorcist* and Shot Myself!' or 'I Saw *The Exorcist* and Gave Up God!' (Quentin Tarantino in Clive Barker 41)

As a startling, fine film, *The Exorcist* touches several major horror keys. The twelve-year-old girl at its heart reminds viewers of the vulnerability of children. Most teenagers seem somewhat possessed by the devil at points during puberty, reject authority, and find themselves as sexual beings, but Regan, at twelve, with her ringlets and nightie, upstairs in her child's bedroom, reminds us of the dangers and the liminal state of the pubescent adolescent. In a particularly invasive assault on one's sense of the safety of the home, the child is pushed out of the limits of 'normality'. Regan is flung about the room, the bed seems animated, she spews green bile, and her head revolves. She is a demon. Demon children represent our fears about normality, the family, and inheritance. Being a young woman, Regan's demonic possession is the most terrible. She's depicted as uncontrollably disgusting. Not only does she vomit, she also masturbates with a crucifix and growls 'Fuck me'. She is the great-, great-, great-granddaughter of the dangerous, perversely sexual women of Webster, the Duchess, punished by her controlling brothers in *The Duchess of Malfi*, and of Vittoria in *The White Devil*. In the context of male fears, women's energies and sexuality have to be expressed as demonic and this fuels the horror and threat represented by Regan, since the patriarchal powers of priest and mother all (helplessly) attempt to control her and restore order to save and 'heal' her. Female sexuality is depicted as spawned by Satan.

The Exorcist sent viewers racing out of the cinema and was buried for years between 1973 and 2000. It is a prime example of body horror—Regan's body is possessed, her demon head swivels, she vomits—and supernatural horror—the demon in the desert. Sequels both revisit and reinforce the tale's/film's effects.

Sequels

Exorcist II: The Heretic (John Boorman, 1977)
The Exorcist III (William Peter Blatty, 1990)

Halloween *(1978)*

John Carpenter's *Halloween* is a deeply disturbing indictment of the complacency of small-town suburban America and one of the most successful low-budget horror movies ever made. *Halloween* spawned a subgenre of what Clive Barker defines as '(mostly inferior) stalk 'n' slash imitations' in the late 1970s and 1980s.

Psychopathic masked killer Michael Myers returns home after fifteen years of incarceration in a mental asylum following his brutal murder of his sister after watching her with her boyfriend. This murder was committed while Michael wore a Halloween mask. When he escapes from the Illinois State Mental Hospital, he returns to Haddonfield, Illinois, followed by Dr Sam Loomis (Donald Pleasance), who once cared for him and knows his likely moves.

Baby-sitter Laurie (Jamie Lee Curtis), hiding in the wardrobe, is menaced by the masked killer. Carpenter stages the brutal (but bloodless) killings relentlessly. It is a strange mixture of local, everyday terror and invasion of the warped normal (like Norman Bates in *Psycho*) and something more supernatural. The psychopathic protagonist, Michael Myers, is finally revealed as a supernatural menace during the gripping climax when he keeps miraculously returning from the dead—a real challenge to the horror audience's need for closure and punishment. The film references science fiction with clips from *Forbidden Planet* (1956) and *The Thing from Another World* (1951) on TV.

In moving horror to the American suburbs, John Carpenter began a new subgenre, which has developed into numerous threatening scenarios, including *Twin Peaks* and David Lynch's other work, and even *Buffy the Vampire Slayer*, with its positioning of an ordinary high school on the Hellmouth.

As with Poppy Z. Brite's disenchanted post-Vietnam war vampire youth, this disturbance is the product of a historically disillusioned period.

'After World War II, suburbia came into being because there was a giant push to normalcy,' explains Carpenter. 'That normalcy was the issue—let's all get normal again. Normalcy can be destructive to the imagination, to creativity, to the intellect, to the soul. The only way we can grow as people is through confronting our dark side because, if all you want is the quiet and the safety, then you are giving up on reality.

. . . Nowadays, maybe because of conditions beyond our control, there is no sanctuary. And I think that is in the audience's mind. So a film-maker, if he plays with that, can create fear. Lots of fear.' (Carpenter in Clive Barker 64–66)

For much of *Halloween*, Carpenter keeps his audience off balance by using clever technical sleight of hand, including a Steadicam camera for the murderer's point of view: 'You have a gyroscopic mount on an operator,' he explains, 'and he can run and move, and that kind of gives you a dreamy, floating quality'. Carpenter used wide-angle lenses and tracking shots to give small-town America a sense of doom. 'Using wide-angle lenses also helps. And if you use the tracking shot, do it very slowly and methodically, be very authoritative about it, then the audience feels there is something strange there' (Carpenter in Clive Barker 64). The nightshots are claustrophobic. The baby-sitter is trapped in the closet, in the night-time house. No one hears or responds to her; the safest of places is inhospitable.

'In *Halloween*,' says Debra Hill, 'Jamie Lee Curtis's character runs for help but the neighbour ignores her and turns out the light. I think that epitomises what happens in suburban neighbourhoods where people are either afraid or in denial that something bad is happening.

'And the role of Donald Pleasance's character was basically to come to this town and say, there's something going on; you have to do something. You can't just keep the door shut, you can't just keep the windows closed.' (Barker 68)

The familiar scenario has been replayed through sequels and in the *Scream* and *Scary Movie* series to name a few. It has been seen as representing all that is unreliable about our complacent investment in local safety and home.

Selected Filmography

John Carpenter
Halloween (1978)
The Thing (1982)
Christine (1983)
Prince of Darkness (1987)
Village of the Damned (1995)

Films related to Halloween
Halloween II (Rick Rosenthal, 1982)
Halloween III: Season of the Witch (Tommy Lee Wallace, 1982)
Halloween IV: The Return of Michael Myers (Dwight H. Little, 1988)
Halloween V (Dominique Othenin-Girad, 1989)
Halloween: The Curse of Michael Myers (Joe Chappelle, 1995)

David Cronenberg (1943–)

David Cronenberg began directing visceral horror films, then moved to more psychological horror. *Videodrome* (1982) explores the morphing of the video players into people in some particularly bizarre scenes. Professor Brian O'Blivion (Jack Creley) develops a TV signal causing brain tumours in viewers. The film also deals with our fears of being controlled by multinationals, under surveillance, and turned into automata (from *1984* [1948], filmed in 1984), to *I Robot*, 2004). Corporations are suspect, particularly Spectacular Optical ('Keeping an Eye on the World'), run by Barry Convex, which manufactures spectacles and weapons systems. Cronenberg is interested in the ways in which science is perverted by corporate interests and how humans can be sucked into science, unaware of the potentially destructive results.

In remaking the classic horror film *The Fly*, Cronenberg uses both fear of science—Dr Seth Brundle develops a matter-transfer device—and body horror, as Brundle, caught in his matter-transfer machine with a small fly, shape-shifts gradually into a fly-human, bringing out the insect in the man. In *Dead Ringers*, Doctors Elliot and Beverly Mantle are crazy gynaecologists, inventing the 'Mantle

Retractor' and 'Gynaecological Instruments for Working on Mutant Women', simultaneously technological devices (variants on the Mantle Retractor) and an avant-garde, sadomasochistic art installation.

Selected Filmography

Shivers (1975)

Rabid (1977)

The Brood (1979)

Scanners (1981)

The Dead Zone (1983)

Videodrome (1983)

The Fly (1986)

Dead Ringers (1988)

Naked Lunch (1991)

Crash (1996)

eXistenZ (1999)

Spider (2002)

David Lynch (1946–)

David Lynch's films and TV series reinforce a sense of the perversity and danger of small-town America. His most notable horror films include *Eraserhead* (1977) and *Blue Velvet* (1986). In *Eraserhead*, Henry Spencer lives in a seemingly abandoned building in an industrial, futuristic town where giant machines work day and night, spewing excessive smoke and noise. People are damaged: Henry's girlfriend Mary X has fits, and the child she bears him is a hideous, terrifying mutant creature. This is a bizarre and powerful film with strange, depressing effects. *Blue Velvet* is a dark, sensuous film focusing on obsession with sex and power. Returning to Lumberton, his small-town American home, Jeffery (Kyle McLachlan), an ordinary and likable man, finds an ear in a field, and because of the ineptness of the local cops, sets out to discover the story behind it. His girlfriend, the girl next door Sandy (a detective's daughter), helps him with his investigation and together they uncover a very seamy, dark side to their town. At the centre of the mystery is a perverse, evil man played by Dennis Hopper, whose drug addiction is second to his playing out of pornographic fantasies on a glamourous, mysterious woman. This is a masterpiece of contemporary film noir, mixing sex and death.

Lynch's *Twin Peaks*, the TV serial, entered the family home on a weekly basis for a very long run in the 1990s, with its strange Fellini-like brew of an evil dwarf, metamorphosis, and dark other sides revealed though the alter ego of a wicked uncle. Starting conventionally with the washed-up body of high school prom queen Laura Palmer, the tale focuses on the initially extremely controlled and controlling FBI agent (Kyle McLachlan) who is sent to discover the killer and engages with a range of dubious histories. Laura turns out to have a dark past, wild partying habits, and possibly a link to something supernatural. The tale intermixes what has become a standard formula of the straitlaced FBI agent who seeks to scientifically prove and track down the source of the crime, and the strange ways in which local notable and family men hide murderous and shape-changing secrets. Stereotypical figures of American soaps or FBI and crime movies (hotel owners and families, the local coffee shop) are not quite as we have previously met them; all have hidden selves and secrets. Drawn into the supernatural, the FBI agent encounters Bill—uncle, double, monster, and embodiment of the untrustworthiness of apparently ordinary life and people. Lynch also produced the impressive, hauntingly unpleasant, seemingly straightforward crime story *Mulholland Drive* (2001).

Lynch's *Mulholland Drive* makes a nearly seamless transition from the mundane to the weird to the horrific. For example, the dialog early in the movie between two men having lunch at a diner reveals that one of them had had a dream in which he saw someone or something through the wall of the diner, an image so terrible that he is relieved that he never has to see it in reality. He explains that, in this dream, his friend was standing by the far wall of the restaurant. At the end of the story, his friend gets up to pay the check; when the other, still seated, turns to look at him, he sees that his friend is standing by the cash register in the same spot where he was in the dream. He then looks into the camera, stands up, and walks over to his friend. The frightened expression on his face reveals that everything is falling to the same position that it was in the dream. (McCrillis, 'Lynching Stephen King' 268)

Lynch, like Stephen King, reveals horror in the quotidian, and shows the normal and abnormal in a state of flux. Nightmares are our normality. No order is restored in Lynch's work, which emphasises how difficult it is to make sense of what goes on around us.

Selected Filmography

Eraserhead (1977)
The Elephant Man (1980)
Dune (1984)
Blue Velvet (1986)
Twin Peaks (TV, 1990)
Twin Peaks: Fire Walk with Me (1992)
Lost Highway (1997)
Mulholland Drive (2001)

The Texas Chainsaw Massacre *(1974)*

Coscripted, produced, and directed by Tobe Hooper, *The Texas Chainsaw Massacre* was followed by several sequels and has been remade in 2004 as a testimony to its lasting effects in our unconscious. One of the most horrible aspects of it is knowing that it is indeed based on fact, on the horrific activities of Ed Gein, who hung victims on meat hooks and cannibalised them.

A group of teens on a visit to a family cabin encounter a brutalised and brutalising backwoods family led by the masked Leatherface. They are relentlessly stalked, and all but one are murdered. The combination of a fear of the unknown in remote areas; never really knowing your dubious, strange neighbours; teen vulnerability; and the relatively hi-tech element of the chainsaw unites psychological and body horror. Clive Barker sees the malevolence and lack of regret to be uniquely modern, yet the nightmarish qualities are timeless since, 'The bad do what the good only dream.' I think that sums up the fascination, not only with Ed Geins but with horror in general. (Schechter in Clive Barker 36)

Wes Craven (1939–)

Writer and director Wes Craven is best known for creating the suburban, stalking psychological horror figure of Freddy Krueger, with his knifed hands and hideous face, in the series of *A Nightmare on Elm Street* films (1984–1994). In *Nightmare*, Nancy has nightmares of a terrifying, scarred figure with a glove of razor-sharp knives for fingers. She discovers her friends are having the same dream, and they begin to die. What is so terrifying about Freddy, apart from his features, is that he breaks through the boundaries of waking life and the dream, entering reality to murder. Craven's popular *Scream* series (three films to date) disturbs the safety of small-town America and the suburbs, relying heavily on awareness of the urban teen slasher movie. *Scream* opens with the phone ringing and fresh-faced, cheery Casey Becker (Drew Barrymore) answering it. Upon hearing a man's voice, she hangs up, but he rings again, and as she moves through the well-lit house eating popcorn, he chats her up. She wonders why he asks if she has a boyfriend and, alarmed, realises he is looking at her. He preys upon her awareness of scary movies to repeatedly ring back and play a game in which her boyfriend, Steve, will die, bringing in details from *Halloween*. The horrifying scream mask is the killer's signature and through the sequels, while Sidney, the protagonist stalked by the killer, remains alone, the tracking down of the killer becomes more complex and contradictory. In the third *Scream* movie, Sidney and friends reunite on the set of 'Stab 3', in which many of the characters have already died. In Craven's *Dracula 2001* (2001), thieves break into a crypt and release Dracula, who happily finds himself in a world of video stores and bright lights. He travels to New Orleans to locate a young woman who shares his dark secret in another updated version of the tale.

Selected Filmography

Swamp Thing (1982)
A Nightmare on Elm Street (1984)
The Twilight Zone (TV, 1985) (multiple episodes)
Shocker (1989)
New Nightmare (1994)
Vampire in Brooklyn (1995)
Scream (1996)
Scream 2 (1997)
Scream 3 (2000)

Quatermass and the Pit

With this TV serial, science fiction horror entered homes in the 1950s. Probably the first sci-fi horror series to appear on U.K. TV, *Quatermass and the Pit* terrified viewers in 1950s BBC serials. Nigel Kneale developed a cult following with a trilogy of live broadcast Quatermass TV plays in the 1950s: *The Quatermass Experiment* (1953), *Quatermass II* (1955), and *Quatermass and the Pit* (1958– 1959). The film rights were bought by Hammer who filmed the first two—*The Quatermass Experiment/The Creeping Unknown* (1955) and *Quatermass II/The Enemy from Space* (1956)—to some acclaim. Kneale borrowed ideas from Arthur C. Clarke's novel *Childhood's End* (1953), which was about a race of aliens resembling classic images of the devil visiting humanity (Scheib 1999, online).

Workmen excavating a London subway extension uncover a large metal cylinder. The Unexploded Bomb Squad is brought in, thinking it a leftover German V2 rocket. Professor Quatermass simultaneously finds a five-million-year-old human skeleton and insect creatures inside the container and there are outbreaks of psychic phenomena. Quatermass deduces that the cylinder is really from Mars, and that Martian insect creatures came to Earth five million years ago and helped humankind to consciousness. The Martian psychokinetic energy lies dormant in humankind and horned insect figures are dimly remembered in human racial memory as the devil. With the uncovering of the spaceship, the dormant powers become active again, coalescing into a giant devil figure hovering over London.

As in the *War of the Worlds* radio scare, Quatermass took hold of the British imagination:

> The three Quatermass TV serials produced by the BBC in the fifties entered the nation's consciousness in what, at the time, was an unprecedented way. Pubs and clubs would empty, the streets would rapidly desert, houses would fall silent as the familiar opening bars of Holst's 'Mars' from the *Planets* suite would fill the living rooms with its insistent, sinister beat.
>
> Monochromatic, flickering images would fill the screen, and for thirty minutes a week, for six weeks at a time, the TV owning population of Britain would be transported to a world of paranoia and alien invasion, with the world being saved at the eleventh hour by the maverick figure of Professor Bernard Quatermass, Director of the British Experimental Rocket Group. (Groome 1997)

TV Series: The X-Files *and* Buffy the Vampire Slayer

Horror enters our homes regularly with a variety of TV series, of which *The X-Files* and *Buffy the Vampire Slayer* are probably the best known internationally. Each deploys familiar horror strategies— shape shifting, something nasty under the bed, mythic creatures come to life, alien invasion, and the transportation of humans for experimental purposes. In using FBI agents Fox Mulder and Dana Scully, *The X-Files* resembles work by David Lynch, matching scientific forensic logic (Scully) with intuition (Mulder) and intruding the weird into the everyday. Paranoia is usually proved to be a legitimate response to the empty ships, body shrinking, and alien contact plotlines, as the governing powers are often either in collusion with events and creatures or deliberately withholding information for their own purposes/to prevent panic, thus placing people in more danger. *Millennium* uses similar plotlines.

Buffy, like *The X-Files*, has a huge cult following, Web sites, chatrooms, merchandise, conferences, and even an online journal, *Slayage*. Vampire slaying is the main activity in *Buffy*, which resembles *Halloween* and work by Stephen King in its location in small-town America, around a high school based on the Hellmouth. Buffy's friends include teens and young people who variously morph into or reveal themselves as witches (Willow), werewolves (Oz), or active/repentant vampires (Spike) of which Buffy's sometimes boyfriend, Angel, is the chief (and who has his own, slightly darker, TV series). Other creatures, including the gingerbread demon (based on the 'babes in the wood' motif), feature in different episodes, which draw upon myth, fairy tale, and the whole range of horror figures and scenarios to be found in Lovecraft, Poe, Blackwood, and others. Plots often rely on the librarian Giles's use of ancient texts to investigate sources, followed by Buffy, using her own superhuman and her friends' human powers to restore order, even if the disorder is located in figures of power such as the mayor, the school principal, and once, Buffy's mum.

With these popular prime-time TV series, horror has become accessible, palatable, and homely, but possibly also retains its mixed Gothic intent and effect of disturbing complacency as well as restoring order.

Japanese Horror Movies

Japanese horror films such as the *Godzilla* series are notable for their monsters, many of which have latterly reappeared in U.S. film versions and even in prime-time cartoons (an episode of *The Simpsons* has the family ignoring Godzilla and another mythic creature fighting alongside their plane). Japanese cartoons, both anime and Manga, carry on the traditions of Japanese horror films that began in 1986, when Komizu Kazuo (aka Gaira)'s *Shojo no harawata* (trans. *Intestines of a Virgin*) and *Bijo no harawata* (trans. *Intestines of a Beauty*) were released. Violent, often featuring rape, torture, and other traditional features brutalising women and the weak (or unlucky), these films are X-rated not because of the violence but that they are *romanporuno*—pornographic movies distributed by Nikkatsu Inc., who named these the 'Splatter Eros' series. Komizu wrote a screenplay for a *romanporuno* film, *Hako no naka no onna: Shojo ikenie* (trans. *A Woman in the Box: Virgin Sacrifice*, directed by Konuma Masaru). The plot is that of a virgin girl caged and tortured by an abnormal couple. Nikkatsu Inc. labeled this film 'Roman X'. 'Splatter Eros' is the next period of 'Roman X' porno films containing extremely violent scenes.

The film regarded as the first Japanese splatter horror film is *Evil Dead Trap* (Ikeda Toshiharu, 1988). In 1992, Matsumura Katsuya made his debut with the violent X-rated *All Night Long*. His second film *All Night Long 2* was released as a video (Hiroaki, Hamasaki, 'SplatterJapan' online).

Muroga Makoto, known as the director of the violent movie *Score* (1995), made a splatter zombie movie (Hiroaki, Hamasaki, film review, 'Junk: Shiryou gari', Let's Enjoy Shooting the Zombies! online).

Manga

The Japanese horror cartoon film that started off the main trend is Katsuhiro Otomo's *Akira* (1988), which features violent gang warfare and mysterious villains often in a futuristic Tokyo cityscape or landscape among trees and rivers in the countryside of a nightmarish Japan and motorbike races through virtual reality cities. Kiteshi Kitane's *Princess Blade* is a Manga tale about a group of vigilantes who kill a leader, then track down the killers with violent sword fights and chases through woodlands. In *Iron Monkey*, a non-Manga Japanese horror movie, a vigilante, feared by the whole of the city, is hunted down by powerful others while he appears in the city at night and is able to hop from roof to roof.

Conclusion

As Lovecraft noted, horror has been with us in the shape of the naturalistic and the weird or supernatural tale in oral cultures and then throughout the great and lesser works of international writers. Latterly, it has become a feature of TV series, merchandising, and children's cartoons, entering our lives on a daily basis. Many, perhaps all, societies have their versions of horror, including vampire tales from India (which has its horror goddess Kali) and Pakistan, ghost stories from Singapore (Catherine Lim) and Malaysia, myths of power from the New Zealand Maori and South Pacific islanders, Darryl Caine's erotic horror (Australia), and Kim Wilkins's focus on demons, vampires, and other creatures (Australia). Horror's grasp on the popular imagination ensures its future.

Chapter Five

Major Themes, Movements, and Issues

This chapter considers favourite concerns or themes in horror. Much horror depends upon destabilising our sense of security, defamiliarising the familiar, and questioning what is seen as an everyday norm—of the body, identity, family relationships, continuity, time, space, boundaries of life and death, alien, Other and self. Horror lies along a continuum in its use of the real, documentary, and graphic, indicating its daily presence in cruel, disgusting acts of violence and disempowerment and invasion into normality, threatening the body and stability. At the other end of the continuum lies the weird or supernatural, its sources in the unconscious, the psyche, and the imagination. Examples of identifiable horror as far back as the Bible and *Beowulf*, and classical mythology, can be identified as lying somewhere on this continuum, and though Lovecraft might valorise the supernatural in horror, schlock, and splatter, the monstrous in the everyday is equally if differently destabilising, entertaining, and thought provoking.

There is frequently a psychoanalytic and philosophical basis to the construction of horror and our responses to it, such as fears about identity and Otherness, fear of bodily invasion or destruction, needing to feel secure with familiar places and faces around you, and feeling threatened by the unknown, the unfamiliar, the displaced, and disturbed. While much horror is conventional and explodes or exposes terrors, embodying them in action, character, and event, then closing them down with a denouement, revengeful climax, and closure, other horror is more radical. While it might use the same formulae, the closure and the 'message' are different, recognising that collusion with convention feeds horror—disgust and terror—and that objects of horror are projections of our own disturbances. Some major themes, tropes, and concerns of horror are:

- Defamiliarisation and the Uncanny
- Supernatural Horror and Weird Fictions
- Gothic Horror
- Domestic Horror
- Slasher and Teen Horror
- The Carnivalesque and Horror
- Ghost Stories
- Split Selves, Body Invaders
- Postcolonial Horror
- Body Horror
- Bug and Reptile Horror
- Objects, Objectification, and Automata
- Women as Objects of Horror
- Contemporary Radical and Women's Horror
- Vampires
- Werewolves

Defamiliarisation and the Uncanny

In the classic *Invasion of the Body Snatchers*, our partners and friends are metamorphosed into aliens that appear identical to those they replace. Those safe people, selves, and places become unfamiliar and dangerous. Those we thought we loved, overtaken silently by aliens, turn against us and would destroy or incorporate us. In *Through the Looking Glass*, every place is like the one back home but somehow different, more threatening. As Alice can be bigger and smaller, bounds and boundaries are changed and challenged. This is potentially liberating, more likely to be terrifying. There is nothing to hang onto when the familiar is defamiliarised, the stable destabilises, and even more so when the subject of this shake-up is one's self. Not surprisingly, defamiliarisation is one of the key themes of horror fictions.

Freud identifies the *unheimlich* or uncanny (1919) as the key horror strategy. In this respect, places, people, our sense of reality and justice, and the comfortable stories we tell ourselves to stay sane and directed are all prime victims for horror's dislocation and destabilisation effect. So, defamiliarisation preys upon our need for secure identities, body wholeness, safe families and neighbourhoods, continuity of identity and self, and shared realities. 'Life as we know it' is the reinforcement of our cultural values (whatever our culture) and our need to have our expectations reinforced. As such, then, defamiliarisation destabilises issues in a range of ways, splitting the self, causing the body to morph, leak, implode, and explode. We might expect dark labyrinthine forests and howling winds, maelstroms, or Gothic castles to loose horror upon us, but we probably feel we should be safe at home.

Supernatural Horror and Weird Fictions

Much horror focuses on everyday brutality, monstrous behaviours, perhaps using documentary realism to confront the reader and viewers with the cruelties and horrors of war, rape, identity theft, and brutal murders. Lovecraft, in his influential *The Supernatural in Horror*, identifies this kind of realistic horror as of lesser worth than that based in superstition and the weird, the psychological, spiritual, imaginative levels of horror that home in on primeval fears and the existence of the imaginary alongside our daily lives. In this respect, Lovecraft is the first serious theorist of horror as a branch of fantasy. Supernatural horror and weird fictions comprise a range of themes and concerns, ranging from split selves and shape shifting (*Skin Folk* 2001), ghost stories, the invasion of dreams and waking life by malevolent nightmare figures (*A Nightmare on Elm Street*), and horror frissons in the burgeoning numbers of tales of the walking dead (*The Sixth Sense, The Others*) who appear to warn and/or befriend us.

Gothic Horror

Horror is a branch of the literary Gothic and, as such, uses many of its settings, atmospheres, fears, and tendency for social critique. Gothic horror preys upon fears of displacement, incarceration, loss of identity, home, heritage, family, friends, and security. In its use of the uncanny, it destabilises what we take for granted and shows the values and certainties in which we invest to be mere constructions, ever vulnerable.

Beginning in the eighteenth century, with Horace Walpole's *The Castle of Otranto* (1764), Ann Radcliffe's *Mysteries of Udolpho* (1794), and Matthew Lewis's, *The Monk* (1796), the literary Gothic explores contradictions and unease in social conventions. It enables readers to question what was taken for granted, such as families, love, and inheritance. It works by using metaphors and imagery, usually of extremes and opposites, gaps, losses, and things hidden, and so exposes contradictions in our lives and in society. Much literary Gothic focuses on romance—its dangers and final rewards. And so, many romantic fictions have used Gothic settings, stories, and stereotypes. Gothic fictions use spaces that are dangerous, at the edge, such as cellars, dungeons, attics, haunted castles, to show us how we, in our minds, push those elements of our lives we worry about into safe, distant places. The Gothic brings them out again, exposes them, and enables readers to explore contradictions before being returned to security. David Punter (*Companion to the Gothic*, 2000) indicates that fragmentation of Gothic elements followed these early texts, so that elements of the Gothic appear in Mary Shelley's *Frankenstein* and in Dickens's claustrophobic settings and disturbing characters. The work of Robert Louis Stevenson (*Dr Jekyll and Mr Hyde*, 1886), H. G. Wells (*The Island of Dr Moreau*, 1896), Bram Stoker (*Dracula*, 1897), and Oscar Wilde (*The Picture of Dorian Gray*, 1891) constitute a late nineteenth-century Gothic revival. Ghost stories are quintessentially Gothic, dealing as they do with the return of the repressed, with phantoms of history, past people, hidden truths and secrets, spectres of the past, and wrongdoings as diverse as hidden family treasure, murder, and genocide. Punter points out:

> Gothic speaks of phantoms: the neo-psychoanalytic ideas of Abraham and Torok are based on a re-description of the phantom. Gothic takes place very frequently in crypts, Abraham and Torok again make the crypt the cornerstone of their psychic topography. The Gothic speaks of, indeed we might say it attempts to invoke, spectres: Derrida for example in *The Spectres of Marx*, chooses the same rhetoric to talk about what we might term 'the suppressed of Europe'. (Punter ix)

This extends our understanding of the Gothic into politics and culture, as well as the individual sense of wholeness or otherwise of self, the domestic and familial. Not everything using these characteristics is Gothic and not everything that is Gothic is horror. While using elements of the literary Gothic, horror is more likely to be or to threaten to be violent and evoke disgust and/or terror. Despite disagreements over modernism's refusal of the past and some critics' reluctance to move beyond recognition of the experimentation and, latterly, the historical connectedness of modernist work, traces of Gothic horror can be found in the recuperated texts of the early twentieth century, the modernist period, in the work of May Sinclair, Charlotte Mew, H. G. Wells, Virginia Woolf, Edith Wharton, and Henry James. In the mid-twentieth century, many horror films in particular use Gothic settings and stories—the British Hammer studio films of the sixties and after, for example. Clive Bloom points out that horror owes its longevity to its perfected translation to film. While readers may struggle to remember individual Gothic or other horror writers, they remember the films:

> As with most popular fiction it has been horror fiction's translation into other media that has guaranteed its survival. Many people remember with a nostalgic affection those Hammer horror movies, filmed with low budgets and uncannily recurring sets upon whose sound stage moved the fledgling stars of television's soap opera. (Bloom, *Creepers* xi)

Gothic-influenced horror, along with other horror types, has, since the late twentieth century, become the mode of choice (vying with science fiction and fantasy with which it frequently overlaps—*Alien, Attack of the 50 Foot Woman, Invasion of the Body Snatchers*, among others) for film and text expression of every kind of exploration and disturbance.

Clive Barker revived Gothic horror in text, TV, and film, Barker's *A–Z of Horror* running on U.K. TV during the late years of the century (1997).

Domestic Horror

Domestic horror picks on an innate need for safety, the complacent assumption that social obedience and common sense reward us. However, as Stephen King points out:

> [T]he good horror tale will dance its way to the center of your life and find the secret door to the room you believed no one but you knew of. (King, *Danse Macabre* 149)

King, in using the location of the home as image, indicates both the horror of place and the horror of self, where the room at the centre of our life is our own identity, our sanity, our sense of stability of self.

The domestic space is a choice location for horror primarily because of the safety, security, and familiarity it promises. Disturbing these fundamentally undercuts identity and ontological security. Jung aligned the self with the house, home, or living space. In horror, there are direct connections between insecurity, stability, identity, and the house or home. Here, horror takes the Gothic fascination with locations straight into our most intimate and personal spaces.

Conventional Gothic focuses on location and its significances, particularly on confined and threatening spaces. Horror frequently exposes and explodes these familiar locations—exposing the family, home, attic, cellar, kitchen, bedroom, toilet, garden, and neighbourhood as danger zones. Women's horror, in particular, often portrays domestic interiors as entrapping, the locus of patriarchal tyrannies. Horror transforms what is considered 'real' through exposing what is feared and hidden and, in doing so, spatial descriptors become important, deploying what Freud defines as 'paraxis'. Explicating how this notion of an underside or alternative space is beyond, beneath, or above the recognisably ordinary is enacted through language, Rosemary Jackson notes:

> Fantasy lies alongside the axis of the real, and many of the prepositional constructions which are used to introduce a fantastic realm emphasize its interstitial placing, 'On the edge', 'through', 'beyond', 'between', 'at the back of', 'underneath' or adjectives such as 'topsy turvy', 'reversed', 'inverted'. (Jackson, *Fantasy* 64)

Domestic horror dramatises the scenes of constriction in the family home and the hints of hidden secrets, other selves, and readings. As such, it concentrates on the spaces and the architecture that represent these, on cellars, attics, lives hidden behind barred windows, behind wallpaper (*The Yellow Wallpaper*, 1899), in locked rooms, and at the end of endless corridors ('Bluebeard'), and its various reinterpretations (Angela Carter's 'The Bloody Chamber', 1979). Like the Gothic, domestic horror often uses adjectives suggesting invasion of those spaces, a cracking of the secure fabric to reveal gaps, fissures, and leakages, indicating contradictions and threats to what then appears a kind of culpably naïve investment in domestic and personal security. Such are the contemporary threats to Middle America and other Western urban and suburban locations, the neighbourhoods of comfortable families, 2.4 children, and their baby-sitters. In horror, such locations harbour axe murderers, psychotics (*Halloween*, *A Nightmare on Elm Street*), terrible secrets, villages of alien children, and plants that pick up their roots, chase, and eat people (John Wyndham's *The Midwich Cuckoos, The Day of the Triffids*), crazed pets (*Cujo*), and demonic domestic appliances or family cars (*From a Buick 8, Christine*). For Stephen King, among others, what is fascinatingly played out is the unsettling character of Middle America, its lurking fears, and the disturbance of its complicity in all that would undermine its façade of order.

The family and domestic and romantic relationships also come under attack. Hitchcock urges us to 'put back horror where it belongs, in the family'. Entrapment, engulfment, monstrous parents and equally monstrous children, skeletons in closets and chopped messes on the kitchen table: These are all features of domestic horror that focus on the oppressive, the threatening, the perverse, and the sickening flip side of 'domestic bliss'.

Edgar Allan Poe, Angela Carter, Joyce Carol Oates, Stephen King, Melanie Tem, Virginia Andrews, and many other horror writers concentrate on domestic horror in fictions, while films depicting family horrors (e.g., *The Shining, The Exorcist, The Omen, Rosemary's Baby,* and *The Village of the Damned*) variously look at mad monster fathers, changeling children—usually the devil's own offspring (or aliens)—and invasion of the domestic home. Domestic horror exposes the contradictions and potential/real unpleasantness of domestic settings and relationships, nuclear and extended families, marriages and parenting. It focuses in particular on the unsafe neighbourhood, the non-nurturing home as a site for horror, and on parents and monster children.

What is terrifying in domestic horror? Why might the family home and parenting be a site for horror when on them depend our sense of safety, continuity, comfort, and familiarity—a reflection of ourselves, of our sense of security, and, to some extent, immortality through our children? Precisely for those reasons. If these qualities are what we desire from domestic life and families, then the removal or undercutting of these is the stuff of horror. We are all concerned with issues of security and the immortality children offer us and so fear parasitic children, domineering husbands, and incarceration in the threatened home. 'Domestic bliss' is not such a perfect dream now after the feminist recognition that 'You start by sinking into his arms and you end up with your arms in his sink'.

House of Horrors

The house and home in domestic horror is a place for confinement. It seems safe and wholesome, but it is threatened from within and without. Gothic horror castles, dungeons, and turrets of the eighteenth and nineteenth centuries have evolved into the labyrinthine claustrophobic home space; of the family house in 'The Fall River Axe Murders' (1981) by Angela Carter, or the hotel in Stephen King's *The Shining* (1977, filmed in 1980 by Stanley Kubrick).

The house and home are NOT a place of safety, horror tells us. Unpleasant creatures, blood, and secrets leak in through cracks in the seemingly secure fabric of the domestic building. Things erupt from the foundations of the house (*The Amityville Horror* [1979] and *Poltergeist* [1982]), up from the cellar, down from the attic, and through the walls and doors (*The Shining*). The spaces erupt and split, allowing in what one hoped to keep hidden, what we feared. The instability of the physical fabric of the family home reflects that of the relationships within the family, and the tenuousness of our security as social beings in a society we might try and believe progresses.

House/home investment is made in the nurturing, identity, and continuity of the family and of social beliefs about harmony, security, and stability. Media myths reinforce the representation of the domestic as a place of safety, the safe haven, 'our house'. You might feel that checking into the Bates motel is a dubious and scary prospect, but you would never predict the invasion of your own home or its implosion into, for example, a festering pit or ancestral burial ground.

Domestic horror dramatises the scenes of constriction in the family home and the hints of hidden secrets, other selves, and other readings. As such, it concentrates on the spaces and the architecture that represent these, on cellars, attics, lives hidden behind barred windows, behind wallpaper, in locked rooms, and at the end of endless corridors. Domestic horror is frequently gendered, as are spaces. In the nineteenth century, medicine was enlisted to support the conservative view that women's intellectual endeavours or creativity, their liberating energies, led directly to physical and mental breakdown, inability to produce and nurture children, and madness. The themes of women's hysteria elided with their creativity spill over into Doris Lessing's mid-twentieth-century *The Summer Before the Dark* (1973), while in a less gendered scenario challenges to any status quo are frequently configured by repressive regimes as the producers of madness. So, in *One Flew Over the Cuckoo's Nest* (1975), hospitalisation is the Stalinesque response to political criticism. What is horrifying in these scenarios is the translation of distinct and alternative political and cultural perspectives into a madness that itself leads to incarceration. Historically, this is the fate that befalls the sister who inherits and marries inappropriately in Wilkie Collins's *The Woman in White* (1890). Her punishment is to be designated mad, incarcerated, disempowered so that her money can be stolen from her. There are no ogres here, no ghosts or alien invasions, just patriarchal oppression, meanness, and disempowerment. As Gothic horror, *The Woman in White* deals in mistaken identity, doubling, incarceration, madness, death, theft, and the denial of human rights. In the twentieth century, there are many disturbing horror scenarios in which the questioning of sanity leads to disempowerment and incarceration, as if one's perception of reality, being

queried, removes one's human rights. Those who recognise friends
and family as alien pods in *Invasion of the Body Snatchers* are seen as
mentally disturbed.

Charlotte Perkins Gilman's *The Yellow Wallpaper* (1899) is a
powerful tale of women's incarceration in the prison of the family
home. Based on Gilman's own period of enforced bedrest accom-
panying postnatal depression, the tale exposes patriarchal nineteenth-century and twentieth-century medical practices that
characterise any female disturbance as hysterical, curable by lack of
activity. Confined in the upstairs nursery with its barred windows,
the protagonist is silenced and denied even the outlet of her writing. Her husband/doctor aligns himself with another doctor and the
sister-in-law, each identifying her as unstable. Locking her up wors-
ens her condition and splitting of the self results. She imagines a
wild woman sneaking out from behind the foul yellow wallpaper,
creeping around the room, tearing strips off, like a trapped zoo animal. She cannot, but the reader can, see this is actually herself. The
language slips to reveal alignment of the wallpaper woman and the
protagonist. Disoriented, split, and falling further into madness, she
'escapes', possibly committing suicide. *The Yellow Wallpaper* offers a
paradigm of ways into which those in power—political, gendered,
economic, and legitimate—enforce certain versions of reality, criticising, devaluing, and denying alternative perceptions and rights.

Male tyranny incarcerates traditional Gothic heroines in *Jane
Eyre* (1846), Jean Rhys's *Wide Sargasso Sea* (1966), *The Silence of
the Lambs* (1988), and numerous horror fictions and films. But
women are dangerous, too. Domestic horror exposes the lies of nurturing paternalism and the ostensible comforts of families, family
history/homes, often indicating societal repression of women's creativity and energy.

Murder in the Family

Angela Carter's 'The Fall River Axe Murders' (1981) and Stephen
King's *The Shining* (1977) build on elements of threat, repression,
and explosion latent in domestic entrapment. A key early text in
domestic, family horror is Edgar Allan Poe's 'The Fall of the House
of Usher' (1849). In Poe's tale of illegitimacy threatening the sta-

bility of lineage, the unsafe, deadly, imploding house is an image of the disturbed self, an index of a sick society. Poe's archetypal tale focuses on the entrapping and self-destructive house, a 'mansion of gloom', with 'vacant eye-like windows' (Poe 138). It matches and represents Roderick Usher's disordered mental state. As his reason cracks, so fissures appear in the house. Mental illness, a family condition, wracks Usher as cracks in the house represent his condition and cracks in the family—fears about heredity, inheritance, and legitimacy, a false heir usurping the head of the house.

> 'Lizzie Borden took an axe
> and gave her mother forty whacks.
> And when she saw what she had done,
> She gave her father forty-one.'
> (Playground verse, Fall River, Massachusetts, 4 August 1892)

The familiar story of the eruption of violence from family claustrophobia is re-told in Angela Carter's 'The Fall River Axe Murders' (1981, all references to Carter's short stories, 1996), building on the playground verse and notorious murders. Locked rooms and endless labyrinthine corridors are the location in this tale of Lizzie Borden's domestic entrapment and the resultant carnage. The incarceration and denial of turn-of-the-century American gentlewomen's lives are embodied in the endlessly linked corridors and locked rooms making up the sheltered existence upstairs in undertaker Borden's household. Lizzie, temporarily released for the customary European tour, returns to a world of sly, staring houses, death in life, her energies constrained. Like Poe's sick house and the fairy-tale Bluebeard's castle, this home hides secrets and represses lives. It is:

> A house full of locked doors that open only into other rooms with other locked doors, for, upstairs and downstairs, all the rooms lead in and out of one another like a maze in a bad dream. (Carter 107)

The claustrophobic middle-class normality of the Borden household in Fall River, Massachusetts, contains lives in the same way as the clothes worn by those who inhabit it constrict their breathing. Ties 'garrotte' wearers. Lizzie and her sister are turned in upon themselves, enclosed in the labyrinthine corridors and rooms of this stiff undertaker's house, 'narrow as a coffin' (104), literally without 'passages' (107), without shared space or ways out: 'it is a dead end' (107). In this as in other domestic horror, from comforts, the maintenance of facades of domesticity and pleasantry, neat petticoats, and family values, extrude haunted dreams of axe murderers stalking lives, broken locks inside and outside the house. We are reminded of its familiarity: 'Don't we all conceal somewhere photographs of ourselves that make us look like crazed assassins?' (119) asks Carter's narrator, inviting us into the scene and events. Her favourite pigeons killed to make her stepmother's pie, the story ends just moments before Lizzie enters with the axe to slaughter her family in a terrible response: 'at home all was blood and feathers' (120).

Hotel of Horrors

Domestic horror takes place in a claustrophobic, snowbound hotel with a terrible history in Stephen King's novel/Stanley Kubrick's film *The Shining* (1977/1980). The oppressive confusions and lurking terrors of conventional Gothic castles, the entrapment of domestic homes, are relocated to a hotel, itself labyrinthine, containing deadly past secrets. Hotels ostensibly represent the comforts of home away from home in a more pampered, perfect setting and atmosphere, so it is unsurprising that the threat they offer is an excess of nightmares hidden behind closed doors. The walls, doors, boundaries, and spaces of the hotel fracture as its terrible past influences the present. Blood and horror seep through the furnishings and fabric, forbidden rooms hiding murderous secrets, and the deadly dynamics of family relationships. Visions of dead twins and blood filling the corridor chill viewer and Danny alike. In the shut 'Overlook' hotel in the midst of a winter snow zone, the vulnerable little boy, Danny, on his bike zooms along the endless shiny corridors. Jack Torrance, the indulged mad/writer father, influenced by the powerful repressed history of the hotel, churns out acres of repetitive nonsense—every writer's fear. He then turns on his wife, accusing her of criticising him. In *The Shining*, the family is a site for tensions and explosions of immense social pressures and expectations. Torrance, mad partly due to problems with being unable to support his family economically, ends up the victim of compulsive and violent behaviour, controlling, deceiving, overlooking, and then abusing wife and child. Godlike, he watches them wander in the garden maze, deceives himself that he is working, dominates and bullies his wife, lies to and terrifies his son, and tries to chop the family into messes in a confined space, the bathroom. Torrance's chilling 'Here's Johnny!' reaches into our imaginations, disturbing our sense of everyday comfort as his axe splinters the bathroom door. The hotel is an incarcerating, fractured space, dangerous and deadly, and Torrance is a monster parent. Each individual is lost in the house/hotel of the self, from which explodes contradictions and violence.

Slasher and Teen Horror

In American suburbia, the end of complacency erupts as stalkers phone up baby-sitters (*Scream*, 1996), deranged relatives return (Michael Myers in *Halloween*, 1978), salesmen ply an evil trade (*Halloween II*, 1981), and creatures of our unconscious enter our homes and minds (*A Nightmare on Elm Street*, 1984; *The Tommyknockers*, 1993).

Teens are like vampires: borderline creatures, undergoing changes, placing them precariously on the edge of normalcy, or not —perfect for horror's disturbances. And our neighbourhoods, built as modern-day castle communities, appear perfectly maintained and safe, but for that very reason are favoured locations for disturbance. Linda Holland-Toll challenges Stephen King's argument that disturbance takes place in horror in order to reaffirm and reconfirm culture's values:

> The most effective horror fiction, disaffirmative horror fiction, is that which subverts and lays bare the cultural assumptions which we use to avoid facing certain unpleasant realities. (Holland-Toll 2)

'Teenage' is a liminal space between the controlled liberties of childhood and the conformities of adulthood. It is a dangerous borderline, wild, allowed a certain free rein, then curtailed as too dangerous. Teenagers have to question all authority in order to construct themselves. Every element of law-abiding daily life is problematised and theorised. How vulnerable our teenagers are, poised in the doubting, creative space between parental controls and being themselves parents. Into this crack seeps the *Scream* movies, teen slashers, splatterpunk, vampire and werewolf tales, and others focusing on the creative, dangerous, deviant energies of metamorphosis that could go horribly wrong (as it does for Kafka's Gregor Samsa, the human cockroach in 'The Metamorphosis') or which can be seized as a moment of self-definition. For Suzy McKee Charnas's athletic teenage girl werewolf in 'Boobs' (1991), seizing one's own powerful self, refusing the debilitating effects of menstruation while enjoying the control of one's body, is a perfect solution to the awkward embarrassment of teenage life, peaking the enjoyment of her werewolf body and devouring the class tease, Billy Linden.

A group of young teen vampires coast the suburbia of small-town America in Poppy Z. Brite's *Lost Souls* (1992). They pick up stray children, vampirising them, turning them against their friends, and destroying them. Nothing, a character adopted by these violent anarchic teens, succeeds in his initiation through murdering his own best friend. These are post-Vietnam generation youth, empty of values and ideals, selfish, destructive, and predatory, as is the culture that spawned then lied to them. Brite's characterisation of these teens as vampires, lost souls, indicts the vacuity of Middle America's complacent investment in the comfort of homes, neighbourhoods, TV, and TV dinners, and a sense that 'God is on our side' in any imperialist conflict abroad (Korea, Vietnam, Iraq).

In horror, the house is not safe; the family is a site for deception, violence, and abuse; and neighbours and neighbourhoods are dangerous or culpably disengaged. *Halloween* brings horror into our homes because no one reaches out to the victim.

It is a cliché that in America people are much more mobile. They can enter and exit towns, driving away on the freeways to another state, across the continent. There are also more suburbs. In locating his films in the suburbs and focusing on what it means to 'return to normal', director John Carpenter developed a new horror subgenre. Putting horror scenarios into the beautifully presented suburbs and middle-class homes suggests that nowhere is safe. The now clichéd invasion of the suburban norm, such as in Wes Craven's *Scream* films, emphasises loss of control and loss of any sense of the real.

Debra Hill, who produced and cowrote *Halloween* (1978) with Carpenter, agrees.

> It looked like the kind of place that you would want to have your children playing in, and the idea was that there was *something* lurking behind those trees. All these identical houses across the street from each other created this kind of claustrophobic effect and a feeling that something was wrong. (Hill in Clive Barker 68)

Translated to the screen, we have a deep disturbance in the neighbourhood that's supposed to be safe for your kids to grow up in, where the houses with white picket fences and lawn sprinklers turn into the least safe environments, invaded by knife-wielding deranged brothers (Michael Myers in *Halloween*), hideous-faced, tramplike old men (Freddy Kreuger in *A Nightmare on Elm Street*, 1984), and passing salesmen selling dubious items for Halloween who you *wouldn't* ask in.

Horror is a safety valve. It is, too, in neighbourhood houses—more particularly so as the genre, in film, begins to substitute parodies of itself—the formulaic reminding us that it is a theatrical performance and to shriek but not *really* be scared. So, we have *Scream* (1996), which is self-referential to the genre—scream masks, baby-sitters, and teen misbehaviour. Degeneration into *Scary Movie* (2000) and its variants renders the genre safe because it becomes amusing, the horrors clinking and clanking as they are wheeled on. But we are reminded of Linda Holland-Toll's concern that disaffirmative horror is the most effective because it refuses to close down the terror at the end of the tale and restore an order. We are left unable to identify the invader of our spaces as the ethnic, cognitive, or economic Other, which has now been dispatched back from whence it came (actually a construction of our own deep-seated insecurities and terrors). Since it is our own product, it will return. The fortresses of suburbia will not protect our vulnerable selves, our young and old.

Hitchcock's *Psycho* (1960) is recognised as the first real slasher movie. The scene in the shower—a beautiful, seductive woman whose sexual morality is (for the time) somewhat in question, brutally murdered by a kitchen-knife-wielding, mother-fixated psychopath approaching her, vulnerable in the shower, and mutilating her body—must be inscribed on the consciousness and subconscious of even those who never watch another horror film. The act of showering is routine, the victim as vulnerable as we all are in the bathroom, the murder bloody, violent, accompanied by the piercing, throbbing, shrieking background noise as each stab attacks her. The scene has been replicated many times and both the *Psycho* remake (1998) and other 'Psycho' films use versions of it to replay that horrific slasher shock moment.

In 1974, another film, *The Texas Chainsaw Massacre*, changed the genre. It has been seen as the most extreme and the best slasher movie. *The Texas Chainsaw Massacre* is a strange mix of the highly realistic and the supernatural tale, utilising body horror, terrible masks (Leatherface), mob and family body groups, and lots of shock. In the drive into Texas, a hitchhiker is picked up, who upsets his hosts when he first cuts his hand and then slashes the arm of one of the boys, so they throw him out. When they arrive at their destination, the abandoned home of the grandparents, the hitchhiker and his very strange family are living next door. This family comprises three generations and includes a mummified grandmother. As out-of-work slaughterhouse workers, they have turned to carving up, butchering, and eating those who foolishly travel through their area. Their home is littered with bodily remains and mementoes, and they dispatch each of the young people except Sally, who, after a terrible night, manages to hitch a lift out of the carnage. A slasher, travelling, body horror cannibal movie, it is a warning about wandering into the rural settlements of America. H. P. Lovecraft's work also warns about going off course and meeting monstrous humans set to destroy you.

The Carnivalesque and Horror

Bakhtin's theory of the carnivalesque lies behind/explains much of this subhuman neighbourhood horror, as it does much horror more generally. When the constraints of everyday working and home life, obedience to the law, conforming in a community, housing, behaviour, time management, childrearing, taxpaying, and so on—the mechanics of an ordered society—are allowed to be questioned and the complacencies destabilised, there is for reader and viewer a carnivalesque moment of release. Traditionally, this appears in actual carnivals, in circuses (Dickens's *Hard Times*, Angela Carter's *Nights at the Circus*), or moments of rebellious revelry (as in Shakespeare's *Twelfth Night* or *A Midsummer Night's Dream*), when laws are overturned, hierarchies and rules turned topsy-turvy, and riot is the order of the day.

The carnival ends and order returns in traditional saturnalia, but we must remember that carnival is a moment for the working classes and others to both riot and rule. Many activities mock the social norms that would maintain subordinate positions. Carnival activities actually reveal much that is flawed or artificial about complacent societies.

> Effective horror fiction holds up a carnival house mirror which reveals the often warped but ironically true image of our society, our community and ourselves. (Holland-Toll 251)

The licensed release of dysfunctional and excessive (often working-class, radical) energies uses both the comic and the horrific for rioting but in a managed space. If order is restored, we could be lulled back into a false sense of security, so undermining the function of horror to not only disturb in a temporary fashion but (true to its Gothic roots) to enable us to question our complacencies and see them as constrictions.

> By concentrating on the skull beneath the skin, on the reality of the skeleton society instead of on its smoothed-out skin, horror fiction lays bare one truth: all of the qualities on which we pride ourselves as Americans are as subject to alienation and subversion as they are to valuation and reaffirmation. (Holland-Toll 251)

For the writers and readers of horror comics in the 1950s, such as *Tales from the Crypt*, through to the scorned lover, Alex, boiling the rabbit in the film *Fatal Attraction*, families, homes, and neighbourhoods are all destabilising and threatening in horror. Traditionally, much domestic horror took the form of ghost stories.

Ghost Stories

Ghost stories dramatise the return of the repressed—people, behaviours, memories, something we would wish to suppress. Interestingly, they range from Maude Ffoulkes's tales and other semidocumented realism, such as TV's *Most Haunted* trips to known ghostly locations. Conventionally, claiming to be honest reports, hiding their fictionality, ghost stories tend to be told by dependable society members whose word we trust. A ghost is frequently a domestic figure, haunting familiar places, threatening where you feel most safe or warning when you feel secure. Restless, the spectre unsettles the settled. It has truly crossed over the borderline between life and death, corporeality and insubstantiality. A ghost cannot be fixed, caught, or photographed and catalogued (though some Victorians certainly tried). Many women of the nineteenth and twentieth century have written ghost stories, based mostly, as David Punter notes, on the 'dialectic between disturbance and comfort' (Punter 315). Nineteenth-century writers frequently overlapped with sensation novels. Julia Briggs identifies ghost stories with romanticism:

> The combination of modern scepticism with a nostalgia for an older more supernatural system of beliefs provides the foundation of the ghost story, and this nostalgia can be seen as inherently romantic. (Briggs 19)

Why are ghosts, horror figures, and ghost stories similar to horror? Because of their dramatisation of what is hidden and repressed. Ghost stories have had particularly bad press as nonsense, old wives' tales, products of an extremely heightened nervous system. It is easier to reject a ghost story precisely because of its contiguity to a documentary realist tale, which also produces its compelling attraction.

Haunting is a familiar expression of latent fears and powers and most often a dramatic phenomenon. Women's supernatural and horror writing becomes more innovative, looks at more women-oriented fears and desires, and breaks down more boundaries at the nineteenth century's turn. Jennifer Uglow (Introduction, *Virago Book of Ghost Stories*) notes the tendency to reveal that danger lies in domestic and patriarchal dominance:

Again and again, with almost shocking repetitiveness, the stories attack the symbolic and actual domination of the father, the husband, the lover, the doctor, the cruel emperor —the men of power. At times there is no escaping the role of victim, but at others the tables are turned. (Uglow xii)

Women's ghost stories frequently deal with a desperate need for love and security:

A different energy, which burns in women's ghost stories, is that of female desire and its more 'feminine' but equally consuming counterpart, the hunger for love. Its desperate force is often perceived as a threat by men and feared by women themselves, but its strength can be conveyed by the lightest touch. (Uglow xiii)

[F]emale fears clustering around vulnerability and margin-ality, sex and childbirth, love and jealousy, intensify the loneliness which marks all ghost stories, whether by men or women. (Uglow xiii)

Sara Maitland (1991) highlights the ways in which ghost stories cross formal and technical boundaries, interweaving the real with the fantastic to give the latter credibility: 'In order for the ghost story to work, the realist elements of it have to be firmly fixed' mix-ing 'the language of social realism and the language of the subter-ranean, the not-explained' (Maitland xi). Like vampire and shape-changing tales:

women come to the ghostly task of writing ghost stories as ghosts (even, for much of literary culture, as dangerous spectres). Our tradition is a tradition in the shadows; our past is lost and misty; our identity as writers and as objects of men's writing, is both owned and denied. (Maitland xiii)

They 'play with the patterns of our own ambivalence'. (Maitland xv)

Although ghost stories can be argued as traditionally a woman's favoured form, they are created by writers of both genders, locating disturbances and unease about identity, history, and repressed fears.

Algernon Blackwood's tale 'The Empty House' (1906) is in many ways a typical ghost story. It also provides the mould for *Most Haunted*. The first-person narrator accompanies his sprightly, aged aunt to spend a night in a known haunted house. Some ghost stories emphasise the similarity between perceiver and perceived, casting light on pretence, instability, and questionable conditions. Suddenly, the aged aunt appears as youthful as the young housemaid hunted out and brutally murdered by a master in the house. The murder is seen and felt by both aunt and narrator as murderer and girl pass through them. They leave the house past midnight into the lightening dawn.

A closer escape and more alienated parallels between narrator and ghost are features of Blackwood's acknowledged second attempt at this kind of tale, 'The Listener', which self-reflexively focuses on a writer who, taking remarkably cheap lodgings, starts to resemble the impoverished, fetid-smelling, disorientated man-creature he sometimes hears or sees/thinks he sees, whose presence is never confirmed by the landlady and servants. The monstrous creature has a leonine head and mane, listens at dawn, appears ahead of the narrator in the snow, but leaves no traces. Just before he dissolves into madness, believing this is clearly something out to get him, the narrator is visited by an extremely rational, dependable, traveller friend, who unpacks the tale. Blount, a leper, lived his last years and died in the house. In the days of empire building, leprosy entering London was as terrifying an idea as Dracula's vampire hordes buying up the suburbs. This is a stock ghost tale, one of foreign, bodily shape shifting, monstrosity (*The Island of Dr Moreau*, *Alien*), fear of contagion (*Dracula*, *28 Days Later*), and terror of the monstrous Other as hidden version of self (*Dr Jekyll and Mr Hyde*, *Frankenstein*, any doppelganger tale).

Twentieth-century writer Susan Hill sets ghost stories in the nineteenth century. In *The Woman in Black*, she explores social oppressions, family power games that imprison and destroy mothers and children. She also looks at life lined with denials and losses—contained futures, a kind of living death. Hill's ghost tales of the dead impinging on the living depict individual feelings and strange confusions of relationships. She creates social microcosms with delicacy, a sense of vulnerability, of threat. Hers is a very English horror of isolated houses, misty English marshes and cobbles, nurseries in which rocking horses rock childless, and graveyards are filled with tiny graves.

The Woman in Black is replete with tension, suspense, Gothic description, and sensitive handling of emotion and narrative. It is a new version of the family ghost story. Jenet Humphrey, a spectral presence mourning her lost dead child, cursing other children and parents, is in many ways a femme fatale. Domestic tragedy resembles a disease caught by the narrator (see chapter 4).

The Others is a powerful, gentle ghost story in which a young woman staying in a house tries to protect her two children who have a disease. Other visitors, butler and housekeeper, visit daily. She has no idea that they are ghosts.

Other contemporary ghost films include *The Sixth Sense* (1999), a slow-moving psychological thriller with a gentle turn, in which Bruce Willis plays a caring social worker/psychoanalyst who is befriended by a young boy considered rather moody, thoughtful, and likely to predict unpleasant events. Actually, the child sees those who will be or are ghosts. The Bruce Willis character believes in him, and the punch line is that he is himself only seen by the boy because he has become a ghost. Many other ghost stories have been filmed, some, such as Henry James's *Turn of the Screw*, several times. The return of departed loved ones was a popular theme at the end of the twentieth century and at the beginning of the twenty-first, with the film *Ghost* and many others trading in on the sense of maintaining contact with a dead loved one, always inside you, and rarely bringing ill will.

Undying Love and Returned Loved Ones

Ghosts frequently return either for malevolent purposes or to continue alongside loved ones, something represented as longed for but often a literally consuming passion. 'The Nature of the Evidence' (in *Shudder Again* Michele Slung, ed., 1994) by early twentieth-century writer May Sinclair is one version of a tale retold by many different authors (Keats, Poe) about fixation upon a powerful, attractive, dead first wife.

Like several others, this tale is built on Poe's earlier 'Ligeia', in which the dead wife returns to haunt the husband and which itself probably derives from Poe's loss of his cousin-wife, Virginia, from tuberculosis.

Sinclair's 'The Villa Desiree' is another couple and ghosts tale (collected in Michele Slung, ed., *I Shudder at Your Touch*, first published in 1926). Like 'Where Their Fire Is Not Quenched' (Sinclair 1923), it is about the banality and danger of unquenched lust. Virginal young Mildred Eve arrives in the south of France to await her extravagantly romantic, sensual fiancé Louis Carson. His last bride died in the room Mildred is to occupy. Carson has 'personal magic, the fascination of his almost abnormal beauty', intensely blue eyes under straight black bars of eyebrows, perfect pure white face suddenly masked by black moustache and small black pointed beard, 'and the rich vivid smile he had for her the lighting up of the blue, the flash of white teeth in the black mask' (Sinclair 105). Sensuality, excess, threat, abnormality, pretence, and concealed viciousness are all suggested in this description. Carson is a suspicious, dusky villain. 'The Villa Desiree' is a Gothic horror tale. Mystery and threat attach to romantic desire and sensuality. Powerless, Mildred is awoken from sleep to sense something else in the room. Her eyes:

> opened under the same intolerable compulsion. And the supernatural thing forced itself now on her sight. It stood a little in front of her by the bedside. From the breasts downward its body was unfinished, rudimentary, not quite born. The grey shell was still pregnant with its loathsome shapelessness. But the face—the face was perfect in absolute horror. And it was Louis Carson's face. (Sinclair, 'The Villa Desiree' 112)

As it closes in on Mildred, examining, she seeks escape. This creature is a birth fantasy, an example of body horror, a prenuptial threat, a remnant of fears of nighttime abuse, monsters in the bedroom. It is highly sexualised, threatening normality and conformity. The beastliness of Carson projects itself, constructed out of his torrid, sadistic relationships with 'other' sorts of women. His lust overwhelms him even at a reasonable distance and the phantasm takes the form of this sadistic lust. This is a tale of the engulfment of romantic love. Later in the century in *The Hunger* (1983), a vampire tale starring David Bowie and Catherine Deneuve, undying love for the serial vampire partners leads to being stored to rot in the attic.

Split Selves, Body Invaders

The figure of the alien Other operates on the borderline between horror and science fiction, body horror and loss of identity. There are many films that figure aliens, monsters, and others invading the body, attacking in outer space or in the home, or that emphasise identity terror and fear of change to the status quo by depicting highly intelligent, evil aliens invading the earth. In *Attack of the 50 Foot Woman*, an alien spacecraft turns the protagonist into a monster woman. *The X-Files* has a plethora of aliens as does *Millennium*, in which aliens are in the guise of bureaucrats, shape shifters who, at important moments, reveal their other selves before shifting back into the oppressive roles and forms everyone recognises.

Probably the best known of these types of films in the latter part of the twentieth century is *Alien* (1979), which builds on the plots of several old science fiction movies (*IT: The Terror from Beyond Space*, 1958; *Planet of the Vampires*, 1965, etc.). The seven crew members of the commercial spacecraft *Nostromo*, awakened from a long-term sleep, are ordered to investigate signals from a nearby planetoid. On its surface they discover the wreck of an alien spaceship and, upon returning to their own craft, unknowingly bring with them on board the deadly life form that wiped out the planet. The film is made more powerful by H. R. Giger's (much imitated) genuinely bizarre alien designs. One of the most powerful moments is the supper scene in which John Hurt's character convulses, and the birth-trauma-originated, monstrous alien Other bursts, screeching, from his chest, while horrified onlookers watch and then wonder where in the ship it has scuttled to and who will be next. Tracing down this and other alien monster children throughout the sequels constantly replays birth traumas, motherhood, and mothering as sites for monstrosity, Otherness, and horror, as well as melding in tales of the unknown in outer space where creatures avoid obeying laws governing Earth (acid for blood, for example). The sequels are *Aliens* (1986), *Alien³* (1992), and *Alien: Resurrection* (1997).

Alien: Resurrection continues the alien theme, but in the merging of Sigourney Weaver's character, Ripley, with the alien itself the film morphs the formula into one similar to that of *Terminator* and its versions. Technology and genetic cloning contrive to represent a body to us that does not seem to be a whole self. Mother (the alien) refuses to attack Ripley—recognising a relative. The film focuses on birthing imagery as both Ripley and metamorphosed alien creatures swim through something resembling amniotic fluid. Elements of horror here include body horror, questioning of identity and self, and disgust at women's procreative abilities: the monstrous mother. Seeing them in glass jars, Ripley, now part-monster, destroys her siblings in a frenzied, disgusted attack.

Doubles

Loss of self and metamorphosis into the Other are a terror familiar in horror. The diabolical other is an early Gothic form in James Hogg's *Confessions of a Justified Sinner* and *Dr Jekyll and Mr Hyde*, while the 'apprehension of the demonic as mere absence' (112) becomes an even greater fear.

Doppelgangers, alter egos, and the Other of the restrained, conformist, socialised self are familiar in Gothic and horror fictions. Hogg's *Confessions of a Justified Sinner* is credited with being the first fiction to explore the expression of the antisocial split self. Here, evil criminal deeds are carried out by an undiscoverable Other who the narrator faces on a hilltop, suddenly recognising himself. The most familiar example of the theme is R. L. Stevenson's *Dr Jekyll and Mr Hyde* (1824), while Wilfred Owen's poem 'Strange Meeting' presents the soldier's murder of a version of himself in the underground trench-killing of the enemy German; this recognition indicts war as a 'trek from progress' and predates Kristeva's identification of ways we Otherise elements of ourselves and project them onto abject Others—women, foreign peoples—when we should instead recognise them as such projections. So, in war, Owen reminds us, we project all that is terrifying, Other, and to be destroyed onto enemies of our own making, 'strangers to ourselves', as Kristeva would have it. Stevenson's *Dr Jekyll and Mr Hyde* has a social and psychoanalytical base. Dr Jekyll, respected Victorian gentleman, does not suddenly reveal a dark and devious side. Instead, he cultivates the opportunity that scientific experiments offer him to act out this side and give it space to be. Although latterly Dr Jekyll fears this savage self is taking him over, he also seems pleased in acting out his atavistic nature.

Grown from 'shilling shockers', 'Christmas crawlers', and sensation fiction, *Dr Jekyll and Mr Hyde* reveals the dark underside of Victorian respectability that is defined by social Darwinism. The tale exposes social fears, which are dramatised and exorcised in the reading, restoring, presumably, an investment for the reader in respectability, sexual norms, and professional trustworthiness. Stevenson's narrative builds on scientific beliefs of the time, so criminal characteristics are recognisable through phrenology and Darwinism, which identified hierarchies of beings and would classify Hyde as underdeveloped, a savage, a throwback. One source of the story's horrors is medical science and experimentation, also explored in *Frankenstein* and *The Island of Dr Moreau*. There are elements of fears here not only of a bestial self but of homosexuality, that hidden other self, in the reading of spaces, names, and places—'Je Kill', 'Hide', and comings and goings through back doors, disguises, and duplicity.

Self and dark Other are polarised. This highlighting of man's animal nature appears in films such as *The Fly* (1958, 1986) and stories of shape-changing werewolves and vampires. Destroying the evil twin/alter ego/alternative creature self/terrifying Other restores order but ignores the inevitable and continuing presence of that twin.

Monsters

It is not only the invasion and leakages, the deformity and disturbance of disease, that evokes body disgust and horror. So, too, does the monstrous body. Deformity frightens; anything in human shape deviating from the norm threatens our sense of identity, safety, and wholeness, causing the turn of abjection. Equal opportunities and diversity legislation coupled with enlightened behaviour counter some of the urges to destroy or stay away from whoever is unlucky enough to be seen as different, deformed, or deviant, as does criminalising the kind of antisocial behaviour that led in the past to extraditing people to the margins of society (up a bell tower, on the edge of a village, in an asylum) or hunting them down and killing them. Horror replays these fears through its monsters, some human, others far from it. *The Hunchback of Notre Dame* (1831) is a 'freak', mistreated and vengeful because of his ugliness. Dr Frankenstein's monster is the paradigm for this. Composed of individual, hideous body parts robbed from graves belonging most often to criminals, the monster inspires only terror and disgust in his parent at the moment of his birth. The innocent, potentially gentle but physically monstrous alter ego of the coldly scientific, obsessive Dr Frankenstein, who would be God and woman (creating life) while carrying out scientific experiments (critiquing post-Enlightenment science), has no future. He is seen as monstrous by the one who put him together. The rejection of this monster is a self-fulfilling prophecy, as Frankenstein's creation disgusts him. Lacking guidance, the monster is led into accidental and then revengeful murderous acts.

The monstrous psychopath roaming the city and neighbourhood streets is a contemporary figure of social dysfunction and mental instability. Monsters range from the psychopathic to the deformed, the latter turned into a figure of horror in our minds because he or she doesn't appear to fit in, from Thomas Harris's Hannibal Lector, intellectual aesthete and cannibal, to Buffalo Bill, who constructs a new skin from that of his female victims (both in *The Silence of the Lambs*).

Monsters in horror are often created through rejection and/or in relation to homosexuality, which is constructed and represented as perverse or deviant in terms of sexuality and sexual practice, thus revealing social fear and denigration of those who do not fit the heterosexual 'norms', a criticism leveled at the figure of Buffalo Bill, as it is at Evan Highland/Julian Lamb in Daniel King's *Mama's Boy*. Forced into incest with his mentally ill mother and rejected from his father's second cosy family, he takes to spying first on his father's new family and later as a CIA agent on families considered politically problematic. He selects happy families, videotapes them, homes in on the secret family language, uses them for sexual release, then butchers them. He must be shot down and killed, as is the fate of most film or TV psychopaths, including the butcherer of families and individuals in Harris's *Red Dragon* (filmed in 1986 as *Manhunter* by Michael Mann), which predates *The Silence of the Lambs* (1988, filmed in 1991 by Jonathan Demme).

Challenges to the rather simplistic equation of the different, deformed, and deviant with the monstrous and evil are born of our psychoanalytically informed awareness of how fear of the monstrous is constructed. But they also come from people who have themselves been Otherised as monstrous—principally women or gay men. Jeanette Winterson's DogWoman in *Sexing the Cherry* (1989) reverses our assumptions that physically monstrous is naturally evil; large women are disgusting, self-indulgent, and non-nurturing; woman's bodily changes through age are monstrous and to be controlled, rejected, and hidden. In this single hideous, enormous, nurturing figure who empowers her adoptive son and makes fools of the Puritans' insistence on restraint, Winterson creates a character who functions to refuse the identifying of the woman's body as abject in itself. 'Large', 'ugly' women (in an economy of formal representation favouring the thin, silent beauty) do not inevitably have to be punished. DogWoman is angry and funny, a celebration of women's variety and right to refuse the kinds of control and constructions that render them powerless and silent.

In *The Life and Loves of a She-Devil* (Fay Weldon), Ruth, the excessively large and clumsy housewife who makes a pact with the devil, remodels herself and takes revenge, another celebration rather than rejection of the constructions of woman as monstrous. Female body horror is exploded by Winterson and Weldon.

The 'Queer' and the Monster   Paulina Palmer and Sue Ellen Case identify a strain of celebratory lesbian Gothic horror in the construction and representation of the lesbian vampire, but much conventional horror figures the lesbian or gay man as a figure of terror, a threat to sexual identity, diseased, and invading normality (whatever that is). Hammer's *Twins of Evil* (1971) is a case in point, where sexual frissons of delight are augmented by disgust in the erotic play of lesbian vampire women. Their predecessors are the voluptuous, excessive, potential lesbian vampires in *Dracula* and the lesbian advances of Sheridan le Fanu's 'Carmilla' (1872). Whatever can be constructed as deviant terrifies whatever sees itself as normal.

The Monsters in The Closet (Benshoff 1997) traces historical representations of gay men and their involvement in filmmaking, and queer theory is used to relate how the boundary-breaking and troubling of horror challenges constructions of gender and sexuality. Queer theory exposes cultural and psychoanalytical bases for the depiction of gay men and lesbians as threatening, devilish Others, and highlights the boundary-breaking potential of gay and lesbian characters, events, and metaphors in horror. Poppy Z. Brite's and Anne Rice's homosexual youth and homoerotic scenes have been recognised as important examples in this change of direction in more mainstream horror as opposed to (see below) radical horror. Discussing German Expressionist film, Harry M. Benshoff notes:

> Many of the German 'Schauerfilme' of the era explored Gothic themes such as the homosexual creation of life (*The Golem*, filmed in 1914 and 1920), while others focused on homoerotic doubles and madness (*The Student of Prague*, 1913), *The Picture of Dorian Gray* (1917), and perhaps most famously *The Cabinet of Dr. Caligari* (1919). One of the leading filmic Expressionists of this era, F. W. Murnau, was homosexual; he made film versions of both *The Strange Case of Dr. Jekyll and Mr. Hyde* and *Dracula*, released in Germany as *Der Januskopf* (1920) and *Nosferatu* (1922). German Expressionism and modern art in general was and still is frequently linked with homosexuality, not only through the historical sexuality of many of its practitioners, but also through its subject matter, and its opposition to "normality" as constructed through realist styles of representation. (Benshoff 21)

James Whale, Universal Studios' director of *Frankenstein* (1931), *The Old Dark House* (1932), *The Invisible Man* (1933), and *Bride of Frankenstein* (1935), was openly gay. Considering displacement of the homosexual or homoerotic, Benshoff notes that in *The Raven* and *The Black Cat*, potential homosexual desire is displaced onto sadomasochistic behaviour using mirrors, facial disfiguration, and a riding crop.

How to Make a Monster was allegedly written by (then stolen from) Ed Wood, a heterosexual male transvestite beloved of B movie fans who enjoy queer-themed films. His independently financed films conflated the monstrous and the sexual. Woods's science fiction/horror films are also gay-themed and range from the camp to hard-core. They include *Bride of the Monster* (1955), *Plan Nine from Outer Space* (1956), and *Night of the Ghouls* (1958). *Orgy of the Dead* in 1965 is described by Benshoff as basically a '"cooch" movie showcasing a series of female strippers within a Gothic frame story' while *Necromania*, in 1971, is 'an X-rated nudie with allegedly hardcore footage shot in a coffin' (Benshoff 157).

In John Carpenter's *Prince of Darkness* (1987), the devil, confined in a glowing green jar by a mysterious order of Catholic priests, begins to leak out and infect people. One such infected woman enters another woman's room at night, and her monstrous attack on the sleeping woman is at first understood by the victim as an unwelcome lesbian advance. As monstrous devil-ooze replaces more natural bodily fluids, the conflation of homosexual and monster is once again fixed in the viewers' minds. Homosexual/AIDS horror is also at the core of *The Kiss* (1988), a film telling the story of a wormlike parasite that must be transmitted from female carrier to female carrier through an open-mouthed kiss. As in both the classical horror film and AIDS discourse in general, the queer threat is constructed in terms both homophobic and racist, since the monstrous contagion is figured as African in origin.

Male homosexuality is often coded in modern horror films as homoerotic sadomasochism. *The Hitcher* (1986) contains an unspoken homosexual threat in the hitchhiker, who, Benshoff notes, 'is obsessively toyed with by an even prettier psychopath' (Rutger Hauer). As usual, the idea of homosexual attraction is displaced into bloody violence and dismembered body parts—one of which, a severed finger, almost makes it into Howell's character's mouth from a bag of French fries' (Benshoff 244).

Postcolonial Horror

Postcolonial horror has only been identified and critiqued in any consistent way in the early twenty-first century, informed by David Punter's elision of Gothic, horror, and the postcolonial in his *Postcolonial Imaginings*. While several postcolonial writers have been mentioned in relation to other themes and reading practises in their own right (see chapter 4), the particular postcolonial take on horror and the subsequent versions of issues and themes that emerge are worthy of special identification. Usurping the laws of other lands, imperialists and colonialists stole mother tongues and silenced peoples, imported and enslaved, disenfranchised, destabilised, and disempowered them, taking over spaces and ways of living. Some insisted on imposing the post-Enlightenment bravado and self-assuredness of the (largely) European conqueror as the best, the only way. The history of postcolonial peoples is one that reeks of the elements of horror: silencing, hauntings of repressed past histories, ghosts, abjection and the split self, colluding with the ruler. Simultaneously, colonised peoples attempt to maintain and revive indigenous or exiled homeland conditions, beliefs, and ways of looking at the world, the imaginary. Punter considers a range of work—that of Chinua Achebe, Derek Walcott, J. M. Coetzee, and Jamaica Kincaid, among others—using the imagery of fossils to describe the objects and elements of an enforced education, noticing hatred, chaos, ruin, and hauntings.

The imagery of Coetzee's *Age of Iron* is undoubtedly that of horror, as he indicts both the deadening enforced law of the Afrikaners in South Africa and the warped comradeship of retaliation, anger, and violence, leading to death. No one wins this battle of hatred, historical oppression, and blood. The dying Mrs Curren, Latin teacher, writes in tones of disgust of control by the Afrikaners, seen on the TV. Language of hammer blows, violence, and silencing present a politicised horror.

> The slow, truculent Afrikaans rhythms with the deadening blows, like a hammer beating a post into the ground. The disgrace of the life lived under them is revealed: to open a newspaper, watch on the television, like kneeling and being urinated on. Under them, their meaty bellies, their full bladders. (Coetzee 9)

But the revolt is iron-willed, death-driven, leading to 'a sea of blood'. Imperialists and colonialists of all kinds emerge as figures of horror rather than discoverers and bringers of light. This is equally true of British, Afrikaner, and American colonial and imperial power. So,

> One place the dream [the American dream] is permitted to perish, with noisy, convulsive death rattle, is in horror entertainment. The American nightmare, as refracted in film and fiction, is about disenfranchisement, exclusion, downward mobility, a struggle-to-the death world of winners and losers. (Skal 354)

Horror is far from being an exclusively American genre, and David Skal's identification of the ways in which horror destabilises the complacencies of twentieth- or twenty-first-century civilization is equally valid for its practice of undercutting such complacencies in modern-day Singapore (see Catherine Lim [*Howling Silence, The Serpent's Tooth*], Japan [cartoons/anime], Australia [Darryle Caine, Kim Wilkins], the Caribbean [Olive Senior, Nalo Hopkinson], and Britain [Clive Barker, Angela Carter]). Horror, a branch of fantasy, is like fantasy expressed in disruptive energies: 'the imagination of the folk involved in a crucial inner re-creative response to the violations of slavery,' such imaginative explorations and projections are liberating, offering alternative readings of history and people's lives so that 'the possibility exists for us to become involved in perspectives . . . which can bring into play a figurative meaning beyond an apparently real world or prison of history' (Wilson Harris 27). The liberating powers of the imagination record different histories and presents, and envision alternative futures.

Toni Morrison uses elements of the ghost story and horror in particular in *Beloved* (1987), in which the unbearable history of slavery is embodied in the presence of a returned baby ghost, Beloved, which acts as a succubus to her mother, Sethe. Her mother had sacrificed the baby in order to rescue her from a return to slavery. Toni Morrison explores the legitimacy of fantasy and horror as modes of expression, particularly appropriate to African American and other black people seeking:

> the tone in which I could blend acceptance of the supernatural and a profound rootedness in the real time at the same time with neither taking precedence over the other. It is indicative of the cosmology, the way in which Black people looked at the world, we are a very practical people, very down to earth, even shrewd people. But within that practicality we also accepted what . . . I suppose could be called superstition and magic, which is another way of knowing things. But to blend these two works together at the same time was enhancing not limiting. And some of those things were 'discredited' only because Black people were 'discredited' therefore what they knew was 'discredited'. And also because the press upward towards social mobility would mean to get as far away from that kind of

knowledge as possible. That kind of knowledge has a very
strong place in my world. (Morrison in Evans, 1984)

Other postcolonial women's horror texts dramatise body horror,
disgust at the Other, and the revitalisation of hidden histories of disempowerment and oppression associated with imperial and colonial
rule. In 'Hantu Hantu', from a colonial viewpoint, Ann Goring
locates disgust, fascination, romance, and horror in the foreign
Other, interrelating genres of romantic fiction, travel writing, and
horror.

In *Crocodile Fury*, Australian Malaysian/Chinese Beth Yahp
explores a postcolonial and gendered reinterpretation of a subju-
gated hidden past, utilising Malaysian/Chinese mythic forms, the
supernatural and magical, along with everyday reality and its
metaphors, to reassess the silenced female histories of subjugation
in the religious, colonised, impoverished, altered histories of the
colonised. The mythic figure of a crocodile emerges from the jungle, representing radical energies and liberation. The crocodile is a
bandit creature. The crocodile fury is that of a silenced subaltern
speaking out against refusals of its own versions of history and life,
and against misinterpretation. The crocodile represents the bandit,
alternative, radical Other as the self—the encroaching jungle and
the slipped shape of an alternative, radical, disruptive, varied, shape-
shifting, energetic female self that refuses the constraints of convent
identity and the female colonised. Turning into the crocodile, the
young protagonist recognises that she represents a radical energy
and finds her voice.

Singaporean Catherine Lim, a threatened journalist, writes
against a repressive regime of sanitised realities, reviving and
embodying memories and histories that have denied the spiritual,
magical Chinese mythic readings of events. Singapore, like Malaysia,
is a country of haunting and supernatural occurrences. In Lim's
novel *The Serpent's Tooth*, old evils are revived. A materialistic wife,
Angela, trying to manage a household in which the living exist
alongside ghostly returns and nightmarish dreams of the dead, finds
her children ungrateful, and she dreams of the domineering old
grand-uncle raping and murdering a bondmaid. Sometimes he
seems to take the shape of Angela's own husband. Grand-Uncle
rapes all the handmaids and servants:

except the old or the ugly, pockmarked ones or the ones known to have disease, for Grand-Uncle was meticulous about his health. He had his three wives brew cleansing herbs for him to ingest or soak in, and one night, in bed, he took a fourteen-year-old virgin by force and she died of the pain and shock. They removed her bleeding body and buried her quietly, but her ghost returned to haunt Grand-Uncle repeatedly. He became impotent, then mad.

. . . Angela could not remember the context, but the details stood out vividly, screamingly; the torn body of the fourteen-year-old haunted her imagination ever afterwards. Once she asked her mother-in-law whether there was any picture of the grand-uncle . . . . When shown the picture of the grand-uncle, she gasped, 'He looks exactly as I imagined him to be—obese, flabby, even down to the mole with the long hairs drooping from it. Now how on earth did I think of a mole with long hairs? It's weird isn't it?' (Lim 105–106)

The returned bondmaid ghosts and the ingratitude of children (referencing *King Lear*) are a subtle threat to the whole family. Serpents in dreams reveal gender and economic power-oriented oppression. Some of the histories of horror of this family return when the grandmother tries to kill herself in a Singaporean death house, once a very real place where old, poor people were sent to end their days.

There is a vulnerable but real freedom for the new generation when Angela's son visits the death house to help rescue the grandmother and attempts to reject both the closed car that his mother has come to collect him in and his mother's nice suburban lifestyle, which has been revealed as a collusive power built on wealth, pretence, violence, and suppression.

These texts negotiate a postcolonial feminist rereading of oppression, suppression, repression, misinterpretation, and selective silencing histories, utilising strategies of horror—body horror, disgust, and abjection. These prove a crucial and inspirational link in theory between the postcolonial and horror—abjection and Otherising—and the vitality of the critical, culturally inflected Gothic, enabling new radical views and expressions, and recognising the supernatural in the everyday, gender equalities, and a rewriting of history to re-empower the hidden and silenced.

Body Horror: Disgust at the Abject Body, Leakages, Lack of Control

Disgust and loathing of the human body is a predominant theme in horror, deriving from ontological insecurity and alienation. Body horror can partly be explained using post-Enlightenment theories that emphasise mind over body, reason, and control over emotional excess; the state of rationality and the sense of the human ability to create order is threatened by the messiness of the body. In the economy of body horror, any excess or lack is terrifying and disgusting.

Significant among many women's interests in horror is that of body horror, and for men, a fear and loathing of the developing or developed female body, which harkens back to the rejection of the mother. Women horror writers often replicate this body horror, as in Ann Goring's 'Hantu Hantu', where bugs invade the body and turn it into a disgusting mess. Some rewrite body horror, recognising and pointing out that it is essentially built on a male fear and loathing, the fear of a vagina dentata, which renders all women's bodies, for some men, the object of disgust and terror, the abject, the rejected Other of waste, taboo, and potential devouring death. Body horror is built on a disgust and fear of the body and its functions, a desire to obliterate or destroy one's own body or other bodies, a desire to be devoured, or an examination of that desire as it appears in traditional tales.

Stephen King's *Carrie* fuses terror at Carrie's extra powers, a kinetic energy and ability to manipulate objects, with body horror. Marginalising her as odd, Carrie's viperous, hateful classmates line up a bucket of blood to pour on her when she and her date win Best Couple at the prom night. Carrie, covered in pig's blood, is an object of loathing and disgust, but her body also represents the power of women's procreative abilities, signified in menstrual blood, a power that manifested itself in those kinetic activities. Carrie's body is monstrous because of her powers and her gender—and these powers allow her to take dramatic revenge—slamming the doors of the hall shut and bringing down the school and its students.

Body horror is manipulated by media insistence on particular versions of ideal body shape, some of which, for women at least, are at odds with good health. Extremely skeletal women over six feet tall are ideal for catwalks but represent versions of women's shape that cause those who don't conform to this ideal to starve themselves, undergo cosmetic surgery, maintain a low self-image, and feel unworthy and unwanted. At the other end of the scale, Web sites devoted to feeders and feedees capitalise on a love of obesity. Here, women are part of a fetishist's pornographic visual industry: Their body size and weight renders them entirely helpless, their skeletal system is unable to bear the weight, and their hearts and vital organs are in peril. The West is obsessed with body image, particularly for women. We should not, then, be surprised to find this the subject of body horror. Cosmetic vampire horror appears in the nineteenth century, with Mary Elizabeth Braddon's 'Good Lady Ducayne' successfully bleeding her young companions to retain her own youthful appearance, and Countess Dracula retaining youth through bathing in the blood of young virgins. Stories about women reaching huge proportions or wasting away are more likely in the second half of the twentieth century, because of the media fascination with women's ideal body shape and size. Both Fay Weldon's *Growing Rich* and Emma Tennant's *Faustine* joke about selling your soul to the devil to develop and maintain an ideal female body shape and eternal youth.

The companion to these cosmetic horror tales are those depicting the monstrous body. Jabba the Hutt in *Star Wars* is an item of flabby, wheezing, liquefied disgust.

Cannibals

The most disgusting version of a response to body horror is the cannibal. Buffalo Bill in *The Silence of the Lambs* mutilates, murders, and skins women to make a new human dress/skin, driven by bodily self-loathing. Disgust and terror mingle in cannibal movies such as *Wrong Turn* (2003), where incest and inbreeding in the backwoods U.S. produce a hillbilly mutant family who capture and eat (and store in the fridge-freezer) hapless tourists. Using barbed wire, they tie and then cart off drivers, partygoers, or lovers of the American outdoors in order to devour them straight away, or (in a parody of domestic planning) store them in the freezer for later. Body horror of the mutant hillbilly family dissolves into that produced by the lack of storage system for many human body parts/frozen dinners. The piling up of farming and car repair instruments alongside jars of brain and body parts and the litter of bones and bloody remains reminds us of 'Jack the Giant Killer' and tales of ogres. These people even sniff out their prey. *Wrong Turn* is disturbingly realistic while also the stuff of horrific fairy tale, the Gothic.

However, one of the bases of the construction and representation of cannibalism is transubstantiation, where, in Catholic beliefs, the body of Christ is actually shared out among his followers and eaten. Another is the imperial and colonial need to figure as subhuman those whose lands were invaded. The veto on eating human flesh was seen as a signifier of civilised and enlightened response. Africans and the people of the Far East Islands (Papua New Guinea, Borneo, and others) were depicted (whether true or not) as cannibals in a manner that terrified travelers because of the otherness of the act of eating human flesh. In fact, as Darryl Jones has declared, cannibalism was rife in Europe into the medieval period and afterwards, sometimes to show power over one's enemies by eating them, to ingest their power, or to ward off starvation. It figures in a variety of texts, including Maturin's *Melmoth the Wanderer*.

Disease

Diseased bodies, creeping sickness from within or without, could overwhelm and destroy us. So leprosy, syphilis, AIDS, radiation sickness, and the plague provide links in a version of body horror between texts as diverse as 'The Listener' (Algernon Blackwood), *Cabin Fever* (2004—a creeping disease overwhelms holidaymakers), *28 Days Later* (a rapidly infectious disease turns people into zombies), *Ghost Ship* (2002), and *Resident Evil* (2002—flesh-eating zombies), to name a few current examples.

Disease and plague tales are narratives of invasion or the explosion of something deadly inside. The location of terror or disgust is the body itself and its responses to whatever takes it over, diffuses it, and destroys it. History has given us a whole range of plagues, most notably in Europe where the Black Death killed up to two million people in 1348, but more recently smallpox, AIDS, and, in Africa, the Ebola virus.

Edgar Allan Poe's 'The Masque of the Red Death' is a model for disease horror narrative. Its direct alignment of immoral acts and hubris on the part of the ruling classes with the invasion of disease fits with people's tendency to view plague as biblical revenge for evildoings. In this tale, the plauge spreads amongst the suffering feudal poor partly because of the selfish excess and evil perversity of the rich. The real Death enters as an unwelcome guest into the castle of the Duke, whose life of artifice and excess expresses itself in a masked ball that features elements of heightened perversity, oppression, cruelty, selfishness, and performance. Death singles out the Duke and his spoilt revellers as necessary victims for that which they tried to avoid by locking their doors tight against the night: the past, disease, and truth. Death decimates the lot. The disgusting signs of their disease spread from reveler to reveler and, as in 'Ring-a-Ring-a-Roses', the Black Death ditty, they all fall down.

The insistence of syphilis rocks the family in Ibsen's *Ghosts*. Disease causes and spreads visible examples of the imperfect body, encouraging dis-ease among readers and viewers. It could happen to us, we fear, so we try to lock it out and deny it, since our deep-seated fears are indeed that, like the biblical plagues of sores, we have unbeknown to ourselves deserved it. Such was the sanctimonious response to the early days of the AIDS crisis in the 1980s and 1990s, when conformist figures could point out a whole rich range of 'deviants', particularly gay men and drug users. As if a perfect example of what horror can conjure up, however, AIDS and HIV refused to be so contained and easily viewed as a scourge. Infected blood products transferred HIV/AIDS to anyone using these products and has decimated enormous numbers of the impoverished and needy in Africa. These numbers are too huge to be convincingly seen as deviant because so many have been devastated by its effects.

Disease is a reality. In horror fictions, we produce the diseases; they spring from our fears, faults, ignorance, and perversity, and Otherising both diseases and those who have them/catch them/harbour them/pass them on/suffer from them hits home every time. If this sounds like a piece of glib journalistic comment, it also replicates the crucial horror 'turn' in which readers recognise the abject Other of horror as of their own production.

Daphne du Maurier's 'The Birds' utilises horror tropes of invasion and engulfment. Invasion by foreigners or aliens is common in horror. They disturb our spatial and bodily securities, disrupt the body's system with illness and destructive forces, whether teeth, blood, or chemicals. Common also are vampires, werewolves, aliens, and other space, body, and blood invaders/destroyers. In 'The Birds', invasion is of both the sacrosanct family home space and the body, through pecking and stabbing. The birds enter through cracks in the windows and down the chimneys. They come into the house through boards that they peck, and through glass that they shatter. They also invade bodily space through pecking at hands and eyes.

Freud's essay 'The Uncanny' (1919) explains some of the story's power and horror, essentially based upon both fear of castration and fear of dismemberment and disempowerment through blinding. 'The Uncanny' analyses E. T. A. Hoffmann's story 'The Sandman', in which the nurse tells of a wicked man who throws sand in the eyes of children who refuse to go to bed and carries their eyes off in a sack, to feed them to his monstrous, birdlike children who:

> sit up there in their nest, and their beaks are hooked like owls' beaks, and they use them to peck up naughty boys' and girls' eyes with. (Freud 348–349)

Bug and Reptile Horror

Many of the favourite figures of horror are derived from insects or reptiles, so Mother in *Alien* is like a gigantic egg-laying reptile. In Ann Goring's 'Hantu Hantu' (Malaysian for 'haunts' or 'ghosts'), one of my favourite horror stories, body horror combines with horror of the Other in the shape both of the foreign or exotic and deadly, as well as of insects. The allure of a strange couple and the promise of love and status overtake Su and Jane on their visit to the Malaysian jungle. The tale concentrates on shape changing, the domestic, and the stuff of social-climbing romantic fictions. Informed that the brother and sister they meet are royal 'golden people', Su is drawn in by the romantic/fateful glance across a crowded room among strangers and the promise of fulfillment of an 'unspeakable emotion'. The sexual emotion is overwhelming and presented with a tinge of fear for Jane, watching her friend entranced. But there is a hint of lesbianism here, adding to the taboos on which horror festers, as the golden sister nearly hypnotises Jane to collude:

I stared from one to the other, reluctantly becoming aware that whatever it was between them—this unspeakable emotion, this sexual, animal compulsion—it was almost palpable on the heavy night air. Like the cloying, clinging waft of perfume from a flower-laden frangipani. The tree invisible, its presence overpowering. (Goring 219)

Staying with them, Jane discovers that the Flit gun, her favorite domestic weapon back home in Singapore, crumbles the whole facade. When she sees Su and her exotic/erotic prince in an embrace, she recognises the smell, revealed only gradually to us. It is the stench of her most (and our most?) loathed bug: of cockroaches. This is a moment of disgust and terror: Household pests and romantic fiction mixed together, a yoke of lies, domesticity, and horror:

His kiss was upon her. I saw cockroaches flow like a brown slithery rushing tide from his mouth into hers. Into her, over her, through her tangled red hair, under her clothes. I saw her writhe and jerk and moan in that last terrible orgasm as they sank, locked together, to the floor. (Goring 226)

When singled out as the next victim, Jane heaves the Flit gun and destroys the lot. But the denouement, the hospital from where the story is told, is a return to the overwhelming power of Charles Smith, who initially brought the couple together. So the threat lingers on.

Objects, Objectification, and Automata

One of the elements of 'the uncanny' is the destabilising and terrifying notion of turning the human into the object, the object into the human. This fear returns in the zombie tale where mechanical, moving, living dead behave like objects with designs upon the living.

Stephen King's 'Chattery Teeth' is an object horror tale in which a travelling salesman buys and ties up a set of toy teeth, lurking on a store shelf. They have wreaked horrible harm on people in the past, but in the case of this salesman, their release prevents him from being murdered by a hitcher he picks up. The teeth maul the hitcher, rescuing the salesman. In Angela Carter's *The Magic*

Toyshop, 'The Loves of Lady Purple', and the screenplay of *The Lady of the House of Love*, Carter exposes a version of patriarchal control and oppression that would turn women into puppets or controlled objects. 'Corpses don't nag and they never want new clothes', notes Henri Blot in the screenplay. Meanwhile, Lady Purple, managed as a marionette in a voyeuristic pornographic puppet show, turns on the puppeteer who puts her through her nightly whorish paces, and in a reversal of the Pygmalion myth, empowers herself, drains him, and walks off to wreak sexual havoc in the town's brothel.

The marionette, the living doll, is central to 'The Loves of Lady Purple', a paradigmatic tale of male fantasy, power, and lust, featuring woman as automaton. A mixture of several familiar social and horror motifs—vampire, flesh-eating zombie, Pygmalion icon, and predatory puppet—Lady Purple is a compendium of horror. She is Queen of the Night, 'the undead' (Carter 43), created from the perverse sexual longings of a wise but untranslatable Asiatic professor, aided by a deaf apprentice and a mute helper. He uses her to dramatise sexual messages, exhibiting her nightly as a 'didactic vedette' (Carter 46). The stories she enacts fill their silences; she herself is literally voiceless. A sideshow for the perverse, Lady Purple is hung up lifeless after each performance. Her 'act' consists of the playing-out of the sexual excesses that supposedly precipitated her 'fall' from humanity into puppet perversities, which in turn objectify her own lovers:

> in the iconography of the melodrama, Lady Purple stood
> for passion and all her movements were calculations in an
> angular geometry of sexuality. (Carter 44)

She is the stuff of their hidden fantasies and fears, written on the constructed body of woman. Lady Purple is an icon of desired and loathed woman, the embodiment of men's longings and anxieties. She is the 'petrification of a universal whore' (44), both a 'nameless essence of the idea of woman' (44) and yet, once involved in her performance, 'the image of irresistible evil' (46). Importantly, she is controllable and static, an ageless marionette whose body parts are hung up nightly after the show like a painted, false coquette. The archetypal horror figure, she embodies all her audience's desire and fear and yet can be conveniently tidied away out of sight for future use. Until, of course, she seizes the initiative, writes her own tale, and comes to life. One night, the Asiatic professor, enamored of his creation, kisses her. Time freezes as the tableau turns into reality. Lady Purple awakens, vampirishly drains him of blood, and walks off to wreak sexual havoc in the town's brothel, vivifying the stories she was constructed to enact.

In the story, the sources of conventional male horror and desire are exposed, enacted, and discarded. However, Carter takes this scenario to its ironic, logical extreme. Lady Purple, the embodiment and repository of the punters' horror, *cannot* be packed away. This monster of their own making will finally neither lie down nor be hung up.

Carter uses paradox, irony, and horror to follow through with both the transferred loathing of female bodies and power that the vampiric femme fatale figure represents and patriarchy's desire to control women entirely, rendering them idealised/disempowered 'living dolls'. Lady Purple embodies these conventional female horror figures and her determined stalk into the village is both a logical conclusion, returning the horror to its sick source, and somewhat celebratory. The living doll has her final revenge.

Stephen King's *From a Buick 8* and *Christine* explore versions of objects that come to life, focusing on the thinking, possibly malevolent car. The legions of dead, mobilised in *Night of the Living Dead*, the mechanical movements of those taken over by pods in *Invasion of the Body Snatchers*, and the Terminator's robotic movements all terrify. There is something unreasoned and unreasonable about the human turned object—a machine, it cannot be made to deviate from its chosen path, and an object animated of its own accord is out of our control. Martin Barker in *Haunt of Fears*, looking at the fifties horror comic strips, deals with with horror as a political weapon or scapegoat providing an opportunity to criticize social flaws.

> In his fine book *Living in Fear: A History of Horror in the Mass Media*, Lee Daniels makes an interesting case that one of the prerequisites for the emergence of horror as a distinct genre was the secularisation of society. (Barker 125)

Religion acknowledges the supernatural and so helped explain terrifying events. But when its power diminished and science failed to fill the spaces, horror took over as a location to dramatise and explore the inexplicable. Barker goes on:

> For no category of horror does this explanation make better sense than for the objects-come-to-life kind. It is still a use of the same formula, still a shock-logic. But now the shock is not necessarily merely an ending that reverses expectations (though it may do that anyway), but more a stepping outside the ordinary, an approach that is maintained throughout the narrative. Many strips at this end of the horror spectrum have a lot to do with raising doubts of a Hamlet kind: there are more things in heaven and earth than are dreamed of in our philosophies. Or at the very least, they have to do with the emotions of uncertainty that surround what that statement entails. Of course, it is a darkness in our hearts that needs expunging by horror—something which Bruno Bettelheim wisely notes about fairy-tales. (Barker 127)

Object horror deeply destabilises our sense of security in terms of what is real, what matters, and what we can trust about ourselves and others. If objects can come to life and people be turned into objects or automata, then some of the fundamental bases of human life—thought, morality, and human relationships—are undermined.

> We are there as victims. It is the sense of helplessness in the face of unpredictable objects and processes that make such narratives work as horror. (Barker 129)

Close to the fear of being turned into an object or of objects coming to life is the dehumanisation represented by the zombie.

Zombies

Shape shifters, werewolves, and vampires challenge what it means to be human through revealing an animal self beneath the veneer of a civilised self. Boundaries between animal and human, mythic creature and human, reappear throughout myth and history. So, too, do tales of the risen dead, from Lazarus, a symbol of Christ's power and Christ himself, to the stumbling, blind, neighbourhood monsters of Romero's *Dawn of the Dead* (1968) and Raimi's *The Evil Dead* (1981). In the early twenty-first century, zombies come in for a real revival, represented as figures of blind obedience, a mindless force, the populace's mind numbed by consumerism, hooked on shopping, or of armies unquestioningly invading and acting like killing machines. As one colleague remarked at the 2003 Fantastic in the Arts conference, it is not so surprising that the United States should embrace the figure of the zombie as metaphor with the reality of a zombie in the White House (the Bush administration).

28 Days Later is in many ways a very conventional zombie film. Beginning with the visionary, it relaxes into horror and plague scenes in a coherent visual style, using the tones of contemporary journalism to expose London, evidencing the artifacts of defunct civilisation. These horror techniques are all recognisable, with stock scenes and chaos. The film mixes plague-ridden zombies, idealistic survivors, and brutal soldiers uniting plague and zombie formulae, indicting the zombie-like activities of the soldiers who intend to manage and destroy the sick. Jim, the protagonist, seems a just man, but he's also like the zombies and persuades viewers to buy into his reading of events. Zombies in *28 Days Later* are an army of the impoverished, seeking, equally, both human flesh and mall merchandise.

While conventional zombie tales and films expose consumerism and social obedience to dangerous, destructive power, there are some examples of the zombie's use in postcolonial critique. Erna Brodber's novel *Myal* (1988) is an example of postcolonial Gothic that uses the zombie myth and figure to explore ways in which imperial and colonial powers disempowered, de-energized, disenfranchised, and silenced colonised and enslaved peoples, taking from them their identities, their histories, language, and the right to imagine and speak. In this powerful novel set largely in Jamaica, Brodber focuses on the early twentieth century, when Ella O'Grady, with her absent Irish white father and her Jamaican mother, begins by mouthing imperialist representations of colonised peoples, delivering Kipling's 'The White Man's Burden' at public shows. Ella then experiences the theft of her history and re-representation of it in a 'coon show', on stage, at the hands of her American capitalist husband, Selwyn Langley (who will not have a child with Ella for fear of miscegenation). Eventually, Ella achieves empowerment in the deconstruction, rereading, and reconstruction of an allegorical tale 'Mr Joe's Farm', a text the adult Ella as teacher is expected to teach to Jamaican children to effectively control their imaginations, their sense of self and identity, enforcing notions of white paternalistic control. Like Orwell's *Animal Farm*, Mr Joe's farm resembles the Stalinist state rather than nurturing authority and avoids democracy. Ella recognises in the teachings of the imperialists and colonialists, which she herself was repeating, the powerful control of language and minds, worldviews and identities. Like Myal, the book itself and the inspirational religion that came from Africa and flourished in Jamaica, Ella reinterprets and so enables others to see they do not need to remain secondary, controlled, and effectively zombies. As Ella's spirit theft dissolves, so, too, does that of her parallel, Anita, who has literally had her spirit stolen by the powerful Mass Levy. Levy's power over Anita is released when a neighbourhood exorcism, led by Miss Gatha, results in his death in the private, seemingly safe place, his outside privy. This gives Anita back her own power, symbolically also releasing others who would have followed her in Levy's serial manipulation of young women's spirits. *Myal* is a complex novel, which politicises the figure of the zombie as bonded sufferer of imperialist and colonial spirit theft, a mind slavery to be thrown off, leaving the ex-sufferer re-empowered. It also aligns itself with postcolonial horror (see below).

Women as Figures of Horror

In horror films and texts, women have conventionally been represented as bimbos, victims, or hags. The categories overlap. Bimbos can turn into deadly femmes fatales or victims. Think of Fay Wray screaming in the arms of giant King Kong, whose love for her endangered his judgement, leading to his death. In *Species* (1995), the beautiful blonde is an alien out to become impregnated so that she can spawn, a true example of disgust at women's bodies and the castrating threat their active sexuality represents, both in their power and in the sex act's danger. Mothers are also monstrous figures of horror, representing their engulfing and devouring powers.

Julia Kristeva (1982) and Luce Irigaray (1985) debate the ways in which women's bodies have been abjected, turned into figures of horror, the womb swallowing and entrapping, even as the mother's personality might overwhelm the child's.

The nineteenth century in particular figured this sexualised, devouring woman as snake, monster, and gaping hole. William Hope Hodgson (*The House on the Borderland*, 1908) describes a yawning abyss: the image of woman as a terrifying pit, wherein the male can be lost, a womblike wild nature with a terrifying smell. A fear of female sexuality pervades the whole:

> Sometimes in my dreams, I see that enormous pit, surrounded, as it is, on all sides by wild trees and bushes. And the noise of the water rises upwards, and blends—in my sleep—with other lower noises; while over all, hangs the eternal shroud of spray. (Hodgson 34)

Cellars, caverns, shrouds of spray, pits, and the relationship of these to fear, enclosure, and self-destruction pervade Hodgson's narratives, though he marginalises the acknowledgement of their sexualised terrors. 'The borders between anxiety and appetite however are never stable, and fear gives way to fascination in a continuum of displaced desire', says Amanda Boulter (in Bloom 35).

Bram Stoker's Jonathan Harker was also fixated on the voluptuous vampire woman's mouth—ideal both for kissing and for biting. In the imagery of a mouthful of teeth lies the male terror of the 'vagina dentata' to castrate and devour the male, as Barbara Creed points out, 'Jaws suggested the vagina dentata which turn-of-the-century men feared they might find hidden beneath women's clothes' (Creed 108).

Bram Dijkstra's study *The Idols of Perversity: Fantasies of Feminine Evil in Fin de Siecle Culture* (1986) collects nineteenth-century images of women as wolves, bears, claws, cats, and devouring creatures. The fear that the New Woman inspired provoked all manner of comments about potential female illness attached to intellectual endeavour and any sort of vigor. However, a more obviously psychological response to this figure, terror of Victorian patriarchy, was to denigrate her as witch, siren, vampire, and monster. Theodore Strong's poem 'The Witch' (*The Smart Set*, August 1900) is an example of this, seeing in her 'lure of moonlight: she brewed a soul's death' in 'the falsehood and the smile/that disguised the wanton guile' (11 no. 2, p. 49). This predatory sexuality draws men in, paralyses, and drowns them like the sea. Bram Dijkstra theorises about late nineteenth-century sirens:

> The male's fantasies of helplessness before the sirens' physical enticements were not infrequently placed with a yearning to be seduced. Such a fantasy of seduction allowed him to combine the pleasures of indulgence with the innocent state of the unwilling victim—thereby placing the responsibility for his weakness once again squarely on the shoulders of woman. (Dijkstra 266)

Commenting on images of women as animals and snakes, as Medusa, in embraces with animals, Dijkstra points out how male fears of woman when other than passive, nun-like, static, even dead, constantly figure her as animal, snake, and monster, the feared Other, the abject.

> It is clear that by 1900 writers and painters, scientists and critics, the learned and the modish alike, had been indoctrinated to regard all women who no longer conformed to the image of the household nun as vicious, bestial creatures . . . the personification of witchery and evil, who attended Sabbaths and dangerous rituals, astride goats . . . . Woman, in short, had come to be seen as the monstrous goddess of denegration, a creature of evil who lorded it over all the horrifically horned beasts which populated man's sexual nightmares. (Dijkstra 324–325)

This devouring animal woman is familiar in Victorian painting and writing, which depicts women as snakes, mermaids, and vampires.

Medusa, snaky-haired, paralysing Gorgon of myth, derives from male castration anxiety. Freud's own retelling of the tale of Medusa helps us explore sexualised terrors in writing of the Victorian, Edwardian, and Georgian eras. Medusa, punished by a goddess for her promiscuity (making her live in a temple), is the snake woman who turns men to stone, the vagina dentata with snakes for waving hair and a murderous stare.

> An interpretation suggests itself easily in the case of the horrifying decapitated head of the medusa . . . a representation of woman as a being which frightens and repels because she is castrated . . . [it] takes the place of a representation of the female genitals, or rather it isolates their horrifying effects from their pleasure-giving ones. (Freud, Penguin ed., vol xiv 273)

Contemporary Radical and Women's Horror

Radical writers have always been rather tangential to, and critically perceptive of, a mainstream that ignored or marginalised them. Radical women horror writers are much more likely to refuse punishment, closure, and the regimes that designate difference as Other, that try to close down variety and debate. Their creative energies reconfigure the vampire, the werewolf, Medusa, sirens, mermaids, and other monsters; expose families and domestic norms as the potential locus for incarceration and lies; and reject those male/female, life/death, and good/bad polarities, revealing existence as much more varied. Like Angela Carter, many use the tropes and trajectory of familiar horror and fairy tale (of the Grimm variety or a similarly disturbing source) from which to deviate and so question the values and norms conventionally restored. These values and norms are questioned and troubled because the reinstatement of a status quo that enforces women's vulnerability and subordination, and that demonises women's sexuality, is rejected. Ambiguity and ambivalence lie at the heart of this reconfiguring.

In the work of Charlotte Perkins Gilman, Virginia Woolf, Sylvia Townsend Warner, and Katherine Mansfield, among others, we find the development of a new and still relatively unrecognised kind of women's supernatural and horror writing. Mansfield and Woolf refuse to define ghosts as abject but instead present them as friendly familiars. Children changing into animals or birds in Mansfield's tales are not feared horrors. There is none of the need to restore an order that rejects the Other and the non-boundaried. Woolf's ghosts in 'A

Haunted House' are not the kind of evil, destructive monstrosities we find in Blackwood's tales; instead, in a familiar, friendly setting, long-dead lovers wander and look for the traces of the love they imprinted on the house. Woolf's narrative envelops us; language is a rhythmic heartbeat confirming security. In most ghost and horror tales, horror enters the domestic space, ghostly, murderous, threatening an invasion, entering the body space. Woolf's 'A Haunted House' defuses this fear. The haunters are a couple who lived there previously. We hear them and live alongside them; they hold no harm or hatred for us.

Similarly, in Sylvia Townsend Warner's *Lolly Willowes*, Laura's recognition of herself as a witch is a moment of celebration and identity rather than terror. Warner's Laura embraces images of spiderlike spinsterhood summed up later by Simone de Beauvoir as creatively transgressive:

> And in truth, cellars and attics no longer entered, of no use, become full of unseemly mystery; phantoms will likely haunt them; abandoned by people, houses become the abode of spirits, unless feminine virginity has been dedicated to a god one easily believes that it implies some kind of marriage with the demon. Virgins unsubdued by man, old women who have escaped his power, are more easily than others regarded as sorceresses; for the lot of women being bondage to another, if she escapes the yoke of man she is ready to accept that of the devil. (de Beauvoir, *The Second Sex* 144)

Women's Erotic Horror

There are probably as many versions of women's erotic rescripting of the horror genre as there are variations on horror itself. I will concentrate mainly on the reconfiguration of the vampire, always related to a rather sadomasochistic version of sexual interaction or action, but I will look briefly at other forms of horror that women rescript to celebrate the erotic, with a certain forbidden *jouissance*.

Pam Keesey's lesbian vampire tales *Daughters of Darkness* (1993) establish a lesbian literary history beginning with the (demonised) 'Carmilla' (1992, first published 1872); Sheridan le Fanu's exploration of a lesbian vampire read in more recent times as representing repressed but potentially positive lesbian relationships. The 'point at which the lines between sexuality and violence become blurred' (Keesey 16) is pivotal for Pat Califia's groundbreaking lesbian sadomasochistic 'The Vampire' (1993). Wasp-waisted, blonde Iduna, whose 'complexion was so pale it was luminous. In the dark she almost seemed to glow' (170), actively seeks out the leather-clad dominatrix Kerry, who takes her male victims literally, beating them past endurance, but refusing the blood she needs. Iduna represents an alternative partner, no victim, freely offering her blood and enjoying the exchange, conditioned and 'well schooled' (183), which she has actively hunted out, as needy as Kerry, adapted to this new kind of vampire relationship of mutual exchange. At the height of vampire passion:

> The venom that had prevented her blood from clotting and closing the wound sang now in her veins, making her see colors behind her closed eyelids, making her warm inside, simultaneously relaxed, alert. No other drug could ever duplicate this ecstasy, this calm. She should know, she had had long enough to search for a substitute. (Califia 182)

Sex, then, is 'not out of the question' (183).

Califia's tale reverses significant elements in the conventional vampire narrative while retaining others. Iduna, the 'prey', seeks out her predator. Like Dracula's female vampires and the women on whom the Count preys, Mina and Lucy, the vampire's seductive act turns the women into voluptuous, lustful, passionate partners. However, in this contemporary lesbian feminist vampire tale, no punishment is necessary; the exchange between Kerry and Iduna is predicated upon them, each being adapted to feed the needs of the other. Energy, self-determination, and sexual choice predominate in their erotic engagement.

Not all women's horror radically rescripts the convention to promote active, equal erotic exchange, however. Some contemporary women's erotic horror concentrates on the kinds of scenarios and relationships that could horrify or disgust women in particular. Highly eroticised, dark, bestial rape fantasies seem to be popular choices for the intermixing of both horror and the erotic personae, which, to many feminists, is problematic to say the least.

A case in point is the Australian Darryle Caine, who tends to play with highly eroticised, deadly scenarios. In 'Predators' (*Screams*, 1996), the predatory couple, the female narrator and Tiger, her boyfriend, indulge in sexual safaris along Surfer's Paradise, picking up and sharing women whose own isolation and slightly under-achieved attractiveness make them succumb easily to flattery and friendship. The language of seduction and destruction—'devour' (16), 'target' (18)—and the erotic foreplay hinting at danger, pales into insignificance once their most recent prey, Elvi (anagram for evil), plays them at their own game, seducing Tiger. The seduction is based on the kind of danger they are used to inventing and con-trolling for themselves. Caine's erotic writing is more like conven-tional (male-produced) pornography. Elvi's inhuman gaze and growing fangs terrify the narrator, who cannot extricate her impal-ing lover:

> Before my very eyes she was transforming into some hideous demon! There were huge fangs, long talons, a rough, reddened hide and wild, stringy hair sprouting from its head. (Caine 20)

This is a hermaphroditic monster, for when it has finished with the dying Tiger, it turns on the narrator:

> I could not guess what sort of gruesome weapon she packed between her legs. For the tatters that remained of his sex looked like he had been having it off with a giant pencil sharpener . . . And then the demon-creature turned on me. It had transformed further, and now a ferocious looking device was protruding from its groin, like some giant, deformed penis weapon. And it was meant for me! (Caine 21)

Imagery of violence, invasion, and destruction characterise sex acts in Caine's work. Her erotic horror fantasies replicate many of the stereotypical abject scenes involving women—Medusa, the Iron Maiden, the vagina dentate—and combine these with horrors specifically designed for women—invading, throbbing, barbed mon-ster penises; inhuman power; bestiality; the helplessness of the female victim, whose life, partner, unborn children, everything, are threatened or destroyed.

The power of the erotic in much women's horror, however, derives initially from that location of terror as a response to the sexuality of women, which conventional horror consistently delivers up to audiences. Contemporary women's erotic horror is more likely to celebrate the erotic. Much of it aims to rescript, re-value, and reinstate the attraction of the erotic, encouraged and enacted by conventionally abject creatures or humans—werewolves, vampires, mermaids, even creepy 'things'.

Vampires

The vampire, once bitten, infects victims with a demonised energy, which breaks out at night, visibly, as another bestial image—the fangs. Conventionally, vampirism is a metaphor for the release and then recontainment of social controls. It is an expression of fears of sexuality walking the night streets, an expression of the taboo of eroticism:

> The ideas in vampire fiction of what sexuality is like—privacy, secrecy, uncontrollability, active/passive—have a complex relationship to the place of sexuality within the social order. Until the 1960's—and, really still today—sexuality was approved within marriage. Vampirism takes place outside of marriage. Marriage is the social institution of the private of sexuality—the vampire violates it, tapping at new windows to get in, providing sexual scenes for the narrator to witness. Marriage contains female sexuality—hence the horror of the female vampire walking the streets at night in search of sex . . . Finally, marriage restricts sexuality to heterosexuality—vampirism is the alternative, dreaded and desired in equal measure. (Dyer 54)

Vampirism enacts sexual license and its social aftermath—dread, disgust, punishment, and death. Richard Dyer concentrates on vampirism as a metaphor for homosexuality/lesbianism, emphasising its transgression. Actually, it is the rather catholic sexual tastes (victims can be of either gender, as long as they are attractive) of vampires that provide part of the *frisson*. The male vampire seeks female victims/partners and often also males, while female vampires, the paradigmatic oversexed demonic women, also traditionally seek both sexes.

> The female vampire is conventionally represented as abject because she disrupts identity and order. (Dyer 54)

> Driven by her lust for blood, she does not respect the dictates of the laws which set down the rules of proper sexual conduct. Like the male, the female vampire also represents abjection because she crosses the boundary between the living and the dead, the human and the animal. (Creed 121)

Of all the figures of horror reappropriated by contemporary women horror writers, the vampire rises into the late twentieth century renewed and reinvigorated. Always associated with the terrors of unleashed libidinal energies, it is imaged in the deadly fanged kiss that conveys ecstasy and then condemns the beloved to an eternity of death in life as victim and victimiser.

The figure of the vampire has been radically reappropriated by contemporary women horror writers such as Anne Rice (*Interview with the Vampire*, 1976), Sherry Gottlieb (*Love Bite*, 1994), Poppy Z. Brite (*Lost Souls*, 1992), Jewelle Gomez (*The Gilda Stories*, 1992), Katherine Forrest ('O Captain, My Captain', 1993), and others. They have reinterpreted the vampire to their own radical ends, investing the figure with all the disruptive power of the erotic and, through the troubling of gender roles, questioning the stability of a range of what is taken for granted as 'normal' cultural and social behaviours.

> . . . the maternal body is an emblem for all vulnerability, for the animal as much as for the human, and this in the animal layers of the psyche. It is in our dealings with the fantasised maternal body that the formation of sadism and masochism appear, in projected and introjected torture as the mother, which is bound back into the circle of fear and desire, but the inseparability of this body from all our hopes of nurture and thus of having a hearing, 'a receptacle for our point of view'. (Punter, *Gothic Pathologies* 14–15)

Julia Kristeva (*The Powers of Horror*, 1982) explores the conventional abjection of mothers and women that grows into both a desire for, and terror of, women's potentially engulfing sexuality.

Contemporary women's horror writing, particularly in the vampire genre, challenges this division into self and Other, this abjecting of the figure of woman, mother, and lover. Instead, it offers a recognition that the Other is part of ourselves, a projection with which we need to come to terms.

The female vampire terrifies because of her ability to transgress the norms and behaviours associated with the different genders: Her actions resemble those of penetration. Most transgressive of all is the lesbian vampire. Not only does her existence as a vampire challenge male power, but her sexual choice is perceived as a threat to normal behaviour, as disgusting and titillating. In making *Brides of Dracula* (1960), the decision to include lesbian scenes, building on the triadic relationship of the three women in Stoker's *Dracula* (1896), produces a response of voyeuristic fascination with what is ultimately considered utterly abject.

Vampire relationships are confusing: They place the lover in the role of a child who both seduces and suckles. The vampire's embrace seems to recall that of the mother and child, but it is deadly. Bodily fluids fortify the one who suckles, but they drain the lifeblood of the one who is suckled—the mother figure.

> Vampirism combines a number of abject activities: the mixing of blood and milk; the threat of castration; the feminization of the male victim. (Creed 70)

Re-reading of the primal birth scene places the vampire as mother birthing (usually) an adult child as victim or new vampire lover. Suckling moves from breast to neck or wrist, and milk is replaced with blood. In vampiric relationships, this breaks the taboo of incest (the 'mother' is briefly the lover). Abjection is present in the body of the mother and in the opening of wounds, indicating leakage, imperfection, and breaching boundaries of the bodily surface. This is a source of horror in conventional vampire texts by male and female writers.

The vampire is more likely to appear as a radical, exciting role model rather than a creature instilling conventional terror and

disgust. The vampire is a subversive figure, one that highlights contradictions, paradoxes, gaps, and fissures in the fabric of a safe and
whole society, a safe and whole self, for which social and psychoanalytic beliefs were/are socially maintained for the sake of stability.
That most ancient of creatures, the vampire, then begins to be
recognised as an essentially postmodern one—the Gothic comes of
age. It is a condition of the postmodern as it is of the Gothic that
dislocation, fragmentation, irony, paradox, contradiction, and deconstruction are features of our everyday perceptions and versions of
ourselves, the world, and its ideas and practices. We accept parody
and paradox, performativity, and the layered variety of any interpretations possible in reading events, people, and texts in many different ways. This very practice and philosophical turn of the
postmodern condition positions the Gothic as its favourite and
inevitable form. The vampire figure breaks through solid selves and
solid buildings, time and space; changes shape; crosses thresholds
and boundaries; is androgynous in nature and encourages; and draws
out of others their own transgressive natures, their own sexual
natures, their nonconformist subversive selves. In these ways, the
vampire can be seen by some as the figure of a dangerous challenge
to order and by others as the figure who, by challenging that order,
shows it up to be the shame we know it is, the construction and performative that it has to be in postmodern mess.

Liberating energies that merely turn the tables do not enable a
fundamental demythologising and remythologising. They do nothing to expose and critique the way the world works. However, the
figure of the vampire in women's writing by Anne Rice, Poppy Z.
Brite, and others actually alters the meanings and relationships of
vampires, particularly vampire women, to radical and liberating
effect. Desire, passion, and sexual activities have, as Foucault points
out, always been regulated and contained by law and language. The
figure of the vampire refuses this containment, liberating the explo-
sive power this generates; breaking down boundaries, behaviours,
taboos, and regulatory practices; denying the constraints of our lives
as they fulfill both the terrors (devouring and death) and the promises (undying love and life) of popular myths and fictions. As Poppy
Z. Brite has remarked, regarding bringing her own vampires to the
screen:

I think the only way to film the book and not have it be a complete disaster would be to blow all the pallid Goth stereotypes out of the water—nothing against Goths, but as far as the vampire thing goes, it's been done to death. Someone should go to the complete opposite extreme and make a kick-ass 'hood' movie out of it, if it's to be made at all. (Ian S. online)

Vampires and Revengeful Living Dolls—Women's Horror Bites Back

In Angela Carter's hands, the clichés are male fantasies of women's sexual power. Female vampires represent male fears of sexually voracious women. That Carter became increasingly fascinated by the parodic potential of horror clichés can be seen in her highly influential reworkings of the vampire myth. Carter's Gothic antecedents include Isak Dinesen, whose interests lay in the perversions and power of decayed aristocracy, Jacobean tragedy's emphasis on mortality and perverse sexuality, and Djuna Barnes's heavily Jacobean, nightmarish, lesbian Gothic, especially *Nightwood* (1937), where nightmare terrors explore and critique gender roles. The focus of much lesbian Gothic is on questions of sexuality and 'normality' raised by such borderline horror creatures as werewolves and vampires.

Carter's vampire tale 'The Lady of the House of Love' explores the vampire figure. The last relative of Vlad the Impaler, the Lady sits in a castle coated in dust and moth-ravaged velvet. Her beauty is intense, ideal, and unnatural. She feasts reluctantly each night on woodland creatures, using her mandarin-length nails to gouge her prey, and carries out the traditional vampiric daily/nightly routine:

> In a white lace negligee stained a little with blood, she lies down in an open coffin. (Carter 196)

Flowers and scents intoxicate and overwhelm the potential victim. Vaginal imagery dominates the excessive descriptions. All the flowers are as voluptuous as any depicted by Georgia O'Keeffe:

> [T]he flowers themselves were almost too luxuriant, their huge congregation of plush petals somehow obscene in

their excess, their whorled, tightly budded cores outrageous in their implications. (Carter 200)

The lady is thin, with a plush mouth, waiflike, and lost, with a 'lovely death's head' (Carter 202), a living contradiction of death and sensuality, her mirror returning no reflection. Her beauty is unnatural. She has:

> an extraordinarily fleshy mouth, a mouth wide, wide full prominent lips of a vibrant purplish crimson, a morbid mouth. Even—but he put the thought away from him immediately—a whore's mouth. (Carter 202)

The young, bicycling World War I soldier who accidentally visits the Countess cannot avoid patriarchal constructions and representations of woman. Consequently, he compares this lovely woman to flowers and whores. But she also seems doll-like, encaged like her pet bird, helplessly fulfilling age-old roles. She was:

> like a great ingenious piece of clockwork. For she seemed inadequately powered by some slow energy of which she was not in control; as if she had been wound up years ago, when she was born, and the mechanism was inexorably running down and would leave her lifeless. The idea that she might be an automaton . . . deeply moved his heart. (Carter 204)

Noble though he might be in appearance, her potential marionette status is still a turn-on for him, and romantic love ironically proves her undoing. The lady falls victim to her own vampire's promise of eternal love when she falls in love with the soldier, letting him taste her blood. He feels lured by the long-nailed countess, an icon of romantic love, into a living monument, 'Juliet's tomb'. The roses planted by her dead mother to thrive in the burial ground of a garden recall those that twine around the castle of the Sleeping Beauty, but the irony surrounding her romantic awakening undercuts all romantic fictions. One kiss from this young man to help heal her wounded hand and, loving, she becomes human, lost. The hero is ironically a celibate match for any charmed tales of virginity as a talisman against evil. The approaching historical moment of great blood loss is the corollary of the eternity promised by vampire lovers. World War I connotes the death of chivalric versions of war, itself a product of the same kind of logic that generated the control of motion by geometry, the bicycle. The young soldier's logical challenge to the superstitions of the Carpathians cannot protect him from future death in the trenches. And he misses the grand fatal passion of the Countess. An English hero, he is far too unimaginative to understand. The vampire's rose he revives back in his quarters feeds on the approaching blood loss of the war. This tale thrives on contraries. The Lady, descendant of Vlad the Impaler, lives in a kind of waking dream:

> She herself is a haunted house. She does not possess herself
> . . . sleeping and waking, behind the hedge of spiked flow-
> ers, Nosferatu's sanguinary rosebud. (Carter 205)

The Countess hovers between life and death, inhabiting a half-life. She both occupies the traditional vampiric role of uniting opposites (life/death, human/animal, etc.) and exposes the destructive oppositions between logic/superstition, male/female, and human/animal that produce wars and romantic lies. The story is also a radio play, 'Vampirella' (1985), a medium that Carter claims better enables that vital mix of the ironic, comic, and the horrific, encouraging both enjoyment and critique. Carter has commented on how radio enables a tension between black comedy and pathos. The dexterities and subtleties of radio allow ambiguities denied the short story. 'The Lady of the House of Love' is a Gothic tale about a reluctant vampire; the radio play 'Vampirella' is about vampirism as metaphor. In the radio play, Count Dracula and the insane, wicked waste of World War I provide a context and set of parameters against which we can measure and relate the life, loves, and decay of the lady vampire.

Both play and tale are full of reversals of the vampire myth. Vampires are more often traditionally male. Reluctant, cursed female vampires emphasise different social points than demonic, powerful male vampires. Their curse can be recognised as the need to remain beautiful, and the kiss of death positions them as femme fatales. The Countess's ancestress Elizabeth Ba'athory, the Sanguinary Countess, so reveled in her legendary beauty that she

feasted on and washed in the blood of young peasant girls to perpetuate it. She was a grim victim to stock cosmeticised female
images.

The tale scrutinises, reverses, and exposes the cultural sources of
fears of vampires and the roles and dramas they usually enact.
Carter's vampire tale combines the blurring of human and animal
with that of human and automaton in both her main horror figures.
The bicyclist thinks of the Countess as doll-like, and Henri Blot, the
radio play character, goes a stage further. He prefers necrophilia:
Women are more tractable, less fuss, as corpses:

> Corpses don't nag and never want new dresses. They never
> waste all day at the hairdressers, nor do they talk for hours
> to their girlfriends on the telephone. They never complain
> if you stay out at your club; the dinner won't get cold if it's
> never been put in the oven. Chaste, thrifty—why they
> never spend a penny on themselves! and endlessly accom-
> modating. They never want to come themselves, nor
> demand of a man any of those beastly sophistications—
> blowing in the ears, nibbling at the nipples, tickling of the
> clit—that are so onerous to a man of passion. Doesn't it
> make your mouth water? Husbands, let me recommend the
> last word in conjugal bliss—a corpse. (Carter, 'Vampirella'
> in *Come Unto These Yellow Sands* 108)

Blot indicts bourgeois husbands who fail to see that their pref-
erences are also for corpselike women. Their living, ostensibly
respectable wives, he suggests, suck them dry while they (the predatory husbands) 'perpetuate infamies'. Women, safer as dolls, are, he
suggests, even more tractable as corpses. Vampirism is, in Rosemary
Jackson's words, 'perhaps the highest symbolic representation of
eroticism' (Fantasy 120). Richard Dyer in 'Children of the Night'
(1988) locates the attraction of the vampire as erotic metaphor in
the private setting—both our beds and our innermost thoughts. The
equation of blood draining with sexual ecstasy, the domination and
swooning, the sensuality, the promise of eternal love and life, make
the vampire motif central to that of romantic love and central to
erotic depiction and imaginings:

> [A] number of writers on the horror film have suggested,
> adapting Freudian ideas, that all 'monsters' in some meas-
> ure represent the hideous and terrifying form that sexual
> energies take when they return from being socially and cul-
> turally repressed. Yet the vampire seems especially to rep-
> resent sexuality . . . s/he bites them, with a bite that is just
> as often described as a kiss. (Dyer 54)

Vampires are popular figures in contemporary women's horror
not merely because of their promise of eternal youth but also
because of their naturally transgressive and so potentially revolu-
tionary nature. Being a vampire metaphorically enables escape from
the destruction inevitable in a world that relies on divisions of space,
on difference, and on boundary disputes that cause world wars.

At the end of the twentieth century/start of the twenty-first century, as at the end of the nineteenth, vampirism has become an over-
whelmingly popular metaphor for the erotic. As metaphor, however,
it has always expressed both the repressions and the terrors. With
Bram Stoker's classic *Dracula* (1897), the eroticised representation
of women was an illuminating unshrouding of Victorian terrors
regarding any kind of active female sexuality. It also embodied the
need to reestablish both a national and a sexual status quo in the
face of 'filthy foreigners' seducing 'our women' and tutoring them
into something too horrible to mention. In the early twenty-first
century, the imagery of vampirism is enjoying a shape-shifting
longevity. Women's narratives of vampires are redolent with a celebration of the body, of blood, beauty, eternal youth, passion, and,
above all, the erotic. The metaphor of vampirism has been reappropriated: It is compulsively attractive for the sexually alive twentieth-
century feminist (though clearly its concrete practical practices,
were they real, would be rather unpleasant!). Eternal beauty and
eternal love, with several opposite or same-sex partners, and a really
rather final answer to women's fears of being reified and disempowered, treated as sexual objects, pushed around by myth and cultural norms, assaulted when walking the night streets, are all enacted
in the female vampire.

Lesbian Vampire Erotic Tales

Some contemporary women writers in the vampire genre deliberately reverse and trouble the forms and figures of the genre and refuse the narrative trajectory that would condemn female and lesbian vampires in particular to a permanent death as a punishment for their transgression.

Lesbian vampire fiction by contemporary women writers rarely chooses to utterly demonise or to destroy the vampire herself. Relationships are frequently sought and felt to be mutually rewarding, based on compacts and companionship. These regulate the otherwise overwhelming desire and the highly charged eroticism of the encounters, which do not carry the conventional taboo. Transgressive eroticism upsets reductive, binary, binding norms of self/Other and male/female.

The use of the erotic in women's horror is also transgressive in order to suggest new ways of behaving and relating in both heterosexual and homosexual love/sex/erotic unions. A mutual recognition of the Other as a subject, however similar or different, is the basis of positive human relations. Some erotic horror explores the creative and celebratory potential of relationships of mutuality, where difference is a reason for celebration not destruction.

In *Bonds of Love: Psychoanalysis, Feminism and the Problem of Domination* (1988), psychoanalyst Jessica Benjamin suggests that healthy relationships and development demand 'mutual recognition, the necessity of recognising as well as being recognised by the other' (Benjamin 23), as well as 'the reciprocity of self and other, the balance of assertion and recognition' (25). Jane Donawerth suggests, however, that there is a separation in our constructions and projections in everyday society, which militate against such mutuality and recognition of the validity, uniqueness, and value of differentiated individuals (Donawerth, *Frankenstein's Daughters* 46). Donawerth says that in our culture, however this process occurs, in particular in the context of gendered relations that idealise the father as the symbol of differentiation and subjectivity (Donawerth 105, 109, 123), and the mother as the symbol of symbiosis (158), 'neither state of mind', warns Benjamin, 'represents real relationships as the truth about gender—as merely an ideal' and 'Either extreme, pure symbiosis or sure self-sufficiency, is represented as loss of balance' (Donawerth 46, quoting Benjamin 158).

In this definition, erotic expression is seen as an element of health. Vampire erotic horror combines the *frissons* of horror with the charged, eternal promise of fulfilled and constantly re-fulfilling desire. What could be more transgressive in a censorious society, and what more celebratory and liberating? There are similar needs for mutual self-recognition in romance fictions and in women's erotic horror fictions.

Melding the genres of science fiction, romance, and horror, and blending the Gothic motif of the vampire with the science fiction motif of the alien Other, Katherine Forrest's short story 'O Captain, My Captain' (1993) utilises the tropes of all three genres to create an erotic horror in which the space captain vampire Drake (Dracula, but the adventurer Sir Francis also), captain of the ship *Scorpio IV*, does not prey upon her travelling companion but instead awakens her to the pleasure of her body in a highly erotic union, graphically, but never tackily, described. The lesbian relationship is initiated by Drake with the military lieutenant, Harper (after Jonathan Harker in Stoker's *Dracula*). It is then entered into mutually with full awareness of what each 'is', what they can offer, and the limitations of this relationship. Vampires in contemporary women's erotic horror do not need to drain their victims unto death; they embrace in a mutually aware exchange that refuses to turn the temporary or long-term mate into a member of the undead.

Forrest and others use the transgressive power and the liberating eroticism of the vampire relationship to suggest and describe new heights of a passion that is mutually sought and exchanged. By using a science fiction location (onboard a space ship travelling to acquire plants beyond a deadly asteroid belt), the formulae of science fiction are also queried. The ship's captain, recognised for her vampire self when she is accidentally caught changing into a bat in the ship, has unique technical powers enabled by her longevity, concentration, and inhuman stamina. Her superintelligence has enabled her to successfully play the game—learning how to forge computerised data.

Unlike much heterosexual erotic horror, lesbian vampire erotic horror is rarely concerned with permanent damage. Drake's vampiric serial monogamy has a positive effect on her partners, one other of whom (Col. Westra—a variation on Stoker's Lucy Westenra) contacts Harper over a confidential video screen. No harm is done. Sensuality and self-awareness are released. Confession, attraction, sexual encounter, and then revelation as vampire partner all adhere to the course of conventional vampire fictions. But here there is no draining of blood, no death. Drake gains her nurturance from the sexual arousal of the other. There is no domination, only mutual recognition and exchange. As Paulina Palmer, in *Lesbian Gothic* (1999), notes:

> Drake, it appears, is not the conventional predatory vampire of popular film and fiction but a vampire with a feminist conscience. She seeks to pleasure her partners, not hurt them and, in order to do so, has succeeded in renouncing the dreaded vampire kiss. (Palmer 115)

Harper, stunned that Drake derives nourishment from sexual juices not blood, asks: "Do you diet between women?" Drake's reply: "Your body is not my food . . . Your pleasure is my food" (Forrest 225), which establishes the relationship as mutually pleasurable and non-destructive. Harper recognizes the sources of her own sexual appetites. Like Pat Califia's (1993) more sadomasochistic partners, they are made for each other. This is a coming-out story that normalises lesbian sex as mutuality and nurturance in a community relationship. It refuses the negatives of the vampire myth. Otherness is welcomed and embraced.

Maternal relationships are explored in the Gothic lesbian vampire writing of Jewelle Gomez. In *The Gilda Stories* (1992), Gomez develops an African-American lesbian vampire narrative in which the erotic elements are a richly queer challenge to much heterosexual erotic writing and to conventional vampire narratives. It is an extraordinary novel, or story sequence, moving through time and different locations, which, in its creative breaking of social and sexual taboos and those of conventional vampire and horror fiction, radically reconfigures the vampire and more conventional erotic exchanges.

In conventional vampire tales, the high romantic offer 'to die upon a kiss' is most often realized, while in contemporary women's vampire writing death is not usually necessary for those from whom the female vampires 'feed or gain nurturance'. Eternal life and relationships in a vampiric community are a definite possibility for the initiated.

As Palmer has explored at length in *Lesbian Gothic,* Gomez's chief radical act in writing *The Gilda Stories,* in terms of the treatment of the eroticism of the relationships of the vampire, is to reappropriate and positively re-value that psychoanalytically conventional abjection of the mother and the mother's body, which we find in so much male-produced horror. In so doing, Gomez dramatises a lesbian erotic that valorises a sensual, sexual, maternal, and erotic exchange between (mostly, here) female vampires. Blood exchange is a moment of high sensuality and the act of suckling equates the maternal with eroticised relationships. In *The Gilda Stories,* blood is a life-giving not an abject-defiling fluid, agreeing with Kristeva's observation that blood represents:

> a fascinating semantic cross-roads, the propitious place for abjection where death and femininity, murder and procreation, cessation of life and vitality all come together. (Kristeva, *The Powers of Horror* 96)

A vampirish encounter that takes place between Bird and Gilda illustrates these contrary associations. Here, Gomez brings together the displaced image of the child suckling the mother's breasts, the act of birthing, and the mother's abject bleeding body. She describes how Bird, making an insertion in the skin beneath her own breast,

> pressed Gilda's mouth to the red slash, letting the blood wash across Gilda's face. Soon Gilda drank eagerly, filling herself, and as she did her hand massaged Bird's breast, first touching the nipple gently with curiosity, then roughly. She wanted to know this body that gave her life. Her heart swelled with their blood, a tide between two shores. To an outsider the sight might have been one of horror: their faces red and shining, their eyes unfocused and black, the sound of their bodies slick with wetness, tight with life. Yet it was a birth. The mother finally able to bring her child into the world, to look at her. It was not death that claimed Gilda. It was Bird. (Gomez 40)

In *The Gilda Stories* the real horror is the racial and sexual violence from which Gilda, originally called 'the Girl', initially fled when escaping the plantation, before being rescued by Bird and the original Gilda, who ran a rather friendly brothel. Gilda witnesses lynchings and escapes rape. Hers is a testimony to racial hatred and male abuse of women. Against the backdrop of these horrors and the growing crises in the 1980s, of homosexual witch-hunting during the early discoveries of AIDS, and the defilement of the planet by pollution, the nurturing vampiric community appears as an alternative maternal force, not one of horror. *The Gilda Stories* is a novel that traverses the various social and cultural configurations, and, in questioning their divisions and the apportioning of blame as abject or tolerance and celebration, causes fundamental questions to be asked about divisions of black/white, male/female, active/passive, good/bad, and life/death.

Lesbian vampire relationships *can* be destructive and invasive, but most often they are not so figured. So in Amelia G's short story 'Wanting' (1994), the exchange is eroticised, the results are not fatal —but a lasting relationship has begun:

> The images I had known were there. 'Are you going to drink my blood?' I asked. 'No, silly.' She threw her head back and her long heavy hair flew up into the air behind her and cascaded down over her shoulders into my breasts like a black waterfall. She laughed and it was the most beautiful music I had ever heard. 'What I need is your wanting, just your wanting'. (G 32)

In many examples of women's erotic vampire writing, death is avoided as the women writers refuse such conventional closure. Transcendence and mutual exchange are more likely endings.

Invasion or destruction of self is one threat of horror. Engulfment is one of horror's worst forms, and the notion of being taken over by one's own other animal self, by devils from inside, or by creatures in some overwhelming shape is a recurrent figure in horror (see *Demon Seed*, 1977; *Rosemary's Baby*, 1968; *Wolfen*, 1981).

Numerous tales of werewolf lovers (for example, Cheri Scotch, *The Werewolf's Kiss*, 1992) further explore the theme and concern over animal invasion or engulfment, the monstrous within us. In contemporary women's horror fiction, however, the Otherness is often recognised within the self and/or embraced. Women in Angela Carter's 'The Company of Wolves' (1981) and Suzy McKee

Charnas's 'Boobs' (1990) are happy to embrace werewolf status as they recognise their maturity and feel comfortable with their (werewolf) bodies.

Hybrid vampire fictions enable questionings of social 'norms' and genre boundaries, as we read and watch romantic fiction/crime vampire stories (*Love Bites*, Sherry Gottlieb), cowboy vampire tales (*From Dusk Till Dawn*; Katherine Bigelow's *Near Dark*, *The Cowboy and the Vampire*), the teen slasher high school soap vampire (*Buffy the Vampire Slayer*), sci-fi vampire ('O Captain, My Captain'), and so on. This is fun, and it's also a product of writers in a postmodern age from particular cultural contexts who have rejected the simplistic assertion behind conventional vampire fictions. Such tales assert that it is easy to spot the abject, the Other, and that the powers of a comfortable, assured, conventional society can so spot it and exorcise it, returning an order we can all buy into—chastity, purity, property, ownership, Christianity, God on our side in all battles, and racial differentiations and hierarchy, of which blood is a key signifier. Many women rewrite vampire tales celebrating the potential for recognising the variety of sexualities they offer.

Werewolves

Werewolves are borderline creatures, shape shifters in the domestic world, figures of the abject who remind us of our animal natures, that which we both loathe and have to acknowledge while we restrain it. The werewolf myth explores or reveals hidden animal selves, deriving from fears that we and those we know and love might not be as we expect, may harbour beneath civilised and loving exteriors some basic, monstrous, uncivilised, bestial behaviours. Historically, in the U.K., the Channel Islands, and Europe, radical religious or political behaviour led to charges of lycanthropy, while traditionally werewolves are shape shifters, acting out the beasts within (usually) man. A mere glimpse of a full moon and metamorphosis into the beast results. After terrorising local people, the werewolf returns to his daylight self, only to be dispatched by a silver bullet.

Over a thousand years old, the werewolf myth appears in many different modes worldwide. In traditional werewolf tales (Romulus and Remus), wolves parented children. In 400 B.C., apparently a werewolf named Damarchus won medals at the Olympics. In A.D. 77, the Roman writer Pliny's Natural History introduced the werewolf's habits and lifestyles, while Virgil identified Rome's elite with lycanthropy. Prince Vseslav, ruler of today's Belarus, was nicknamed 'the magician' for his apparent ability to transform himself into animals.

Like the vampire, the werewolf is a creature of the night, a product of our deadliest fears, both of invasion by others, as the werewolf's bite infects, turning prey into werewolves, and of expression of the inner beast. Unlike vampires, werewolves particularly haunt forested areas, rural peasant territory, part of the terror of dark nights before electricity. Werewolves represent bestial others lurking beneath the civilised self.

The fairy tale 'Little Red Riding Hood' explores 'the threat of being devoured' within an Oedipal conflict: 'But the wolf is not just the male seducer, he also represents all the asocial, animalistic tendencies within ourselves' (Bettelheim, *The Uses of Enchantment* 169, 172). Bettelheim notes that, unlike 'Hansel and Gretel', which it otherwise resembles in its concerns with morality and fears of being devoured, 'Little Red Riding Hood' marginalises female monstrosity (the cannibalistic witch, the grandmother), foregrounding the masculine sexuality embodied by the wolf. Marina Warner suggests a deeper link between witch and wolf:

> The wolf is kin to the forest dwelling witch, or crone; he offers us a male counterpart, a werewolf who swallows up grandmother and then granddaughter. In the witch hunting fantasies of early modern Europe they are the kind of beings associated with marginal knowledge, who possess pagan secrets and are in turn possessed by them. (Warner 181)

In the middle of the nineteenth century, the Rev. Sabine Baring-Gould, an English clergyman on a walking holiday in western France, was injured. As the sun was about to set, Baring-Gould hobbled to a nearby hamlet. These being the Celtic provinces, it was only with difficulty that Baring-Gould made himself understood to the villagers, who spoke only Breton. He sought out the priest who in turn led him to the mayor:

'Monsieur can never go back to-night across the flats because of the—the', and his voice dropped; 'the loups-garoux . . . If the loup-garoux were only a natural wolf, why, then, you see'—the mayor cleared his throat—'you see we should think nothing of it; *but*, M. le Cure, it is a fiend, a worse than fiend, a man-fiend,—a worse than man-fiend, a man-wolf-fiend.' (Baring-Gould 2–4)

Baring-Gould walked, survived, and went on to collect numerous werewolf tales. Some of these have informed werewolf stories in horror, while other representations of the werewolf relating to a fascination with the beast within emerge from Darwinism and Freudianism. Nineteenth-century eugenics identify those of other than white races as inferior and less developed, and figure beast-men as throwbacks to an earlier stage of development (Wells, Haggard, Stevenson), leading to werewolf tales and latterly films, some of which figure invasions of the foreign. Freudian-derived fantasy builds on Freud's case of the wolf man 'from the history of an infantile neurosis' (Freud 234). Witnessing the primal scene between his parents seriously harmed the boy who, as later Wolf Man, a neurotic adult depicted by Freud as a feral child, exhibited a fear of castration and anal eroticism. His 'sexual aim could only be cannibalism—devouring' (Freud 347). In Darwin-inspired werewolf tales, the invasion of the foreign or Other is uppermost. A bite from a Tibetan beast, Yogami, in Carl Dreadstone's *The Werewolf of London* damages Dr Wilfred Glendon, botanist. He is followed by and kills the evil invading Tibetan in London, then is shot himself by the police. Freudian-inspired tales tend to focus on an explosion of the beast from within and include *The Wolf Man*, in which Larry Talbot's sexual frustration over his relationship with Jenny Williams is augmented by his sexual competitions with his own young father.

Traditional werewolf tales and films depict werewolves as figures of terror and horror. The existence of the beast inside the man is a metaphor for real fear and disgust, and the werewolf, though cursed, must be destroyed, cannot be allowed to continue or love because he represents (and it is always a he) a threat too great to civilisation. However, in the 1961 film *The Curse of the Werewolf*, starring Oliver Reed, a more radical edge appears. Informed by social Darwinism, bestiality and poverty are linked from the terrible opening scene, and the peasantry, Reed's character Leon the lycanthrope chief among them, are seen as constructed by vile, unjust economic inequalities.

Latter-day films and tales somewhat question what we take as normal and civilised and so use the figure of a werewolf as part of this problematising. One of the key movements to begin this questioning is *An American Werewolf in London* (1981), a comic horror film where young students walking alone among the North England moors are chased by a werewolf in an area where the locals pass on the kind of warnings so prevalent in vampire films about not wandering around at nighttime, fearing strangers, and so on. One of the students is killed by the werewolf, the other bitten. The dead friend returns to warn and haunts his friend, who gradually turns into a werewolf in the middle of London, with some stirring, saddening, and poignant moments.

In *Wolf*, Jack Nicholson, a bitten, sidelined editor, turns into a werewolf. In revealing his wolf self, he finally celebrates his urge to go back to nature and reject the untruths, pretences, and artifices of civilisation. Central Park is a favourite haunt. He is a New York type recognising his own bestial powers—releasing the beast in man.

Werewolf tales home in on our terrors of the defamiliarisation of the everyday and familiar friends, on the *unheimlich*, or uncanny. Traditionally, they have been male, predatory, dominant, and emblematic of the sexual stalking and devouring of the powerful male. In Suzy McKee Charnas's story 'Boobs', there is a direct link between the onset of puberty, menstruation, and breasts and the metamorphosis into a werewolf. The girl does not revel in her body, for which she is loathed, longed after, and ridiculed by the boys at school, particularly Billy, who calls her 'Boobs Bornstein'. But, overcoming the disgust with menstruation, she recognises new powers, controlling her changing in a more positive way than the anorexic Edie Silver, who has internalised male loathing of the female body and starved herself to death:

> I felt myself shrink down to a hard core of sort of cold fire inside my bones, and all the flesh part, the muscles, and the squishy insides and the skin, went sort of glowing and free-floating, all shining with moonlight, and I felt a sort of shifting and balance-changing going on. (McKee Charnas in Tuttle 21)

Kelsey really admires her strong muscular body, the fur, even the lolling tongue:

> My face was terrific, with jaggedy white ripsaw teeth and eyes that were small and clear and gleaming in the moonlight. (McKee Charnas 25)

And of course, she can run, and fears nobody and nothing. As she seizes a new delicious power in her own body, she finds she turns, willingly, into a werewolf. Unlike the traditional versions of werewolf stories, she is pleased and at home in her alter self, and wreaks revenge on suburban pets as well as teenage pests, particularly Billy. She devours him warm, having lured him through his own lust:

> [W]ho would think that somebody as horrible as Billy Linden could taste so *good*? (McKee Charnas 35)

This is an amusing and empowering tale that reverses werewolf trajectories—identifying with the views of the werewolf and realising that the myth itself could be one for sexuality, power, and relishing rather than suppressing and fearing the beast in humankind.

Werewolves also frequent several of Angela Carter's short stories. 'Wolf Alice' and 'The Company of Wolves' focus on the sexuality and powers that inhabit the figure of the werewolf.

Anne Rice's sister Alice Borchardt has written several werewolf tales, largely set in ancient Rome exploring Romulus, Remus, and wolf-related cultural myths. A daughter's domestic prison of sexual abuse is exposed in Karen Joy Fowler's 'The Night Wolf' (1990), where the father's nighttime 'visits' to his terrified daughter Anna are described by her as those of a wolf. A shape changer, a domestic werewolf, he acts the considerate father but breaks through the chair propped against the door to keep him out at night. Anna's social, personal, and psychological space is invaded; she is trapped in her own room and within the lies and family behaviours that govern the daytime world and 'normal' family relations. He denies her the power to name what happens to her.

Werewolves are creatures of the borders, of the abject: horrific constructions built from our fears of the proximity of 'normal' human and animal natures. By figuring her father as a werewolf, Anna exposes the invasion of her sexuality and her vulnerability

within patriarchy. The father transgresses both physical and personal space. Like the cracking wallpaper in Charlotte Perkins
Gilman's story, Anna's ceiling cracks change shape:

> Sometimes the cracks on Anna's bedroom ceiling turned
> into a wolf's head. It wasn't always easy to see. (Fowler in
> Tuttle 59)

And although her mother cannot see the cracks and helps move the
bed, these cracks widen to let in the wolf figure. The abject invades
the bedroom's ostensible safety:

> Anyway by then it was too late. By then the wolf had found
> his way into Anna's room in the middle of the night, in the
> middle of her dreams, and especially on those nights when
> the moonlight was bright. By then the wolf had found his
> way to Anna and he came any time he wanted to. (Fowler
> in Tuttle 59)

Her father tries to silence her: "God knows, the world can always
use a few more women who can't talk" (Fowler in Tuttle 63). This
links him with the invading wolf whose breath and smell she recognises and who, unlike any real wolf, can clearly turn the door handle. Linguistically, the daylight shape of the friendly father is linked
with the nighttime wolf who would be exposed were the sunlight
to hit him. Speech, light, and space are essential in the repression of
this abuse. Anna determines in her imagination to either defend her
own space or to turn it into a space of danger for her invading
wolf/father. Her thoughts of traps would force fixity on the shape-
changing and value-shifting situation, she hopes. The trapped wolf
would be exposed in the sunlight of the everyday morning:

> The trap would hold him until night and the darkness were
> over. Until hard, bright sunlight found him in his vulnera-
> ble sunshine shape. (Fowler in Tuttle 63)

The abject werewolf is a particularly appropriate figure for terrors
associated with father-daughter rape.

One deep-seated horror is shape shifting, which threatens the
identity, wholeness, and continuity of self. In werewolf tales, shape

shifting is frequently connotative of extrusion of the disgusting animal nature. Socially unacceptable, werewolves, although often the sad victims of their own sexuality/bestiality, must be flushed out and dispatched with a weapon every bit as phallic and powerful as the stake that impales a vampire, the silver bullet. The werewolf transformation, the disgusting revelation of the beast beneath the civilised skin, is often eroticised in popular literature. As the beast breaks out from the containment of human form, there is an exciting violence and self-recognition of the bestial abjected Other, which has been hitherto a hidden, taboo part of the self.

The Werewolf's Kiss (Cheri Scotch, 1992) reverses this terrified disgust and celebrates the werewolf in an erotic transformation that brings the protagonist in touch with himself. Recognising that he has been born a *loup garou* (werewolf), Achilles decides to find his repressed self. After some foreplay from Mae, who meets him down at the bayou, he starts to metamorphose. Like the moments during and after a vampire's transformation, there is a high intensity of sensual experience and awareness. Achilles is happy and wants to cry, blinded by the beauty of the moon, his new mistress. First, however, there is suffering: 'the pain is a birth agony' (Scotch 202). He compares this metamorphosis to that undergone by caterpillars changing into butterflies (a comparison also made by Carmilla the vampire in Sheridan le Fanu's 1872 novella):

> I feel like every muscle in my body, every nerve, is being stretched and changed. The ends of my fingers start to tingle and burn as they lengthen. The surface of my skin heats up as the pelt starts to grow. But in the middle of this, I begin to feel a great strength. (Scotch 202)

The discovery of the hidden Other in the self is a revelation of the beast beneath the skin of conventional horror:

> I'm a loup-garou now, in body as well as in spirit. Half man half wolf, more powerful than either, more cunning. I have supernatural powers, I can see for miles in the dark, every little detail comes clear, I can smell a million scents and will learn to differentiate between them all. I can move almost as fast as I can think, and I have a strength that's truly

frightening. I'm not immortal, but will live for hundreds of years, the moon's gift to her lovers. (Scotch 203)

It would be hard to determine what the down side of being a full-fledged werewolf was from this! The *loup garou* wants to change and is happy in his powerful body. Bonds and ties of love and affection surround the werewolf family and friend group; the lone hunter is not their sort. In this tale the transformation is positive and exhilarating, the companionate and sexual relationship rewarding. It is a real romantic fiction.

Chapter Six

Key Terms

Abjection

This is a term coined by Julia Kristeva in her *Powers of Horror* (1982). The term *abjection* is developed in response to Lacan's theory of the development of the 'mirror phase', in which the infant comes to recognise him- or herself as an individual subject, through rejection of whatever is not self. Faeces are the first things to be rejected and excreted from the body of the infant, so that he or she can define him or herself. The second rejected influence and body is that of the mother in particular, who threatens to engulf and overpower the infant, preventing him or her from identifying him- or herself as a separate being. The mother's body, therefore, comes to be associated with that which is repulsive, definitely Other, disgusting, overwhelming, disempowering, and potentially destructive. This is contradictory, since the mother's body is also a nurturing one. Kristeva argues that a psychoanalytically inspired rejection of the disgusting and abject Other's body is extended in the adolescent and adult male's need, it seems, to both fear and desire the different body of woman and to feel threatened by it as Other, different to self. This dichotomous and perversely contradictory response is woman's fate: to be desired and to be identified as the cause of all destructive and disgusting powers. From this grows the image of the femme fatale, Medusa, the devouring mother, the monster woman.

While woman is the first obvious rejected Other, the abjection or disgusted rejection of the Other, 'the not self', is also transferred onto anything that is not the self—particularly those who are foreign. In this, foreignness can include alien Others and peoples from

other countries or other religions. Kristeva's theory of horror, therefore, links the psychoanalytic with stereotyping and abjection. This
explains the infant's need to determine its own individual self,
rejecting what is not self; the ways in which men are attracted to
and then reject and blame females; and ways in which people reject
as Other, disgusting and threatening, people who differ from them
in any of several significant ways. This Otherising in horror transfers
in science fiction into a disgust towards and destruction of the alien.
One of the political and radical strategies of less conventional horror is to highlight this abjection and question it by exposing its origins in definitions of self.

The Literary Gothic

Beginning in the eighteenth century with novels by Horace Walpole,
The Castle of Otranto (1765) and Ann Radcliffe, *Mysteries of
Udolpho* (1794), the literary Gothic explores contradictions and
unease in social conventions. It enables readers to question what is
or was taken for granted, such as families, identity, love, and inheritance. It works by using metaphors and imagery usually of extremes
and opposites, gaps, losses, and things hidden, and so reveals contradictions in our lives and in society. Much literary Gothic focuses
on romance—its dangers and final rewards. And so, many romantic
fictions have used Gothic settings, stories, and stereotypes. Much
Gothic uses spaces that are dangerous, at the edge, such as cellars,
dungeons, attics, and haunted castles, to show us how we, in our
minds, push those elements of our lives we are worried about into
ostensibly (temporary, of course) safe, removed places. The Gothic
brings them out again, exposes them, and enables readers to explore
contradictions before being returned to security. In modern times,
many horror films in particular use Gothic settings and stories, such
as the British Hammer studio films of the 1960s and after.

Monster

The mention of monsters and the creation of the monster is the
stock-in-trade of myth. The minotaur is half-human, half-bull, con-

demned to live in a labyrinth, fed on youthful victims, adolescents not cursed with his kind of affliction. Medusa is seen as a monstrous woman not merely because of her sexual inclination but more particularly because her snake-haired appearance turns men to stone. Monsters typically are aberrant versions of ourselves, the human gone wrong, something we are terrified of because it is quite close to us. They are horrors who prey upon and emerge from ourselves, and which ultimately must be destroyed so that a kind of normality can continue. To recognise that the monster is within us and projected without us as a construction of our own fantasies, hopes, and fears is an appreciation of elements of the self. Embracing the monster in ourselves and others is popular in some feminist and other radical texts, such as Jeanette Winterson's *Sexing the Cherry*, in which the monster figure of the huge Dogwoman celebrates the figure of a woman whose size does not negate her sexuality or her mothering capacity. Fay Weldon's *The Life and Loves of a She-Devil* explores a similar theme, where the ugly, sidelined housewife Ruth decides to take revenge upon the system that would marginalise her for her domestic and cosmetic defects. She blows up the family home, offloads the children onto the lover of her wayward husband, and gets in league with the devil. This questions the way in which we and society construct and deconstruct what is seen to be monstrous.

The Monstrous-Feminine

Barbara Creed's *The Monstrous-Feminine* (1993) focuses on a range of constructions and representations of woman as monster, femme fatale, and female castratrix. It seems that the stereotypical imagination, as indicated in myth and popular film, constructs a representation of woman as monster in order to identify that terrifying and desirous Other against which to defend itself. In its fear and disgust, the monster female is likely to have a vagina dentata. This represents a castration anxiety. Either visually displayed or more subtly in the figure of a vampire or Medusa figure, she turns men on, and she turns them to stone. Female monsters from the Gorgons and Medea to Scylla and Charybdis haunt myth, and they appear throughout the visual works collected by Bram Dijkstra in the

Victorian and Edwardian periods. They also appear in the figure of Alex in the movie *Fatal Attraction*, and in film noir women are both perpetrators and victims, and are punished for their deviant attractiveness—they are culpable flirts in their beauty and play tempting roles.

Splatter

Splatter horror conjures up scenes of gore, mess, and uncontrollable destruction. Apparently originating with Romero's *Night of the Living Dead*, which used graphic violence and gore, spatter/splatter films are now commonplace and include *The Texas Chainsaw Massacre* and its various sequels. Splatter films do not pretend to restore social and cultural order but prefer manic montages full of 'subject camera . . . cross-cuttings from hunted to hunter, and ominous juxtapositions and contrasts' (Fraser 46). Fragmented narrative (and direction), then, is intrinsic and not only an intellectual response to a splatter text but also an emotional response; the fragmentation itself displaces the viewer in relation to the film and causes a sense of the uncanny (Freud's *unheimlich*) or 'that which make you feel uneasy in the world of your normal experience' (Prawer 11). The most notable contributions to splatter horror are such films as *I Spit on your Grave, Maniac, I Hate Your Guts*, and *Henry: Portrait of a Serial Killer*. They provoke disgust followed by an examination of conscience. They 'force you to reveal your hand . . . and then they cut it off' (Prawer 169).

Uncanny

The German term *unheimlich* informs Freud's 1919 coining of the term the 'uncanny', explored at length in Nicholas Royle's book *The Uncanny* (2003), to suggest not something deeply strange but strangely familiar. By emphasising whatever is more or less taken for granted as rather strange and unfamiliar, the notion of the uncanny aligns itself with defamiliarisation and with ghostliness, disturbance, and disease. Royle and others identify its origins as lying in the Enlightenment, and its manifestations as involving a whole range of experience and situations. One very common one is the related fear of losing genitalia or/and eyesight, expressed in E. T. A. Hoffmann's tale 'The Sandman'. But this fear also suggests threats to body parts, cannibalism, signs of disturbance, and unease at a variety of disabilities or their threats, fits, trances, ecstasy, and the possibility of being turned into an automaton or doll, with human will removed. To have a body that operates without life and choice questions whether something is animate or inanimate. Such moments of anxiety are elements of the uncanny that underlie many horror figures and scenarios.

Vampire

The vampire is an undead creature of myth and legend that is a threat to our sense of definitions and boundaries because of its crossing between life and death. Latterly, in the more radical fictions of the type, it also crosses between male and female. Vampires appear in all cultures, from India and Egypt to Transylvania, Ireland, and Europe. Initially, literary vampires entered mythology and then literature, particularly with the figures of *Varney the Vampire* (Lord Ruthven), 'Carmilla' (Sheridan le Fanu), and most famously *Dracula* by Bram Stoker. Dracula the vampire becomes associated with sexuality and excess that needs to be curtailed for the perpetuation of social order. Vampires in literature have commonly been used as cultural indices. Whatever is feared and perhaps rather desired by humans is transferred in the literary vampire invader of property and body space, particularly the body space of woman. Latterly, in the twentieth century, vampires enjoyed a renaissance with Bela Lugosi's marvelous depiction of Nosferatu, the undead, hideous, humpbacked, claw-handed creature, who visits the young woman in her sleep to drink her blood and is himself vulnerable to the light at sunrise.

The Hammer horror film studios made Dracula and his minions famous with a series of B movies focusing on patriarchal controls on deviant sexuality and vulnerable young visitors to foreign mansions (usually set in Surrey or Sussex). With Anne Rice's *Interview with the Vampire* (1976), the cult figure of the vampire was revived and revisited. Now he or she returns as a variety of dangerous potentially liberating deviant figures, ranging from androgyny and sophisticated cultural pretensions, accompanied by dangerously deviant practice (David Bowie and Catherine Deneuve in *The Hunger*); radical lesbian alternatives (Pat Califia, Nancy Collins, and Poppy Z. Brite); film and TV series and novels that focus on the dangerous destructiveness of the vampire to be hunted down; and his/her vulnerability as a creation of the night, often with a potentially more deserving and amicable side—Buffy the Vampire Slayer's exploits destroying the zombielike vampires around the campus but recognising the fallen in Angel.

Werewolf

Amongst the legions of Others, werewolves represent the beast in humankind, which emerges at the full moon, when those cursed as werewolves change from human, usually man, to beast, usually a wolf. Shape shifters, whose history is seen in the metamorphosis of the ancients into bats, bears, and a number of animals, appear in many early accounts, including those of Native Americans. Of these, werewolves have been configured in popular culture to represent those attacks upon self and others that are products of the expressions and energies of Otherness hidden beneath the conformist social self.

Zombie

Also known as 'The Walking Dead', zombies have a factual basis in the voodoo ceremonies of Haiti. There are documentary accounts of these activities in William B. Seabrook's *The Magic Island* (1929) and Wade Davies's *The Serpent and the Rainbow* (1985). They mostly appear in the cinema, beginning with Bela Lugosi's 'Murder Legendre' orders to the corpses of plantation workers in *White Zombie* (1932), latterly followed by Val Lewtons's *I Walked With a Zombie* (1943), George Romero's *Night of the Living Dead* (1969), *Dawn of the Dead* (1978), and *Day of the Dead* (1985). *Dawn of the Dead* was most recently remade, followed by a spoof, *Shaun of the Dead* (2004). The best collection of zombie stories is Stephen Jones (ed.), *The Mammoth Book of Zombies*, featuring Ramsay Campbell, Clive Barker, H. P. Lovecraft, and others' treatment of the figure.

Zombies disgust and terrify because they are reanimated corpses, emptied out of thought and feeling, bound to do the duty of their masters. Only recently has the zombie figure been used to express a critique of ways in which oppressive or mind-deadening regimes operate with collusive followers to valorise brutality and mindless consumerism, each seen as death-in-life. Hence, shoppers, consumers, and armies have each been seen as comprised of zombies. Religious resurrection does not need to or seem to lead to zombification, as it is reanimation as opposed to soulless emptiness.

Chapter Seven

Horror Criticism and Ways In

> The business of sustained critical analysis of Gothic horror
> could not take place until practitioners and critics took the
> genre seriously and were concerned not to divide the essen-
> tial art of its craft and symbolism. (Bloom in Punter, *A*
> *Companion to the Gothic* 157)

This chapter looks at the views of several theorists—David Punter,
The Literature of Terror (1980); Ken Gelder, *Reading the Vampire*
(1994); Mark Jancovich (1992); Clive Bloom (1993); Clive Barker
(1997) on horror genre development; and Barbara Creed (1994)
and Julia Kristeva, *Powers of Horror* (1982), on women, abjection,
and questioning the gender of horror. In so doing, this chapter
defines ways in which horror interrogates what we take for granted
in our lives and in society, and introduces readers to the idea of
'abjection', getting rid of things that are not our self, destroying or
rejecting these—making them the 'Other'—the disgusting, terrifying stuff of horror. Horror is fantasy exploration, expression, challenge, and a contribution to social, cultural, and political comment.

The horror genre is paradoxical in terms of its relation to theory,
or the relation between society, writer, text, reader, and theory, for
it is at those intersections that horror is constructed and perceived
as engaging at all with any kind of theory. Indeed, one of the main
problems we might have with reading, understanding, and discussing horror is its seemingly relatively untheorised position.

Serious critical study of horror in Britain began with Edith
Birkhead (1921), Eino Railo (1927), and Montague Summers
(1915), who studied vampire fictions. The first major text that
located and defined supernatural horror was H. P. Lovecraft's
Supernatural Horror in Literature (1927). More recently, David

Punter's *The Literature of Terror* (1980) and subsequent books have identified the ways in which horror, as a branch of the engaged literary Gothic, acts in part as a mirror to reflect what societies and individuals desire and fear at any point and place, and in part as cultural critique of the complacencies and real fears of the time. Lovecraft's own definitions separate out the horror of the realistic, the everyday, and horror based in the supernatural. However, horror is still scarcely respectable, despite this theorising and engagement. Even today, a noted African-American woman horror writer, Tananarive Due, can feel worried about being taken seriously:

> I needed to address my fear that I would not be respected if I wrote about the supernatural. (Tananarive Due, interview)

Some of the main strands of horror criticism are those based in psychoanalysis, following Freud and his identification of the uncanny (1919). Others, like that of Martin Barker, identify a political and cultural engagement with the production, reading, and censorship of horror. David Punter (1999) traces it as a flowering of the twentieth/twenty-first-century Gothic. Lovecraft, who differentiates between the realistic and the supernatural, finds the latter more imaginatively sound. In his 1982 study, *Danse Macabre: The Anatomy of Horror*, Stephen King classifies three stages of horror effects in novels. The first conjures up terrors of things suggested by the unseen '[I]t is what the mind sees that makes these stories such quintessential tales of terror' (King 36). The second level is that of 'fear' and the 'horrific', able 'to invite a physical reaction' (27–28), and the third is mere revulsion. King, too, prioritises the psychoanalytically based, the weird rather than the disgusting or realistic, though his own work mixes them. Many writers of horror, including Henry James, Edgar Allan Poe, and Edith Wharton, wrote tales of terror or lingering ghost tales but did not theorise their intentions or effects and seemed somewhat embarrassed when they were pigeonholed in the Gothic horror genre. This is all part of the historical and cultural marginalising of the genre, until the latter part of the twentieth century and the rise of contemporary Gothic horror, particularly through the horror film.

In considering critical approaches to horror, we find that beyond the distinctions and definitions, the discussions about kinds of horror in terms of the genre's Gothic antecedents, the study of horror is flourishing. There are now a large number of horror critics who look specifically at the effects of the films, at Gothic horror, the revival of the ghost story, and at particular kinds of horror, such as suburban horror with its destabilising threat of the ordinary people next door as potential cannibals, rapists, and murderers (*The Amityville Horror, Poltergeist, Halloween*), of those who invade reality from our dreams (*A Nightmare on Elm Street, Candyman*), and of retribution, featuring the devilish, the devil, or human evil (*Angel Heart, Cape Fear, Fatal Attraction*). Some write of horror the way it utilises the same kinds of fantasy strategies found in mythic tales and science fiction —from *Lord of the Rings* to the *Alien* series. There has been horror criticism that is politically focused (Martin Barker) and other types, such as that by Barbara Creed, Carol Clover, and Lisa Tuttle, which focus on horror's abjection of women, representation of women in horror, and, latterly, women writing back. Picking up an entertaining Mammoth, Giant, or Penguin book of horror we now find introductions that identify the development of aspects of the genre (zombies, vampires, werewolves, and so on), the kinds of cultural fears they home in on and debate, as well as a sense of how they might be enjoyable—from psychological thriller to splatter.

A Couple of Thoughts about Horror Readers and Examples

In the 'Estates' office the young woman on the reception counter hands out keys, lends maps, and files things. During her breaks she reads Stephen King avidly, one novel after another. Is she enjoying the severed hands, the strung-out deaths, the oppressive power, the undead? What's going on in her head? Should I be a little worried about getting normal clerical responses from this woman deriving from simple requests and questions? Is her head filled with strange images all the time?

My dissertation student is visiting me for the first time. She has chosen to write on nineteenth-century and twentieth-century literary vampires. She comes in. She is dressed in black. 'Why do you want to do your dissertation on vampire writing?' I ask.

'I love vampires! I think I might be a vampire; my boyfriend certainly thinks I might be a vampire!'

Ah, enthusiasm, but I continue:

'What is it about the nineteenth-century literary vampire that has interested you—what do you think he or she might represent? Is there any kind of message or argument that any of your authors might be using in choosing the figure of the vampire?'

Silence.

No. This is not the level we should be working at. This is enthusiasm, not theorising.

But why should an entertainment genre used to scare young children into obedience to protect them (?), to give us all a spine-tingling *frisson* of disturbance, explosion, catharsis, and a sense of peace—a rush like a ride on Space Mountain at Disney World followed by the sweet sense of safety when you are back on the ground —need to be theorised? Be at all theorised? What has it got to do with anything except entertainment?

In a local Cambridgeshire village, at the height of summer, two ten-year-old girls, friends, are abducted by someone they trust, abused, murdered, their bodies burned and left in a ditch, found covered with maggots only when the farmer opened his sluice gates. Their bodies were discovered by someone walking in the field. They were murdered by the safest of people, the young, friendly, police-advising school caretaker.

Someone sneezes in a lift in Hong Kong. Soon a deadly, seemingly untraceable, incurable, difficult-to-diagnose respiratory disease invades a 'fruit and veg' market. Airports spray travellers and take their temperatures; public areas are deserted; students refuse to sit next to other students. SARS.

And a friendly local family doctor finally commits suicide while serving a life sentence for murdering at least twenty but probably thousands of trusting elderly folk who depended on him—the biggest serial killer of all time is a local GP, Dr Harold Shipman.

These everyday monstrous events have a lot to do with the reader in the Estates office and my dissertation student—but theorists and critics of horror are divided about exactly what. In terms of reader response theory or reception theory, that which looks carefully at the interaction between the intentionality of the author, the written/filmic text, and its engagement with viewers or readers, horror has been the public scapegoat for all ills. The question is crucial. If readers or viewers are untheorised and uncritical, if they merely take the fantasy or near-reality mimicked before them as truth, and not merely as truth but some kind of guidebook or blueprint for action, then the censorship of horror might well be justified. Taking a chainsaw round the suburbs to those you don't like or to casual strangers (*The Texas Chainsaw Massacre*); leading toddlers away to torture them and leave them to die on a railway track (*Child's Play 3*, the James Bulger case); and picking up young men, drugging and forcing them to be sexually submissive, murdering them, chopping up their limbs and eating bits of them while putting the rest in the freezer for later (Jeffrey Dahmer, cannibal films, such as *Wrong Turn*) all ask whether horror films are a terrible mirror to events or an incitement to them. The reception theory (Wolfgang Iser) and the censorship that surrounds horror argues this precise case. It argues a similar case for romance insofar as early second-wave feminists argued that women reading romance believed in it, invested everything in the honeyed scenario of sinking into his arms and finding eternal protection, perfection, and passion. Later feminists (Radway and others), on the other hand, perceived that not all housewives were total mugs; many were capable of choosing fantasy as an imaginative liberation while recognising its difference from the mundane, enjoying romantic plots, acknowledging the need for a licensed, managed escapism, but discovering that the fantasy itself enabled them to put their own lives into some perspective.

Genre fictions are the butt of censorship and intellectual arrogance, but they are also very powerful and amazingly widespread popular mirrors to ourselves, measures of our imaginative lives, projections and versions managed or unmanaged of the beliefs, desires, and fears of the times, places, humankind, and individuals. It is at the juncture of this particular debate about social realities, intention, writing practice, and reading, with the awareness of representation and significance, that critical discussion of horror lies. It is not just copying reality but the use of story, image, event, and character to construct, represent, deal with, offer, suggest, negotiate with, and engage readers in their own imagination and such things as serious, social, and political as their ethics, their sense of social connectedness, and their humanity, that makes horror in particular an influential and ever present genre. It samples from all the others, appears in all the others, and negotiates in a way that westerns really cannot, for instance, a crucial line between entertainment and engaged response, literalness, and the recognition of significance.

Horror is politically and culturally engaged as a representation and a comment on the social and political rootedness and contextualisation of us as people, in shared environments, governed by others. It can have an edge, critiquing the conservative, encouraging the radical, depending on the writer—but it also has its roots in fairy tale, myth, parable, and tales that teach.

Here, the dark fairy tales of the Brothers Grimm are set alongside the political exposition of Martin Barker, who recognised the link between the horror comics trial of the fifties, the crushing collusiveness of McCarthyism, and any kind of antiradical and antipolitically enabling regime. Other roots of horror are in psychology, the mind, and in our imaginations. In this, Freud is the key figure— and the Grimms again—the notion of 'the uncanny' is the chief theoretical instrument. Defamiliarisation of what we take for granted unquestioningly destabilises, disturbs, and enables us to question; prevents dangerous complacencies; enables imaginative escapes from real oppressions; and enables problematising of givens and some distance, some problem-solving strategies. It is a mirror to our desires and fears and a crucible in which the fantastic and the real mix, so we might work out their origins and perhaps address them (not necessarily crushing them, perhaps giving them rein).

As everyday readers, we might not need to engage with any theorising underpinning our reading, but if we are studying a genre then it is important to identify the critical versions and interpretations of it.

Freud and the 'Uncanny'

Freud is not exactly a critic of horror, but his theories do lie behind our understanding of how horror operates and how disturbance operates in us. As such, these theories enable a critical understanding of horror, its intentions, representations, and the ways we read it. Freud is credited with recognising the origins of psychological horror and its basis in the uncanny, in dream. His groundbreaking essay 'The Uncanny' (1919) (the *unheimlich*) identified the particular effects of defamiliarisation, where the familiar becomes strange and the strange more familiar; where whole bodies seem mechanical, sick, uncontrollable; where boundaries between what we take for granted and strange events destabilise our sense of solid reality and communication through language. Freud's essay is possibly the earliest piece of formal theorising that begins to enable us to explore the genre's origins, locations, and effects. 'The Uncanny' exposed horror's strategies for defamiliarising the familiar, threatening us where we feel most secure. It exposes dread, 'that class of the frightening which leads back to what is known of old and long familiar' (Freud 219). Dictionary definitions of *uncanny* suggest the supernatural or inexplicable. Freud goes on to list what might be seen as uncanny:

> We have now only a few remarks to add—for animals, magic and sorcery, the omnipotence of thoughts, man's attitude to death, involuntary retention and the castration complex comprise practically all the factors which turn something frightening into something uncanny. (Freud 365)

People are uncanny if we expect something evil of them. Distinctions between the imagination and reality tend to be erased within the uncanny. These are strategies and expressions of horror. The castration anxiety derives from E. T. A. Hoffman's 'The Sandman' (1916), a terrifying tale of children's eyes being pecked out by the sandman, who then falls in love with Olympia, an automaton. Kaja Silverman (*The Acoustic Mirror* 14) identifies the castration problem. Man fears woman as castrated man, as if woman's lack can somehow harm or transfer to him. Woman seems fearful because there is something unpleasantly familiar about her (*i.e.*, woman). Desiring to debunk this rather negative view of women (and sexuality), Silverman is concerned with 'dislodging woman from the obligatory acting out of absence and lack' (14). Nicholas Royle's *The Uncanny* (2003) traces the origins, critics, and theorists who deal with the uncanny and where we can find it, in everything from ghost stories and tales of being buried alive to déjà vu and doubling, as well as the feminist-critiqued castration anxieties and Othering. Royle identifies many of horror's disturbance strategies that leave us feeling uneasy and questioning.

David Punter—The Gothic and Horror

David Punter's *The Literature of Terror* (1980) made horror criticism respectable. In exploring a historical development of the literature of terror, the Gothic, and how it evolves into horror, Punter combines the psychological and the historical/cultural. Latterly, his movement into the postcolonial Gothic (*Postcolonial Imaginings*, 2000) unites the two differing standards of what is considered 'abject', that is, Otherised and rejected—the stuff of horror—recognising the similarity of gesture of Otherising and rejection in the construction of a 'dark continent' as well as a 'dark side'. Punter's work looks at the dark Gothic of Maturin's 'Memnoth the Wanderer', Baudelaire, Poe, and Angela Carter, among others, and in his work examines what causes terror and how the Gothic differs from its more violent, pathologically informed branch, horror. He focuses on literary texts, both poetry and prose. Reading Punter's work, we can find Gothic horror characteristics in a range of literature, from romantic poems including 'Christabel', 'la belle dame sans merci', to Angela Carter's contemporary domestic horror and rewriting of fairytales

Chris Baldick and Fred Botting are also theorists of the Gothic who incorporate and explore horror as a major feature and development of the Gothic, especially in the twentieth and twenty-first centuries.

Many horror theorists are also horror writers. Lisa Tuttle and Anne Rice are two authors who, like Poppy Z. Brite, among others, theorise about the sources of their own horrors—loss of a child, awareness of gendered space and the threats of this. Stephen King, probably the most popular horror writer, is well aware of the sources of horror in the social, the psychological, and particularly in the mid-America of our minds.

Horror is a branch of the Gothic, more violent and more excessive in its ability to evoke fear and disgust. It utilises and identifies Gothic conventions such as dangerous, split selves, the exposing of the contradictions in convention, and highly physically and mentally threatening scenarios residing in the everyday. Horror lurks most happily in the familiar, in the family home, seemingly safe relationships, the stability of identity and comfort with which we surround ourselves—families (*The Shining*), high school proms, (*Carrie*), teen partying on a lake at the end of summer ('The Raft'), and hospital procedures (the TV series *Kingdom Hospital*). Stephen King spatialises and familiarises horror, comparing its success with intrusion upon the house of the self.

This kind of narrative structure is claimed to have specific ideological effects that poststructuralism offers to analyse. Mark Jancovich's criticism both explores a variety of themes and concerns and identifies the characteristics of horror in terms of its effects on audiences:

> The narrative closure of horror texts is not only claimed to repress and contain elements which are disturbing to the dominant ideological order, but is also supposed to produce specific psychological effects within the audience. It gives the members of the audience a sense of themselves as individuals (or subjectivities) by suppressing psychological conflicts or contradictions which might threaten their sense of themselves as unitary or coherent identities. This process is referred to as 'the positioning of the subject within ideology', and is said to be politically undesirable regardless of the ideology within which the subject is positioned. The reasoning behind this argument is that while we appear to express our own thoughts through the use of language, the very way in which we think is determined by the structures of language. The subject, or the sense of individuality and identity, is merely a product or function of ideology. In positioning the subject within ideology, this sense of identity is made to appear natural and inherent. It makes what is social, constructed and historical appear to be individual and natural. (Jancovich 9)

The form as well as the content of horror can be conservative, challenging, alternative, or radical depending on the writer and reader's engagement with ideology. This politicised interpretation is in alignment with that of Martin Barker.

Political Horror—Martin Barker, *Haunt of Fears*, 1984

In the 1980s, radical philosopher Martin Barker developed ideas about the relationships between horror and politics, censorship, and the Otherising of anything seen to challenge the political status quo. He raised issues of whether and where horror is conservative, or radical, and where this resides—in the intentionality, the expression, or reader reception. Barker explored the interesting phenomenon of the horror comic campaign in which American, imported horror comics—*Tales from the Crypt* and *Haunt of Fears*, to name a couple— were being banned for inciting young people, particularly children, to immoral and evil behaviour. Horror comics were seen as disgusting and directly linked to the encouragement of violence—a replication of the nastiness in real life of threats in the texts. Alongside the moral speakers, the U.K. Communist Party revolted against this American import—horror comics were then seen as American culture spread over everyone and making everyone the same. The political argument that developed, however, was that communist conspirators were trying to turn people against America in banning the comics (Barker 45). In his analysis of horror comic characteristics, Barker scrutinises the strip 'The Orphan', in which an unpleasant girl sets up her mother to take the blame for the murder of her drunken father, of which she is actually guilty, and winks at the readers when the mother and boyfriend are electrocuted. Critics said the comics taught that crime pays, but Barker found them actually much more disturbing than that, and therefore more interesting and culturally necessary: '[H]orror comics are typically not an exercise in degradation but in doubt' (Barker 139). Their meaning is slippery; they can be interpreted and produced differently at different times. This very instability is what worries the moral arbiters and what enables the comics to encourage a healthy dose of question and doubt. Banning the comics, however unpleasant, was effectively preventing a kind of space and opportunity to imaginatively question the seeming security of the status quo and, by facing up to and dramatising what disturbs, to manage responses to it. Barker compares these comics, which open up debate, to war comics, which unquestioningly reinforce the American way of life as normal, with no space for communists or contradiction. This communist vilification was ironic since the British Communist Party had itself turned against horror comics. Barker suggests it should have scrutinised the room for doubt, the space left to debate rather than insist without question.

This early critical work aligns horror with lively, imaginative critique and a very necessary ability to question what is taken for granted and safe. This is a fundamental drive in horror texts, aligning them with the culturally critical Gothic.

Horror is all around us and resides in the everyday familiar. Hitchcock suggests that we should 'put horror back where it belongs, in the family'. Power, oppression, silencing, and repression are the stuff of horror, deriving from our essential fears of being forced, denied, controlled, and displaced out of ourselves into constraining roles and constricting places, unable to resist or refuse:

> Throughout its history, horror has been concerned with forces that threaten individuals, groups, or even 'life as we know it'. It has been concerned with the workings of power and repression in relationship to the body, the personality, or to social life in general. (Jancovich 118)

Horror often threatens or enacts violence. It opens the door to expose that of which we are afraid, the door to a hidden room we would possibly rather ignore. What is hidden and suppressed in what is familiar is most horrifying. Subversive horror is frequently spatialised and quite literally looks beneath the surface, into the cracks, below the floorboards, or up in the attic, and in the corners. Virginia Andrews incarcerates children in an attic (*Flowers in the Attic*, 1979); Caitlin R. Kiernan has spiders creeping up from hell into and out from the cellar (*Silk*, 2002), invading the body and transmuting or entwining it. What results is a projection from the familiar—something bursts or creeps out, something lurking, monstrous, something repressed bodied forth in a demon spirit, ghost, or monster.

Outward projections of split selves and the questioning of seeming social and cultural givens are embodied in horror in ghosts and terrifying events. What can also emerge in horror is an alternative self, the animal beneath the skin, the werewolf or vampire, the lurking death in us all, mummy, or zombie. We might be terrified of that which emerges from the cracks and fissures, from beneath the skin, but equally, what is subversive questions cultural conventions and can offer alternatives. It is in this liminal position that horror works its contradictory magic: it exposes and undercuts, and through these cracks emerge many other readings, other possibilities. It is in the seizing of the radical wealth of other constructions and readings that much contemporary horror and particularly contemporary radical women's horror flourishes. It erodes cultural barriers and differences that position some as excluded to the margins and destroyed, and others centrally positioned and celebrated, which clearly defines that which is clean/unclean, good/bad, black/white, which actually acts critically, as Rosemary Jackson, fantasy critic, indicates:

> Far from constructing this attempt at erosion as a mere embrace of barbarism or chaos, it is possible to discern it as a desire for something excluded from cultural order—more specifically, for all that is in opposition to the capitalist and patriarchal order which has been dominant in Western society over the last two centuries. (Jackson 176)

Confronting that which horrifies and disgusts and recognising ourselves in it is a way of overcoming our fears and owning up to them, admitting to their place in our own lives, as parts of us.

Julia Kristeva, the French Feminists, and Women in Horror

Women in horror tend to be represented as weak victims shrieking in the arms of King Kong, or brutalised and left, raped, for dead, innocent or worthy of the destruction; other times they appear as the bad mother, the wicked stepmother, the deceptive old woman who seems motherly but who instead locks up little children ('Babes in the Wood', *The Blair Witch Project*). Mark Jancovich evaluates the ways in which horror has been seen to denigrate women, as if this were an inevitable element of its formulae.

> [R]ecent forms of post-structural psychoanalytic criticism have claimed that the horror genre degrades and denigrates women. These forms of criticism have attempted to shift

the focus of study from the individual artist or text to the system of signification itself. They stress that *all* cultural activities have rules and codes, whether of language or visual imagery. As a result, they claim that it is not the individual author who should be seen as the source of meaning, but these rules and codes. In fact, they maintain that our sense of ourselves as individuals (or our subjectivity) is a product of these systems of signification: it is not we who speak language but language which speaks us. Though we seem to express our own thoughts through the use of language, the very way in which we think is determined by the structures of language itself. (Jancovich 8)

While much conventional horror represents women as the figures who produce the response of terror and disgust, therefore identifying and punishing the woman and restoring order in which she is put in her place, some more radical women's horror, by refusing the closure and punishment, the restoration of order, insists on this recognition of ourselves as women in the construction of that which has conventionally been seen as Other, as disgusting and rejected, as abject.

French feminists and psychoanalytical philosophers Julia Kristeva, Luce Irigaray, and Hélène Cixous develop their theories post-Lacan and Freud, critiquing the construction and representation of women as figures of abjection and horror. They urge the liberation of energy, and reversals and refusals of conventional representations of women. They explore, explode, and produce the energies of the body and of carnival, indicating subversion and reclamation of varieties of self. This is a full-blown, theorised deconstruction of the bases of conventional horror in terms of the representation of women.

French feminist, ex-colleague of Lacan, psychoanalytic critic Julia Kristeva explores the psychoanalytic turn that leads to the figuring of woman as dangerous and/or victimised, Other, ideal, and/or figure of terror, stereotyped. In her work on horror, Kristeva (1982) defines the abject as those substances that the body needs to reject, make Other, in order for the subject to be able to recognise itself, literally have space for itself. And the first object of rejected abjection is the mother, prefiguring the extradition of women from predominantly male social territory to the borders of the imagination, either idealised or demonised but definitely 'Other', to be restrained or destroyed. Kristeva argues:

> Fear of the archaic mother proves essentially to be a fear of her generative power. It is this power, dreaded, that patrilineal filiation is charged with subduing. (Kristeva 92)

The mother and sexually aware woman are terrifying; and women's bodies are a focus of fear and loathing.

Victor Burgin (1990) expands this arguing, that Otherness produces idealisation, rejection, and marginalisation:

> This peripheral and ambivalent position allocated to woman, says Kristeva, has led to that familiar division of the field of representations in which women are viewed as either saintly or demonic—according to whether they are seen as bringing the darkness, or as keeping it out. (Burgin 116)

Luce Irigaray (1977) has a very different sense of the psychic from that of Kristeva. She argues of the relation between women and what is considered Other, that woman ultimately represents death:

> In this proliferating desire of the same, death will be the only representative of an outside, of a heterogeneity, of an other: women will assume the function of representing death. (Irigaray 27)

Death, it seems, can be rendered a manageable concept if the terrifying female figure, the monstrous Other, is rendered powerless.

Julia Kristeva's Powers of Horror (1982) and Strangers to Ourselves (1988)

Julia Kristeva engages on a feminist and psychoanalytical level with the ways in which horror identifies the human response of abjection, seen by Freud and Lacan as a natural stage of development. While this may be a natural stage in which we identify who we are as distinct from other bodies, other beings, and so wish to reject or eject that Other, when somewhat pathologised and transferred into perceptions and actions that abject others—women, the culturally different, those with disabilities—it becomes an identified source of acts of destruction and repulsion in daily life. Its expression (newspapers, TV) emerges as the narrative, content, and tone of horror, leading to the recognition that women are dangerous and fatal (the femme fatale), so must be controlled and possibly either tamed or destroyed, and that foreigners wish to invade and defile the purity of those settled and indigenous (*Alien*, *The Others*, *Dracula*, tales of plague). Anyone who differs from ourselves (white middle-class Western males?) is dangerous. Kristeva moves on beyond recognising this abjection as Otherising to identifying its reign in our own fears, in ourselves. She indicates psychoanalytic maturity as lying in this recognition, which, once reached, would enable us to avoid the need to Otherise, fear, and destroy.

By recognising the Other and the abject as part of ourselves, and refusing that borderline and opposition, we can, Kristeva argues, overcome the need to find victims, scapegoats, and enemies. Kristeva's *Strangers to Ourselves* (1988) provides a political exploration of the way the West treats foreigners based on an examination of racism in France. Here, she links the need to expose the boundaries, rejections, and repressions of western patriarchal-based horror with the need for equality, both racially and politically:

> Our disturbing otherness . . . is what bursts in to confront the 'demons', or the threat that apprehension generated by the protective apparition of the other at the heart of what we persist in maintaining as a proper, solid 'us'. By recognising *our* uncanny strangeness we shall neither suffer from it nor enjoy it from the outside. The foreigner is within me, hence we are all foreigners. If I am a foreigner, then there are no foreigners. (Kristeva 192)

This aligns itself with David Punter's explorations (2000) of ways in which postcolonial Gothic criticism identifies strategies of horror engaging at the level of abjection in colonial and imperial texts to render colonised, foreign subjects as objects, as Other. Identity construction and representation and psychoanalytically based theories explain the abjection of women and foreigners and their representation as victims or monsters.

This recognition of the Other, the impulse to abject, can be turned to positive effect in more radical horror, perhaps the horror written by those considered abject—women, colonial peoples, anyone who does not fit with a white male middle-class family-oriented conservative conformist 'norm' if that is what horror, as it seems, aims to applaud. Contemporary women's horror and horror produced by postcolonial Others are less likely to replicate the Otherising of the more conventional examples of the genre. In so challenging some of the underlying values, which emerge in the construction and representation of character and event, and most particularly in the reading of the horror and monstrosity of character and event, horror by Others or more radical writers can be both disturbing and enlightening. It can expose its designs upon us as readers and help critique and problematise some of the social, political, personal, psychological, cultural, and mythical givens with which we are familiar and with which our lives might well be governed, albeit often subconsciously. Those givens are the 'mind forged manacles' of everyday cultural myths of which Angela Carter ('Notes from the Front Line' 1984) speaks and which she exposes, troubles, and destroys.

Kristeva's *Strangers to Ourselves* is a key theoretical text in this endeavour, as is David Punter's *Postcolonial Imaginings*. Recognising that the Other is our other half, that we offload fears of invasions, engulfment, monstrosity, and death onto this Other, this monstrous female or colonial construction can liberate. Celebrating our Other is empowering. It can undercut binary oppositions by showing they are twin sides of the same: yoked. For some writers this yoking of opposites is actually enacted through the language, as in Angela Carter and other women Gothic and horror writers. Theirs is often confrontational, oppositional, and carnivalesque contemporary women's horror. In such work, horror provides an entertaining and provocative vehicle for interrogating gender representations and assumptions, as well as other configurations of power.

Barbara Creed

Following Kristeva, Barbara Creed, the film and cultural critic, in *The Monstrous-Feminine* (1993) focuses on myth, film, and image, popularising the psychoanalytic and literary work of Kristeva and the other French feminists. Focusing on Medusa (as does Cixous), Creed identifies that films are filled with female monsters drawn from primeval fears, myths, and nightmares. They include:

> the amoral and primeval mother (*Aliens* 1986); vampire (*The Hunger* 1983); witch (*Carrie* 1976); woman as monstrous womb (*The Brood* 1979); woman as bleeding wound (*Dressed to Kill* 1980); woman's possessed body (*The Exorcist* 1973); the castrating monster (*Psycho* 1960); woman as beautiful but deadly killer (*Basic Instinct* 1992); aged psychopath (*Whatever Happened to Baby Jane?* 1962); the monstrous girl-boy (*Reflection of Fear* 1973); woman and non-human animal (*Cat People* 1942); woman's life in death (*I Spit on Your Grave* 1978). (Creed 1)

We can add many other examples to each of these categories, including the angry monster woman (*Attack of the 50 Foot Woman*, 1958), woman as enraged bug alien or serpent (*Species, The Wasp Woman*), and woman as automaton. Stephen Neale in his book *Genre* (1980) utilises Laura Mulvey's (1975) notion of the male gaze to identify two main focus points for horror, the monster and castration anxieties, where fear of castration is predicated upon woman's lack. Neale notes that:

> In this respect, it could well be maintained that it is woman's sexuality, that renders them desirable—but also threatening to men, who constitute the real problem that the horror cinema exists to explore and which constitutes also and ultimately that which is really monstrous. (Neale 61)

Creed explores Susan Lurie's work 'The construction of the castrated woman in psychoanalysis and cinema', Karen Horney (1967), David J. Hogan in *Dark Romance* (1986), and James B. Twitchell's *Dreadful Pleasures* (1985), looking at female monsters and the interpretation of their origins in castration anxiety as the basis for her exploration of the monstrous feminine in the range of films cited above. Her work provides a very useful exploration of the dark side of patriarchally based anxieties that produce and replicate the films' focus on the castrating sexually dangerous female monster, using an accessible psychoanalytical approach that leads the reader to Kristeva.

Carol Clover's *Men, Women and Chainsaws: Gender in the Horror Film* (1992) identifies some of the same areas as Creed but focuses on a variety of films and produces many new ideas, including the figure in the teen slasher movie of the 'final girl' (Clover 44), who watches her friends turn into corpses and outlives them (Sydney in the *Scream* trilogy). She looks, too, at 'the demonising influence that the city-revenge films have inherited from the western' (Clover 135). Revenge films such as *Deliverance*, *Hunter's Blood*, and *The Hills Have Eyes* feature the losing battle of city dwellers approaching the country, hopeful of expiating their guilt over some loss of contact with nature and their selves. Clover characterises as victims or predators a range of Americans, including rednecks, movie Indians who live in the hills and wear headscarves, and marginalised hippie types, such as those who appear in *I Spit on Your Grave*. Clover's approach is steeped in film studies and her identification often overlaps between horror and westerns, locating related themes and concerns, most often with very different conclusions. Her work on the male gaze resembles that of Creed, but when she turns her attention to female violence revenge movies it deviates and raises the debate of whether the genre is always to be seen as horror or not, depending, Clover argues, on the gender and views of the viewer. In this discussion, *I Spit on Your Grave* and *Thelma and Louise* can be seen by some as terrifying examples of violent women committing crimes, or, alternatively, as revenge duly justified. Theorising blockbusters, Clover laments the loss of low-budget films in Hollywood.

Ken Gelder

Ken Gelder's *Reading the Vampire* (1994) focuses on the figure of the vampire, a favourite late-twentieth-century horror hero/heroine/villain. The vampire as a figure is particularly popular in the kind of revisioning that enables an undercutting of Otherising, or making the different monstrous. Gelder identifies the popularity of the vampire in contemporary horror partly in its use to flout some of the notionally established psychoanalytic readings of human development, security, and identity. The vampire myth undercuts the binary divisions of life/death, male/female, and day/night with which we are most familiar.

> Especially in the vampire myth, the attempt to *negate* cultural order by *reversing* the Oedipal stage constitutes a violent countercultural thrust which then provokes further establishment of repression to defeat, or castrate such a thrust. The centre of the fantastic text tries to break with repression, yet it is inevitably constrained by its surrounding frame. Such contradictions emerge in graphic form in the many Gothic and fantastic episodes which break into nineteenth century novels, erupting into the calm surface and bland face of their realism with disturbing reminders of things excluded and expelled. (Gelder 122)

Gelder discusses how powerful *Dracula* has become through its consumption—reading and viewing, which has led to repetition and reconfiguration, the tale retold in different times and circumstances by writers and more popularly by filmmakers. Of the fascination with the vampire, David Skal notes:

> A completely straightforward academic history would simply not do the subject matter justice: the Dracula legend rudely refuses to observe conventional parameters of discussion and touches upon areas as disparate as Romantic literature and modern marketing research, Victorian sexual mores and the politics of the Hollywood studio system. (Skal 7)

In line with Freud's uncanny, the vampire is both familiar, culturally located, and beyond culture, unfamiliar. This disturbance is a gap with which different readers and writers or filmmakers play to enable the vampire to carry so many interpretations. Gelder brings together a number of critics on the vampire in his discussions of its versions and uses. Critiquing Francis Ford Coppola's *Dracula*, Geoffrey O' Brien notes that:

> The narrative possibility of vampire lore is so intimately familiar that Coppola can get away with casting a commercial blockbuster as a self-consciously postmodernist palimpsest.

He does not so much reinvent the horror movie as reinventory it . . . *Dracula* functions concurrently as a faithful adaptation and a caricatural pastiche, while linking its interests with portentous contemporary tie-ins (AIDS, drug addiction). (O'Brien 63)

Reading the Vampire is the first serious, critical, book-length study of the popular vampire figure. One of its great strengths is its consistent and consistently accessible theorising, as it moves from *Dracula* through to Poppy Z. Brite, a number of popular films, and Anne Rice, in each instance culturally and historically contextualising the texts and introducing theorists and critics whose work can help illuminate our reading. Thus, Gelder's work embodies the ways in which writers in different times and places construct vampires to represent their own culturally, psychoanalytically, personally, and historically inflected disease/unease.

Queer Theory

Horror troubles boundaries and questions, undermines, and sometimes restores what different cultures and societies construct and represent as 'normal', including versions of sexuality, identity, and power. In its consideration of problematising 'normality', queer theory can be most enlightening when we think of the ways in which horror dramatises what is frightening because different in some way, challenges and breaks boundaries, and then, in conservative horror, reinforces and replaces these boundaries, while more radical horror refuses their reconstruction. Queer theory in itself challenges and breaks a whole variety of boundaries. This aligns it with the main intentionality and narrative trajectory and outcomes of much horror. In his *The Monster in the Closet* (1997), H. M. Benshoff explores the alignment between queer theory and the horror genre and the representation and participation of gay men and lesbians in the horror industry.

As Robin Wood has identified, horror can be 'reducible to three variables': normality (as defined chiefly by a heterosexual patriarchal capitalism), the Other (embodied in the figure of the monster), and the relationships between the two. (Benshoff 4)

Racial, ethnic, religious, political, gender, disabled, and sexual monsters can be identified in this critical formulation, and, as such, much horror can be seen as the exploration or embracing of any of these troubling Others into the comfortable world of whatever is considered 'normal'. Benshoff applies queer theory to his discussions of the ways in which horror operates to Otherise expressions of sexuality other than heterosexuality, most usually representing it as a terror, particularly in films. Benshoff's development of the term *queer* is one that goes beyond the identification of that which is different from normative heterosexuality to question the normative and celebrate the different. In this manner, queer theory enables recognition of the liberating energies of breaking boundaries of a variety of kinds—between male and female, gay and straight, life and death, passive and active. Such theorising is aligned with the questioning of polar opposites of a philosophical and social system consisting of binaries, as explored in Hélène Cixous's feminist text 'The Laugh of the Medusa'.

> Queer can be a narrative moment, or a performance or stance which negates the oppressive binaries of the dominant hegemony (what Wood and other critics have identified as the variables of 'normality') both within culture at large, and within texts of horror and fantasy. (Benshoff 4)

Its insistence that issues of race and sex can be addressed, and its political theory, links queer theory with horror. This is particularly the case as horror moves into fantasy forms to explore in a positive way expressions of Otherness, and to question structures of normalcy.

Foucault's recognition (1977) that sexuality is constructed by society through a variety of discourses illuminates this argument. In film, in particular, the very expression of being gay or lesbian helps to construct what it might mean to be heterosexual, by opposition. So a marvelously transgressive act in film or literary text would be to side with the gay or lesbian point of view and to recognise that while society seems to have to construct its own homosexual monsters (among others), queer theory, by its psychoanalytic and social critique, can expose it as just that, a chosen construction. Through this exposure can be seen the potential or alternative representations, constructions, and readings that refuse to demonise the homosexual.

Paulina Palmer focuses on horror in terms of its lesbian, Gothic traces and antecedents, considering the constructions of lesbians as Other and figures of horror. In particular, she considers the construction of lesbian vampires as outsiders. This feature, she argues, is relevant in conventional texts, popular fictions deriving from patriarchal outlooks and forms, but is radically challenged and reconfigured in the lesbian vampire tales of many contemporary women. Relying on the critical work of Sue Ellen Case's homage to the lesbian and queer as vampire, 'Tracking the Vampire', Palmer identifies the critical turn that leads to celebration rather than denigration. The lesbian vampire 'revels in the discourse of the loathsome, the outcast, the idiomatically-proscribed position of same-sex desire', 'attacks the dominant notion of the natural', 'is the taboo-breaker, the monstrous, the uncanny', and 'dwells underground, below the operatic overtones of the dominant; frightening to look at, desiring, as it plays its own organ, producing its own music' (Case 3).

Palmer identifies Case's reconfiguration of desire, and of the cultural questioning of lesbians, identifying their outcast position as one similar to that of vampires and noting how radical contemporary feminist writers frequently celebrate the nurturing and enabling qualities of lesbian communities through representing them as communities of outsiders, most popularly as vampires (however Melanie Tem's short satire *Wilding* [1992] depicts a non-nurturing lesbian family as werewolves). Palmer argues that:

> By reclaiming perversity and monstrosity as rightfully hers, Case's lesbian/queer (as) vampire re-presents and subverts the frameworks from which her invention as monster initially originated. She demands to know how the queer can appear 'when the visible is not in the domain of the queer, when the apparatus of representation still belongs to the un-queer' (9), and she simultaneously questions the politics of establishing reductive binary distinctions between the visible and the invisible, the queer and the un-queer.

Her ambiguity, her hybridity, and her multiple border crossings predicate modes of representation and interpretation which can locate the lesbian/queer (as) vampire. (Palmer 102)

Palmer's main example is that of Jewelle Gomez's *The Gilda Stories*:

A tale of 'loneliness, love, families, and heroism' (Gomez, 'Lye Throwers and Lovely Renegades', 109). A complex portrait of a sympathetic black lesbian vampire's journey through a variety of African American female identities across time, 'perpetually seeking that sense of family, something she could commit to' (Gomez 'Transubstantiation' 74). (Palmer 102)

Palmer sees *The Gilda Stories* as:

An imaginative leap intended to 'recast the mythology', to take us beyond our limited and limiting fictions of the vampire as white, European, aristocratic, and male, as exploitative, violent, unsympathetic, and horrifying. A tale of horror, indeed; yet one that challenges traditional presumptions about the nature of horror. (Palmer 102)

The powerful turn that *The Gilda Stories* manages is to enable readers to shudder not at the female vampires in their brothel in the southern states of America but at the plantation owners who brutalise African-American women, and the comfortable white males who use, discard, and destroy them. The tale invites readers to reject the constructed notion of the Other that figures women and black women as loathsome (or desirable), projecting onto them inner terrors. Benshoff, Palmer, Richard Dyer, and Case utilise queer theory first to expose the alignment between conventional horror and homophobia, then to realise the radical potential of horror in its troubling of a variety of boundaries, to centre stage the gay and lesbian as politicised, radical, and celebratory.

Horror and Criticism: Theorising Sexuality

Issues engaged in by feminist critics and queer theorists are also related to questions of politics, culture, and sexual politics more generally. Perhaps it has been in the exploration of sexual politics and its expression in the horror genre that some of the most highly theorised critical response to the genre has been developed. Let us take this as a significant example of the ways in which theorising the popular cultural genre of horror enables a critically enlightened and responsive intersection between genre fictions and culture, gender, power, identity, politics, language, and forms of expression.

For many poststructural critics, horror is founded upon a patriarchal fear of female sexuality. They claim that it is female sexuality that is ultimately defined as monstrous, disturbing, and in need of repression. However, they arrive at this conclusion from a variety of often conflicting claims. According to critics such as Barbara Creed and Clare Hanson, the horror genre presents women (and particularly mothers) as monstrous, all-devouring figures who threaten men. Steven Neale, on the other hand, claims that most monsters are male, not female, going on to argue that women are their primary victims.

> For some critics, the pleasure of horror is based on a male desire to see sexually active women contained. Women are punished by the male monster for sexual activity and only saved by the male hero if they are willing to subjugate themselves to his patriarchal authority. Not only do these critics claim that horror is patriarchal in its ideology, they also claim that it is 'primarily, produced and consumed by men.' (Jancovich 9–10)

> [D]istinctions between the genders produce different psychological anxieties and problems, and by addressing specific anxieties and problems, specific genres are supposed to appeal to specific genders. For [Clare] Hanson, horror is supposed to address male anxieties. It repeats the 'repression of the maternal semiotic and of the desire for the mother' which is performed by males within the Oedipus complex, and is necessary for their construction as masculine subjects or identities. For this reason, she argues that horror is 'a kind of obverse of the romance'. (Jancovich 10)

The importance of this form of criticism is, at least in part, that it attempts to take cultural forms such as horror seriously rather than simply dismissing them, as had been the tendency in earlier or highbrow criticism. However, there are problems with poststructural psychoanalysis. Some of this resides in the definitions of the form and content, as well as the subject matter, of horror, since many critics still view popular fictions as reproducing dominant ideologies unquestioningly. Genres such as horror may not be fixed structures, but they are still defined as 'systems of structuration' (Jancovich 11). With academic literary critics such as David Punter, more popular film-oriented critics, psychoanalytical and feminist theorists, and writers who are also explainers of their own work, such as Stephen King, we now have a range of critical views on what has been dismissed as merely entertaining and low-budget dross: the horror film and text. Together, this variety of critics enables an exploration and expression of horror as both entertaining *and* an index of versions and representations of the dominant anxieties, diseases, and potential alternative versions growing from the location —cultural, gendered, and historical position—of the writing and its reception.

Chapter Eight

Key Questions

The key questions related to our reading of horror, whether in text or film, popular culture or embedded in high art, tend to home in on a range of crucial issues centering around its entertainment and/or educative, engaged intentions and achievements, which link, of course, to how we read horror as well as how it is written.

Is horror entertainment? Is it voyeuristic, pornographic, unpleasant, disgusting, a reveling in the deliberately nasty for its own sake? Or is it, as well as being entertainment, something that enables social comment and critique? Does it, in fact, have a culturally engaged, socially and ethically useful, even an educative, role in the continuum of horror writing from pulp vampire magazines and video nasties to the provocative use of horror by, for example, the Romantic poets (Keats, Coleridge) and contemporary, culturally engaged, postmodern, complex writers such as Angela Carter and Tananarive Due? What is the relation of horror to our imagination and the popular imaginary? to our own psychology as humans? to society and belief, behaviour, values, actions, conformity, and rebellion, complacency, and radical awareness? Horror enables spotlights to be cast upon all of these issues. Its balancing of entertainment and education, problematising and reinforcement, certainty and uncertainty, feeds into the ways in which such essentially human and social concerns, everyday realities, and deep-seated questioning of beliefs can be positioned and recognised as continual rather than polar opposites.

In developing from its roots, the literary Gothic, horror can be seen to be socially and culturally engaged, and engaged also with fundamental questions of what it means to be human; what is reality, identity, continuity of self; what really matters. It does not provide answers except perhaps in the more conventional formula of the blockbuster movie. *The Day After Tomorrow* unleashes a horror scenario of global warming, the end to civilisation as we know it, a drowned and frozen New York, only to valorise comradeship, integrity, entrepreneurial activity, and family and friendship values in action, returning much of the world (less a few million drowned people) to order, with some lessons learned about tampering with nature (not good) and investing in the value system of family and friends (good). It fundamentally asks us to question what we take for granted and to problematise what seems safe and familiar. In so doing, it destabilises complacent conformities and investments in all those safe bets:

- Identity, family relationships
- Reality, time, and space
- Law and order
- Empire, clinical power
- Gender and case in relation to hierarchies
- Political rights and writing and any kind of constriction, representation, or insistence upon any set reading and rules related to any of these categories: identity, family relationships, reality, time, space, solidity, logic, law, and order

In postmodern times, the destabilisation of many of these ostensible givens is almost commonplace, particularly if we align postmodernism with feminist and postfeminist critique, such as one finds in the writing of Kristeva and Cixous. Many of the destabilising elements actually have their originals in an earlier, complacent era—the Victorian period, when Poe, Stevenson, Wilkie Collins, Braddon, Stoker, and Shelley were writing. But the parallel sense of investment in the status quo that gave Victorians their complacent sense of reality, bolstered up by explicable science, respectability, and certain social certainties based on class, family, and identity, are as questioned today in a variety of locations. One of the horror writers I have enjoyed is Singaporean Catherine Lim, whose supernatural, ghostly tales spring from her mixing of traditional Chinese mythologising, a spiritual subtext and layer companion to everything taken as real, and the necessity of critiquing the complacent climate of conformity and complicity that characterises the firm grip of the government on Singapore's millions. Postcolonial Gothic horror is a branch of the genre that enables a fundamental under-cutting of the kinds of certainties that led to empire building and maintenance, imposition of religion and mores and customs by one country on another in the name of Enlightenment, and at the costs of difference and energy. Readers and writers might be terrified at the destabilisation and questioning, liberation, or several points in between.

Abjection, Otherising

These lie at the heart of horror. A key question is that of identifica-tion of self and Other and the seeming necessity to construct hier-archies, exclusions, and acceptances around this Otherising. Kristeva's theorising is central to understanding this area.

The Uncanny and Defamiliarisation

What is familiar and what is unfamiliar or defamiliarised? How can horror operate to defamiliarise? Is this a positive, constructive set of questions that leads to the problematising of given complacent thoughts? Does it provide entertaining *frissons* of unease? Does defamiliarisation work to destabilise us and, if so, to what ends?

Reception and Reader Response

Does reading, writing, and viewing horror lead to a need, desire, and inevitability of enacting it, having proved yourself unable to distin-guish fantasy and dramatisation from an action in the real world?

Is it harmful? What is the role of reader response and reception theory here?

Much research and work has been done on the role of 'video nas-ties' in encouraging copycat violence. This branch of horror has come in for particular criticism in the U.K. since the death of little James Bulger, drawn away from his mother in a Liverpool shopping centre and tortured to death by two young boys only a few years older than him, who claimed they were influenced by the film *Child's Play*. One key question in horror has been whether its blurring of boundaries between the imaginary and the real (whatever that might be) encourages those without a clear sense of right and wrong or the value of the preservation of life to feel they can play with others less powerful than themselves and that there will be no harm done (in cartoons such as 'Roadrunner' or 'Bugs Bunny' the victim reinflates and carries on). Also, does horror totally remove any social sense of right and wrong and the value of life? Does horror then legitimise, even valorise, acts of violence? Does its contingency with fantasy remove the sense that there will be real punishment and deadly results from actions seemingly safe, wrapped up in the deadly but playful space of a horror movie? Does it actually encourage, through modeling, monstrous behaviour? These are powerful reader-response theory-influenced questions and answers that are relevant to our reading of, for instance, Swift's 'A Modest Proposal', whose horror features include the suggestion that the problem of starvation can be overcome through devouring children (a metaphor, a satirical shot at British, deliberate ignorance and culpability—taking literately the ways in which political and cultural behaviours were leading), as they are in contemporary blockbusters such as *Armageddon*, which warns of ignoring seemingly distant comet activity at our peril, or films buying into documentary realism, such as that in *Ted Bundy*, which reminds us that the real killer is the friendly bloke next door, part of our everyday world. Is the fantasy element a release of seemingly safe, legitimated, horrific actions? Can the frame of the film and text suggest that anything is possible, but all will be well in the end? Socially, this is both a possible release—face up to the worst and you might be able to decide on ways of imagining how you could avoid it or deal with it—or it acts as a model for inhumane, monstrous behaviour.

Although reading horror enables us to face up to the worst, perhaps it provides dangerously elusive safe answers, reinforcing a status quo that has in no way provided us with the imaginative skills to work with and avoid what could go wrong (invaded by a fire-breathing beast released from beneath the ground, or the terrible behaviours of our ancestors emerging as vengeful ghosts from beneath suburban homes, as in *Poltergeist* and *The Amityville Horror*).

What Is the Effect of Cultural Context? How Does Postcolonial Horror, African-American, and Afro-Caribbean Horror Differ from Others and Why?

Different contexts for horror produce different styles and focal points—different cultures and genders might well find terrifying and disgusting different locations and events, characterisations and emphasis. In postcolonial horror, for example, the historical legacy of colonial and imperial oppression of slavery, disempowerment, and loss of identity can be figured as ghosted horrors that can recur to be expressed and exorcised. In Toni Morrison's *Beloved*, the returned baby ghost is the lived presence of the guilty and destructive memory of slavery, a memory that horrifies, terrifies, and lingers with those who have experienced it, who have been part of it, or who might be victims or perpetrators of it. The exorcism of the ghost and the latent guilt and silencing enabled a movement forward into a shared world of freer speech and self-awareness, and thus, in this context, horror enables the facing up to the unimaginably dreadful history and tackling of its legacy, and moving on. This is an exorcism and is an act of identification and growth.

How Does Women's or Feminist Horror Differ and Why?

In horror produced by women, black and white, we find the depiction and enactment of scenarios, contexts, and events that terrify and disgust women in particular. Lisa Tuttle points out that 'territory which to a man is neutral is for women mined with fear' (1990), so certain urban spaces—the dark parking garage, the blind alley—represent untold horrors for women because of the history and everyday reality of their attack and disempowerment in such spaces. Definitions or lack of them terrify and disgust women; if you have a history of being denied a separate identity and naming, then the possibility that horror can reenact this is very real. While women have, in horror, to learn to face up to their fears of being raped and disempowered, and of having their identity and individuality removed, so, too, as they work their way through horror, they learn to develop radical forms of writing that focus on overturning conventional closures and reward strength and individualism.

What are the lines and differences between horror and pornography, the erotic horror and the sadistic, masochistic, pornographic, slasher/splatter movies and snuff movies? How can horror be said to be political? What role then has *Tales from the Crypt* to play?

Chapter Nine

Bibliography and Further Reading

Works Cited

Andrews, V. C., *Flowers in the Attic* (New York: Pocket Books, 1979).

Antti, Näyhä, 'Touched by the Hand of Goth: Classics of Gothic Horror Cinema', www.student.oulu.fil~sairwas/frameX/horror, accessed 4 October 2001.

Arnzen, Michael, 'Diving In', in *100 Jolts: Shockingly Short Stories* (Hyattsville, MD: Raw Dog Screaming Press, 2004).

———, 'Gardener', in *100 Jolts: Shockingly Short Stories* (Hyattsville, MD: Raw Dog Screaming Press, 2004).

———, 'How to Grow a Man-Eating Plant', in *100 Jolts: Shockingly Short Stories* (Hyattsville, MD: Raw Dog Screaming Press, 2004).

———, 'Introduction: Minimalist Horror', in *100 Jolts: Shockingly Short Stories* (Hyattsville, MD: Raw Dog Screaming Press, 2004).

Atwood, Margaret, *The Robber Bride* (Toronto: McClelland and Stewart, 1993).

Austen, Jane, *Northanger Abbey* (New York: Modern Library, 2002 [1798]).

Baldick, Chris, *The Oxford Book of Gothic Tales* (Oxford: Oxford University Press, 1993).

Baring-Gould, Sabine, *The Book of Werewolves* (Guernsey: Studio Editions, 1995 [1865]).

Barker, Clive, *The Books of Blood*, Vol. 3: 'Son of Celluloid'; 'Rawhead Rex'; 'Confessions of a (Pornographer's) Shroud'; 'Scapegoats'; 'Human Remains', www.clivebarker.dial.pipex.com/blood barker.html, accessed 2004.

———, *Clive Barker's A–Z of Horror*, compiled by Stephen Jones (New York: HarperCollins, 1997).

———, 'Clive Barker's Shadows in Eden', 25 February 1987, UCLA talk.

———, *The Hellbound Heart* (New York: HarperTorch, 1991).

———, 'The Horror!' www.clivebarker.dial.pipex.com/ bloodbarker.html.

———, 'Night Visions 3', www.clivebarker.dial.pipex.com/ hellboundhbarker.html, accessed 10 January 2004.

———, 'The Tragical History of Dr. Faustus' [1988], from 'Horror: 100 Best Books', www.clivebarker.dial.pipex.com/ hellboundhbarker.html, accessed 10 January 2004.

Barnes, Djuna, *Nightwood* (London: Faber and Faber, 1979).

Benchley, Peter, *Jaws* (New York: Doubleday, 1974).

Benjamin, Jessica, *The Bonds of Love* (New York: Pantheon Books, 1988).

Benshoff, H. M., *Monsters in the Closet: Homosexuality and the Horror Film* (Manchester: Manchester University Press, 1997).

Bettelheim, Bruno, *The Uses of Enchantment* (London: Penguin Books, 1978).

Bierce, Ambrose, *The Ambrose Bierce Satanic Reader: Selections from the Invective Journalism of the Great Satirist*, Ernest Jerome Hopkins, ed. (Garden City, NJ: Doubleday 1968).

———, *Black Beetles in Amber* [1892] (Temecula, CA: Reprint Services Corp, 1989).

———, 'The Boarded Window', in *The Complete Short Stories of Ambrose Bierce*, Ernest Jerome Hopkins, ed. (Lincoln, NE: University of Nebraska Press, 1985).

———, *The Complete Short Stories of Ambrose Bierce*, Ernest Jerome Hopkins, ed. (Lincoln, NE: University of Nebraska Press, 1985).

———, 'The Death of Halpin Frayser', in *The Complete Short Stories of Ambrose Bierce*, Ernest Jerome Hopkins, ed. (Lincoln, NE: University of Nebraska Press, 1985).

———, *The Fiend's Delight (The Principle Works of Ambrose Gwinette Bierce)* [1872] (Temecula, CA: Reprint Services Corp, 1989).

———, *Ghost and Horror Stories of Ambrose Bierce* (New York: Dover, 1964).

———, *The Letters of Ambrose Bierce*, Bertha Clark Pope, ed. (New York: Gordian Press, 1967).

———, *An Occurrence at Owl Creek Bridge* (Harmondsworth: Penguin Books, 1995).

———, 'One Kind of Officer', in *The Complete Short Stories of Ambrose Bierce*, Ernest Jerome Hopkins, ed. (Lincoln, NE: University of Nebraska Press, 1985).

———, 'A Psychological Shipwreck' [1870], in *The Complete Short Stories* (New York: Ballantine Books, 1971).

———, 'The Secret of Macarger's Gulch', in *The Complete Short Stories of Ambrose Bierce*, Ernest Jerome Hopkins, ed. (Lincoln, NE: University of Nebraska Press, 1985).

———, *Tales of Soldiers and Civilians and Other Stories* (Harmondsworth: Penguin Books, 2000).

———, 'A Wireless Message' [1870], in *The Complete Short Stories* (New York: Ballantine Books, 1971).

Birkhead, Edith, *The Tale of Terror: A Study of the Gothic Romance* (London: Constable & Co. Ltd., 1921).

———, *The Tale of Terror: A Study of the Gothic Romance* [1921] (New York: Russell and Russell, 1963).

Bleiler, E. F., ed., 'Introduction to the Dover Edition', in H. P. Lovecraft, *Supernatural Horror in Literature* (Mineola, NY: Dover Publications, 1973).

Bloom, Clive, *Creepers: British Horror and Fantasy in the Twentieth Century* (London: Pluto Press, 1993).

Borchardt, Alice, *Night of the Wolf* (New York: Ballantine, 1999).

Botting, Fred, *The Gothic* (London: Routledge, 1995).

Braddon, Mary Elizabeth, *Good Lady Ducayne* (London: *The Strand Magazine*, 1896).

Briggs, Julia, *Night Visitors: The Rise and Fall of the English Ghost Story* (London: Faber and Faber, 1977).

Brite, Poppy Z., *Courtney Love: The Real Story* (London: Orion, 1998).

———, *Drawing Blood* (originally called *Birdland*) (New York: Delacorte Press, 1993).

———, *Exquisite Corpse* (London: Orion, 1996).

———, *The Lazarus Heart* (*The Crow*) (New York: HarperCollins, 1998).

———, *Love in Vein* (New York: HarperCollins, 1995).

———, *Plastic Jesus* (Burton, MI: Subterranean, 2000).

———, *Seed of Lost Souls* (Burton, MI: Subterranean, 1999).

———, *Self-Made Man* (formally published as *Are You Loathsome Tonight?*) (London: Orion, 1999).

———, *Swamp Foetus* (Harmondsworth: Penguin Books, 1981).

———, *Wormwood* (formally published as *Swamp Foetus*, 1994) (New York: Bantam Doubleday Dell Publishing Group, 1996).

Brodber, Erna, *Myal* (London: New Beacon Books, 1988).

Bronte, Charlotte, *Jane Eyre* (Harmondsworth: Penguin Popular Classics, 2003 [1846]).

Bronte, Emily, *Wuthering Heights* (London: Penguin Books, 2003 [1847]).

Burgess, Anthony, *A Clockwork Orange* (Portsmouth, NH: Heinemann, 1962).

Burgin, Victor, 'Geometry and Abjection', in *Abjection, Melancholia and Love: The Work of Julia Kristeva*, John Fletcher and Andrew Benjamin, eds. (London and New York: Routledge, 1990).

Burns, Robert, *Tam O'Shanter*, Joseph Shearer, ed. (Ayrshire: Alloway Publishing, 1992).

Caine, Darryle, 'The Inheritance' and 'Predators', in *Screams*, Madeleine Kinhill, ed. (Queensland: AMS Ironbark publication, for Wild Child, 1996).

———, 'The Trouble with Organs', in *Scream Again*, Madeleine Kinhill, ed. (Queensland: AMS Ironbark publication, for Wild Child, 1997).

Califia, Pat, 'The Vampire', in *Daughters of Darkness: Lesbian Vampire Stories*, Pam Keesey, ed. (San Francisco: Cleis Press, 1993).

Carroll, Lewis, *Through the Looking Glass* (London: Macmillan, 1872).

Carter, Angela, *Burning Your Boats: The Collected Short Stories* (London: Chatto and Windus, 1995).

———, 'The Fall River Axe Murders', in *Black Venus* (London: Picador, 1986).

———, 'The Lady of the House of Love' [screenplay of short story], in *The Bloody Chamber and Other Stories* (London: Gollancz, 1979).

———, 'Notes from the Front Line', in *On Gender and Writing*, Michelle Roberts, ed. (Ontario: Pandora, 1984).

———, 'Vampirella', in *Come Unto These Yellow Sands* (London: Bloodaxe Books, 1985) (first published as a play for *Radio 3*).

Case, Sue-Ellen, 'Tracking the Vampire', in *Writing on the Body: Female Embodiment and Feminist Theory*, Katie Conboy, ed. (Columbia University Press, 1997).

Cixous, Hélène, 'The Laugh of the Medusa' [1975], in *The Signs Reader: Women, Gender, and Scholarship*, Elizabeth Abel and Emily K. Abel, eds. (Chicago: University of Chicago Press, 1976).

Clareson, Thomas D. and Alice S. Clareson, 'The Neglected Fiction of John Wyndham: 'Consider Her Ways', Trouble with Lichen and Web', in *Science Fiction Roots and Branches*, R. Garnett and F. J. Ellis, eds. (London: Macmillan, 1990).

Clover, Carol J., *Men, Women and Chainsaws: Gender in the Modern Horror Film* (London: British Film Institute, 1992).

Clute, John, *The Encyclopaedia of Science Fiction*, John Clute and Peter Nicholls, eds. (New York: St. Martin's Press, 1993).

Coetzee, J. M., *Age of Iron* (London: Penguin Books, 1998).

Coleridge, Samuel Taylor, 'Ancient Mariner' and 'Christabel' [1819], in *Samuel Taylor Coleridge: The Major Works*, H. J. Jackson, ed. (Oxford: Oxford University Press, 2000).

Collins, Wilkie, *The Woman in White* (Oxford: Oxford University Press, 1996 [1860]).

Cook, Judith, *Daphne, a Portrait of Daphne du Maurier* (London: Corgi, 1991).

Corliss, Richard, 'King of Creep in Hollywood: The world's top spooky storyteller gets all the credit—and no respect', *Time* 139: 17 (27 April 1992), p. 62.

Creed, Barbara, *The Monstrous Feminine: Film, Feminism, Psychoanalysis* (London: Routledge, 1993).

Dahl, Roald, Interviewed in *Twilight Zone*, January/February 1983.

Daniels, Les, *Living in Fear: A History of Horror in the Mass Media* (Philadelphia: Da Capo Press, 1983).

Darrach, B., 'Stephen King (20 Who Defined the Decade)', *People Weekly* 32, (Fall 1989), p. 90.

Davis, Wade, *The Serpent and the Rainbow* (New York: Simon and Schuster, 1986).

de Beauvoir, Simone, *The Second Sex* (New York: Vintage Books, 1989 [1949]).

Dell, Shawn, 'Daria Dangerous', in *Dark Angels*, Pam Keesey, ed. (San Francisco: Cleis Press, 1995).

Derrida, Jacques, *The Spectres of Marx* (Paris: Editions Galilée, 1993).

Dickens, Charles, *Hard Times* (London: Bradbury & Evans, 1854).

Dijkstra, Bram, *The Idols of Perversity: Fantasies of Feminine Evil in Fin de Siecle Culture* (Oxford: Oxford University Press, 1986).

Donald, J., 'What's at Stake in Vampire Films?', *in Sentimental Education: Schooling, Popular Culture and the Regulation of Liberty* (London: Verso, 1992).

Donawerth, Jane, *Frankenstein's Daughters* (Syracuse, NY: Syracuse University Press: 1997).

Due, Tananarive, Interview, 17 March 2002, www.tananarivedue.com/interview.htm.

du Maurier, Daphne, letter to Maureen Baker-Minton, 4 July 1957.

Dyer, Richard, 'Children of the Night: Vampirism as Homosexuality, Homosexuality as Vampirism', *in Sweet Dreams: Sexuality, Gender and Popular Fiction*, Susannah Radstone, ed. (London: Lawrence and Wishart, 1988).

Eliot, George, *The Lifted Veil: Brother Jacob* (Oxford: Oxford University Press, 1999 [1859]).

Evans, Mari, ed., *Black Women Writers* (London: Pluto, 1984).

Fein, E. B., 'Book Notes: King on Horror', *The New York Times* (18 November 1992) on the Web, www.nytimes.com/books/97/03/09/lifetimes/kin-v-booknotes.html.

Finney, Jack, *Invasion of the Body Snatchers* (New York: Warner Books, 1954).

Forrest, Katherine, 'O Captain, My Captain', in *Daughters of Darkness: Lesbian Vampire Stories*, Pam Keesey, ed. (San Francisco: Cleis Press, 1993).

Forster, Margaret, *Daphne du Maurier* (London: Chatto and Windus, 1993).

Fowler, Karen Joy, 'The Night Wolf', in *Skin of the Soul*, Lisa Tuttle, ed. (London: Women's Press, 1990).

Freud, Sigmund, 'From the History of an Infantile Neurosis' (The Wolfman) in *Three Case Histories*, [1918], New York: Touchstone, 1996.

———, 'The Uncanny' [1919], in *The Standard Edition of the Complete Psychological Works of Sigmund Freud*, Vol. XVII, James Strachey, ed. and trans. (London: Hogarth, 1953).

———, 'The Uncanny', 273, Vol. XIV (London: Penguin, 1919).

Friend, B., 'Virgin Territory: The Bonds and Boundaries of Women in Science Fiction', in *Many Futures, Many Worlds: Theme and Form in Science Fiction*, Thomas D. Clareson, ed. (Kent, OH: Kent State University Press, 1977).

Gelder, Ken, *Reading the Vampire* (London: Routledge, 1994).

Gerard, Morgan, 'Clive Barker: The Horror!', in *Graffiti* 4:1 (January 1988) www.clivebarker.dial.pipex.com/bloodbarker.html.

Godwin, William, *Caleb Williams* (London: B. Crosby, 1794).

Gomez, Jewelle, 'Lye Throwers and Lovely Renegades', in *Forty-Three Septembers: Essays* (Ithaca, NY: Firebrand Books, 1993).

———, 'Transubstantiation', in *Forty-Three Septembers: Essays* (Ithaca, NY: Firebrand Books, 1993).

Goring, Ann, 'Hantu Hantu', in *Skin of the Soul*, Lisa Tuttle, ed. (London: Women's Press Ltd., 1990).

Gottlieb, Sherry, *Love Bite* (New York: Warner Books, 1994).

Grimm, Jacob and Wilhelm Grimm, 'Hansel and Gretel', in *The Complete Fairy Tales of the Brothers Grimm* (New York: Bantam, 1992).

———, 'Little Red Riding Hood', in *The Complete Fairy Tales of the Brothers Grimm* (New York: Bantam, 1992).

Groome, Tim, 'Quatermass and the Pit: A Theatre Experience', first published in *The Last Hurrah*, number 2, September 1997. Retrieved from www.outlanders.fsnet.co.uk/tlh0208.htm.

Gullette, Alan, 'Edgar A. Poe: In the Valley of the Shadow', www.creative.net/~alang/lit/horror/poebio.htm, accessed 14 October 2004.

Harris, Wilson, 'History, Fable and Myth in the Caribbean and the Guianas' (Edgar Mittelholzer Memorial Lectures) (Georgetown, Guyana: National History and Arts Council, 1970; rev. and updated ed. Wellesley, MA: Calaloux, 1995).

Heller, E. Lee, 'Frankenstein and the Cultural Uses of Gothic: A Cultural Perspective on Frankenstein, What is Cultural Criticism?' retrieved from www.usask.ca/english/frank/heller.htm, 2004.

Heller, Joseph, *Catch-22* (New York: Simon and Schuster, 1996 [1955]).

Hiroaki, Hamasaki, 'Junk, Shiryan gar: Let's Enjoy Shooting the Zombies', www.fjmovie.com/horror/column/001.html.

———, 'Splatter Japan', www.fjmovie.com/horror/column/001.html.

Hoffman, E. T. A., 'The Sandman', in *Weird Tales of E. T. A. Hoffmann* [1885, 2 vols.] (New York: Scribner, 1963).

Hogan, D. J., *Dark Romance: Sexuality in the Horror Film* (Jefferson, NC: MacFarland and Company, 1986).

Hogg, James, *Confessions of a Justified Sinner* (London: Panther, 1970).

———, *Kilmeny. The Oxford Book of English Verse: 1250–1900*, Arthur Quiller-Couch, ed. (Oxford, Oxford University Press, 1919).

Holland-Toll, Linda, *As American as Mom, Baseball and Apple Pie: Constructing Community in Contemporary American Horror Fiction* (Bowling Green, OH: Bowling Green State University Popular Press, 2001).

Hope Hodgson, William, 'A Tropical Horror' [1905], in *The Grand Magazine Masters of Terror*, Vol. 1 (London: Corgi Books, 1977).

———, 'The Voice in the Night' [1907], in *Masters of Terror*, Vol. 1 (London: Corgi Books, 1977).

Horney, Karen, *Feminine Psychology*, Harold Kelman, ed. (New York: W. W. Norton, 1967).

Hughes, W., 'James, Montague Rhodes (1862–1936)', *The Handbook to Gothic Literature*, M. Mulvey-Roberts, ed., (Basingstoke: Macmillan, 1998), 143–144.

Hugo, Victor, *The Hunchback of Notre Dame* (New York: Modern Library, 2002 [1831]).

Ibsen, Henrik, *Ghosts* (Copenhagen: Gyldendalske Boghandels Forlag, 1881).

Irigaray, Luce, *Speculum of the Other Woman*, C. Gill, trans. (Ithaca, NY: Cornell University Press, 1985).

———, *This Sex Which Is Not One* [1977] (New York: Cornell University Press, 1985).

Jackson, Rosemary, *Fantasy: The Literature of Subversion* (London: Routledge, 1981).

James, M. R., 'The Mezzotint', in *The Collected Ghost Stories of M. R.. James* [1904] (London: Edward Arnold and Co, 1931).

———, 'Oh, Whistle, and I'll Come to You, My Lad', in *The Collected Ghost Stories of M. R. James* [1904] (London: Edward Arnold and Co, 1931).

Jancovich, Mark, *Horror* (London: Batsford, 1992).

Jones, Darryl, *Horror: A Thematic History in Fiction and Film* (London: Arnold, 2002).

Jones, Stephen, *The Mammoth Book of Zombies* (New York: Carroll and Graf Publishers, 1993).

Kafka, Franz, *The Metamorphosis* [1915] (San Francisco: Cleis Press, 1996).

Kagarlitsky, Julius, 'John Wyndham', in *Twentieth-Century Science-Fiction Writers*, 2nd Ed., Curtis C. Smith, ed. (London and Chicago: St. James Press, 1986), 818–820.

Keesey, Pam, *Daughters of Darkness: Lesbian Vampire Stories* (San Francisco: Cleis Press, 1993).

Keesey, Pam, ed., *Women Who Run with the Werewolves: Tales of Blood, Lust and Metamorphosis* (San Francisco: Cleis Press, 1996).

Kiernan, Caitlin, *Silk* (New York: Penguin Putnam, 2002).

King, Daniel, *Mama's Boy* (New York: Pocket Books, 1993).

King, Stephen, 'Chattery Teeth', in *Nightmares and Dreamscapes* (London: Hodder and Stoughton, 1993).

———, *Christine* (London: New English Library, 1983).

———, *Cujo* (New York: Viking Books, 1981).

———, *Danse Macabre: The Anatomy of Horror* (London: Futura, 1982).

———, *The Dark Tower II: The Drawing of the Three* (Hampton Falls, NH: Donald M. Grant, 1987).

———, *Dreamcatcher* (London: Hodder and Stoughton, 2001).

———, *From a Buick 8* (New York: Schreiber, 2002).

———, *Gerald's Game* (New York: Viking Press, 1992).

———, 'The Glass Floor', in *Startling Mystery Stories* (fall 1967, reprinted in fall 1990 issue of *Weird Tales*).

———, *Pet Sematary* (London: New English Library, 1983).

Kipling, Rudyard, 'The White Man's Burden', *McClure's Magazine*, 12 February 1899.

Kristeva, Julia, *Abjection, Melancholia and Love: The Work of Julia Kristeva*, John Fletcher and Andrew Benjamin, eds. (Warwick: Warwick Case Studies in Philosophy and Literature, Routledge, 1990).

———, *The Powers of Horror: An Essay on Abjection*, Leon Roudiez, trans. (New York: Columbia University Press, 1982).

———, *Strangers to Ourselves* (New York: Columbia University Press, 1991).

Lamming, R. M., 'Walls', in *Skin of the Soul*, Lisa Tuttle, ed. (London: Women's Press, 1990).

Laplanche, Jean and J. B. Pontalis, *The Language of Psycho-Analysis* (London: Hogarth Press, 1983).

Le Fanu, Sheridan, 'Carmilla', in *In a Glass Darkly* (London: R. Bentley and Son, 1872).

Lehmann-Haupt, Christopher, 'Books of the Times', *The New York Times* (17 August 1979) on the Web, www.nytimes.com/books/97/03/09/lifetimes/kin-r-dead.html.

Leigh, Janet, *Psycho: Behind the Scenes of the Classic Thriller* (New York: Harmony, 1995).

Lessing, Doris, *The Summer Before the Dark* (New York: Vintage, 1983).

Lewis, Matthew, *The Monk* [1796] (Oxford: Oxford Paperbacks, 1998).

Light, Alison, *Forever England: Femininity, Literature and Conservatism between the Wars* (London: Routledge, 1991).

Lim, Catherine, *The Howling Silence* (Singapore: Horizon Books, 1999).

———, *The Serpent's Tooth* (Singapore: Times Books International, 1982).

Lodge, David, *The Modes of Modern Writing: Metaphor, Metonymy and the Typology of Modern Literature* (London: Edward Arnold, 1977).

Lovecraft, H. P., 'At the Mountains of Madness', in *At the Mountains of Madness and Other Tales of Terror* [1948] (New York: Ballantine Books, 1971).

———, 'Cthulhu Mythos', in *Tales of the Cthulhu Mythos* (New York: Del Rey, 1998).

———, *Supernatural Horror in Literature* [1927, 1933–1935] (Mineola, NY: Dover Publications, 1973).

Lurie, Susan, 'The Construction of the Castrated Woman in Psychoanalysis and Cinema', in *Discourse* 4 (Winter 1981–1982), 52–74.

Machen, Arthur, *The Great God Pan* [1894] (New York: Creation Books, 1993).

Maitland, Sara, 'Introduction', *Virago Book of Ghost Stories* (London: Virago, 1989).

Maturin, Charles, *Melmoth the Wanderer* [1820] (London: Bentley and Son, 1892).

McCrillis, M. P., 'Lynching Stephen King', *World and I* 18:7 (July 2003), p. 268.

McEwan, Ian, *The Comfort of Strangers* (London: Vintage, 1981).

McGrath, P., 'Poe's Dank Vaults', in *Critical Fictions: The Politics of Imaginative Writing*, Philomena Mariana, ed., Seattle Center for the Arts (Seattle: Bay Press, 1991).

McKee Charnas, Suzy, 'Boobs', in *Skin of the Soul*, Lisa Tuttle, ed. (London: Women's Press, 1990).

McRobbie, Angela, *Feminism and Youth Culture: From Jackie to Just Seventeen* (Basingstoke and London: Macmillan, 1991).

McWilliams, Carey, *Ambrose Bierce: A Biography* [1929] (Boston: Little, Brown and Co., 1967).

Mew, Charlotte, 'A White Night', *Temple Bar* CXXVII (1903), 625–639.

Morrison, Toni, *Beloved* (New York: Vintage, 1997).

Morrow, W. C., *The Ape, The Idiot and Other People* (New York: HarperCollins, 1997).

Mulvey, Laura, 'Visual Pleasure and Narrative Cinema' [1975], in *Visual and Other Pleasures* (Bloomington: Indiana University Press, 1989).

Neale, Steve, *Genre* (London: British Film Institute, 1980).

Nesbit, Edith, *Five Children and It* [1902] (Oxford: Oxford Bookworms, 1996).

Oates, Joyce Carol, *American Appetites* (New York: E. P. Dutton, 1989).

———, *Foxfire: Confessions of a Girl Gang* (New York: E. P. Dutton, 1993).

———, *The Rise of Life on Earth* (New York: W. W. Norton, 1991).

———, *Them* (New York: Vanguard Press, 1969).

———, *Where Are You Going, Where Have You Been?* (Ontario: Ontario Review Press, 1993 [reissue]).

———, (as Rosamond Smith), *Lives of the Twins* (New York: Simon and Schuster, 1987).

———, *Nemesis* (New York: Dutton, 1990).

———, *Soul/Mate* (New York: Dutton, 1989).

O'Brien, Geoffrey, 'Horror for Pleasure', *New York Review of Books* (April 1993).

O'Connor, Richard, *Ambrose Bierce, A Biography* (Boston: Little, Brown and Co., 1967).

Orwell, George, *Animal Farm* (London: Secker and Warburg, 1945).

Palmer, Paulina, *Lesbian Gothic: Trangressive Fictions* (London: Cassell, 1999).

Perkins, Charlotte Gilman, *The Yellow Wallpaper* [1913] (London: Virago, 1981).

Perrault, Charles, 'Bluebeard' [1697], in *The Blue Fairy Book* (New York: Dover, 1965).

Plath, Sylvia, 'The Applicant' [1962], in *The Collected* Poems, Ted Hughes, ed. (New York: Harper and Row, 1981).

Poe, Edgar Allan, 'Metzengerstein', *The Philadelphia Saturday Courier*, 1832.

———, *The Narrative of Arthur Gordon Pym of Nantucket* [1839] (Harmondsworth: Penguin Books, 1999).

———, *The Raven and Other Poems* (New York: Wiley and Putnam, 1845).

Prawer, S. S., *Nosferatu: Phantom Der Nacht* (London: British Film Institute, 2004).

Punter, David, *A Companion to the Gothic* (Oxford: Blackwells, 2000).

———, *Gothic Pathologies: The Text, the Body and the Law* (Basingstoke: Palgrave Macmillan, 1998).

———, *The Literature of Terror: A History of Gothic Fiction from 1765 to the Present Day* (New York: Longman, 1980).

———, *Postcolonial Imaginings: Fictions of a New World Order* (Lanham, MD: Rowman and Littlefield, 2000).

Radcliffe, Ann, *Mysteries of Udolpho* [1794] (Oxford: Oxford University Press, 1998).

Radway, Janice, *Reading the Romance: Women, Patriarchy and Popular Literature.* [1984] (Chapel Hill: University of North Carolina Press, 1991).

Railo, Eino, *The Haunted Castle. A Study of the Elements of English Romanticism* [1927] (New York: Gordon Press, 1974).

Rance, Nicholas, 'Not Like Men in Books: Murdering Women: Daphne du Maurier and the Infernal World of Popular Fiction', in *Creepers*, Clive Bloom, ed. (London: Pluto, 1993).

Rashkin, Esther, *Family Secrets and the Psychoanalysis of Narrative* (Princeton: Princeton University Press, 1992). Quoted in Punter, *A Companion to the Gothic* (Oxford: Blackwells, 1999).

Rice, Anne, *The Feast of All Saints* (New York: Simon and Schuster, 1979).

———, *Lasher* (New York: Alfred A. Knopf, 1993).

———, *Memnoch the Devil* (New York: Random House, 1995).

———, *Merrick* (New York: Random House, 2000).

———, *The Mummy* (also known as *Ramses the Damned*) (New York: Ballantine Books, 1989).

———, 'On the Film, *Interview with the Vampire*', www.maths.tcd.ie/~forest/vampire/morecomments.html, accessed 30 July 2003.

———, *Pandora: New Tales of the Vampires* (New York: Random House, 1998).

———, *Servant of the Bones* (London: Chatto and Windus, 1996).

———, *The Tale of the Body Thief* (New York: Alfred A. Knopf, 1992).

———, *Taltos: Lives of the Mayfair Witches* (New York: Random House, 1994).

———, *The Witching Hour* (New York: Alfred A. Knopf, 1990).

———, *Vittorio the Vampire* (New York: Random House, 1999).

Royle, Nicholas, *The Uncanny: An Introduction* (Manchester: Manchester University Press, 2003).

Ruddick, N., 'Deep Waters: The Significance of the Deluge in Science Fiction', *Foundation* 42 (Spring 1988), 49–59.

———, *Ultimate Island: On the Nature of British Science Fiction* (Westport, CT: Greenwood Press, 1993).

Scheib, Richard, 'Invasion of the Body Snatchers', www.moria.co.nz/sf/bodysnatchers78.htm, 1994.

———, 'Quatermass and the Pit' (aka 'Five Million Years to Earth'), www.moria.co.nz/sf/quatermass3.htm., 1999.

Schonhorn, Manuel and Daniel Defoe, *Accounts of the Apparition of Mrs. Veal* [ca. 1705] (New York: Ams Press, 1992).

Scotch, Cheri, *The Werewolf's Kiss* (New York: Diamond Books, 1992).

Seabrook, William B., *The Magic Island* [1929] (St Paul, MN: Paragon House Publishers, 1989).

Silverman, Kaja, *The Acoustic Mirror: The Female Voice in Psychoanalysis and Cinema* (Indiana: Indiana University Press, 1988).

Sinclair, May, 'Hurst of Hurstcote', in *Shudder Again: 22 Tales of Sex and Horror*, Michelle Slung, ed. (Harmondsworth: Penguin Books, 1993).

———, 'The Token', in *The Virago Book of Ghost Stories*, Richard Dalby, ed. (London: Virago, 1989).

———, 'The Villa Desiree', in *I Shudder at Your Touch: 22 Tales of Sex and Horror*, Michele Slung, ed. (Bergenfield, NJ: New American Library, 1991).

———, 'Where Their Fire Is Not Quenched', in *Witches' Brew*, Marcia Muller and Bill Pronzini, eds. (Basingstoke: Macmillan, 1984).

Skal, David, *The Monster Show: A Cultural History of Horror* (London: Faber and Faber, 1993).

Smith, Andy W. and Lucy Nevitt, '"This is where you get off": The Problem of Ambivalence in Early Episodes of *Buffy the Vampire Slayer*', *Diegesis: Journal of the Association for Research in Popular Fictions* 7 (Summer 2004) (Liverpool: John Moores University).

Stevenson, Robert Louis, *Dr Jekyll and Mr Hyde* [1886] (Harmondsworth: Penguin Books, 2004).

Stoker, Bram, 'Dracula's Guest' (Co. Kerry: Brandon, 1990 [1897]).

———, 'The Duties of Clerks of Petty Sessions in Ireland' [1876], in *Collected Works of Bram Stoker* (John Falconer, 2000).

———, 'The Snake's Pass' (Co. Kerry: Brandon, 1990 [1891]).

———, 'The Way of the Vampire by Professor Abraham Van Helsing' [1897], in *Dracula* (Harmondsworth: Penguin Books, 1979).

Strong, Theodore, 'The Witch', in *The Cowboy and the Vampire*, Clarks Hays, Kathleen McFall, ed. (St. Paul: Llewellyn Publications, 1999).

Summers, M., *The Gothic Quest: A History of the Gothic Novel* [1915] (New York: Russell and Russell, 1938).

Swift, Jonathan, *A Modest Proposal* [1729] (Essex: Prometheus Books UK, 1994).

Tem, Melanie, 'Wilding', in *Women Who Run with the Werewolves*, Pam Keesey, ed. (San Francisco: Cleis Press, 1996).

Tem, Melanie and Steve Rasnic Tem, 'Mama', in *Sisters of the Night*, Barbara Hambly and Martin H. Greenberg, eds. (New York: Warner Books, 1995).

Tennant, Emma, *Faustine* (London: Faber and Faber, 1992).

Tuck, Donald H., 'Harris, John B', in *The Encyclopaedia of Science Fiction and Fantasy*, John Clute and Peter Nicholls, eds. (New York: St. Martin's Press, 1993).

Tuttle, Lisa, ed., *Skin of the Soul* (London: Women's Press, 1990).

Twitchell, James B., *Dreadful Pleasures: An Anatomy of Modern Horror* (Oxford: Oxford University Press. 1985).

Uglow, Jennifer, 'Introduction', in *The Virago Book of Ghost Stories*, Richard Dalby, ed. (London: Virago, 1989).

Verne, Jules, *Twenty Thousand Leagues Under the Sea* [1870] (Harmondsworth: Penguin Books, 1994).

Walpole, Horace, *The Castle of Otranto* [1764] (Oxford: Oxford University Press, 1998).

Warner, Marina, *From the Beast to the Blonde: On Fairy Tales and Their Tellers* (New York: Farrar, Straus Giroux, 1996).

Webster, John, *The Duchess of Malfi* [1623] (Whitefish, MT: Kessinger Publishing Co, 2004).

———, *The White Devil* [1612] (Otterup: Scholar Press, 1971).

Weldon, Fay, *Growing Rich* (London: Flamingo, 1992).

Whitehead, John W., 'Invasion of the Body Snatchers: A Tale for Our Times', www.gadflyonline.com.

Wilde, Oscar, *The Picture of Dorian Gray* [1891] (Harmondsworth: Penguin Books, 2004).

Winter, Douglas E., *Faces of Fear* (New York: Berkley Publishing Group, 1990).

Winterson, Jeanette, *Sexing the Cherry* (New York: Grove Press, 1989).

Wisker, Gina, 'At Home All Was Blood and Feathers: The Werewolf in the Kitchen—Angela Carter and Horror', in *Creepers*, Clive Bloom, ed. (London: Pluto, 1993).

———, ed., *FEMSPEC* 4:1(San Francisco: Caddo Gap Press, 2002).

—————, 'Horrors and Menaces to Everything Decent in Life: The Horror Fiction of Dennis Wheatley', in *Creepers*, Clive Bloom, ed. (London: Pluto, 1993).

Wollstonecraft, Mary. *A Vindication of the Rights of Woman* [1792] (Mineola, NY: Dover Publications, 1996).

Wood, R., 'Returning the Look: "Eyes of a Stranger"', in *American Horrors: Essays on the Modern American Horror Film*, Gregory A. Waller, ed. (Urbana and Chicago: University of Illinois Press, 1987).

Woolf, Virginia, 'A Haunted House', in *A Haunted House and Other Short Stories* (Orlando, FL: Harvest Books, 1966).

Wymer, Rowland, 'How "Safe" is John Wyndham? A Closer Look at His Work, with Particular Reference to The Chrysalids', *Foundation* 55 (Summer 1992).

Yahp, Beth, *The Crocodile Fury* (North Ryde: Angus and Robertson, 1992).

Filmography

20,000 Leagues Under the Sea, dir. Richard Fleischer, 1954.

28 Days Later, dirs. Danny Boyle and Andrew MacDonald, 2003.

Akira, dir. Katsuhiro Otomo, 1988.

Alien, dir. Ridley Scott, 1979.

Aliens, dir. James Cameron, 1986.

Alien³, dir. David Fincher, 1992.

Alien: Resurrection, dir. Jean-Pierre Jeunet, 1997.

All Night Long, dir. Matsumura Katsuya, 1992.

All Night Long 2, dir. Matsumura Katsuya, 1995.

American Werewolf in London, An, dir. John Landis, 1981.

Amityville Horror, The, dir. Stuart Rosenberg, 1979.

Angel Heart, dir. Alan Parker, 1987.

Armageddon, dir. Michael Bay, 1998.

Attack of the 50 Foot Woman, dir. Nathan Hertz, 1958.

Basic Instinct, dir. Paul Verhoeven, 1992.

Blair Witch Project, The, dir. Daniel Myrick, Eduardo Sanchez, 1999.

Bram Stoker's Dracula, dir. Francis Ford Coppola, 1993.

Bride of Frankenstein, The, dir. James Whale, 1935.

Bride of the Monster, dir. Edward D. Wood Jr., 1955.

Brides of Dracula, dir. Terence Fisher, 1960.

Brood, The, dir. David Cronenberg, 1979.

Candyman, dir. Bernard Rose, 1992.

Cape Fear, dir. Martin Scorsese, 1991.

Carrie, dir. Brian De Palma, 1976.

Cat People, dir. Jacques Tourneur, 1944.

Child's Play, dir. Tom Holland, 1988.

Child's Play 3, dir. Jack Bender, 1991.

Clockwork Orange, A, dir. Stanley Kubrick, 1971.

Crash, dir. Charles Band, 1977.

Cujo, dir. Lewis Teague, 1981.

Curse of the Werewolf, The, dir. Terence Fisher, 1961.

Dark Half, The, dir. George A Romero, 1991.

Das Kabinet des Doktor Caligari, dir. Robert Wiene, 1919.

Dawn of the Dead, dir. George A. Romero, 1968.

Day After Tomorrow, The, dir. Ronald Emmerich, 2004.

Day of the Dead, dir. George A. Romero, 1985.

Day of the Triffids, The, dir. Steve Sekely, 1962.

Deep Rising, dir. Stephen Sommers, 1998.

Deliverance, dir. John Boorman, 1972.

Demon Seed, dir. Donald Cammell, 1977.

Desperation, dir. Mick Garris, 2003.

Dolores Claiborne, dir. Taylor Hackford, 1995.

Don't Look Now, dir. Nicholas Roeg, 1973.

Dracula (Der Januskopf), dir. F. W. Murneau, 1920.

Dracula, dir. Tod Browning, 1932.

Dracula, dir. Terence Fisher, 1958.

Dracula, dir. John Badham, 1979.

Dracula 2000, dir. Wes Craven, 2000.

Dreamcatcher, The, dir. Edward Radtke, 1999.

Dressed to Kill, dir. Brian De Palma, 1980.

Et Mourir de Plaisir, dir. Roger Vadim, 1960.

Evil Dead, The, dir. Sam Raimi, 1981.

Evil Dead Trap, dir. Ikeda Toshiharu, 1988.

Exorcist, The, dir. William Friedkin, 1973.

Exorcist II: The Heretic, dir. John Boorman, 1977.

Exorcist III, dir. William Peter Blatty, 1990.

Fall of the House of Usher, The, dir. Roger Corman, 1960.

Fatal Attraction, dir. Adrian Lyne, 1987.

Final Conflict, The, dir. Graham Baker, 1981.

Firestarter, dir. Mark Lester, 1984.

Fly, The, dir. Kurt Neumann, 1958.

Frankenstein, dir. T. S. Edison, 1910.

Frankenstein, dir. James Whale, 1931.

Friday the 13th, dir. Sean Cunningham, 1980.

From Dusk to Dawn, dir. Robert Rodriguez, 1996.

Golem, The (Der Golem), dir. Paul Wegener, 1920 (1914).

Gothic, dir. Ken Russell, 1986.

Green Mile, The, dir. Frank Darabont, 1999.

Guinea Pig: Devil's Experiment, Unearthed Films, 1985.

Halloween II, dir. Rick Rosenthal, 1981.

Hellboy, dir. Guillermo del Toro, 2004.

Henry: Portrait of a Serial Killer, dir. John McNaughton, 1986.

Hills Have Eyes, The, dir. Wes Craven, 1977.

Hitcher, The, dir. Robert Harmon, 1986.

Horror of Dracula, dir. Terence Fisher, 1958.

How to Make a Monster, dir. Herbert L. Strock, 1958.

Hunger, The, dir. Tony Scott, 1983.

Hunter's Blood, dir. Robert C. Hughes, 1987.

I Hate Your Guts (aka *Intruder, The*), dir. Roger Corman, 1961.

Interview with the Vampire, dir. Neil Jordan, 1994.

Intestines of a Beauty (Bijo no harawata), dir. Komizu Kazuo (aka Gaira), 1986.

Intestines of a Virgin (Shojo no harawata), dir. Komizu Kazuo (aka Gaira), 1986.

Invasion of the Body Snatchers, dir. Don Siegel, 1956.

Invasion of the Body Snatchers, dir. Philip Kaufman, 1978.

Invisible Man, The, dir. James Whale, 1933.

Iron Monkey, dir. Yuen Woo Ping, 1993.

Island of Dr Moreau, The, dir. John Frankenheimer, 1996.

I Spit on Your Grave, dir. Meir Zarchi, 1977.

It, dir. Tommy Lee Wallace, 1990.

It! The Terror from Beyond Space, dir. Edward L. Cahn, 1958.

I Walked with a Zombie, dir. Jacques Tourneur, 1943.

Jaws, dir. Steven Spielberg, 1975.

King Kong, dirs. Merian C. Cooper, Ernest B. Schoedsack, 1933.

Kiss, The, dir. Pen Densham, 1988.

Kiss of the Vampire, dir. Don Sharp, 1964.

La Maschera del Demonio, dir. Mario Bava, 1960.

Le Frisson des Vampires, dir. Jean Rollin, 1970.

Lodger, The, dir. Alfred Hitchcock, 1926.

Long Walk, The, dir. Alan Bibby, 1998.

Lord of the Rings: The Fellowhip of the Ring, dir. Peter Jackson, 2001.

Lord of the Rings: The Two Towers, dir. Peter Jackson, 2002.

Lord of the Rings: The Return of the King, dir. Peter Jackson, 2003.

Lost Boys, The, dir. Joel Schumacher, 1987.

Manhunter, dir. Michael Mann, 1986.

Masque of the Red Death, The, dir. Roger Corman, 1964.

Misery, dir. Rob Reiner, 1987.

Near Dark, dir. Kathryn Bigelow, 1987.

Night of the Demon (aka *Curse of the Demon*), dir. Jacques Tourneur, 1957.

Night of the Ghouls, dir. Edward D. Wood, Jr., 1958.

Night of the Living Dead, dir. George A. Romero, 1969.

Nosferatu, dir. F. W. Murneau, 1922.

Occurrence at Owl Creek Bridge, An, dir. Robert Enrico, 1962.

Old Dark House, The, dir. James Whale, 1932.

Omen, The, dir. Richard Donner, 1976.

One Flew Over the Cuckoo's Nest, dir. Milos Foreman, 1975.

Others, The, dir. Alejandro Amenadar, 2001.

Pet Sematary, dir. Mary Lambert, 1989.

Picture of Dorian Gray, The, dir. Albert Lewin, 1945.

Pit and the Pendulum, The, dir. Roger Corman, 1961.

Plan 9 from Outer Space, dir. Edward D. Wood, Jr., 1959.

Plant, The, dir. Alexandre Gavras, 1991.

Poltergeist, dir. Tobe Hooper, 1982.

Prince of Darkness, dir. John Carpenter, 1987.

Princess Blade, The, dir. Shinsuke Sato, 2003.

Psycho II, dir. Richard Franklin, 1983.

Psycho III, dir. Anthony Perkins, 1986.

Quatermass and the Pit, dir. Roy Ward Baker, 1967.

Rabid, dir. David Cronenberg, 1976.

Raft, The (Creepshow 2), dir. Michael Gornick, 1987.

Rage, dir. David Cronenberg, 1977.

Raven, The, dir. Roger Corman, 1963.

Reflection of Fear, A, dir. William A. Fraker, 1973.

Requiem for a Vampire, dir. Jean Rollin, 1973.

Resident Evil, dir. Paul W. S. Anderson, 2002.

Ring, The, dir. Hideo Nakata, 1998.

Ring, The, dir. Gore Verbinski, 2002.

Rosemary's Baby, dir. Roman Polanski, 1968.

Running Man, The, dir. Paul Michael Glaser, 1987.

Salem's Lot, dir. Tobe Hooper, 1979.

Scary Movie, dir. Keenan Ivory Wayans, 2000.

Score, dir. Muroga Makoto, 1995.

Shaun of the Dead, dir. Edgar Wright, 2004.

Shining, The, dir. Stanley Kubrick, 1980.

Silence of the Lambs, The, dir. Jonathan Demme, 1991.

Species, dir. Roger Donaldson, 1995.

Strange Case of Dr Jekyll and Mr Hyde, The, dir. F. W. Murnau, 1920.

Tales from the Crypt, dir. Freddie Francis, 1972.

Talisman, The, dir. John Carr, 1966.

Ted Bundy, dir. Matthew Bright, 2002.

Terminator, The, dir. James Cameron, 1984.

Texas Chainsaw Massacre, The, dir. Tobe Hooper, 1974.

Thelma and Louise, dir. Ridley Scott, 1991.

Tomb of Ligeia, dir. Roger Corman, 1965.

Twins of Evil, dir. John Hough, 1971.

Underworld, dir. Len Wiseman, 2003.

Vampire Lovers, The, dir. Roy Ward Baker, 1970.

Van Helsing, dir. Stephen Sommers, 2004.

Village of the Damned, The, dir. John Carpenter, 1995.

Wasp Woman, The, dir. Roger Corman, 1960.

Whatever Happened to Baby Jane? dir. Robert Aldrich, 1962.

White Zombie, dir. Victor Halperin, 1932.

Wolf, dir. Mike Nichols, 1994.

Wolf Man, The, dir. George Waggner, 1940.

Wolfen, dir. Michael Wadleigh, 1981.

Woman in the Box: Virgin Sacrifice, A (*Hako no naka no onna: Shojo ikenie*), dir. Konuma Masaru, 1915.

Wrong Turn, dir. Rob Schmidt, 2003.

Televisionography

Addams Family, The, executive producer David Levy, 1964.

Bates Motel, Richard Rothstein, 1987.

Buffy the Vampire Slayer, creator: Joss Whedon, 1997.

Bugs Bunny, Warner Brothers, 1941.

Kingdom Hospital, creator: Craig R. Baxley, 2004.

Millennium, creator: Chris Carter, 1996.

Most Haunted, creators: Karl Beattie, Yvette Fielding, 2002.

Psycho IV: The Beginning, creator: Mick Garris, 1990.

Quatermass and the Pit, creator: Nigel Kneale, 1953.

Roadrunner, Warner Brothers, 1952.

Suspicion, creator: Alfred Hitchcock, 1941.

Tales from the Crypt, creator: William Gaines, 1989.

Tommyknockers, dir. John Power, 1993.

Twilight Zone, The, creator: Rod Serling, 1985.

X-Files, The, creator: Chris Carter, 1993.

Further Reading/Films

Michael Arnzen

'Diving In', 'Gardener', 'How to Grow a Man-Eating Plant', and 'Introduction: Minimalist Horror', in *100 Jolts: Shockingly Short Stories* (Hyattsville, MD: Raw Dog Screaming Press, 2004).

Martin Barker
A Haunt of Fears: The Strange History of the British Horror Comics Campaign (London: Pluto Press, 1984).

Ambrose Bierce
'A Cold Greeting', 'A Fruitless Assignment', 'A Horseman in the Sky', 'An Arrest', 'At Old Man Eckert's', 'Beyond the Wall', 'George Thurston', 'The Affair at Coulter's Notch', 'The Applicant', 'The Damned Thing', 'The Empty House', 'The Haunted Island', 'The Isle of Pines', 'The Man and the Snake', 'The Other Lodgers', The Spook House', The Vine on a House', 'Two Military Executives', and 'The Coup de Grace' in *The Collected Works of Ambrose Bierce* (New York: Gordian Press, 1966).

'A Diagnosis of Death', 'A Jug of Sirup', 'John Bartine's Watch', 'Moxton's Master', 'One of Twins', 'The Middle Toe of the Right Foot', and 'The Stranger' in *Can Such Things Be?* [1893] (PA: Wildside Press, 2002).

'Killed at Resaca', in *In the Midst of Life* (London: Chatto and Windus, 1964).

The Enlarged Devil's Dictionary, Ernest Jerome Hopkins, ed. (New York: Doubleday, 1967).

Algernon Blackwood
'A Haunted Island', in *Ancient Sorceries and Other Weird Stories* [1927] (London: Penguin, 1974).

'Ancient Sorceries', 'Secret Worship', 'Smith: An Episode in a Lodging House', 'The Empty House', 'The Insanity of Jones', 'The Listener', 'The Man Who Found Out', 'The Wendigo', and 'The Willows' in *Best Ghost Stories of Algernon Blackwood* [1973] (Thirsk: House of Stratus, 2002).

Robert Bloch
Psycho, 1959.
The Scarf, 1947.

Poppy Z. Brite

Are You Loathsome Tonight? A Collection of Short Stories (Colorado Springs, CO: Gauntlet Press, 1998).

His Mouth Will Taste of Wormwood and Other Stories (Harmondsworth: Penguin Books, 1995).

Lost Souls (New York: Delacorte Press, 1992).

John Carpenter

Christine, 1983.

Halloween, 1978.

Angela Carter

'The Loves of Lady Purple', 'The Company of Wolves', and 'Wolf Alice', in *The Bloody Chamber and Other Stories* (London: Gollancz, 1979).

Nights at the Circus (London: Chatto and Windus, 1987).

The Magic Toyshop (London: Virago, 1967).

The Sadeian Woman (Harmondsworth: Penguin Books, 1979).

Wisker, Gina, 'At Home All Was Blood and Feathers: The Werewolf in the Kitchen—Angela Carter and Horror', in *Creepers*, Clive Bloom, ed. (London: Pluto, 1993).

Wes Craven

Nightmare on Elm Street, A, 1984.

Scream, 1996.

Scream 2, 1997.

Scream 3, 2000.

David Cronenberg

Dead Ringers, 1988.

Dead Zone, The, 1983.

Fly, The, 1986.

Videodrome, 1983.

Tananarive Due

The Living Blood (New York: Washington Square Press, 2001).

My Soul to Keep (New York: HarperCollins, 1998).

Daphne du Maurier

The Birds and Other Stories (London: Arrow, 1953).

Don't Look Now and Other Stories (Harmondsworth: Penguin Books, 1971).

Rebecca (London: Arrow, 1992).

Cook, Judith, *Daphne, a Portrait of Daphne du Maurier* (London: Corgi, 1991).

Forster, Margaret, *Daphne du Maurier* (London: Chatto and Windus, 1993).

Rance, Nicholas, 'Not Like Men in Books: Murdering Women: Daphne du Maurier and the Infernal World of Popular Fiction', in *Creepers*, Clive Bloom, ed. (London: Pluto, 1993).

William Friedkin

Exorcist, The, 1973.

Jewelle Gomez

The Gilda Stories (Ithaca, NY: Firebrand Books, 1991).

Thomas Harris

Hannibal (London: Heinemann, 1999).

Red Dragon (New York: Random House, 1981).

The Silence of the Lambs (New York: St. Martin's Press, 1988).

Susan Hill

The Mist in the Mirror (New York: Vintage, 1992).

The Woman in Black (New York: Vintage, 1983).

Alfred Hitchcock

Birds, The, 1963.

North by Northwest, 1959.

Psycho, 1960.

Rebecca, 1940.

Steps, The, 1935.

Vertigo, 1958.

William Hope Hodgson
The Boats of the "Glen Carrig" (London: Chapman and Hall, 1907).
The Ghost Pirates: Famous Fantastic Mysteries 6 (New York: Frank A. Munsey, 1944).
'The Hog', in *Carnacki, the Ghost-Finder* (St. Albans: Panther, 1974).
The House on the Borderland (London: Chapman and Hall, 1908).

Nalo Hopkinson
Brown Girl in the Ring (New York: Time Warner International, 1998).
'Greedy Choke Puppy', in *Dark Matter*, Sheree R. Thomas, ed. (New York: Warner, summer 2000).
Skin Folk (New York: Aspect, 2001).

M. R. James
Casting the Runes [1911] (Oxford: Oxford University Press, 2002).
The Ghost Stories of M. R. James (Oxford: Oxforud University Press, 1987).

Stephen King
Carrie (New York: Doubleday and Co., 1973).
The Dead Zone (New York: Signet, 1979).
Dolores Claiborne (London: Hodder and Stoughton, 1993).
The Green Mile (London: Simon and Schuster, 2000).
Misery (London: New English Library, 1987).
Salem's Lot (New York: Signet, 1975).
The Shining (New York: Signet, 1977).

Vernon Lee (Violet Paget)
'A Phantom Lover', 'A Wicked Voice', and 'The Virgin of the Seven Daggers', in *Hauntings: The Supernatural Stories* (British Columbia: Ash-Tree Press, 2002).
For Maurice: Five Unlikely Tales (London: John Lane, 1927).

H. P. Lovecraft
'The Call of Cthulhu', 'The Dunwich Horror', 'The Lurking Fear', 'The Music of Erich Zann', 'The Rats in the Walls', and 'The

Shunned House', in *The Lurking Fear and Other Stories* (London: Panther, 1970).

The Colour Out of Space (New York: Lancer, 1963).

The Lurking Fear and Other Stories (New York: Ballantine Books, 1971).

David Lynch
Blue Velvet, 1986.

Eraserhead, 1977.

Mulholland Drive, 2001.

Twin Peaks, 1990.

Arthur Machen
The Hill of Dreams (Holicong, PA: Wildside Press, 2002).

The Novel of the Black Seal [1907] (Milton Keynes: Lightning Source UK LTD, 1965).

The Novel of the White Powder (London: Transworld, 1965).

The Terror [1917] (Milton Keynes: Lightning Source UK LTD, 1965).

The Three Impostors [1890] (Holicong, PA: Wildside Press, 2004).

The White People (Milton Keynes: Lightning Source UK LTD, 1965).

Joyce Carol Oates
Because It Is Bitter, and Because It Is My Heart (Harmondsworth: Penguin Books, 1990).

'The Doll', in *Haunted: Tales of the Grotesque* (Harmondsworth: Penguin Books, 1994).

Heat and Other Stories (Harmondsworth: Penguin Books, 1991).

We Were the Mulvaneys (New York: E. P. Dutton, 1996).

Zombie (New York: Plume Books, 1995).

(As Rosamond Smith), *Snake Eyes* (New York: E. P. Dutton, 1992).

(As Rosamond Smith), *Starr Bright Will Be with You Soon* (New York: E. P. Dutton, 1999).

Edgar Allan Poe
'Annabel Lee' [1849], 'Cask of Amontillado' [1846], 'Ligeia' [1838], 'Never Bet the Devil Your Head' [1850], *Tales of the*

Grotesque and Arabesque [1840], 'Tales of the Folio Club' [1833], 'Tamerlane' [1827], 'The Balloon-Hoax', 'The Black Cat' [1843], 'The Fall of the House of Usher' [1837], 'The Gold Bug' [1843], 'The Masque of the Red Death' [1850], 'The Murders in the Rue Morgue' [1841], 'The Mystery of Marie Roget' [1843], 'The Oval Portrait' [1850], 'The Pit and the Pendulum' [1850], 'The Tell-Tale Heart' [1843], and 'The Raven' [1845] in *Edgar Allan Poe: Poetry and Tales* (New York: Library of America, 1984).

McGrath, P., 'Poe's Dank Vaults', in *Critical Fictions: The Politics of Imaginative Writing*, Philomena Mariana, ed., Seattle Center for the Arts (Seattle: Bay Press, 1991).

Anne Rice

Blood and Gold: The Vampire Marius (London: Chatto and Windus, 2001).

Interview with the Vampire (London: Macdonald Raven, 1976).

Queen of the Damned (New York: Alfred A. Knopf, 1988).

The Vampire Armand (New York: Random House, 1998).

The Vampire Lestat (*Vampire Chronicles*) (New York: Alfred A. Knopf, 1985).

Eli Roth

Cabin Fever, dir. Eli Roth, 2002.

Mary Shelley

Frankenstein [1818] (London: Penguin Books, 2003).

M. Night Shyamalan

Signs, 2002.

Sixth Sense, The, 1999.

May Sinclair

'The Token', in Virago Book of Ghost Stories, Richard Dalby, ed. (London: Virago, 1989).

Bram Stoker
'The Burial of the Rats' [1914], in *Best Ghost and Horror Stories* (Mineola, NY: Dover Publications, 1997).

Dracula [1897] (Harmondsworth: Penguin Books, 1979).

The Lady of the Shroud [1909] (London: Arrow Books, 1974).

The Lair of the White Worm [1911] (Holicong, PA: Wildside Press, 2001).

Melanie Tem
Blood Moon (London: Women's Press, 1992).

'Lightning Rod', in *Skin of the Soul*, Lisa Tuttle, ed. (London: Women's Press, 1990).

Sylvia Townsend Warner
Lolly Willowes [1926] (London: Random House, 1993).

Fay Weldon
The Cloning of Joanna May (New York: HarperCollins, 1996).

The Life and Loves of a She-Devil (New York: HarperCollins, 1996).

H. G. Wells
The Island of Dr Moreau [1896] (Mineola, NY: Dover Publications, 1996).

The Time Machine [1896] (New York: Signet Classics, 2002).

The War of the Worlds [1898] (Mineola, NY: Dover Publications, 1999).

Dennis Wheatley
The Devil Rides Out [1934] (London: Century, 1988).

The Haunting of Toby Jugg [1948] (London: Arrow, 1961).

The Ka of Gifford Hillary [1956] (London: Arrow, 1974).

The Satanist [1960] (London: Arrow, 1969).

To the Devil a Daughter [1953] (London: Century, 1988).

Wisker, Gina, 'Horrors and Menaces to Everything Decent in Life: The Horror Fiction of Dennis Wheatley', in *Creepers*, Clive Bloom, ed. (London: Pluto, 1993).

John Wyndham

The Day of the Triffids [1951] (London: Penguin Books, 1956).

Chocky [1968] (Norwich: Aflex Books, 1970).

The Midwich Cuckoos (London: Penguin Books, 1969).

Clareson, Thomas D. and Alice S. Clareson, 'The Neglected Fiction of John Wyndham: "Consider Her Ways", Trouble with Lichen and Web', in *Science Fiction Roots and Branches*, R. Garnett and F. J. Ellis, eds. (London: Macmillan, 1990), pp. 88–103.

Wymer, Rowland, 'How "Safe" is John Wyndham? A Closer Look at His Work, with Particular Reference to The Chrysalids', *Foundation* 55 (summer 1992).

Index

A

abject 41, 184, 217, 218, 237
abjection 12, 46, 213, 217, 237, 253
Alice Through the Looking Glass 146
alien 3, 128, 129, 141, 153, 188, 217
Alien 5, 149, 167, 241
Amityville Horror, The 34, 152
Andrews, Virginia 31, 151, 235
  Flowers in the Attic 45
anime 175
Arnzen, Michael 23, 122–123
attic 8
Austen, Jane 54
automata 183

B

Ba'athory, Elizabeth 201
Barker, Clive 4, 29, 117, 121, 134, 138–139, 149, 225, 226
Barker, Martin 9, 10, 19, 28, 69, 185, 230, 233, 234–235
Bates, Norman 126–127
beast 4
Beloved 175, 255
bestial 193
Bierce, Ambrose 76–78
Blackwood, Algernon 70–73, 74, 164, 180, 192
Bladerunner 48
Blair Witch Project, The 25, 44, 226

Blatty, William Peter (*The Exorcist*) 10, 11, 20, 131
Bloch, Robert (*Psycho*) 20, 92–93, 125
Bloom, Clive 149, 225
Bluebeard 25
body horror 7, 83, 118, 129, 130, 131, 178
body snatcher 110
Book of Werewolves, The 34, 36, 40, 100
border 189, 199
Botting, Fred 3, 4
Bowen, Elizabeth 19
boundaries 82
boundary-breaking 172
Braddon, Mary Elizabeth 64, 179
Brite, Poppy Z. 2, 22, 31, 46, 60, 105–110, 133, 158, 172, 196, 198, 222, 232, 244
Brockden Brown, Charles 15
Brodber, Edna 187
Buffy the Vampire Slayer 67, 128, 133, 141–142, 209
bug 182
burial 200

C

Campbell, Ramsey 21
cannibal 1, 125, 130, 160
cannibalism 180
'Carmilla' 17, 192, 215, 221

carnivalesque 46, 146, 160
Carpenter, John 133, 134, 158
Carter, Angela 20, 21, 31, 46, 96–
    98, 151, 152, 154, 155, 161,
    183–185, 199, 202, 208, 213
    'The Company of Wolves' 34
censorship 6
Charnas, Suzy McKee 60, 158,
    209, 212
Cixous, Héléne 237, 245, 252
Clover, Carol 242
coffin 1, 81
cockroach 183
Coleridge, Samuel Taylor 39, 43
Collins, William Wilkie 153
colonialism 50
Corman, Roger 125
corpse 109, 125, 184, 202
corridor 8
cowboy vampire 209
Craven, Wes 20, 139
Creed, Barbara 22, 219, 225, 227,
    240, 241, 248
Cronenberg, David 21, 135
Crowley, Aleister 19
curse 201

D

death 1, 2, 67, 108, 181
decadent 67
decay 88
defamiliarisation 84, 146, 147,
    220, 230, 252
dehumanisation 128, 129
demon 8, 80, 82, 114, 131, 143,
    192, 194
demonic 11, 88, 121, 132
demonically 121
demonology 42
demythologising 198
desire 6, 13
destabilise 147, 220
devil 89, 90, 102–103, 114, 132,
    140, 192
devilish 42

diabolical 52
Dinesen, Isak 199
disease 7, 13, 180, 181
disempower 119
disgust 12, 195
domestic 119, 146, 150–157
doppelganger 103
Dracula 44, 55–61, 123, 124, 139,
    148, 164, 171, 193, 201, 203,
    205, 221, 239, 242, 244
Dr Jekyll and Mr Hyde 148,
    164, 168
Due, Tananarive 115–115, 226, 251
Du Maurier, Daphne 54, 81–88,
    125, 181,
    Rebecca 54, 81, 86–88
dungeon 8, 54, 125

E

ecstasy 202
Eliot, George (*The Lifted Veil*)
    31, 39
engulfment 181
entrepreneur 119
erotic 112, 143, 193, 195, 202,
    203, 204, 205
eroticism 118
eternal 203
exorcise 38, 131
exorcism 131
Exorcist, The 10, 11, 151

F

fairytale 4, 26, 39
familiar 2
fantastic 36, 41
fantasy 1
Fascism 4
Fatal Attraction 161, 220
fear 2
feminist 36, 41
femme fatale 27, 31, 105
Finney, Jack 127

Fly, The 7, 9, 21, 135, 169
Foucault, Michel 198, 245
Frankenstein 9, 12, 19, 32–33,
　　47–50, 60, 123, 124, 148,
　　169, 170, 172
Freud ('The Uncanny') 146, 182,
　　220, 230–232, 243, 253
Freudian analysis 4

G

Gelder, Ken 22, 225, 241, 242, 243
gender 13
genetic engineering 50
genre 5
ghost 54, 62, 73, 75, 78, 79, 103,
　　104, 105, 148, 153, 162–167,
　　191, 254
ghostly 65, 104, 220
Gilman, Charlotte Perkins 154,
　　191, 214
Godzilla 142
Gomez, Jewelle 22, 32, 114–115,
　　196, 206–208, 247
Goth 199
Gothic 3, 7, 8, 9, 11, 13, 26, 29,
　　33, 37, 43, 44, 45, 47, 48, 54,
　　58, 65, 69, 78, 80, 104, 108,
　　111, 121, 123, 124, 142, 146,
　　147–148, 150, 161, 168, 172,
　　180, 187, 199, 205, 218, 226,
　　232, 235, 239, 242, 246, 251
Gottlieb, Sherry 196
Gould, Sabine Baring 210
Grimm 5, 230

H

hag 188
Halloween 133–135, 139, 151,
　　157, 159
Hammer Horror studios 53,
　　124, 149
Hannibal Lecter 1, 130, 131
Harris, Thomas 170

haunt 104
haunted house 7, 192
hellish 121
Hellmouth 41
Herbert, James 21
Hill, Susan 21, 103, 164–165
Hitchcock, Alfred 93, 125–127,
　　159, 235
Hoffmann, E. T. A. ('The
　　Sandman') 221, 231
Homosexuality 195
Hope Hodgson, William 75, 189
Hopkinson, Nalo 116–117, 147
horror comic campaign 9, 10, 19,
　　28, 69, 185, 230, 233, 234–235
Hunger, The 166

I

identity 38
imagination 2, 3
imaginative 6
imperialism 50
incest 67
Invasion of the Body Snatchers
　　127, 149
Irigaray 45, 237
I, Robot 48

J

Jacobean 40, 96
James, Henry 17, 165
James, M. R. 17, 74, 79
Jancovich, Mark 225, 233,
　　236–237, 248
Japanese horror films 142
Jaws 2, 5

K

Keats 39
Kiernan, Caitlin 23, 31, 106, 235
King Kong 188

King, Stephen 60, 118–121, 138, 141, 150, 151, 152, 154, 156, 157, 178, 185, 226, 227, 233, 241, 249
   Kingdom Hospital 9, 19, 20, 23
   The Shining 55
Kreuger, Freddy 139
Kristeva, Julia 12, 21, 41, 45, 207, 217, 218, 236–238, 239, 240, 252

L

Lacan 41, 237
Lee, Christopher 124
Lee, Vernon 16, 17, 63
Le Fanu, Sheridan 16, 172, 192, 215
lesbian 115, 192, 195, 197, 199, 204, 244, 245, 246
Levin, Ira (*Rosemary's Baby*) 20
Lim, Catherine 176, 252
liminal 107, 157
Lovecraft, H. P. 2, 4, 18, 19, 40, 51, 66–70, 92, 107, 121, 147, 160, 225
Lugosi, Bela 124
Lynch, David 133, 136–138, 141

M

Machen, Arthur 17, 19, 23, 74, 123
mad science 129
mad scientist 7
magic 114
maleficent 3
malicious 88
masochism 196
McCarthy 128, 230
Medea 44, 219
Medusa 3, 27, 190, 194, 217, 219
mermaid 190
metaphor 113
Middle America 119, 121
minimalist 122

monster 3, 25, 32, 39, 49, 50, 126, 169, 190, 218, 219
monstrous 7, 89, 173, 228
murder 1, 4, 82, 187, 191, 228
Murnau, F. W. 16, 60
myth 26
mythic 113, 142, 218
mythology 112

N

necromancer 64
Nemo 3
Nesbitt, E. 64
New Orleans 108, 109, 111
New Woman 59, 189
nightmare 1, 2, 13, 61, 83, 119, 131, 143, 147
Nightmare on Elm Street, A 139, 147, 151, 157, 159
nightmarish 176
Nosferatu 124

O

Oates, Joyce Carol 20, 94–95, 151
object horror 147, 167
Other 2, 3, 12, 43, 46, 56, 58, 113, 145, 167, 168, 190, 191, 197, 208, 215, 217, 218, 222, 232, 238, 239, 240, 242, 245, 253
Others, The 147, 167, 239

P

pain 2
paranoia 141
patriarchal 248
patriarchy 36, 50, 59, 82, 88, 96, 98, 189
penis 94
perversity 68
Pitt, Ingrid 124

Poe, Edgar Allen 16, 51–54, 60, 92, 125, 151, 154, 165, 180, 226, 232, 252
Polidori 48
Poltergeist 54
popular culture 6
pornographic 142, 194
pornography 27, 252
postcolonial 173, 177, 187, 239, 240, 253, 255
postmodern 14
Price, Vincent 125
primitive 2, 4
Psycho (see Bloch, Robert) 126–127, 159, 160
psychoanalysis 204
psychopathic 93
Punter, David 13, 23, 59, 148, 174, 196, 225, 226, 232, 239, 240, 249
Pulp 252

Q

Quatermass and the Pit 140
queer 171, 244, 247

R

Radcliffe, Ann 12, 15, 43, 48, 148, 218
radical 36
rape 4, 13, 193, 255
repulsion 88
revenge 53, 96
revengeful 121
revulsion 6
Rice, Anne 20, 21, 110–114, 196, 213, 221, 232
ritual 71, 99
romance 28, 202
Romantic poets 43, 47, 48, 252
Romero, George 20, 222
Rymer 'Varney the Vampire' 16

S

sadism 196
sadomasochistic 136
SARS 228
science fiction 46, 128, 140
serial killer 30, 254
sexuality 8, 36, 56, 57, 82, 197
Shakespeare 15, 45, 142
Shelley, Mary 9, 12, 15, 32–34, 44, 47, 252
Shipman, Dr Harold 228
Silence of the Lambs, The 5, 130–131, 154, 179
slasher 146
sorcerer 192
soucouyant 116
spectral 105
spectre 148
spirit theft 188
spiritual 113
splatter 122, 142, 145
split self/selves 9
Steele, Barbara 124
Stevenson, R. L. 16
Stoker, Bram 16, 17, 18, 55, 252
Straub, Peter 21
succubus 39, 175
suicidal 109
Summers, Montague 225
supernatural 2, 15, 33, 74, 75, 77, 111, 120, 121, 133, 137, 145, 147, 176, 186, 226
Supernatural Horror in Literature 5, 147

T

taboo 57, 99, 178
Tales from the Crypt 8, 10, 28
Tem, Melanie 100–102
terror 6, 11, 84, 99, 145
Texas Chainsaw Massacre, The 44, 138–139, 160, 229
torture 1, 13, 125, 142

tragedy 104, 105
transgressions 88
transgressive 82, 130
28 Days Later 44, 164, 180, 187
Twin Peaks 133, 137

U

uncanny 2, 146–147, 239

V

vagina dentata 189, 194
vampire 1, 25, 31, 34, 39, 56–57,
    100, 101, 106, 107, 109,
    110–117, 130, 124–125,
    141–142, 143, 145, 157, 158,
    167, 179, 182, 184, 185, 189,
    190, 191, 193, 195, 197, 198,
    200, 201, 202, 203–208, 209,
    210, 228, 243, 246
Van Helsing 70
Verne, Jules 3, 4, 10
victim 75, 108
Vietnam War 29, 107, 133, 158
violence 8, 27, 29, 68, 94, 97
violent 82, 94
virgin 192
Vlad the Impaler 201
voodoo 109

W

Walpole, Horace 15, 148, 218
Warner, Sylvia Townsend 64, 191

War of the Worlds 141
Webster, John 15
weird 2, 5, 10, 33, 69, 147
Weird Tales 5
Weldon, Fay 102–103, 171, 219
Wells, H. G. (*The Island of Dr
    Moreau*) 9, 19, 61–62, 148
werewolf 3, 142, 146, 182, 191,
    208, 209, 210–216, 222, 246
werewolfishness 37
Whale, James 49
Wharton, Edith 3, 39, 149, 226
Wheatley, Dennis 54, 67, 188–191
Winterson, Jeanette 171, 219
witch 27, 110
witchcraft 119
wolf 35, 56
Woolf, Virginia 31, 149, 191
Wrong Turn 44, 229
Wyndham, John 91–92

X

xenophobia 59
X-Files, The 128, 141–142

Y

Yahp, Beth 176

Z

zombie 121, 143, 184, 186–188,
    222–223

green
press
INITIATIVE

Continuum Publishing is committed to preserving ancient forests and natural resources. We have elected to print this title on 30% postconsumer waste recycled paper. As a result, this book has saved:

4.9 trees
229 lbs of solid waste
2,080 gallons of water
450 lbs of net greenhouse gases
836 kw hours of electricity

Continuum is a member of Green Press Initiative, a nonprofit program dedicated to supporting publishers in their efforts to reduce their use of fiber obtained from endangered forests. For more information, go to www.greenpressinitiative.org.